John Vize was born in London and educated at King George V College in Southport. Following a commission in the Royal Air Force as a pilot, he held a marketing management role in Ford Motor Company before co-founding a successful advertising agency. He retired after selling the business and now spends his time travelling, writing and throwing himself into numerous active projects. He lives in rural Northamptonshire with his wife, Judith. To balance the restful pursuits of gardening, poultry and bee-keeping, he remains a keen yachtsman, canoeist and aerobatic pilot.

Seems like he's living the life everyone wants

Chapter One
Without Due Care

My affair with Alice had lasted for almost a year when it happened. *affair?*

The alarming incident and the close shave with the law could have landed me in gaol had I not wriggled out with some reckless deception. I soon shrugged it off at the time but little did I realise the eventual impact it was to have on my selfish, carefree life. *OK?*

I usually take Thursday mornings off to visit her at home whilst husband, Ken, attends a weekly sales meeting in the Midlands. We can rely on his regular attendance as he's his company's sales director, and it's very convenient too that he likes to instil in his team a work ethic that requires a full day after a very early start. *omg!*

It isn't a love affair, neither of us wants that. It is just pure sex. She is twenty-five, blonde and beautiful and not concerned at all about the age difference between us. *what age difference?*

Alice insists that she loves her husband and never criticises him or complains about him in any way. She made it clear from the start that our liaison is just for fun. She has a single man's attitude to sex. I'm very fond of her but I don't love her and she doesn't love me. But we have such fun. In the past year I've had more sex in more ways and in more places than ever before in my life. It is fantastic and I can't believe my luck. She is spectacularly beautiful, has the body of a porn star without the implants and she fucks like a rattlesnake. There is no emotion, no tears, no rows, no jealously; just wonderful, compulsive, energetic shagging. *wk? ''*

The only slight disappointment for me is that surprisingly my lovely porn princess's orgasms are almost completely silent. She comes at least twice during our assignations but at her climax emits only a muffled squeak. It's as if she's a mouse worried about waking a cat sleeping nearby. *hmm?*

11

I always wait for her but often have to ask, "Was that it? Have you come?"

"Yes!" she answers with mock irritation and a sharp pinch of my arse, painful enough to prompt my instant ejaculation or postpone it for minutes. "Several times. Didn't you notice?" *No wl*

I wonder if perhaps, perversely she thinks that giving me the satisfaction of full volume would be a greater infidelity. Perhaps she limits the unfaithfulness by saving her orgasmic cries for Ken alone. *thats sad*

It happened on a cold damp Thursday early in March. I was on my way to Alice's spacious home in the leafy suburbs, although there wasn't a leaf to be seen in the naked avenue as spring very definitely had not yet sprung. Not a bud had so far emerged on the urban trees and I pondered whether nature had gifted them with inverted buds, an arboreal equivalent of the nipples I'd be taking into my mouth so soon, awaiting the kiss of warm sunlight to coax them from inactive hibernation.

It was just before one o'clock as I drove down the High Street and I was even more than usually excited. She had suggested that we 'have lunch first'. This was a new game and I just knew she was going to tease me for an hour before we romped. Alice had left a voicemail an hour earlier saying that she was going to buy a dozen scallops and six Madagascan prawns and to ask me if she should pick up a Gewürztraminer, or go to the better stocked wine shop to find a more appropriate Muscadet, to wash down our crustaceans. Whilst I must confess she has taught me a lot about women and sex that even I didn't know, I have in return taught the lovely airhead to appreciate fine wine and good food.

It was customary for me to call when ten minutes away for an always unnecessary final check that the coast was clear, that no unwelcome neighbour had dropped in for girl talk about unsatisfactory relationships or troublesome children.

The seat belt gave a little as I raised one buttock in the driving seat just sufficiently to make room for me to shove a hand down my trousers. I was getting a hard-on in anticipation and had to reposition my cock to take the bend out of it before it got too painful. Oh, what a wonderful life! *glad , dont have*

It was a short call to respond to her suggestion about the wine, a brief conversation that I knew would as ever end with an exchange of sexual innuendo, when he stepped from the kerb. Simultaneously, I felt and heard him hit the front bumper with a sickening crack and caught a glimpse of his agony as his body rolled along the bonnet towards me, slowing momentarily to face me accusingly

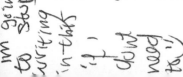

To my late mother, Eileen Joan Vize.

has she got missed
he peirod?

John Vize

BEST SUPPORTING ACTOR

AUSTIN MACAULEY PUBLISHERS™

LONDON ★ CAMBRIDGE ★ NEW YORK ★ SHARJAH

A CIP catalogue record for this title is available from the British Library.

ISBN 9781528992725 (Paperback)
ISBN 9781528992732 (Hardback)
ISBN 9781528992749 (ePub e-book)

www.austinmacauley.com

First Published (2021)
Austin Macauley Publishers Ltd
25 Canada Square
Canary Wharf
London
E14 5LQ

To Sam Street for her invaluable advice and encouragement, to those who have inspired this fictional tale and to my wife, Judith, for her patience during those summer holidays in Greece that I spent typing rather than touring. Thanks also to my daughter, Claire, for her calm and expert IT support.

I want you're life mate

Table of Contents

through the windscreen before disappearing over the roof of the car. I don't think I'd had time to brake before I saw him in the rear-view mirror rolling in the road behind me. The whole tragic, frightening episode lasted only two seconds but will haunt me for life. *you hit someone!?! dum biccch*

I got out of the car and approached the crowd gathering noisily around the silent figure lying in the gutter. I was too shocked even to notice that I had wet my pants. I started shivering uncontrollably. It was obvious to me, just by the unnatural angle of his head, that he was dead. *omg*

The police arrived within minutes and the unnecessary ambulance within quarter of an hour. A paramedic with a ridiculous ginger Mohican hair style knelt *lol* by the body. He looked more like a children's entertainer on his way to a kiddies' party than a healthcare professional. I knew I'd seen him before somewhere but in my state of shock, I could not remember where. He didn't even bother to open his lifesaving box of tricks. The body was respectfully covered with what looked like a duvet provided by a passing motorist. It was a children's bedspread, printed predominantly in pink, featuring happy images of the *Hello Kitty* brand. A small bloodstain appeared in the area of the victim's mouth, bizarrely coinciding with the image of the cartoon character's face, making it look as though it was the cat's nose that was bleeding. The gory patch didn't spread for long.

Despite my obvious state of shock and the fact that the accident was plain for all to see clearly his fault, the police treated me as a criminal from the start. I was pushed into the back seat of the patrol car with that practiced manoeuvre they must teach at Henlow; firm downward pressure on the crown of the head ostensibly to give the impression that it's to protect the prisoner from banging their bonce on the roof of the car rather than to remove any chance of escape.

I was breathalysed; thank God I was on my way to Alice's rather than on my way home and then arrested.

At the police station I was interviewed briefly by a uniformed sergeant with an apparent I.Q. of less than fifty, cautioned for causing death by dangerous driving and put in a cell, having first been deprived of my belt and shoes. I had been wearing slip-ons and the thick twat seemed unsure of whether I could keep them, as the normal practice evidently was just to remove the shoelaces. He decided to confiscate my shoes and issued me with a pair of paper moccasins to replace them. *ewww*

I was allowed just one phone call and chose to spend the privilege on contacting my solicitor rather than Alice who I could picture by then impatiently watching through the leaded windows of her lounge for my overdue arrival, concerned that my late appearance might upset the careful and practiced timing of our assignation and run the risk of us being found together should hubby arrive home early. I was certain she'd be in one of her sulks by now and wondered how she'd explain the unusual meal of scallops, prawns and fine wine to the returning Ken. Doubtless she'd position it as a spur of the moment romantic surprise dinner.

My only previous contact with the aptly named Wills & Payne had been on a financial contract matter involving a property purchase, so they felt it more appropriate to send to my rescue a newly appointed partner, a young female solicitor, Philippa Stapleton, assuring me of her undoubted expertise. She'd have me out of there within an hour I was promised.

As predicted, I was released very shortly after Philippa's intervention, pending further investigation. I had been too shocked to enquire about the careless pedestrian who had landed me in all this trouble but the witless sergeant was determined that I should learn who it was that I had killed. I don't remember his name but apparently, he was a local bank manager. Oh Shit

Philippa Stapleton impressed me greatly; in more ways than one.

She dealt with the police as if she were talking to children with learning difficulties. It was patently obvious, she asserted, that this was an unfortunate accident for which the careless victim was entirely responsible. Yes, a man was dead, but that was no reason to treat her client, clearly himself in shock, in such an insensitive way. The sergeant attempted to quote 'normal procedure' but was no match for the young lawyer and I was out of the cell and into an interview room, coffee in hand and restored to my own footwear within ten minutes of her arrival on the scene. Want her

Philippa established that the police already had a witness to the accident, the woman who'd provided the *Hello Kitty* bedspread, who would testify that Oliver Purkiss, 'clearly in a hurry' had 'dashed out between two parked cars. The driver didn't have a chance to avoid him. There was nothing he could have done.'

This it seemed was enough to ensure my release from custody that day but my car was impounded for evidence although the sergeant in more moderate tones explained that was normal practice in the event of a fatality. After a procedural discussion with Ms Stapleton he advised that I would be cautioned for the lesser offence of driving without due care and attention pending further investigation. Philippa told me not to worry about that as she was confident there would ultimately be no action taken against me. However, neither she nor the police were aware that I'd been using my phone at the time of impact and I was extremely worried forensic examination might reveal that. I asked if my phone could be returned to me in hope of preventing this analysis but was told that the car and everything in it would be held until due process was completed. I could only hope that the forensic cops were as inept as the duty sergeant.

The young lawyer sensed my concern, insisted that we should confer in private and once alone asked if I had been on the phone at time. I lied convincingly and gave her some bullshit about expecting a vital business call within the hour and after a few seconds of deliberation, during which she fixed me with a searching stare, said she'd do her best to recover it for me. I heard a one-sided argument between Philippa and the sergeant in which she reminded him that I was the innocent party in this tragedy and suggested he put her through immediately to a certain Chief Superintendent of her acquaintance. My phone was reluctantly handed back to me on the understanding that I'd return it next day. I did, having replaced the sim card with one from another phone I use exclusively for business.

The other way in which Ms Philippa Stapleton impressed me was somewhat less to do with her professional expertise. At first meeting I guessed her age at somewhere between thirty and thirty-eight, about ten years my junior. She appeared to be very confident, as all lawyers do, though as I was later to discover she was racked with self-doubt and a fear of failure. However, as I've always found in my twenty odd years as a property developer, the outward appearance of confidence is more important, and certainly much more common, than the reality. She was tall, about five eleven, giving me a three-inch advantage, slim with what appeared to be very tiny tits, barely discernible through the regulation black business suit favoured by most women in the legal profession. I was later to discover to my immense pleasure that they were small but perfectly formed as they say, in perfect proportion to her slender body with legs that seemed to stretch from her ankles to her armpits. Her face was not unattractive once one came to appreciate the strange beauty of the abundant freckles that accompanied her auburn hair. Yes, she certainly had been kissed by the fairies, and all over too, for the intriguing discolouration covered her entire body. Her best feature though without doubt were her fascinating, expressive eyes, cobalt blue pupils set in porcelain white that evidenced clean living, a healthy lifestyle and an almost total abstinence from alcohol. ok, Just dont fuck her

I think I decided right back then, at first meeting, that I'd have a crack at it, provided, of course, that I didn't end up in gaol. I sensed that she was single and nearly got off on the wrong foot by clumsily enquiring, "Are you single or do you just choose not to wear a ring?" The withering look from those serious yet compelling blue eyes told me unequivocally that she was totally resistant to charm and that I'd have to considerably up my game to bed this challenging woman. She was evidently in a different intellectual league from all of my past conquests. Yes, Philippa Stapleton would require a totally different approach and without doubt a deal more respect into the bargain. *Don't fuck her!*

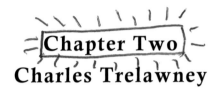

Chapter Two
Charles Trelawney

Oh, I haven't introduced myself, have I? ~no~ ~45?!!~

I'm Charles Trelawney, a young forty-five-year-old, successful businessman, attractive, tall, single, well-heeled with a g.s.o.h. I have all my own teeth and a fine head of hair. ~mhm ...~

Sorry! I'm so used to describing myself in less than one hundred and fifty characters for the contact mags and dating websites; for you I'll be a little less brash. ~ok, old man .....~

Some say I have a mega ego. I wouldn't necessarily agree but what's wrong with that anyway? I'd prefer to say that I'm supremely confident. Most women like that. ~I dont ... oh yeah im not a woman lol~

I have been accused of being the world's most arrogant man, but only by feeble women lacking any trace of self-esteem. ~r ught oh ...~

The problem is, when you're a good-looking bloke who's kept himself in great nick, with a few quid to his name and a reputation for being a bit of a hit with the ladies, women find you irresistibly attractive. They always go for the 'bad boy heartbreaker' just to prove they're the one who can tame you; then when it's all over you're suddenly a bastard. They boast to their girlfriends that they've pulled you and then lie about who ditched whom, concealing their devastation by claiming you were no good in bed anyway. ~prob wasnt~

I've never married; don't see the point. I used to do all that ball-aching socialising bit, going to parties, even dances in my youth. I spent years chatting up birds, dating them, romancing them, wining and dining them, spending a fortune on them. Then, bang! along comes the internet and takes all the fag out of it.

No, I never married. Too busy having fun and making a fortune. ~i wish~

~im ghia arrowd to say that you aint gay~

I did live with a girl for almost a year in my late thirties. She was a real looker but moody and over-sensitive. I don't really understand why she left. I just happened in passing to point out a minor quality control problem in the ironing of my shirts and when I got home that night found she'd packed her bags and moved out. She didn't leave a note but I did find my best silk shirt with a huge burn mark in the front of it.

I started out straight from college, joining the RAF as a pilot. Much to everyone's surprise I got a commission too. Pilot Officer Charles Henry Trelawney, at your service ma'am. Yes, I've even got a parchment scroll to prove it, signed by Her Majesty; well, rubber stamped probably. Can't see Liz finding the time to sign all those autographs.

'To our Trusty and well-beloved Charles Henry Trelawney,
Greeting:
We, reposing especial Trust and Confidence in your Loyalty, Courage, and good Conduct, do by these Presents Constitute and Appoint you to be an Officer in Our Royal Air Force. You are therefore carefully and diligently to discharge your Duty as such in the Rank of Acting Pilot Officer or in such Rank as We may from time to time hereafter be pleased to promote or appoint you to and you are in such manner and on such occasions as may be prescribed by Us to exercise and well discipline in their duties, such Officers, Airmen and Airwomen as may be placed under your orders from time to time and use your best endeavours to keep them in good Order and Discipline. And We do hereby Command them to Obey you as their superior Officer and you to Observe and follow such Orders and Directions as from time to time you shall receive from Us, or any superior Officer, according to the Rules and Discipline of War, in pursuance of the Trust hereby reposed in you.'

A scroll signed by the Queen makes you proud, doesn't it?

Well, no actually. I've always been a staunch republican but joining the RAF is the only way you can get your hands on a military jet.

I didn't last long in the service, about three years before I got chopped for a 'disciplinary matter'. In those days they were a bit snobbish about officers shagging other ranks and I was a serial offender. The WAAF officers were a bit 'Plain Jane' and too stuck up for me, but those doe-eyed young airwomen in their

rough textured blue-grey uniforms and RAF issue sensible knickers, God, what a time we had! OK, ~~beautiful~~

It was so easy too. Just like nurses entering the medical profession to marry a doctor, those little scrubbers set their sights on catching an officer and ideally a pilot. Yes, an officer's uniform and a pilot's brevet was a real leg-opener in those days. Some young ACWs and SACWs had several of us on the go at once. Sadly it all came to an end when one got pregnant and named six pilots _she'd been shagging._ The MO reported it to the Station Commander but only after he'd established that as many as eight girls were involved. All of us got a bollocking, one guy was posted to another station but I was made an example of and suspended; probably because I was named by all eight. I can't see why they made such a fuss. After all, I had promised the Queen I'd, '_Use my best endeavours to keep them in good Order and Discipline,_' and I certainly did my duty in that respect. yeah right...

The 'Station Master' was livid, puce with rage. I've never seen a man so angry. I think he'd have been less upset if we'd all been found to be Russian spies. I was invited to resign my commission to avoid a court martial for 'conduct prejudicial to the maintenance of good order and discipline'.

In hindsight I think I was a marked man and that they'd been waiting for any opportunity to give me the chop. Just like the stupid air force; do themselves out of a bloody good flyer rather than accept an individual a bit different from the herd.

I remember a few incidents from training days that tested the military sense of humour almost to the limit. During a question and answer session at the end of a briefing about the electrical system of a Jet Provost, I was asked,

"So, Trelawney, what's the main indication of a total electrics system failure?"

Playing to the crowd I answered, "The total electrics system failure warning light comes on, sir." As always that drew satisfying laughter from my fellow junior officers but a dark scowl from the instructor and no doubt another black mark on my course records

On another occasion, during a combat survival lecture in which we'd been instructed in the use of various pieces of life-saving kit to be found in our one-man life rafts, I recklessly indulged in what I viewed as harmless banter. The kit included rudimentary fishing tackle, presumably to be deployed in the event that one remained un-rescued by dinner time. The point being stressed was that if there were any indications of shark activity in the area, one should immediately draw in the line and stop fishing, so as to avoid the attention of the unwelcome predator.

"So, Trelawney," started the instructor, picking on me again. "There you are bobbing somewhat uncomfortably in your dinghy, awaiting rescue. Under what circumstances should you stop fishing?"

"When the dinghy is full of fish, sir?" I ventured.

On that occasion the instructor couldn't stifle his own laughter but I saw a note being made of my flippant response nevertheless.

In Ground School, we studied numerous aeronautical subjects; navigation, signals, aviation medicine, aerodynamics, aircraft technical systems, and in my view less relevant subjects such as geo-politics, service administration and organisation, and air force law.

I scraped through the ground exams with average grades but did much better in the air. High altitude and low-level flying, tail-chasing, formation and navigation all I took in my stride, but the element in which I excelled was aerobatics. I couldn't get enough of it. Invariably when briefed for a solo 'general handling' sortie in which one was supposed to practice various elements of the syllabus for an hour, I'd instead just go and perform aerobatics, not if I'm honest to hone my skills but just for the sheer joy of it. Loops and rolls, Cubans and half Cubans, stall turns and horizontal eights, spins and stalls, I loved it all. Pulling 'g' is something mere mortals never really experience, apart perhaps in limited doses on the more advanced fairground rides. I simply couldn't get enough of it and filled my boots.

Early in training, I read a poem that for me encapsulates the joy of flight. Written during the war by a young Canadian pilot, who although seeing action was later killed in a flying accident, it simply sums it up. You'll either get it or you won't.

'Oh! I have slipped the surly bonds of earth,
And danced the skies on laughter-silvered wings;
Sunward I've climbed, and joined the tumbling mirth
Of sun-split clouds, and done a hundred things
You have not dreamed of,
Wheeled and soared and swung
High in the sunlit silence.

Hov'ring there
I've chased the shouting wind along, and flung
My eager craft through footless halls of air,
Up, up the long, delirious, burning blue
I've topped the wind-swept heights with easy grace
Where never lark or even eagle flew,
And, while with silent lifting mind I've trod
The high untrespassed sanctity of space,
Put out my hand, and touched the face of God.'

John Gillespie Magee 1941

Apart from that God bit at the end, I got it. I got it in spades; every phrase, every line, every nuance.

To this day there are flights I remember clearly as if it were yesterday.

I recall a high-altitude sortie one winter's day. Briefed to climb to thirty thousand feet to experience the handling characteristics in thin air I entered cloud almost immediately after take-off. Climbing through the murk with no external references whatever I concentrated on the blind flying instruments until eventually I burst through into bright blue sky like a leaping salmon breaking the surface of a river and looked over a pure white landscape at twenty-eight thousand feet. The cloud now beneath me stretched to the horizon like a vast flat snow covered plain for as far as the eye could see.

I made some steep turns, noting how much less manoeuvrable my jet was compared with its performance at lower levels and marvelled at the long white condensation trail of water vapour I'd drawn in the sky. Then I entered a shallow dive and levelled out so that my aircraft was just sinking into the top of the cloud layer, like a shark with its dorsal fin just breaking the surface. As I sped along, the cloud ahead of me opened up in a furrow as if moved by an invisible ploughshare.

Looking ahead I saw a black dot on the horizon moving swiftly towards me on a reciprocal course, itself dragging virgin white contrails of its own. Within seconds, the Victor tanker passed four hundred yards off my port wing and just two hundred feet higher, its curling contrails elongated whirlpools of vapour which spun for a while before running out of energy and forming a static stripe of man-made cloud across the sky.

I remember returning to base at the end of night flights in cool stable air, listening to the calm reassuring voice of the final approach controller advising adjustments to heading and rate of descent to keep me on the glide path, the aircraft trimmed perfectly, almost hands-off down the radar slope, then emerging through the cloud to see the runway lights ahead. Safely down, safely home.

Before the days of weather satellites providing real time images from space, Royal Air Force stations across the country would send up an early morning 'weather-ship', an aircraft despatched to climb to altitude and radio back the heights of the various layers of cloud they encountered. The data was then aggregated to form a national picture to assist the Meteorological Office in producing the day's forecast. It was an irksome chore as it not only involved getting out of bed very early in order to take-off at first light but was a pretty tedious job too. Consequently, members of the squadron would take it in turns to man the weather-ship. The upside was that after forty minutes or so of this dull duty one had the pleasure of a free hand with the rest of the sortie. On one occasion I chose to return to base via our designated low flying area before it opened for daily operations. Flashing along at two hundred and forty knots, just a hundred feet over a large forested area, I suddenly caught sight of a cluster of khaki tents in a large clearing at the junction of two firebreaks crossing each other at right angles. It was an army contingent on a field exercise. A long queue of men lined up in front of a big camouflaged marquee. I pulled up into a steep climbing turn and doubled back, keeping the camp in sight as I did so. I then dived down and at barely fifty feet flew along the firebreak over the heads of the soldiers. I was so low that I could see the knives and forks in their hands as they queued for breakfast, many diving to the ground as I roared overhead. Great fun but alas the cause of another black mark in my record as, no doubt much to the delight of the squaddies, the blast from my jet wake ripped away the canvas screen around the officers' latrine where a Major was enjoying his early morning dump.

I enjoyed life in the Officers' Mess where in contrast to the strict discipline in the air the service seemed to tolerate the most boisterous behaviour. The devil-may-care antics of the young airmen letting their hair down when off-duty during the Second World War seemed to have passed into RAF tradition. The drunken Mess Games that followed the monthly Dining-in Nights drew stark contrast to the preening and polite conversation over pre-prandial sherry in the Anteroom and the formality of the dinner itself. Port was unfailingly passed hand by hand to the left and the Madeira to the right with neither decanter allowed to touch the table-top until a full circuit had been completed. The end of the meal was marked by the Loyal Toast when 'Mr Vice' invariably the youngest or most junior officer present, would get to his feet and propose, "Gentlemen, the Queen." All would stand, raise their glasses and repeat simply, "The Queen."

It would have been a cardinal sin, probably punishable by imprisonment in The Tower, to add any embellishment such as, "Gawd bless her."

Unhampered by the smart Mess Kit comprising blue-grey trousers, a short silk-lined 'bum-freezer' jacket with gold buttons and rings indicating rank on the sleeves, blue waistcoat or cummerbund, starched bib-fronted white shirt and bow tie around a stiff winged collar, the after dinner revelry would rapidly deteriorate into rough and tumble of one kind or another.

This might start with the construction of a human pyramid built like a multi-layered rugby scrum to support a reclining officer at the summit for the purpose of planting a footprint on the ceiling. Such a mark would be found in almost every mess in the country and those overseas.

I recall one member of the squadron, a tall Yorkshireman whose drunken party piece in the bar after Dining-in Nights was to stop the revolving ceiling fan with his head. He'd stand on a chair and from a stooping position slowly raise himself until his head interrupted the spinning metal rotor. He'd invariably appear in the morning none the worse for wear but sporting a number of Elastoplast strips across his forehead.

An energetic team game, usually played later in the evening after the senior and more sober officers had retired, was 'The Tunnel'. Two rows of armchairs would be positioned opposite each other and then tilted forward to form a long tunnel. Opposing teams would enter from opposite ends with the objective of emerging at the other end whilst hampering the progress of their on-coming opponents. The team first completing the escape would be declared the winners. That rarely happened as the fighting in the confines of the tunnel as the groups met head-on, often hampered by beer being poured by onlookers through spaces between the armchairs, usually resulted in its collapse before either team could claim victory.

It was amazing how few were the injuries sustained in this boisterous activity which we put down to the relaxing and anaesthetic properties of the accompanying alcohol. The one exception I recall was when two young officers attempted a knightly joust on bicycles along a corridor wearing empty fire buckets on their heads, employing the handles as chinstraps. They approached each other at speed, armed with mops for lances and in the inevitable collision both sustained injuries requiring a week in the station Sick Bay.

That incident, in which I was not personally involved, indirectly caused a sufficiently high number of black marks being added to my burgeoning account the very week of my disciplinary interview the Station Master.

He'd called a Mess Meeting to forbid any future 'Unseemly, juvenile, public schoolboy pranks' such as the recent jousting and went on to read the riot act about the excessive speed in which some officers were driving their cars into the parking area in front of the building.

The assembly of young men, all biting their lips and trying to avoid each other's gaze for fear of bursting into fits of uncontrollable laughter listened as, mustering the angriest voice to match his puce complexion he warned, "This reckless behaviour will no longer be tolerated."

The Mess boasted a beautiful gravel drive which circled an ornamental fountain in front of a short flight of steps leading to the entrance. I was late for the meeting, in fact totally unaware of it and not only approached the building at speed but made a handbrake turn to a standstill that sent a shower of gravel clattering against the tall windows of the anteroom in which he was giving his admonishing speech. In fact, I was later informed by highly amused friends that my timing was perfect. The shower of gravel struck the window as the words 'will no longer be tolerated' left his tight lips. It proved to be the last straw and within a week, I was encouraged to resign my commission.

I loved the flying, it was absolutely fantastic, and the camaraderie too but the rest of the bullshit just wasn't my style. I wasn't really cut out for all that yes sir, no sir, saluting nonsense, the stuffy formality and the discipline. I guess I'm too much of a rebel, too much the individual.

I don't regard getting chopped from the air force as a massive disappointment, in fact I think fate dealt me an even better hand. Without the enforced career change I wouldn't be where I am today. I certainly wouldn't be rich. A good few of my air force contemporaries were killed and some stayed the distance but were in ground roles by the time they reached thirty-five. The vast majority though left to fly holiday jets for Thomson, EasyJet and the like; probably the most boring job in the world, in my view. Mind you, to all accounts an airline pilot's gold-ringed epaulettes have the same effect on the stewardesses as the wings on an RAF uniform.

No, I wouldn't have missed it for the world. You simply couldn't buy it. You could be John Bloody Paul Getty Junior and you still couldn't buy it. They taught me to fly and I still do to this day. I have my own high-performance aerobatic aircraft and I'm still regularly pulling 'g' in the skies over Kent just like a Battle of Britain ace in his Spitfire.

I have a Pitts Special S2B and I love it. It's a two-seater and as it turns out has proved really popular with the ladies too. But more of that later.

Chapter Three
Mid-Life Crisis?

The comfortable, selfish, bachelor years had not prepared me. I was content in my ignorance. Love nor the want of it hadn't troubled me, hadn't conquered and consumed me.

But that's the past, my previous self has surrendered without a fight. I'm different now and I can't wait to tell you how much my life has changed. It's changed forever and now I'm quite possibly the happiest man alive.

I'm 63, although you wouldn't know it. I look much younger; at least I think I do, and inside I'm still just twenty-five. OK, I'm greying a bit at the temples; well, quite a lot really. In fact I'm almost completely grey and although Wendy my hairdresser does her best to conceal it, that final moment when she holds up the mirror for me to compliment her artistry, reveals the early stages of male pattern baldness. You know, the kind that starts on the crown and spreads outwards inexorably like a slow-motion tsunami.

For my sins, I'm a corporate bank manager. I've been with the bank since I was eighteen and I've hated every boring minute, every tedious day, every mind-numbingly predictable month, every ball-aching, life-wasting year. With hindsight I should have sought a role better suited to my adventurous nature. Something more glamorous, more romantic. Perhaps I could have been a steely-eyed fighter pilot. I think that would have suited my temperament much more closely. Pulling 'g's in mock dogfights, looping and rolling my fast jet around the clouds, firing my cannons on the range, zoom-climbing to forty thousand feet, then back to the mess for afternoon tea with the chaps, before we all pile into a vintage Bentley for a night on the town.

Yes, it really has been a wasted life; so far. But there is one glorious consolation. I'm loaded!

I've squirreled away around three million quid although not from my meagre salary I can assure you. No, those greedy fuckwits in Corporate HQ have got that sorted. The life-changing bonuses start just one rung up the career ladder from me. My boss, George, earns twice my salary and can match that with his annual management performance bonus. 'Performance bonus' my arse! The 'performance' is all achieved at my level.

Now I know what you're thinking; he's an embezzler. He's pulled off some almighty scam and now he's off somewhere with no extradition treaty from where he can poke two fingers at the establishment and spend the rest of his life lying to attractive young women about his daring exploits in skies of Iraq or Afghanistan.

Well, you'd be wrong. I've made it all honestly. I saved around a quarter of a million from salary over the years, not having had a wife and kids to spend it for me but the rest I've made from careful, incisive investments. When I say 'incisive', to be honest I mean through discreet insider dealing, taking advantage of confidential information from our corporate clients. And when I say 'careful' I mean that I've bought and sold through my Aunt Margaret, bless her. I do look after her though, the wonderful old lady, for I owe her the greatest of debts.

The big problem with being rich whilst working at my level in the bank is trying so hard not to show it. I've lied about the house and ten acres, saying it was left to me by my mother, and I say the top of the range Jaguar is courtesy of a close friend in the industry who arranged for me a generous employee discount. It's worked well 'til now. Apart from that and a penchant for quality suits, shirts, shoes and silk ties I've studiously avoided any overt signs of opulence. Don't want those evil fuckers from Central Audit on my case.

There's another passion too that has had to be kept a bit quiet. But I'll tell you more about that later.

Indeed the world is my oyster, or at least it could be. I'm young enough and fit enough and certainly wealthy enough. So, why don't I jack it all in and go out to play? Why don't I do all of those things I've dreamed of during those ageing, unchallenging, dreary years as a banker? Why don't I resign in a spectacular way that's talked about for decades in the stale meeting rooms of Head Office by the outwardly confident but inwardly terrified executive lackeys, and around the photocopiers of the branches by the dim and unimaginative clerical zombies throughout the division? Why don't I do that before it's too late and dedicate the rest of my days to adventure, to hedonism, to self-gratification, to feasting on all the joys life has to offer?

I've always fancied being a professional treasure hunter. Not one of those 'anoraks' with a metal detector scouring farmers' fields imagining hordes of Viking gold under their feet and finding only horseshoes and rusty iron nails. No, I mean real treasure hunting, for sunken gold in Spanish galleons. That would have every element of adventure. The painstaking research in locating wreck sites, the commercial cut and thrust in putting together a consortium of investors to fund the venture, the careful negotiation of salvage rights, and the application of the very latest technology to increase the chances of success where others have failed. With schoolboy enthusiasm I'd enjoy the weeks at sea in a purpose-built salvage vessel equipped with robotic submarine cameras and all the specialist kit that has probably made more designers and manufacturers rich than the treasure hunters who buy or lease it. I would, of course, leave the donkey work of labouring on the seabed, hoovering up shells, silt, stones and fish shit to ubiquitous bearded Aussie back packers or journeymen divers but I'd be there to watch the pay dirt come aboard. And, of course, to pick out any highly startled scallops that survive intact after being rocketed to the surface from their tenuous grip on the seabed. I'm very partial to scallops.

In another fantasy I run a unique variety theatre dining club, for a clientele even richer than I and possibly as mind-numbingly bored. The food would be exquisite and like the wine, expensive way beyond its merit. Loyal members would be regularly rewarded with the most bizarre stage acts.

The objective would be to surprise and delight with the sheer absurdity of the acts and the comedic juxtaposition of real talent and the utterly ridiculous. I would, of course, personally audition the artists attracted through advertisements in appropriate media ranging from *The Stage* to *Viz* and *Tattoo Your Bum Monthly*.

I imagine talented naked lady cellists who could pass muster in any symphony orchestra delivering dead-pan virtuoso renditions of the Warsaw Concerto; opera singers note perfect despite the hindrance of wearing 'sensible knickers' over their faces; tap dancers silent in fluffy pink bedroom slippers, and concert pianists straining through the most challenging passages from Rachmaninov's Piano Concerto No.3 on a sabotaged grand piano from which every fifth wire has been removed and with a soft pedal that emits the noise of a submarine's klaxon. To contrast with those more cultured acts there would be contortionists who from seemingly impossible positions could play the national anthem or a medley of popular Christmas carols on a kazoo. The possibilities are endless.

I'd MC the performances in formal Edwardian evening wear and would close the show each night by inviting to the stage the most inebriated diner willing to improvise an act for the amusement of the audience and to emphasise through stark contrast the brilliance of the professionals.

Yes, why don't I jack it all in and do something like that?

Another such daydream birthed between the drafting of countless ever so unctuous, 'looking forward to a long and fruitful association with your company', totally fail-safe, well securitised, personally guaranteed facility offer letters, and the impassionate 'deeply regrettable but my hands are tied, freezing your account do not issue any more cheques' foreclosure letters, was a more philanthropic solution. Perhaps I should select a suitable charity and devote to the cause my undoubted organisational and management skills, so wasted all these years at the bank.

The trouble is I'm very definitely a 'frontline' sort of guy. Working for a charity in an administrative role would be no different from the tedium of banking. And the front line in any worthwhile charity would almost inevitably involve the ardour of roughing it in some mosquito-infested third world hell hole miles from a decent restaurant.

No, on second thoughts, I'll keep up the regular donations to *Oxfam* and leave the implementation to those with less sensitive nostrils.

So why don't I resign from my tedious toil as a banker and get on with my life?

Why do I sit there listening to a depressing procession of eager youngsters with their hopeless business start-up ideas, supported by the most optimistic financial projections all doomed to failure? I suffer the pleas for extended facilities from existing clients with their slick computer presentations full of the latest business bollocks, trying to convince me that, 'with the appropriate investment' the mega contract with Global Conglomerates Inc. will double the company's turnover in six months, when I know darn well they have an unsurvivable cash-flow crisis because Ford and General Motors to whom they supply widgets are stretching them to the limit before resourcing the business to their equally fawning rival.

Is it perhaps because I have such an easy life reporting to George, my Regional Manager? I certainly don't get any pressure from him, and he keeps Head Office off my back too, now that we have 'an understanding'.

George is as pompous as he is unimaginative having attained his salary grade through mastery of the conflicting skills of corporate arse-licking whilst keeping his nose clean. He is happy to sit on his ample backside until retirement on his more than adequate index-linked pension and the proceeds of a few investment tips I put his way. Put his way not out of generosity you'll understand but as a little insurance should any hint of insider dealing arise.

No, George leaves me alone to do as I please simply out of fear of his wife, Hilda, the unwitting accomplice in my power over him. Hilda is a shire horse of a woman. She has the thighs of a Sumo wrestler, a bosom so massive her brassieres are doubtless bespoke made by a marquee manufacturer and it would take a brave man indeed to stand between her backside and a rutting rhinoceros in mating season. Massive though her suffocating breasts appear, they would not be the first part of her ample anatomy to touch the wall should she try to do so full frontal, owing to the matching enormity of her belly. Combined with a permanent facial expression of extreme annoyance the whole package is as intimidating as the Llanelli back row scrumming down in a needle match when a point behind with five minutes to play. This formidable harridan however has brought more joy to me than she has to poor old George.

If she heard of George's 'indiscretion' or worse still, God forbid, saw the photographs, his hopes of a peaceful and prosperous retirement would be dashed even if he did manage to survive being hoisted waist high by the scrotum. In Hilda's case of course the reference to her waist is, like the Equator, an entirely theoretical line.

Although my hold over George is absolute, I'm at pains to appear deferential not just in the presence of clients and colleagues but even when we're alone. He's grateful for this I know and I do my best to limit his terror. He always provides me with a glowing annual performance report, eagerly signs off my expense claims which are of course always a few pence under his authorised signatory level and turns a blind eye to my absences for long lunches. I suppose for him it's like being blackmailed by a member of the family rather than by the Mafia.

So what was George's indiscretion? What allows me to wield this degree of control?

Well, despite being physically unattractive, he could pass for his wife's brother, and despite an impressive aversion to risk worthy of a Health and Safety Officer electing to live in a padded cell, an inclination that qualifies him admirably for his senior role within the bank; it is, of course, sex. Yes, amazing as it may seem, I have video footage of good old George, pompous old George, old Blubber Butt, shagging a prostitute.

Chapter Four
Aunt Margaret

Aunt Margaret was my surrogate mother. She had taken me in before I was a year old and understandably I have absolutely no recollection whatsoever of her sister, Elisabeth, thirteen years her junior and my birth mother, who simply could not cope with bringing up a baby on her own. Whether she'd had much choice in the matter with mature reflection I seriously doubt. My birth certificate revealed that she'd been just fifteen at the time of my unwanted arrival into the world and it recorded too that my father's name was 'unknown'. My grandfather Albert Purkiss, I'm told, spoke not a single word to her after hearing the shattering news of his favourite daughter's pregnancy. In those days, the social stigma of an illegitimate birth was immense and girls unfortunate enough to find themselves in that position were often removed from the family home in disgrace and put into Mother and Baby Homes, where they made up for their 'sin' by learning to raise their babies in shame, hidden away from a society that couldn't cope with the uncomfortable reality of an accidental pregnancy out of wedlock.

Albert's sympathy for his eldest daughter, Margaret, was, although not on the same scale, very limited too. She'd been engaged at the age of twenty to a pilot killed in 1940 during the Battle of Britain and although at the time Albert had been so proud of his daughter's relationship with the brave young airman displayed a cruel impatience with her inability to get over his death. Margaret at twenty-eight still showed no inclination to seek the company of other young men. She was he concluded destined to be 'left on the shelf' and the father-daughter relationship had faded year by year like the pages of a ration book steadily depleted as coupons were cut from their dull and curling pages. Margaret had dedicated her life to work and was one of the first women to break into mainstream journalism becoming a reporter at the *Daily Mail* where in the 1950s she covered women's issues and also compiled a twice weekly feature giving guidance on how to keep your husband happy and the essential skills of homemaking on a budget. She earned a little over half of the salary paid to her male colleagues and by practising what she preached about good housekeeping, though without any experience or even inclination to find out what was required to keep a man happy, she was able to enjoy a standard of living more comfortable than the majority of her readers. Home for Margaret then was a rented flat over a greengrocer's shop in Camden High Street which she gradually decorated and furnished as tastefully as she could with second-hand furniture and brightened with colourful posters promoting rail travel to English seaside resorts, given to her by an admirer in Print Liaison hoping to curry favour with the much-admired young journalist whose private life was a mystery to all of her colleagues.

Where Elisabeth spent her first year of motherhood was a mystery to the family. She fled the austere confines of the mother and baby prison after just two weeks and was never seen or heard of again by any member of the family, apart from her sympathetic sister Margaret. She arrived unannounced at Margaret's Camden flat sporting a black eye and bruises to both arms. Though unwilling to say how she'd come by her injuries, the cause was so obvious to her sister as to be not worth questioning. My mother had asked to be allowed to stay for just a couple of nights; a couple of nights that lasted until just before my first birthday.

Auntie Margaret didn't tell me until I was in my twenties that she had returned home from the office one evening to find a brief but emotional note from her sister saying that she could cope no longer and was leaving to start a new life with a wonderful man she'd met just a few weeks earlier. It was love at first sight and that day 'her life had changed forever and she was now the happiest woman alive'.

The pencilled note, smudged possibly with tears, ended with a P.S. *'Oliver is at Mrs Mason's. Please take care of him. I know you will love him more than I can'.*

I was fed, clothed, educated and I'm sure loved by my aunt throughout my childhood although she was insistent that I called her 'Auntie' and never claimed me as her own, making it clear to all at first meeting that she was not my mother. As a very young boy, it made no difference to me as I worshipped the holy ground my goddess stood on. She was playful and kind, amusing and thoughtful, though kept cuddles very brief and woundingly returned kisses only to my cheeks. Always verbally affectionate but ever shrugging off my attempts at more intimate contact, she trained me to accept love on her terms not mine. The nearest we ever came to physical closeness was when as a five-year-old, I'd sought sanctuary from a nightmare by climbing into her bed. Surprisingly, she did hold me gently to her warm if not welcoming bosom and let me sleep in that heavenly secure embrace, although in the morning I instinctively knew she'd been tense all night and hadn't slept. I feared that level of loving experience would never be repeated, and sadly I was right. By the age of eight though, I wanted more. More cuddles and more recognition that I really was her son. Often I'd refer to her as 'my mother' when talking to the parents of school friends and became most adept at deciding to whom I would spread the lie, dividing all into two groups, those who would come to know the truth and those with whom I could perpetuate the lie by ensuring they never met my aunt.

I enjoyed a truly happy childhood with Aunt Margaret, initially in our little flat in Camden and later in the spacious 1920s' semi in Kingsbury. The utility furniture was replaced by new more stylish items as Margaret was promoted to an editorial management role eventually even being paid the same as her male colleagues of equivalent status. Whilst the furniture was upgraded and the posters replaced by tasteful prints and paintings bought from second-hand shops, the ever-present photographs of a young pilot in RAF uniform never left her bedside table, her dressing table or the dresser in the hall upon which was also placed a telephone, a status symbol the envy of my friends.

As a boy of six, I had asked Margaret who the 'soldier' was and such was my love for the woman even at that age I could see the pain in her eyes and detect the very slight change in her voice as she understated the connection by simply replying, "Oh just someone Auntie used to know."

I wanted for nothing, materially that is, and attended the local grammar school deservedly receiving accolades for excellence in English aided by my early interest in reading, avidly encouraged by Margaret. When my imaginative essays were criticised for their split infinitives or for sentences starting with a subjunctive clause, she would raise her nose in mock derision and say that while I should pay attention to my teachers' instructions in the use of good grammar, they'd be unlikely to appreciate superior literary style. "Good journalism," she'd say, "breaks all the rules. Extend your vocabulary and select exactly the right word. And always check your spelling."

She taught me so much that has proved of value in my life but if the influence of this wonderful and accomplished woman has in any area been negative, it might by some be argued that it was the snobbery with which I was so successfully and perhaps deliberately imbued.

By the age of five, I was encouraged to believe in my social superiority over many of the people I met. She once overheard a playmate say to me in puzzlement at a question I put to him, "Eh? What do you mean?" I noticed that familiar disapproving look she kept handy at all times, to be used at a moment's notice to admonish the bad manners of others in situations in which a sarcastic remark would in itself be bad manners; or more usually when she didn't credit the transgressor with the wit to understand.

When 'Eh?' then very briefly entered my five-year-old vocabulary, I was told gently but very firmly, "Don't say 'Eh', darling, it's frightfully working class. Say 'I beg your pardon' instead, it's much nicer."

Thanks to Auntie, by the age of seven I had a well-developed understanding of 'class'. I knew which jobs were working class and which were middle class. I was able to categorise the people I met by the way they spoke, the way they dressed and the way they behaved. I was taught too that there was no better test of class than indicated by a person's table manners. If they ever held their knife like a dagger or put their elbows on the table, they were very definitely working class. The sin though was magnified to unforgivable proportions if the forearms were kept rooted to the table when eating, necessitating the head to be lowered to the food rather than the cutlery raised to the mouth. 'Eating like a nodding dog' Margaret would describe it. 'Almost as bad as licking your knife' she'd say with a sneer as if it were an imprisonable offence.

Tilting their soup bowl towards them to collect the last spoonful rather than tilting it away was apparently another sure sign. Pudding bowls, everyone knew could, on the other hand, be inclined towards one, although use of the word pudding rather than dessert in those days was in itself pretty marginal. The ultimate table sin and the surest sign of all was a person's use of the fork when eating peas. They should be crushed onto the back of the fork I was firmly instructed, clearly requiring more skill, rather than being scooped up with the concave side, or worse still stabbed onto the tines.

At the age of five, on seeing a Western film in which an actor eating casually, elbows on table, a fork in one hand and using it as a spoon, I asked, "Why is that man not using his fork properly, Auntie?"

"Because he's an American, darling," Margaret replied in a tone implying that my enquiry was entirely superfluous.

"Don't Americans have the same table manners as us, Auntie?" I enquired.

"It's not a question of 'the same table manners', darling; one could say they don't have any at all. Auntie met several very nice American officers during the war but none could use cutlery properly. It isn't their fault, they clearly have never been taught."

Another of Margaret's dining etiquette rules was not to sully the table with any labelled jars or bottles. Marmalade was 'brought forward' into a moulded ceramic dish in the shape of an orange with a lid complete with a leaf and stalk which acted as the handle. The jelly was dispensed with a silver-plated spoon also decorated to match the dish with an indented design depicting a cluster of oranges. No doubt she considered it not only 'frightfully working class' but also unhygienic to dip a buttery knife into the pot. Even HP sauce and mustard were served with miniature silver ladles from tiny little glass dishes. Very wasteful yes, but no doubt regarded as a small price to pay for maintaining standards.

I learned too that manners extended beyond table etiquette encompassing the correct behaviour in all social situations. I was taught that when calling at a friend's house I should always go the back door rather than the front and when leaving always to say to my friend's mummy, 'thank you for having me.' I was made to understand too that if Auntie was talking to a friend or any adult, I should not butt in but touch her gently on the elbow to indicate that I had something to say.

At her knee I learned that all things working class were bad and to be avoided and all things middle class were good and to be emulated and safeguarded against those who would allow standards to drop and cause the world to become a rougher place.

My pre-school childhood in Margaret's care was wonderful, happy and secure. I clearly remember one hot summer's day the front door being wide open to allow in some cool air when the phone rang. Rushing to answer it she left me sitting on my chamber pot in the bathroom waiting to have my bottom wiped. I called out as I'd been trained.

"Auntie, I've finished!"

Deep in conversation for twenty minutes she didn't notice that in my impatience I had shuffled on my pot to the front door, down the steps, out onto the pavement and was a hundred yards away before the naked child was spotted by a neighbour and carried home, no doubt with the contents of the chamber pot still in place.

Another example of latent escapology occurred at the age of five on my first day at school. The mothers of a number of five-year-olds locally had arranged a daily coach hire to take the children to school and bring them home at half past three. A roster of mothers was drawn up to ensure one was present to accompany the children each way. To deal with any first day nerves a number of parents came along on the initial run. Margaret was not one of them, investing in me some self-reliance beyond my years.

I was bitterly disappointed that first day to find that none of the exciting and brightly coloured toys on display during the previous week's preparatory visit were in evidence. Instead it was clearly to be the end of carefree days of play and the beginning of disciplined learning. Our form teacher was a terrifying witch-like woman who frightened us all into silence.

On leaving the bus at school that morning, we were all told to congregate at the end of the day exactly where the coach had dropped us off and that one of the mothers would be there to ensure we all got home safely. What they neglected to tell us was that whilst we'd be having 'school dinners' many of the older children would be going home for lunch. In my first day terror I had not heard or hadn't understood this and at noon saw so many children heading for the gate that I assumed the school day was over. I was swept out of the playground by the crowd. Dutifully returning to where the coach had earlier been parked, I of course found it and the promised parent missing. I was convinced that the school day was over and that for some reason the coach hadn't come or was parked elsewhere. There was nothing for it but to find my way home.

I set off having memorised the three-mile journey, crossed several main roads and eventually reached home where Margaret, relaxing with a glass of sherry answered a knock at the door and was astonished to see me there in tears.

"The coach didn't come, Auntie," I sobbed.

If my adventure had alarmed her, she certainly didn't show it. She calmly made me a sandwich after telephoning the headmistress to explain my absence. Astonishingly, I hadn't been missed.

I remember wonderful endless summer days of fun in the garden and trips with several of Margaret's work colleagues and their children of all ages in a convoy of cars for picnics at Mill Hill and Stanmore common. Playing cricket, hide and seek and collecting newts in empty jam pots with string handles tied around the neck of the jars.

On one such trip, as a five-year-old, I had my first brush with alcohol. The picnic party stopped on the way home at a pub with a large garden and the adults sat at wooden tables as the children played, stopping occasionally for a Coca Cola or orange juice slurped from a glass or noisily sucked through a straw. Tiring of the play I sought refuge on Auntie's lap and listened to the parents chatter and laughter. Without her noticing, I took a sip from Margaret's sherry and a minute or two later, another. It was very nice and sweet.

I then began to circulate, hopping from lap to lap and being welcomed with a cuddle whenever I settled. Each time I stole a sip, sometimes spotted and sometimes not.

My last recollection of that day was being undressed and put to bed but I recall Margaret, perhaps a little tipsy herself, running her fingers gently through my hair as she unconvincingly chastised me for being so naughty.

Although Margaret wasn't a religious person and later in life, I was to learn that she was, in fact, an atheist, as a toddler she taught me a little prayer to say before bed every night. Perhaps she thought it her duty as my guardian or perhaps she was just hedging her bets.

'Gentle Jesus meek and mild,
Look upon this little child,
Pity my simplicity,
And suffer me to come to thee.
God bless Auntie and Mummy who had to go away,
And make me a good boy.
Amen'

As soon as she stopped watching over me as I prayed, I dropped the line about Mummy. In my eyes Margaret was my mummy, with no competition from anyone present or absent. I put all traces of my birth mother out of mind and never once thought about her or asked Margaret about her. She had left me and I only had love for her sister.

It was Margaret's influence with an unrequited suitor that landed me my first job, as a trainee at the bank. In those days it was a respected profession and mere mortals applying for a passport, shotgun certificate or driving licence were directed by the authorities to prove their identity by obtaining the countersignature from someone of status in the community, a pillar of society such as a Justice of the Peace, policeman, school teacher, military officer or bank manager. I guess they could have specified instead 'a middle-class person' but in post-war Britain with the rise of socialism that would have been politically incorrect even before the birth of that ridiculous concept.

Forgiving this great disservice my debt to her is endless and to this day I love her dearly. Until the day she died, I visited her regularly in Kingsbury where, never having married, she lived with the youthful pictures of a halted life.

I have in some small way repaid a little of the great debt I owe her through skilful management of her investments. Not only has this given me great satisfaction in its own right but it has also, through discreet use of new bank accounts and my recent powers of attorney, provided the cover I need for my own careful financial manoeuvrings.

Chapter Five
Time to Tell

I left unanswered the question of why I don't just jack it all in, leave the bank and dedicate my life to self-indulgence, 'going out to play' and spending both my time and my wealth as I please.

I explained that it wasn't my enjoyment of the job, nor my desire for more money, or even the comfort of my professional rut protected by my failsafe guardian and the incriminating photographs.

So why don't I quit? Why do I stay in this unnecessary if comfortable prison cell when my release papers are safely in my possession?

The answer sits just outside my office door, in the beautiful and supremely elegant form of my Chief Clerk, Hermione Nightingale.

At forty-two and divorced, she is my heart's desire. I love every inch of her body and every ounce of her being. I love her bones. I love the shape of her, the sound of her, the smell of her and I know I'd love the taste of her too, although to my immense frustration I've not got that close in the two years since she has owned my heart.

It certainly wasn't love at first sight and the age difference of twenty-one years wouldn't have even put her on my radar had I been looking. She had been with the bank for many years at another location and our paths had not crossed until she was promoted and posted to the Commercial Division and assigned to me as my Chief Clerk. I thought she was pleasant enough, certainly stylishly dressed, very elegant, well-groomed and I will confess to noticing that she was slim and very attractive for her age, although on the office sex fantasy stakes there were several younger females more likely to raise the sap in a middle-aged bachelor. Hermione, though, didn't 'display' as they did, encouraging the young men to try their luck and teasing the older ones with looks that said 'bet you wish your wife was young like me'. She seemed to be carrying an imaginary banner proclaiming to all the men in the office 'I'm here to work and quite happily single thank you, so spare yourselves the disappointment'. I remember admiring that immensely. She was her own woman in the way that I was my own man.

No, it certainly wasn't love at first sight although there was an intellectual attraction from the start. I've always thought that sense of humour is a great indicator of intellect and we often shared unspoken amusement at the expense of others, acknowledged between us with just a wry smile or raised eyebrows. We enjoyed too, a vocabulary way beyond the reach of our colleagues, mine from a lifetime of reading thanks to the interest sparked in me by my aunt. In Hermione's case, I speculated it came from a private education and the influence of a sophisticated mother determined to equip her daughter for the challenges of a career in a male-dominated world.

I was also much impressed to meet someone of her age with a total grasp of the use of the apostrophe. Simple enough but seemingly beyond the ken of everyone I encounter below the age of forty-five. She also shared with me a religious fervour for accurate spelling. For my part I always checked carefully every letter, report or email I originated to ensure there were no spelling mistakes, or typing errors that might embarrassingly appear as spelling mistakes, as I would have been mortified if one should slip through. Not that many of the recipients would have noticed I fear but it was in any event a point of principle. Hermione I noticed, through the half open panels of the integral Venetian blind in the double-glazed panel that separated her workstation from my office, would occasionally pull from her drawer a well-thumbed copy of Collins Dictionary and dexterously flick to the appropriate page, I'm sure only to confirm that her doubt was unfounded.

So neat and tidy was she, and so careful with her possessions, that I mused that this dictionary was probably the one she used throughout the sixth form at boarding school and at university too. The public-school education would have accounted too for the sassiness that on reflection I found attractive from the very start.

No, I didn't fall for her straight away. I'd been working with Hermione for at least a year before it happened. It was a totally wonderful, life-changing accident. Suddenly, from some unknown, unused, hitherto dormant place deep within my ageing anatomy, a neglected organ secreted a trickle of rare hormone into my bloodstream. It must have been waiting for more than forty years to fulfil its vital role in nature's grand plan. It must have wondered whether it would ever get the chance to escape whichever gland is responsible for its creation and cause havoc with my senses. A unique and exquisite sensation, gone in a second, but remembered for ever, it showed me there was indeed a meaning to life that I'd been unaware of until that moment.

We were to entertain a client to lunch and I invited Hermione to attend as I thought her presence might score points with a dreadful 'thirty-something' businesswoman of a strong feminist persuasion. Not that she would have felt in any way intimidated by a male only party from the bank. Good Lord no! She was one of those modern, pushy, loud, aggressive individuals brought up to believe that confidence or at least the consistent outward exhibition of it was more important than substance. The sort of useless mega ego that the researchers of *The Apprentice* television series seek to find through auditions, looking for opinionated cretins who are naïve enough to actually believe that the sort of outdated bullying management style acted out by Alan Sugar is for real. How the fawning arse lickers tremble in his presence before returning to the house to resume their pathetic self-reassuring boastfulness. Personally, I wouldn't employ a single one of those I've seen in the entire history of the fascinating show, and I'll bet my pension that as soon it's over, Sugar pays the winner to fuck off rather than employ them.

During lunch, Hermione was uncharacteristically quiet. Later, she became both quiet and pale.

"Excuse me, I need some air," she said. "I'm just popping outside for a while."

We saw her go out of the front door of the restaurant to seek some fresh air alongside a group of smokers who had gone in search of some not so fresh air. After five minutes and with none of my colleagues showing any concern whatsoever for the poor girl, I excused myself saying that I'd better just see how she is. Outside the restaurant, Hermione was leaning against the window looking even paler still. Clearly grateful for my concern she managed a smile as I approached.

"Are you feeling any better?" I enquired.

"Not really," she replied, before her knees buckled as she fainted. I caught her before she hit the ground and lifted her to her feet. She was as limp as a rag doll requiring me to hold her more tightly than I'd have thought appropriate for a boss-assistant clinch. Then it hit me. That wonderful nanosecond of supreme pleasure. She regained consciousness very quickly allowing me to loosen my grip although she still needed my arm around her slender waist for balance. Then that incredible secretion hit my bloodstream again, this time for ten seconds or more. My blushes felt hot enough to burn her face as I steadied her on her feet before letting go.

Wow! What was that? How embarrassing. How amazing. How ridiculous! I want more.

My life had changed in an instant and for weeks I analysed what had happened. What was this incredible force, so strong, so addictive and yet so tender? That first time it had lasted just a second followed shortly afterwards by a longer burst that had coursed through me like a shot of morphine. Since then it thrills and torments me daily, whenever our eyes meet or as she performs some quite normal movement while undertaking a routine office function, unnoticed by others but far from normal in its effect on me.

Sometimes it's just the slightest movement; a slow turn of the head that causes her hair to fall in a certain way, or a casual stroke with her elegant fingers as she sweeps it back behind an ear in a thoughtful moment as she concentrates on her computer screen. At other times it's sparked just by the sight of one of her catalogue of fascinating feminine shapes. Her mouth, her compelling, captivating, kissable mouth that so often distracts me to the point where I no longer hear what she's saying. I watch the beauty of its changing shape as she speaks and smiles and laughs, treating my heart to very brief glimpses of that perfectly pink tongue. How I long to touch it gently with my own.

There are times too when the sound of her voice literally strikes a chord within me. As a child, Margaret taught me how one could stand by a piano and sing or shout a note that would cause the wires to reverberate mimicking the sound. It's the same effect. I wonder if that's what's meant by 'tugging at the heart strings'. If so, these strings may be anchored at the heart but they certainly reach all the way down to my balls; or loins as Aunt Margaret would certainly prefer me to put it. "Don't be vulgar, Oliver darling, it's so unbecoming."

My 'loins' are stirred too by the outline of her small but perfectly shaped breasts, her graceful neck and the tantalising shape my angel's most perfect bum. One day, she'll sleep with it gently pressed to my stomach as I hold her in the spoons smelling her hair and counting her every breath. If she'd been born without a brain, Hermione could have made a fortune modelling lingerie or women's trousers. Oh what a perfect posterior; Kylie Minogue 6, Hermione Nightingale 10. When following her up a flight of stairs in the office or in restaurants I have to ration myself to the briefest of glimpses for fear of instantly imitating a pole-vaulter on Viagra.

My jealous eyes watch Hermione's elegant fingers nimbly stroking her undeserving keyboard. I love her slender hands, her perfectly manicured clear varnished nails and those sexy dimples lying between the base of her thumbs and her slim wrists that she sometimes, when concentrating, gently touches with the tip of her finger as if taking her own pulse. How much slower it would be than mine.

Feeling these sensations and emotions for the first time in my life I was invaded by the new, exciting, unsubtle blend of lust and love. How the curve of her exquisite bottom even fully clothed can instantly ignite my libido whilst to look into her eyes for no more than three seconds brings such tender feelings of love. The two together I've learned is a rare and beautiful gift to be enjoyed for as long as you can and cherished and remembered for ever. Better to have loved and lost than never loved at all.

What is it about your lover's eyes? How do they capture and hold one's focus only to betray your helplessness? Do the pupils that let in the light let out your spirit too? Is that it? Is it a sure and silent route into your lover's soul? And if that is the case, how can the eyes that take your breath away see nothing in your own?

I suppose it was my addiction to the thrill from Hermione's beautiful eyes that eventually gave the game away. We had become friends naturally and without motive. We liked each other. I liked her for her intellect, her humour, her determination, her sassiness and her unwavering sense of justice and fair play. In me I think she saw a man with whom she'd made an intellectual connection, a safe, sexually unintimidating friend, someone who mirrored her interest in books and politics and shared with her a view of the world formed by our own judgement rather than a lazy acceptance of the contemporary mind-set.

We shared also a delight in good food and as an alternative to the plastic stodge of the office canteen or the over-salted sandwiches offered by a nearby supermarket, I'd occasionally invite her out for a 'decent lunch'. It became a catchphrase between us. I'd slip the invitation into a business discussion as my concentration wavered during a split second of overexposure to those eyes.

"Fancy a decent lunch?"

I began to take her out regularly, enjoying her restaurant conversation, her wit and insight. I learned about her life and she about mine.

Hermione spoke with some sadness about her family; a mother she hadn't seen for years and a 'high-flying' sister, a lawyer with whom she now met only at Christmas when her younger sibling dropped in with a present for her son, Tristan. They had little contact apart from that and a surprise phone call would only mean an enquiry as to whether or not she'd also received an invitation to a relative's wedding or funeral. My enquiries about her father were met with dismissive words and a cold stare. Clearly, no love lost there. I soon sensed the contrast with my own happy upbringing which made it a topic not conducive to happy lunchtime chit chat. Gradually, my thirst for that elusive hormone became a craving. On occasions the very thought of her would initiate a bubble of whatever it was and send it I don't know where, but it was so good, so intoxicating. I'd drive to work in the morning full of serotonin and smiling at the world and my good fortune. She had made me feel so happy and had changed my life but there was no signal from her that she felt in any way the same. And why should she? How could she? The very thought of it was ridiculous. How could such a beautiful young woman, young enough to be my daughter find me in any way attractive let alone feel for me what I'd come to feel for her? I kept my sweet and painful secret.

After six months, our weekly lunches became more regular. I contrived to see her socially too taking any opportunity to look at her beautiful face and drown in the pool of her magnetic eyes. Inevitably, those snatched glances became uncamouflaged looks which in turn became unbridled stares. I hadn't yet confessed but she clearly knew. One day, I just blurted it out. We were talking business over lunch and the words just left my mouth as the precious wave hit me again.

"You do know that I love you, Hermione, don't you?"

She said nothing in return; absolutely nothing. It was as if my stupidity had gone unheard, as if the words were so outrageous that her ears had bounced them straight into a junk mail file unopened. She had after all never in word or gesture ever encouraged me or indicated she might feel the same.

Weeks went by and our friendship carried on as if nothing had happened. I began to wonder if perhaps she hadn't heard my unbelievable confession.

I was desperately embarrassed and made great effort to avoid any hint of the mounting attraction I felt. Then a glass too much of wine weakened my resolve and I started to stretch the nanoseconds of eye contact into fractions and then units and then tens.

"Please don't look at me like that," she said with compassion.

It was the day before Valentine's Day and I took a reckless gamble. I would send Hermione a card. Not one of those ridiculous pink satin jobbies designed for monosyllabic morons who think the bigger the card the greater the love. Not one with a pathetic message in rhyming couplet form about undying love. And very definitely not one of those crude ones full of sexual innuendo designed for men who probably couldn't utter the words 'I love you' even in orgasm. No, I would select one with a humorous cover so that she wouldn't be instantly repulsed but I would staple into it some words of my own. In my despair I had written a poem about her. A bloody poem for Christ's sake, you stupid wanker! Won't you ever get the message? She doesn't want to know!

I know, I know I know! I know that but I'm going to do it anyway.

I opened the password protected file in my office computer, the file in which I kept the encrypted records of my insider dealing, and the photo images of George as his dual moment of ecstasy and horror was captured by the camera in my phone.

'Oh! I just love your face,
Could look at it for hours,
But soft impassive it ignores
And coldly often glowers.
Then sudden smile the surface breaks,
To remind me how I love your face.

I just love your smile,
So quickly hidden by a hand
Or as you turn your head a strand,
Of hair to hide it while,
You reclaim your coolest style.

And I just love your laugh,
Explosive, fast, mouth wide,
But why turn away from me to hide?
As if to share it might betray a secret denture,
Or accelerate my sad dementia.'

I committed it to the post and wondered how it would be received. I felt sure Hermione wouldn't be cross because she seemed to have come to accept the situation with a kind of sympathetic amusement. But that was her; that was the wonderful, stimulating, self-assured person I had fallen for. She enjoyed my company, she liked to be wined and dined, she was appreciative of the outings I arranged with her and her son but she didn't love me and it was my unfortunate hard luck to be in love with her. End of.

At the start of each working day Hermione would join me in my office for a coffee and to discuss the business of the day. The morning after Valentine's Day was of course no exception, after all nothing of import had happened to justify a change in her routine. Her words to me as she entered my office, a cup of coffee in each hand requiring her to push open the door with her entrancing bottom were clearly chosen to put me in my place and pierced my foolish heart.

"Thanks for your card. It made me laugh."

That's all. Nothing more. Not even a friendly dig about the poor metering of the verse.

On another occasion during lunch, I was again overcome by the sheer beauty of this wonderful woman, my aching heart's desire. The sap began to rise and the familiar bubbles began to emerge slowly and in haphazard groups like ripe dandelion seeds in ones, threes and fives swept by a late summer breeze.

"Hermione, what would you do if it was the other way around?" I enquired, trying to make it sound like an overture to an intellectual discussion about life rather than the last utterings of a man being laced into his straitjacket.

"What would you do if you loved someone desperately and they didn't want to know?"

"I'd just get over it," she replied, without a nanosecond of hesitation, the comment cut short as she forked an undeserving scallop between her perfect lips into her perfect mouth, to be rolled around by that perfect tongue.

I was becoming ever more embarrassed by my pathetic situation, the hopeless gulf between our relative romantic perspectives and the unlikelihood of any satisfactory outcome but I simply couldn't give up hope. She was the one for me and however irrational the prospect of life with her would seem to any sane man, I had to pursue her until she told me finally to fuck off and die.

The cruel injustice I had to be man enough to accept was that although I adore her, although she fills my thoughts day and night, although I see my future clearly mapped out to spend the rest of my life with her, she doesn't feel the same. We have become close friends, we trust each other, we share our secrets but she doesn't love me, can't love me, won't love me.

That's the reason I can't leave. I can't make her love me but I need to be near her to collect my daily dose of serotonin that sustains both my happiness and my misery; the love drug that comes with a built-in downer.

Chapter Six
All Is Forgiven

By the time I was released by the police and had made arrangements to visit Philippa at her office a couple of days later, it was too late to call Alice to explain what had prevented me from meeting her, as Ken would almost certainly already be home or well on his way. She has no qualms about leading a double sex life but perhaps like an actress appearing in two shows at the same time, needs an hour or so to clear her head of one part before assuming the other role.

I have no doubt which of the two parts is more important to Alice, she's made that clear on many occasions, and that suits me fine. That is something though that I have to always keep in mind, her respect for Ken. I'm careful never to make any derogatory comment about him and listen without revealing any negative vibes when she talks about him, as bizarrely she quite often does. She is obviously intensely loyal to him and I'm mystified how she can romp with me with such enthusiasm and abandon whilst being so evidently devoted to her husband. Maybe I'm looking for logic where none exists, as my lovely Alice for all her physical beauty is a bimbo of the first order.

Such air-headedness though is most endearing in a beautiful mistress, if not in a wife, and quite often I find myself having to suppress my laughter at her ignorance and tales of misadventure for fear of hurting her feelings.

Alice has had several jobs in the nearly twelve months since we started our affair and each has ended in dismissal for reasons she has either failed to understand or regarded as a significant over-reaction to a trivial incident.

When I met her, she was working in the telesales office of a small local newspaper. I'd placed an ad in the *Men Seeking Women* section of the personal columns but owing to an error on Alice's part it had instead appeared in the *Women Seeking Men* section. Fortunately, the wording of the ad made my heterosexual credentials absolutely clear so no harm was done although I did receive a couple of replies from optimistic bi-sexual men looking for a challenge. The incident did though give me the opportunity to speak to Alice when I phoned to point out the error and we had a drink together that evening on her way home. I was in her bed within the week.

During that first date, she confided in me that her misplacing of my ad was not the first time she had made a mistake in handling 'Lonely Hearts' customers as she embarrassingly put it. In fact, just two issues previously she'd made a more serious error when trusted with the forwarding of responses to specific box numbers. Alice had introduced the girls in the office to the totally illegal but highly amusing practice of steaming open some of the lonely hearts replies and reading them out loud before forwarding them to their eager recipients. She'd mimic the unfortunate characters, ranging from the sex-starved 'sixty-something' lady, to the stuttering pervert and have the girls in stitches. Unfortunately on one occasion when resealing the envelopes she inadvertently forwarded a letter from a lesbian seeking no-strings sex with an adventurous twenty-something and elaborating on the unimaginable fetishes only hinted at in her ad, to a seventy-something lady seeking a respectable non-smoking gentleman for friendship and long country walks.

It turned out that the seventy-something lady did not have the g.s.o.h. that she had claimed and following an internal investigation, during which 'the ugliest girl in the office grassed me up', Alice was fired.

Prior to the newspaper job, Alice had been employed briefly as a receptionist in an advertising agency whose plush regency offices were situated on three floors in the High Street above a hairdressing salon housed in the basement. The agency suites were plush and tastefully decorated and approached by half a dozen impressive stone steps up from the pavement. The salon was approached by a dozen steps down from it and although not as exquisitely decorated attracted a well-heeled clientele.

Alice had been working there only a week when she first got into trouble with Shutter, the pompous Client Services Director, who quite understandably insisted that all staff, 'of no matter what level' exuded the agency's brand values. Alice didn't know what 'brand values' were of course but guessed it meant smiling at anyone who came into the stylish reception area and adopting the poshest voice she could muster. She was bright enough though to know that with absolutely no previous experience of reception work, she had most likely been employed for her decorative qualities, or as she put it, 'having the best tits in town.'

It took my little sex goddess most of the first day to master the simple switchboard and building in confidence daily she fancied herself as the new face of the agency by Thursday.

"Good morning! Shutter Tomlinson Rounce Edwards Welch Taylor Hampton," she'd chirp, "Alice speaking, how may I help you?"

Occasionally, she'd get the names in the wrong order, sometimes miss out one or more, but rarely did she manage to stifle a snort of laughter as she said 'Hampton'.

The Administration Manager, Carol, liked Alice's bubbly personality and was probably responsible for her selection, so proved to be very helpful and protective in the early days. It was Carol who suggested that, when answering the outside lines, Alice look up and read the names from the massive framed logo board, or 'ego board' as Carol termed it, occupying virtually the entire wall facing the reception desk.

Initially though Alice had difficulty differentiating outside calls from internals and rapidly became a figure of amusement throughout the agency as she'd slowly answer, reading from the logo, "Shutter. Tomlinson. Edwards, oh no I mean Rounce. Edwards. Welch and Taylor Hampton," to staff simply enquiring if the post had arrived.

On the Friday of her first week, she incurred the wrath of Tomlinson, the exaggeratedly camp Creative Director, when he overheard her say to a caller asking for Shutter,

"I'll try his line for you, but I'm sure he's still in the toilet."

On instructions from above, Alice was admonished by Carol, who could barely keep a straight face. Characteristically, though, Alice failed to understand what had been wrong in her words and wondered why all to whom she recounted the tale either cringed with embarrassment or laughed heartily.

Her downfall had come in the third week of employment. Alice had been asked to water the flowers in the five window boxes that adorned the tiny first-floor balcony that decorated the entire frontage of the building. Not wide enough to actually stand on, the balcony was simply an Edwardian architectural flippancy and so the window boxes could only be reached by leaning out of the sash windows beneath which each was positioned. Alice was fully aware that the picture she made in her very short skirt whilst leaning out of each window with outstretched arm guiding a five-litre watering can, was a delight to the male account executives and of great amusement to their bitchy female counterparts, and she played to the gallery, with false modesty keeping one had behind her back fussing at the hem of her skirt in a deliberately futile attempt to limit their view of her scanty knickers.

Carol had briefed Alice to give each box just half a watering can, but failing to appreciate the relevance of the odd number, of course, she found herself with a whole can of water when approaching the final window. *Never mind*, thought Alice, *what's the harm in a bit of extra water*, and gave it the whole five litres. The window box soon overflowed and half a gallon of muddy water ran over the edge of the balcony and, as if in a perfectly timed circus act, straight onto the head of a matronly lady emerging from the salon below, whilst admiring her brand new perm reflected, very briefly it must be said, in the glass of a cabinet containing images of perfectly primped models much younger and prettier than herself.

Her screams could be heard throughout the agency, even bringing boyish art directors and copywriters to the windows of their more spartan offices on the third floor.

They were heard too by the unctuous Hampton in the Conference Suite just as he was summing up a client presentation to the global brand leader in umbrellas and 'rainwear' by reiterating the ground-breaking new customer proposition, "Stand out in the rain."

As Carol, followed by a posse of curious staff and clients descended the stairs to establish the cause of the commotion they'd all heard at ground level, she met Alice coming up, wiping her hands together in a gesture indicating she'd proudly sorted out a difficult task.

"It's all right," said Alice. "Some old Biddy got 'er hair a bit wet and was making a fuss. It's OK, I told her where to get off!"

Sadly, Alice was told where to get off too and was dismissed on the spot by a red-faced Hampton in front of the sniggering clients, for whom the new strap line would probably never quite work in the way intended.

I left my call to Alice until after nine on the morning following the accident to be sure that Ken had left for work. I was keen to excuse my failure to arrive the previous day and worried that her inevitable sulk might delay the resumption of normal service.

She was more than understanding and genuinely concerned at the news. Interestingly too, she was the only one to enquire if I had been hurt in any way. I was urged to hurry round that very morning and although the scallops and monkfish had been consumed the night before by a very impressed husband there was other business to attend to and within the hour I was sucking on those delightful nipples without the frustration of any pre-prandial foreplay, whilst hearing of the latest misadventure to befall my little porn star.

Following a most satisfying romp that elicited no fewer than three little squeaks from Alice which I interpreted as orgasms but couldn't really be sure, we lay together on the bed in the guest room staring at the ceiling and making small talk. It was the habitual set for our passion as she admirably denied me access to the matrimonial bed.

Whilst idly gazing at a set of bookshelves fitted into an alcove alongside a chimney breast, I noticed that the books were laid on edge rather than upright in library fashion. It seemed so incongruous that I was moved to ask why they'd been stacked in that way.

Alice had on several occasions in the past, without ridicule, mentioned her husband's lack of prowess at D.I.Y. and I guessed I was looking at such an example.

Sure enough, as I suppressed the urge to laugh; she, absolutely dead pan, explained how it had become necessary.

Ken had decided to build the bookcase himself, and being a thorough sort of chap prepared a detailed sketch of the job, first measuring all of the books and sorting them into groups by size; that is by height, in order to calculate how far apart the shelves needed to be positioned.

There was to be a shelf for the seven-inch books, another for the ten inch, and so on. He then allowed half an inch finger space so that the books to be extracted easily, and another quarter inch for the thickness of the wood he'd use for the shelves. All good stuff which I'm sure had Alice beaming with admiration as he explained the plan.

Unfortunately, he hadn't allowed for the one and a half inch batons upon which the shelves were to rest and the end result was that the shelf spacing wasn't suitable for any of the books at all. Consequently, the pragmatic Ken simply stacked them horizontally rather than upright and no doubt considered the job a success.

On another occasion, Alice had described how her husband had spent a Bank Holiday boarding the loft to provide extra storage space. He'd borrowed a trailer to go to the builder's yard so that he could buy large pieces of chipboard. At six by four feet, they would make the job speedier by increasing the area covered by each board and hence reduce the number of boards to be laid. It was only after carrying one if the boards up to the landing that he discovered the first snag. The loft access was just short of two feet square.

Ken, a patient fellow, after further calculations went to B&Q to buy a circular power saw. He then cut all of the boards into three pieces, each two by four. Alice then helped get them into the loft by passing them diagonally through the two by two aperture to Ken perching in the un-boarded loft.

Snag number two was that the spacing of the joists was such that a four-foot board whilst more than long enough to span two joists was inadequate to span three, requiring an unsupported join between boards rather than a solid one that could be securely nailed to a joist at both ends. The pragmatic Ken pressed on.

With the loft fully boarded and Ken now sitting in the far corner having methodically worked progressively away from the trap door, he had a bright idea. Recognising that the unsupported joins would present a hazard to future unwary visitors to the loft, he would carefully mark the position of the joists beneath the boards with a marker pen and install a notice inside the lid of the trap door declaring that one should only walk on the areas indicated by the hachured lines. Alice fetched a suitable marker pen and Ken completed the task and sat, feet dangling from the trap door as he admired his handiwork.

Snag three became evident only weeks later when together they attempted to shift boxes of junk too useless to be of use but too valuable to throw away, into the newly prepared storage area. Ken, careful to observe his own instructions neatly written on the upper surface of the trap door, treading only on the lines marking the joists, dropped the first box into position only to hear the chipboard split under its weight. He'd bought half inch chipboard instead of three-quarter inch, totally unsuitable for the purpose.

Hearing these and other amusing stories of Ken's D.I.Y. incompetence, usually delivered by Alice not in a mocking manner but almost in admiration of her husband's willingness to tackle such brave challenges, I always managed to keep a straight face, that is until she told me about the clothes post.

Alice had wanted a 'proper clothesline' to replace what she described as the 'stupid roundy-roundy thingy' they'd inherited from the previous owners of the

54

property. Ken rose to the challenge and planned thoroughly for the weekend's project. On Friday he bought the Rolls Royce of clothes posts, a galvanised nine-foot steel pole that would last a hundred years, complete with a pulley mounted the top and a cleat lower down to tie off the end of the washing line. On Saturday morning he bought ready mixed concrete and that afternoon dug a hole of exactly the dimensions specified in the surprisingly detailed instruction sheet which was of course printed in sixteen languages all translated from the original in Cantonese. Whilst the words were more confusing than useful, the diagram was all Ken required.

The pole was first placed in the one cubic foot hole he'd accurately measured and carefully dug, and then it was braced with a temporary tripod of diagonal supports to ensure it was absolutely vertical. Ken's eye had been true and very little adjustment had been necessary after checking its stature with a spirit level that he had bought especially for the purpose.

Ken mixed the prescribed amount of water with the concrete in a wheelbarrow and stirred it with a spade until it was the consistency of thick ice cream, rather than 'jelly' as called for in the instruction sheet. He then tipped the liquid concrete into the hole. It surrounded the centrally positioned pole and exactly filled the hole to ground level. *What a perfect job,* he must have thought as he admired his completed work through the leaded windows of the kitchen and again as he checked the setting concrete before retiring to bed that night.

Like a child on Christmas Day, dressed only in his slippers and pyjamas, he eagerly rushed into the garden before breakfast to inspect his new creation. Sure enough, the concrete had set perfectly and the pole stood firmly anchored and absolutely vertical. He brimmed with pride. At last a D.I.Y. job completed without a snag.

It was only when Alice arrived on the scene tearing away the shrink-wrap packaging from a brand new washing line, that the thought occurred to Ken that perhaps he ought to have threaded the line through the pulley at the top of the pole before setting the now eight feet high post, in concrete. No matter, he'd shin up the pole and thread it through. Feeling somewhat self-conscious he first took a furtive glance around the upstairs windows of the adjacent houses that overlooked the garden to ensure he wasn't being watched. Gripping one end of the plastic-coated clothesline between his teeth he reached up with outstretched arms whilst squeezing the pole firmly between his knees and gradually hauled himself up the pole to within reach of the pulley. Alice looked up with an admiring smile. Ken had to increase the grip with his knees in order to let go with one hand and then expertly threaded the end of the line through the pulley at the first attempt. Mission completed. He then started slipping slowly down the pole in a controlled descent. Then came the snag. The cleat for tying off the end of the clothesline was positioned exactly thirty-eight inches above the ground but Ken's inside leg measurement was only thirty three inches, and he let out a startled squeal as he hooked his scrotum on it. He was stuck. He could limit the pain only by trying to pull himself up using his arms to reduce the pressure and by standing on tiptoe. Like a man clinging to a high ledge by his fingertips he realised it was a battle between the pain of hanging on and the inevitable catastrophe of letting go. To avoid castration he had to ignore his aching biceps and his screaming calf muscles that had never before been called upon to stand for so long like a ballet dancer on his toes. In fact ballet shoes might have a helped a little but sadly Ken was in his blue denim carpet slippers.

Unable to move up or down, in fact not daring to move in any direction poor Ken was painfully stranded. He couldn't climb the pole as any movement upwards would have first required a movement downwards to achieve the necessary spring. And movement downwards was too painful to contemplate.

Alice, although concerned, saw the funny side and was in a fit of hysterical laughter as she tried in vain to give him the necessary bunk up. Recounting the story to me she did of course giggle when using the words 'bunk-up'. Ken was rescued after Alice had sought assistance from two male neighbours who managed despite their laughter to lift him down but only after teasing him with mock negotiations involving car washing and lawn mowing for the rest of the year. By mid-afternoon, the story, no doubt embellished at every telling, was known throughout the neighbourhood.

Chapter Seven
Philippa's First Flight

I'd wondered from first meeting her whether Philippa Stapleton would be a laugher or a screamer. Whenever I take a woman flying for the first time I always ask if they'd like to try some simple aerobatics. They always say 'Yes' in order to appear daring but in some you can see a just a little doubt in their eyes. I ask if they like fairground rides and if they answer in the affirmative, I know they'll enjoy the aeros. If there's any hesitation, I know that they will not. This is always disappointing as I've found that invariably those who enjoy aerobatics will be adventurous in bed too.

Any who failed the fairground test would not be invited to fly because, apart from the obvious reason, the interior of the Pitts has far too many nooks and crannies in which puke can collect and be difficult to remove completely. This would spoil the evocative cockpit aroma that has excited me and generations of pilots throughout the world, the unique and wonderful blend of hot metal, petrol, oil, rubber, leather and sweat.

During the flight, the women will fall into one of three categories. They will turn green and stay silent, they will laugh out loud or they'll scream with delight. I had a strong feeling that despite her prim appearance Ms Stapleton would turn out to be a screamer. I certainly hoped so.

We'd met in her office on only two occasions since the accident, once to outline her strategy to expedite a 'no case to answer' decision from the police and subsequently for her to proudly read to me a response to her letter of complaint to The Chief Constable about the totally unacceptable treatment of her client and the extreme incompetence of his staff. I was in the clear. It was over.

We'd had a celebratory drink that evening in a nearby wine bar frequented by some of her colleagues. God, and they say I'm arrogant. What a bunch of public school tossers. Timothy, Guy, Hugo and Tarquin. Tarquin, for fuck's sake!

She felt obliged to join the group when invited and I tried to make polite conversation but it was clear they were taking the piss. Maybe they didn't think I was good enough for their female stablemate, or more likely they were jealous at seeing her out with a good-looking bloke worth a few bob. They weren't at all impressed about my commission in the RAF, nor about my aerobatics. I bet they all would have been green and silent types anyway.

Philippa could sense I was irritated by their presence and we moved away to a quieter corner with the excuse that we had business to discuss. We were not, however, out of earshot and could hear their juvenile banter of which I was clearly the brunt. I heard the whispered words 'Flash tosser' leave Tarquin's smirking mouth and would have instantly filled it with my fist but for Philippa's calming presence. I chose instead to impress her with my mature self-control but whilst she fiddled for something in her handbag I took the opportunity to momentarily make eye contact with him and with the thinnest of smiles and a menacing nod of the head convey the message that without doubt he'd be paying a price for it later.

Four attractive young women in their late teens or early twenties entered and settled on stools at the opposite end of the bar from the junior lawyers. Simultaneously Tarquin nudged Guy with his elbow and Hugo made a parallel gesture to Tim.

"Hairdressers!" they all snorted in unison as if it were a tie breaker in a pub quiz.

The embarrassed girls pretended not to hear the comment and avoided eye contact with the group who embarked on an adolescent and no doubt regularly practiced game of 'Impress the Bimbo'. It was as predictable and embarrassing as it was banal.

First Hugo's mobile rang, with the musical ringtone of *'I'm in the Money'* which he answered in a voice deliberately loud enough to be heard not just across the bar but throughout the pub as he turned away, a finger in one ear with his back to the group without leaving it.

"Hugo…yeah, go," and after pretending to listen for a few moments interspersed with, "yeah…of course…yeah, that's what I expected," he responded to the non-existent caller.

"Buy half a mil the moment the market opens and sell all my Glaxo! Got that? Yeah, all of it. Yeah cheers."

He then re-joined the conversation whilst the others supported him with body language implying they were suitably impressed.

I was waiting for it and sure enough Guy's phone rang next with the classic bass guitar sequence from *'The Chain'* by *Fleetwood Mac,* the signature tune used for TV coverage of Formula 1 motor racing.

"Hello, mate…about bloody time. Just tell me it's ready!"

After a brief pause he continued.

"For fuck's sake Buddy, how long does it take to do an oil change on a Ferrari? OK. OK, but must have for the weekend, got a house party in Gloucestershire. Don't let me down. Sure. Bye."

The 'hairdressers' were amused but not at all taken in by the act and giggled girlishly, invitingly. I looked at Philippa and asked if this was a regular party piece by her young colleagues.

"Oh yes," she exhaled, raising her eyebrows and nodding her head in a tired gesture she might use to comment on the annoying behaviour of someone else's persistently naughty children.

"What galls me, though, is that it actually works!"

The next mobile to ring was Tarquin's.

Tarquin evidently was a little more subtle than his peers and rather than perform a previously rehearsed and doubtless well-used act, improvised a response clearly designed to take the piss out of me as well as to impress the girls who were by now whispering to each other, no doubt discussing how to respond to the inevitable forthcoming advances.

"Listen James," he said in a weary and exasperated tone, "I appreciate it's my turn to do the test flights but I need to know, if you don't mind, that the fucking wings aren't going to come off again!"

I had to struggle not to laugh at that one myself but Philippa did, so I responded with a grin and gestured to her to call my phone.

The comedians moved to approach the young girls, who repositioned their stools in a welcoming gesture and to allow them to filter in boy, girl, boy, girl in expectation of further entertainment or, I hoped, just free drinks for the rest of the evening before their burly rugby playing boyfriends arrived with less of a sense of humour.

My phone duly rang with the factory-set ringtone, which made me feel just a little unadventurous I must confess but I answered casually without looking at the giggling group at the bar.

"Speaking," I said to the imaginary caller as if confirming my identity.

Philippa looked nervous as if worried that I'd say something too provocative but I reassured her with a mischievous smile and a barely perceptible shake of the head. After a short pause I spoke for the benefit of the girls at the bar, in a mock whispering tone, but loud enough to be heard by all.

"Yes, all four of them are here now, in The Butcher's Arms in the High Street. Tarquin clearly has missed his medication today, Guy has managed to get out of his straight jacket and Tim has clearly been self-harming again. Hugo looks comatose…yes, I know it's hard to tell. They have all been drinking, so I'd get here as soon as you can."

One of the boys looked across and with a smirk said, "Tosser!" but I was rewarded to see that two of the girls appeared uncertain and the little party began to break up before it had started. Hugo defeated, simply raised a defiant middle finger in my direction.

I was bored with the banter by then and keen to progress things with Philippa.

I started to make small talk about the bar, its proximity to her office, the frequency of her visits there and her typical working hours but was interrupted when her phone rang.

"Excuse me please," she said with a polite smile, "This looks important."

She tilted her head away so that she could look into space whilst taking the call.

"Yes, it is…OK…yes, tomorrow at ten would be most convenient."

I was impressed with her confident tone and professional manner as she clarified a few details of the next day's business with an evidently important Client.

"Yes, you too. Until tomorrow then… Thank you, Prime Minister."

The boys at the bar applauded the performance acknowledging they'd been well and truly trumped. I clapped silently too, although I didn't confess that I'd fallen for it hook, line and sinker.

What a surprise, the lady had a great sense of humour!

I was also surprised how friendly and open Philippa appeared that evening. In fact I must say I was surprised that she'd even agreed to come out for a drink as in all three of our past meetings she had appeared cool and distant with an air of superiority that permeated the usual thin veneer of lawyer client cordiality.

After graciously accepting my gratitude for obtaining justice for me, or as she bluntly put it, 'getting me off', the circumstances of our meeting were never mentioned again. It was as if this intellectually intimidating blue stocking had shed her professional aloofness with the closing of the file. She started to make conversation as if I were an old friend, or more particularly as if I had suddenly become potential boyfriend material. Laughing at my jokes and seemingly impressed by my flying stories, she held my gaze just a nanosecond longer than one might have expected at that stage and every minute or two swept her hair back with one hand and a girlish toss of the head. Yes, I felt sure she was inviting an indication of interest from me and perhaps cruelly I decided to keep it cool for a while and play hard to get. It was a conscious decision and a first for me. I was of course as ever eager to get the new target into bed but felt I'd bide my time and see how far she was prepared to go in making the running.

We talked for hours. I wanted to take her out for dinner but judged that would be a step too far given my intended strategy. Instead we just sat there and drank and talked and drank some more.

I learned an awful lot about Philippa Stapleton that evening. She opened up to me to a degree I've never experienced before, even on a proper first date let alone a casual drink.

I got virtually her whole life story. She was the younger of two daughters of a committed career woman dedicated to her job as an international fashion buyer for a major chain of high street stores, and a part time journalist and freelance advertising copywriter. Mummy and Daddy had divorced when Philippa was eleven and although legally in the care of her mother was sent to a boarding school at the expense of her father, an arrangement he clearly resented as his ex-wife earned easily four times his salary. Home life was almost non-existent with alternate holidays spent either with grandparents or with an aunt and uncle in Hastings.

By the time she was fifteen, Mummy had remarried in a wedding to which her disappointed daughter hadn't been invited, and moved to New York. They'd had no contact since.

Philippa was then old enough to hope that perhaps her father would welcome the increased share of his little girl's time if not the added responsibility, but his advancing alcoholism, prevalent in his profession, made him less able to cope with relationships particularly one with a teenage daughter.

During the summer of her sixteenth birthday, Daddy offered to take her on holiday to a remote part of Majorca where she hoped to enjoy her father's attention and some recognition for her academic successes to date. Her elder sister had very much disapproved and Philippa's insistence on accepting caused a rift between the siblings that had lasted to this day. During months of anticipation before the holiday Philippa planned outings and adventures, mountain walks and countryside picnics, grown-up candlelit dinners and rural rides in an open-topped car. Accompanied by her House Mistress she made several shopping trips to *Feva* in Cheltenham for swimwear, thin summer dresses and elegant evening wear. It was to be a wonderful renaissance of the relationship with her father. She was convinced she'd soon feel again the warmth she'd been deprived of since the break-up of the family home.

Philippa's father sadly had a different perspective of the forthcoming holiday. It would consume time and more particularly money that he could ill afford. He'd lied too about the accommodation he'd booked. Rather than the romantic small hotel in a picturesque village of his earlier description, Philippa was disappointed to discover Daddy had taken two rooms in a small hillside smallholding run by a non-English speaking elderly couple. The local village had a small bar 'entirely unsuitable for a girl of your age' at which her father spent most of the first three days of the vacation. On the fourth day, he didn't get out of bed and on the fifth day he didn't return from the bar, sending a hastily written message that he had been urgently recalled to the office and that his daughter was old enough now to find her own way home. Accompanying the note was a birthday present evidently as hurriedly wrapped as it was no doubt purchased. It was a bracelet made up of five plain one-inch pieces of silver each joined by two small silver links. It was still wrapped in the paper bag bearing the jeweller's brand which her father had simply folded over and sealed with sticky tape. I learned that it was the last thing she ever received from him.

After a day and night of painful sobbing, ignored by the farmer and his wife, Philippa did indeed muster the courage to find her own way back to England, back to school and to an independent life.

Summer holidays, half-term breaks and Christmases for the next two years were spent at school with the kindly House Mistress, Miss Forbes, who cared for Philippa until she left for university and showed her more love in that time than either parent ever did. The two became very close, so close in fact that her cruel classmates openly speculated about what the teacher had actually been schooling her in during the holidays. Miss Forbes cried bitterly on the day she left and begged her to return whenever she could. The new Philippa Stapleton, however, never went back.

I also learned on that first evening out that Philippa had only ever had one boyfriend, at university, in her final year. She'd lived in halls of residence until then, seriously applying herself to her studies but desperate for a little freedom accepted the invitation from a fellow law student to share one of a pair of two bedroomed flats over a launderette in Cambridge. She described him as a handsome young fellow who pestered her to share his bed until in the final term she relented. They were photographed together side by side on graduation day throwing their mortar boards into the air. They kissed goodbye and had not seen each other since. At least that's how she described the relationship. I later came to doubt her account and that she'd ever had sex with a man.

During the evening I invited her to come flying one weekend, a prospect that seemed to excite her and she readily agreed.

We parted with a handshake and a peck on both cheeks which seemed appropriate given the professional nature of our meeting but the mutual gestures shared during that evening had hinted of something more.

We met at the airfield a week later and had a coffee in the clubhouse where I briefed Philippa about the intended flight, not about safety issues as they do on airlines but about the various stages of the trip I'd planned. I assured her that we'd only do aerobatics if she was entirely happy and that if not, we could simply fly around the area on a sight-seeing tour.

I was pleased to note that she'd heeded my advice on what to wear. She was dressed in jeans and a stylish leather jacket. Her hair was tied neatly in a ponytail which protruded through the rear strap of a baseball cap.

I always enjoy strapping women into the front seat of the Pitts. Firstly you have to help them into the cockpit, it might appear out of chivalry but more importantly it's to ensure they tread only on the reinforced footplate at the wing root and not on the fragile fabric covering the wing. They often need a hand to get their leg over the coaming too as the angle of movement required is not one that any but the fittest might experience outside of the gym. Once comfortably seated in front of the impressive array of instruments, you have to ensure they are securely held in by the five-point harness. Two shoulder straps and two padded lap straps meet a negative g strap emerging from beneath the seat in a central locking device which sits across their abdomen. The negative g strap has first to be adjusted to the right length to ensure they don't lift in the seat during inverted flight. There's nothing more likely to give a novice the feeling that they are falling out of the aeroplane than any slackness in the negative g strap. The process of strapping in is quite intimate in that the harness straps need to be finely adjusted to suit the individual passenger. Whilst the shoulder and lap straps can be adjusted by most men, the lack of leverage in such a confined space makes it almost impossible for a woman unpractised in the operation. The negative g strap passing up between their legs, tight into their crotch requires particular care as you can imagine. I always say, as they anticipate the proximity of my hand reaching down there,

"Now, keep very still while I do this."

It always elicits a nervous giggle and sometimes a more revealing suggestive comment which all goes to test the lie of the land. When I first took Alice flying her response had been whether she could reach my dick from there and if so would it count for membership of *The Mile High Club.*

I asked Philippa to remove any loose change from her pockets and anything else that could come adrift and cause problems. She asked if she should remove her silver bracelet, but I didn't think that would be necessary at it seemed securely fastened. I'd already got the Pitts out of the hangar, refuelled it and completed the pre-flight checks so that all that all I had to do was show her how to climb into the front cockpit.

Philippa sat absolutely motionless in her seat. The shoulder and lap straps were adjusted without comment but as I moved slowly to fasten the negative g strap she shivered noticeably and insisted that she was more than capable of doing it herself. She tried but failed and I told her to relax as I carefully secured the strap without touching her in any way.

After ensuring that she was both safely strapped in and as comfortable as it's possible to be when trussed up like an oven-ready turkey, I strapped myself into the rear cockpit behind her and completed the pre-starting checks. The engine roared into life and as we taxied out, I made small talk to calm her nerves as we journeyed towards the runway. I described the planned flight, explained that after take-off I'd level out and allow her to get used to straight and level flight before we did anything more exciting. I repeated that we could limit it to a few gentle turns if she wasn't happy to start aerobatic manoeuvres and instructed her to give me plenty of warning in the unlikely event that she should feel sick, as it only gets worse, never better. Finally, I told her where she would find the sick bag in the cockpit's side pocket should it get to that stage, joking that in that eventuality I'd be more than grateful if she'd hang onto it securely until we were back on the ground.

We took off and I climbed away gently rather than zoom climbing as I would have done if showing off to a male passenger. We levelled out at two thousand feet and I turned south towards a bank of stratocumulus clouds which are great fun to fly around as they give you the most amazing sensation of speed and freedom of three-dimensional control.

I asked over the intercom if she was feeling OK but got no response. I turned up the volume and asked again. No response. I tapped on her motionless head in front of me but the canvas helmet made no movement. I realised she was frozen with fear. I loosened my straps to allow me more movement, leaned forward and shook her head gently but firmly. "Can you hear me, Philippa," I called, "Are you feeling OK?"

"I don't like it!" she replied, "Can we go back please? Now." Ten minutes later we were safely on the ground. The propeller jolted to a halt as I pulled the mixture fully lean and as silence returned, I heard her retch into the sick bag.

She evidently didn't like flying, let alone aerobatics. I began to wonder if perhaps she didn't like sex either.

Chapter Eight
George's Indiscretion

It started with a night out entertaining corporate clients following an informal meeting to review their borrowing facility. The renewal was a formality and they knew it, and whilst the procedure was well within my level of responsibility George invited himself along as he was keen to foster a good personal relationship with them, and for he and his oversized spouse to continue to enjoy regular and lavish hospitality in the client's executive box at Cheltenham Race Course.

We'd met for dinner at my favourite Italian restaurant where the perfection of their Scallops Mornay is trumped only by the most heavenly monkfish and lobster ensemble ever to grace the table of a restaurant anywhere in the world. I booked the table personally to ensure that we were given the best position in the house and to make it absolutely clear that if any member of staff should show even the slightest hint of recognition, I would cancel my standing booking for Wednesday lunch.

Kir Royales were followed by my favourite Gewürztraminer, what else could so perfectly complement the scallops that I had briefed the head waiter to recommend? I ordered a cheeky Frascati to accompany my monkfish, and an inexpensive Montepulciano D'Abrusso for the three clients and George who'd all unimaginatively opted for the Tournedos Rossini. It was all part of my continuing bluff to appear at this stage unknowledgeable about wines. I was of course unaware at the time that the events that were to follow that evening would see George unflinching in his approval of my expenses for 'working lunches' in this and other quality restaurants for many months to come. Working lunches to which he knew only too well no client would ever be invited.

I asked the attentive proprietor, Luigi, to recommend a red wine worthy of our guests to follow the Montepulciano and he responded with the pre-arranged suggestion, an excellent though overpriced Lamborghini Campoleone IGT 1999. Adhering diligently to his brief he asked if I'd like to taste it, giving me the opportunity to say that I rarely drink red and, "Mmmm, I say, yes that really is very nice. I'll join you gentlemen if I may."

What nectar, but rather wasted on my fellow diners; like feeding pigs with cherries as Aunt Margaret was often heard to comment in such situations.

The second bottle was followed by a ridiculously over-honeyed dessert wine sweeter even than the tiramisu chosen by all but myself. I asked for 'the standard house port' instead, and Luigi's double tap with a finger against the side of his nose went unnoticed by the others now assailing their undiscerning palates with the sickly stodge.

"Whooge for coffidge?" slurred George.

His face had been getting redder and his sips had become slurps about halfway through the Campoleone. His voice had been getting progressively louder too, and his jokes more blue. His surprising repertoire, he admitted to my astonishment, came in emails forwarded by his boss in Corporate HQ. Now's there's something worth a mental note in writing, I thought to myself.

Two of our guests took their leave, thanking us for our 'continued support' and for the 'excellent meal'.

The remaining client, Terry, in his early thirties the youngest of the group and as Financial Controller junior to his colleagues in status too, had been buttering up George unsubtly throughout the meal. An Essex lad with appalling syntax, he laughed at George's blue jokes and countered with some of his own in what became a tasteless contest between the two of them to include more obscenities than the other. I'd never before seen George behave like this and had never dreamed he possessed this side to his character.

I was ready to leave. The business had been completed and I had enjoyed a superb meal at my favourite restaurant at the bank's expense without the secret of my regular patronage being revealed. Mission accomplished. I was now bored with my fellow diners and all I wanted was to take a taxi home to bed.

George's ambitions were very different. No doubt the years of hen-pecking had made him very determined to extract the most pleasure possible from the rare opportunity of a night on the town, without the intimidating presence of his personal, un-uniformed prison camp guard.

Terry took us to 'a great bar I know' and while unnoticed, I regularly swapped glasses with George to limit my intake and double his, my unwanted companions became more and more drunk. After an hour it was as if the two were the best of friends, young bucks out on the beer after a rugby match and up for anything.

"Ever been to a massage parlour, Georgie?" Terry enquired.

If he'd been sober, George would have flinched at being called 'Georgie' by the young upstart but either the alcohol or his astonishment at the question allowed the insolence to pass unchecked.

"Not in this country," answered George, assuming the air of a much-travelled modern day Lord Byron. "But more than a few in Thailand, I can tell you," he lied.

George expounded his view about oriental women being the best in the world, the most accomplished in the art of sex.

"It's in the culture. Their mothers teach them from an early age how to please a man. Did you know that?"

"Is that so, mate?" Terry responded in a tone that had me betting George was being set up for cruel joke at his expense.

"I bet you'd be showing us the sights tonight if we were out East, leading me and Oliver astray and getting us all laid."

"I certainly would, old chum," replied George lapsing further into the phoney colonial caricature.

"They don't call it Bangkok for nothing you know."

"You're all talk chum," said Terry in a challenging tone. "I could take you to a knocking shop not a mile from here Georgie Boy, where all the girls are from Thailand. Absolutely top-grade pussy, the sexiest totty you can imagine."

I couldn't believe my ears. This guy was actually suggesting that we went and paid for sex. Whether I had significantly misjudged George, or whether he'd simply gone too far in the sexual bravado to turn back I don't know, but I could sense he was going to agree. That left me with just one imperative; how could I escape?

I'd never even dreamt of paying for sex and Aunt Margaret had instilled in me a total belief that all prostitutes had 'VD' as she called it. She hadn't elaborated in any way, as that would have been unseemly, but had convinced me without any graphic reference at all that such folly was strictly for the working classes and would inevitably result in my precious member dropping off or becoming festooned with awful brightly coloured incurable carbuncles oozing puss.

"Bring it on!" said George in an astonishing switch from the nineteen twenties' vocabulary of a minute ago to the street speak he can only have heard on his daily commute to work on the Tube.

"Count me out," I interjected speedily, wanting to nip this ridiculous escapade in the bud before things got out of hand. "You two can catch a dose of clap if you like, but not me."

"Don't be a wimp, Olly mate," Terry countered. "It's perfectly safe. Anyway you don't have to have a shag. You can just get a blow job…with a condom on if you want."

"That way you won't even risk a dose of penile halitosis," George commented, laughing loudly at his own joke, encouraged by Terry almost doubled up in mock amusement and accentuating his phoney rapture by beating the bar with his fist.

Terry was obviously a veteran at this game and continued to sell the alternatives.

"Or two of them get in the bath with you, and you all rub soap over each other. That way you get some girl on girl action too."

"Yes and they change the bathwater at least once a week," joked George as they mercilessly poked fun at my inexperience and lack of adventure.

I visualised the squalid scene.

"Or they'll just toss you off," the Essex boy crudely continued. "Talc or baby oil, the choice is yours."

I have to confess, looking back I think it was the mention of girl on girl action that made me waver. I hadn't agreed but I nevertheless found myself following a short distance behind the two of them as they headed into the back streets of town, on what was I'm sure a well-trodden path for the Essex idiot.

We entered the *Thai Palace*, through a heavy door, its only ground level frontage in a parade of shops. It sat between a hardware store and a pet shop. Both were closed for the night with wrought iron security grilles across the doorways, no doubt an indication that the proprietors were fully aware of the contrasting clientele roaming the area after dark. A bright sign above the door advertised the establishment as a 'Sauna', and another across it in a flickering neon tube spelled the word 'Massage'. An intermittent electrical fault caused the sign to emit a loud buzzing sound as if it threatened to burst into flames at any moment. In my fearful state I could imagine the local newspaper headline, *'Bank Bosses in Brothel Fire Rescue'*. We'd never live it down.

Terry led George up a steep flight of stairs and I followed tentatively several steps behind, my heart pounding nervously and a voice in my head asking what the fuck was I letting myself in for? My mind was racing to find an escape route, an excuse to avoid the risks I felt Terry was leading us into.

Are you a man or a mouse? I asked myself almost audibly. *Just turn and go!*

My excited curiosity, the excess alcohol in my bloodstream and the image in my mind of a pair of soap covered, young, slim, naked, oriental beauties attentively stroking my body answered the question for me. I was indeed a mouse. What's more I was now a mouse with a stonking great hard-on that was already making it difficult for me to climb the stairs.

I'd half expected to be greeted by a fearsome oriental kick boxer or sinister muscle-bound triad enforcer but to my surprise we were welcomed by a well-dressed and attractive Thai lady. It was as if we had just entered a restaurant. I was half expecting her to say, 'A table for three gentlemen?' I couldn't gauge very accurately how old she was but the oriental female aging gene that George had educated us about not half an hour earlier, evidently hadn't yet kicked in so I guessed she was under forty. Her perfect English suggested that she was either a second-generation immigrant or that she'd had a very well-spoken language teacher. An image of Aunt Margaret came instantly to mind. What would she think if she could see me now?

"Good evening gentlemen," said the slim and elegant receptionist. She was wearing a tight-fitting, knee-length red silk dress embroidered with dragon motifs in gold thread. Her small breasts barely caused a bulge in her shiny costume but her deportment oozed sexuality. She smoothed the creases from her silk by caressing her stomach and her inner thighs with the palms of her hands, running her outstretched fingers from her snake hips to her knees, her thumbs separating only as they described her mound. Her jet-black hair was decorated with a red flower attached to an unseen Alice band that perfectly matched both the colour of her dress and the gloss of her lipstick.

"Hello Terry, good to see you. And you've brought some friends I see."

"Yes Suzie, a veteran, and a virgin," the moron joked, indicating with a flick of his head my tentative presence in the doorway.

"That makes me the veteran," George jokingly asserted, his words a slur and his face almost as red as the silk dress he was slowly scanning with a lecherous leer I'd never imagined he could muster, and one no doubt Hilda hadn't encountered for years, if ever.

Terry was really getting on my nerves by now and I decided in an instant that there would be a price for him to pay both for his ignorant manner and for leading me into this frightening misadventure.

I smiled at the unwarranted insult but it occurred to me that it might just present an explanation for my hurried exit should I decide to turn and run.

"We have lovely girls for you lucky boys tonight. Very beautiful and very sexy."

She gestured towards a shabby sofa with an elegant sweep of a slender hand revealing long, neatly manicured fingernails, lacquered to match her silk. The colour co-ordinated concubine offered her cheek to Terry, who kissed her like he would his mother but touched her bottom in a way he wouldn't. George sank into the sofa which through years of use by paying visitors gave way much more than he'd anticipated and he rolled back lifting his feet off the floor in an involuntary half backward roll. Terry remained standing and I squatted on the arm of the yielding sofa in an attempt to limit my embarrassment by concealing the aching bulge in my trousers.

Summoned by an unseen signal from Suzie, five gorgeous young women slipped silently into the room through a door to our left.

They looked so young! This couldn't be right. Two of them were probably aged nineteen and the others could only have been in their early twenties. They lined up and each put their hands together as if in prayer and nodded a little bow of greeting but the giggles and body language indicated no trepidation, no reluctance, and certainly no disinclination to have sex with a stranger, even one old enough to be their father.

I suppose it was their obvious willingness to play the sordid game that kept me squatting there, and to be entirely honest also the fact that my knob, caught in the fold of my underpants painfully needed readjusting in my trousers to at least point up rather than out. I tried to arrange this by leaning forward and twisting from side to side but it was clear that at this stage it would require nothing less than a bold hand down the pants to achieve even this compromise.

The five girls were all dressed just like their madam in silk dresses of various colours but with much higher hemlines. Intriguingly, like Suzie they were all virtually flat-chested too, and I was amused by the sudden thought that George's man-boobs were without doubt the largest tits in the room. It was evident from their halting English that, unlike Suzie, they were not second-generation immigrants and I wondered how long they had been in the country. I wondered too if when they'd set out on their journey to Britain they'd known the profession they were going to enter, or were they perhaps tricked into it by exploitative relatives. I doubted the word 'prostitution' featured on their work permits, if indeed they possessed one between them. I began to have serious qualms about what my companions and, quite possibly, I were about to do.

Terry took the hand of arguably the prettiest and almost certainly the youngest looking girl and I realised then that this line up was for the purposes of partner selection. Terry's girl giggled as she hugged him around the neck, and as he swept her up, she wrapped her legs around his waist like a six-year-old jumping into the embrace of playful father. Her little silk dress rode up her hips showing her pale white bottom and the thin strand of her g-string held between the parting cheeks of her bum. This evidently wasn't the first time they'd met and I volunteered a sarcastic comment,

"Clearly you two have already been introduced."

"Never seen 'er before in me life," Terry joked as he carried the giggling girl towards the door from which she'd emerged, clearly familiar with the building and knowing exactly where they were going. Before disappearing, he turned and said,

"Suzie; the 'virgin' wants some girl on girl bath action."

Immediately two of the remaining four turned to me, or more precisely, on me. One grabbed my tie and using it as she would a dog lead, seductively pulled me to my feet, and in a co-ordinated action the girls pressed themselves to me, one on each side, grinding their bony pubic mounds high into my thighs. Each had one arm around my neck and the other across my chest, a hand gently probing for a nipple. It was as exhilarating as it was humiliating. I stood there being molested wonderfully from both sides whilst concealing my erection with both hands like a footballer in a defensive wall facing a free kick.

Suzie now approached me, standing so close that I could feel her vulva too, gently touching the back of my clasped hands, although her face showed no acknowledgement of the contact, in the way she might tolerate the elbow of a fellow passenger on the Tube in rush hour. This was absurd! My first and unintentional visit to a 'Sauna' and here I was, within two minutes of crossing the threshold in intimate proximity to no less than three fannies!

It was crazy. It was bizarre. However, my options were somewhat limited. I could rush for the door, but with my erection-enforced stoop and my centre of gravity now displaced painfully forward, I'd be in great danger of falling headlong down the stairs. Or I could stay, and see what happens next.

"This is Kalaya," she said, her face six inches from mine and nodding with her head to the girl on my left. Despite the amount of alcohol I had consumed that evening, my senses were suddenly remarkably sharp. I could smell menthol cigarette smoke on her breath and differentiate between the competing perfumes of the scent on her neck and another in her hairspray. They combined to deliver a pleasant but confusing blend of odours. It was like walking through the cosmetics section of a department store and being assailed by individually captivating perfumes that combined into an overpowering chemical mix.

"And this is Lalana," nodding to my right.

"They will join you in a bath for half an hour. That's fifty pounds; for each girl. And anything else you want, fifty pounds also; for each girl. You don't have to say now, you can make up your mind later."

I was speechless. I was embarrassed. I was excited. I was indecisive.

Kalaya moved her fingers from my chest and slid them behind my palms, breaking the protective box of my clasped hands. I was instantly decisive. I would stick around to see what happens next.

As the lovely, slender, silky girls led me to the door, I could see Suzie turning her attention to George, one girl already on his lap and the other alongside him on the sofa but leaning back in an alluring pose. They were clearly in competition for George's custom. The girl at his side lowered her eyes and pushed out her lower lip in a sulky girlish gesture of mock disappointment and retreated to the corner of the sofa. The look, clearly designed to encourage George to take them both, spurred her competitor into immediate action. Giggling, she leapt from the fat banker's lap and tugged at his tie in an attempt to haul him to his feet, in the way Kalaya had taken control of me a moment earlier.

Aided by George's enthusiasm, she managed to get him half standing, pivoting on the balls of his feet, before gravity overcame their joint efforts and sent them both crashing back onto the sofa. George's bulky backside came down like the hind quarters of a circus elephant heavily onto the recumbent girl's legs causing her to scream in pain.

As I was led from the room via the door through which Terry and his temporary companion had exited a minute earlier, I was sickened by the sight, so sickened that my eager erection deflated like a bouncy castle in a power cut. In an instant the crying girl was no longer the sensuous sex kitten of a moment earlier but a petulant teenager in a tearful tantrum. The welcoming Madam had become a scornful headmistress berating her for the over-reaction, and the young woman lying across George's disgusting fat carcass with her yellow silk dress up around her waist revealed the small white bottom of a barely post-pubescent teenager.

This was wrong. This was awfully wrong. They were far too young. I had to escape.

The two girls led me into a room lit by dim pink up-lighters and concealed spotlights illuminating a number of small sculptures of nude oriental couples in erotic tangles and demonstrating the skills of well-practiced contortionists.

It was gaudy in the extreme. The floor covering was a deep pile red woollen carpet and my nervousness was lightened for a moment as I laughed aloud at the bizarre thought, *Is this why they call it shag pile?*

The centrepiece was a large raised rectangular Jacuzzi lined with tiny white and pink mosaic tiles. The red carpet extended up the outer walls of the tub which was edged in black leather on all four sides. I pondered how many delicate female bottoms and fat, spotty, male arses had rested there over the years and hoped their cleaner was as proficient at her job as were the girls now so focussed on my pleasure.

I was again overcome by a sudden sense of sadness, wondering what circumstances had led these two youngsters into this situation, my mind racing with guilt and thoughts of complicity in their exploitation. But in contrast they actually seemed to be excited and enjoying their role, without any reluctance whatsoever. Their evident enthusiasm left me morally dithering, in a trance, too concerned to go on but too excited to leave before seeing what happens next.

Both girls stripped naked speedily like drunken skinny dippers determined to beat their fellow revellers into the pool, their clothes abandoned where they fell. Again this conjured a vision of an untidy teenager's bedroom, an image that nagged at my conscience, yelling at me to leave, but my returning erection and the beauty of their nakedness dispelled any resolve to go. Could I just perhaps enjoy the experience a little longer without violating these young women? Would I really be exploiting them or merely helping them to earn a good living in a way they preferred to toiling in a sweat shop on the other side of the world? Was I looking for a way out, or looking for a justification to stay?

Lalana stooped to double press the start button on the side of the jacuzzi and so small were her breasts I detected only the slightest change in their shape as she bent over. I was also strangely embarrassed that they were smaller than mine. Her mound was shaven into a tiny half-inch vertical strip and her little pink nipples were like embryonic acorns taking their first peep at the world in late summer. She stood up and faced me, pushing her hands onto my shoulders inside my jacket just as Kayala standing behind me tugged at both cuffs removing the garment in a smooth and co-ordinated operation, placing it tidily over the back of an armchair. Lalana unbuckled my belt and unzipped my trousers before pulling them to the ground complete with underpants in place. I'd have willingly stepped out of them but for the fact I was still wearing my shoes. The eager pair pushed me back into the armchair and set about removing my shoes, socks and trousers laughing as the process was delayed by a knotted shoelace. I was left naked apart from my shirt which in contrast to the previously hurried stripping was removed slowly and seductively. Lalana sat on my lap and twisted her slender body towards me, looking me straight in the eyes and panting the word 'yes' as if in fake orgasm as she slowly released each button. It was so ridiculous that I laughed heartily at each step of her walking fingers moving down my chest as she slowly attended to each button. I found myself fighting her off, not to avoid being left completely naked but because it tickled. I was wriggling like a young boy being teased by an elder sister. It was a performance and one the girls clearly acted out so regularly that there was no embarrassment whatsoever on their part. The shirt was folded neatly and placed tidily with the rest of my clothing in complete contrast to the abandoned dresses and g-strings of my willing handmaidens. Any plans I may have had to leave disappeared with the removal of my clothes. A hasty exit now would see me dressing on the run like a married woman's lover escaping barefooted through an upstairs window with his clothes under his arm as the unexpected husband arrives home.

My dick pointed the way to the bathtub as I rose from the chair quite keen to conceal it quickly under the bubbling water of the jacuzzi. The girls jumped in after me and took up position on the submerged ledge one on each side of their nervous client. Lalana stood up and stretched across me to reach for a bottle of bath oil placed on the floor behind us. It was a slow and deliberate move which she prolonged by pretending the bottle was just out of reach causing her body to writhe all over mine. Her tiny breasts rubbed to and fro across my forearm as her stomach played the same game across my lap, and her delightful little bottom just breaking the surface of the pounding water drew my hand like a magnet.

Kayala stood in front of me between my parted legs, her fanny just visible above the energetic waves lapping over the other girl's soft white bottom. She produced a bar of soap and worked up a lather between her hands before gently massaging it first into her tits and then over Lalana's pert little bum. At her touch Lalana purred with exaggerated pleasure before rolling onto her back, still across my lap. What a wonderful sight. Two slim and slippery beautiful naked girls smiling and laughing as if they were really enjoying themselves.

With an unmistakable gesture, they invited me to soap them both and I filled my boots. I eagerly ran my hands over their intriguing little breasts, their gorgeous flat stomachs, their skinny backs and their soft white bottoms. I soaped their hips, their inner thighs, their calves and even their elegant feet, and they did the same to me, though they took care not to touch my penis which frequently broke the surface like the periscope of a hunter-killer submarine as we romped.

Then they turned their attention to each other, kissing and caressing; licking soapy nipples, stroking soapy buttocks and patting soapy fannies, all accompanied with girlish laughter and exaggerated sounds of sexual pleasure.

With hindsight I think the whole episode was choreographed to meet the time constraints indicated by Suzie because suddenly the activity changed from lathersome foreplay to sexual proposition. The girls moved close to me, sitting on the ledge, one on each side, warm wet and womanly. I shuddered with anticipation as the two-girl team went into action. Lalana reached down and cupped my scrotum in her little hand, squeezing it gently as if testing an avocado for ripeness, and Kalaya put both arms around my neck and whispered in my ear.

"You want fuck me now? You want fuck us both?"

"Or you want blow job?" asked Lalana gently squeezing my shaft.

"That feel good? How that make you feel?"

How that make me feel? In an instant I realised exactly how that made me feel.

The bouncy castle suffered another power cut, this time a total blackout. It had made me feel like their uncle, a wicked uncle.

Whether it was the booze wearing off or a sudden pang of conscience I don't know, but I realised perhaps too late that even if these lovely young girls were there of their own free will and had chosen to earn a living in this way, I could not be part of it. I could not go any further.

I was dreadfully ashamed and summoned the will to take control, of myself and of the situation, and leave as quickly as I could.

I uttered the most ridiculous words that make me blush with embarrassment to this day when I recall them.

"Thank you, ladies, that was very nice but I must go home now."

I thought too of the marvellous, virtuous woman whose respect I had recently won and how disgusted she would be if she ever learned of my unforgivable behaviour that night. What would she think of me? I'd been led astray like a teenager egged on by others and felt embarrassed that I hadn't shown the strength of character to opt out of the ridiculous escapade. I blamed Terry and resolved to get even with him as soon as I could although at that precise moment I did not know how. I determined that George would live to regret it too as without his complicity in the misadventure I could have escaped home immediately after leaving the restaurant.

I was very surprised that the girls offered no resistance at all to my decision to leave, and I concluded that perhaps it was a common occurrence for punters to either lose their nerve at the last minute or more likely, to be too drunk to continue. There was no argument and no attempt at persuading me to stay, enjoy more, and pay more.

As I stepped out of the jacuzzi, Lalana and Kayala were as attentive as they had been throughout. They produced two large, newly laundered, fluffy white bath towels and set about drying me, one attending to the front and the other to my back. As they rubbed me dry, tiny drops of soapy liquid flew from their arms and beads of water ran down their bodies accentuating their feminine curves.

I have always found the naked female form even more sexy when wet, whether it was a partner stepping from the shower or a stranger emerging from the sea. I put the thought quickly out of mind. When Lalana attempted to dry my tackle by wrapping the whole bunch in the towel as if she were drying a teapot, I felt the lust returning and snatched the towel from her and pulled away from Kayala too. I stepped a few paces back from them as if the added distance would proportionally reduce both the measure of my indiscretion and the temptation to stay.

The girls were dressed even before I had finished drying myself and left the room without assisting me to regain my clothing. I was in such a hurry that I tried to put on my socks whilst my feet were still damp and struggled to slip into them as if they had suddenly shrunk several sizes. Once dressed, I returned to the reception area hoping desperately that no other customers had arrived fearing I might bump into someone who'd recognise me. I intended to pay whatever I owed to Suzie and slip away before Terry and George emerged from whatever activity they had chosen from the erotic menu.

"No extras, sir," said the elegant gatekeeper in a tone revealing no disappointment whatsoever in the girls' inability to sell the additional services expected of them. "Just one hundred pounds please." She spoke as if she were a hotel receptionist attending to the guest next in line to check out.

I shuddered at the thought that I might not have enough cash to pay. I was sure she'd accept a credit card but I didn't want that on my statement. How would it appear? 'Personal services £100?', 'Massage?', 'Quick bath but no shag?'

I thumbed through my wallet and with great relief found enough notes to settle the bill.

I was on my way to the door when I remembered that I'd left my tie over the back of the armchair by the jacuzzi. I hesitated as I thought about abandoning it, literally rocking back and forth several times in my indecision. It was an expensive Italian silk that I'd be loath to lose but regaining it would delay my escape. A vision of Lalana arriving at the bank to return it came to mind and I could hear the receptionist's words over the intercom in my office.

"Mr Purkiss, there's a young woman here to see you."

Without bothering to explain to Suzie for fear she might intercept me, I almost ran back to the scene of my delightful embarrassment. I recovered my tie and as my hands felt its smooth texture perversely, I knew it would always remind me of the two silky girls I'd encountered that night. I would never wear it again, but I'd keep it forever.

As I made my way back to reception, at a much slower pace than I'd left it a few moments earlier, I very suspiciously checked my pockets. I knew that my wallet was intact having just paid Suzie, and as I tapped each pocket to confirm the presence of my phone, I immediately felt embarrassed at my distrust. It was inconceivable that the lovely young girls would have robbed me. Strangely this thought made me even more ashamed of myself than my brief role as the wicked uncle. As I flicked on the phone to check the time, I heard George's excited voice through a door to my left and the unmistakable sound of his fat belly slapping against the firmer flesh of one or both of the girls that I'd last seen lying over and under him on the reception sofa. He was evidently close to the vinegar stroke as a female voice was encouraging him with a crescendo of squeals as she faked an extended orgasm. From where the thought came I can't imagine but the motive was clear. Now was my chance to settle the score with Blubber Butt. I pulled out my phone, switched to video mode and pushed open the unlocked door.

George was lying on his back on what looked like a brown leather massage table in the centre of the small room. The youngster was sitting on his cock facing away from him, performing rising trots like an energetic teenage girl in a gymkhana. The words of a nursery song came instantly to mind as the rider, completely unperturbed at my presence quickened her pace from a trot to a canter. 'This is the way the farmers ride. Jogglety! Jogglety! Jogglety! Jog!'

As my camera caught the pair of them in flagrante delicto, George's face displayed an amusing mix of expressions in quick succession, surprise, shock, anger, fear and extreme embarrassment. My intrusion could not have been timed better. His grunt of climactic pleasure was cut short as he unsuccessfully tried to jerk his fat carcass upright in an instinctive attempt to reduce his exposure to my unwanted presence, and more especially that of my menacing camera. What terrifying thoughts must have raced through his mind. Thoughts of implications, thoughts of ruin, thoughts of Hilda.

He did not, of course, have sufficient strength in his abdominal muscles to unseat his rider and his attempts to do so produced only asthmatic coughs from him and an amusing extended fanny fart from the girl. Oh joy! I hoped the video would pick up the sound as well.

I had the presence of mind to switch the phone to camera mode and took another six images as I retreated backwards towards the door. George having unsaddled from his mount got to his feet, staggering with dizziness no doubt caused by the sudden change of position, his recent physical exertion and his inebriated state. I've never seen a man sober up so quickly in my life. I think it crossed his mind to boldly remonstrate with me there and then and to make an attempt to snatch the phone, but his disgusting nakedness, the wrinkled condom now dangling from his deflated penis and the open door behind me evidently dissuaded him from such action.

As I withdrew to the reception area, planning to make an immediate exit from the premises I bumped into Terry, fully clothed and ready to depart. He seemed even more drunk than when we'd arrived. The young girl was no longer hanging from his neck and he was carrying a half empty bottle of champagne which slipped from his hand and fell to the floor ejecting a spurt of foaming bubbles as it landed upright before rolling over spilling what remained onto the carpet. He appeared not to notice and made no attempt to pick it up. Judging by his barely successful attempts to remain upright I suspected that he had consumed it all himself rather than sharing it with the clinging girl. His sexual encounter had obviously been as brief as my bath and I wondered if George was the only one of us to expend any bodily fluids that night. Ugh, what a thought!

"Well, 'Virgin', how'd it go?" he enquired. "D'you fuck 'em both?"

"It was an experience I shall never forget," I replied.

"Where's Georgie? Is 'e coming for a drink?" he slurred.

I then witnessed an amazing sight. As he spat out the words, he also accidentally spat out a set of upper dentures. A pink plastic palate complete with a row of seven or eight false teeth splattered with sputum fell from his mouth and chinked against the champagne bottle lying on the floor. Terry laughed as he stooped to pick them up and drunkenly lurched against the sofa losing his balance while using one hand to reinsert the errant teeth as he attempted to rise.

My mind raced as I pondered whether a further drinking spree, the last thing in the world I wanted at that point, might actually provide me with an opportunity to exact my revenge. I probably wouldn't be seeing Terry for another year, so this might be my only opportunity to get him arrested for indecent exposure, run over by a street-cleaning truck, or placed on a mail train to Glasgow.

There was also merit in leaving the building without George as his first priority I felt sure would be to attempt to secure my phone with its incriminating and highly valuable images.

"I think he's already left," I said. "Yes, I'm up for a nightcap. Let's go back to that great bar you took us to earlier."

The words had left my mouth like the well-rehearsed set-up line of an experienced hustler hooking his mark and I ushered Terry towards the stairs having picked up the champagne bottle from the foaming ring it had made on the carpet and handing it to Suzie.

"I take it you've paid, Terry?" I called after him as he made a move for the door.

Suzie answered for him confirming that indeed he had. Such was his familiarity with the place and my ignorance of the industry that I'd wondered if perhaps he'd had a credit account there.

I paused at the top of the stairs to let Terry go ahead. I didn't want him falling on top of me and I thought there was an even chance he might trip and break his neck. Miraculously he did not stumble on the stairs and my unsuspecting victim and I emerged onto the street and into the cool night air.

As I walked and Terry zig-zagged our way back to the dreadfully noisy bar we'd left just an hour earlier, I contemplated the possibilities for revenge. It would have to be nothing illegal and nothing that could be traced back to me of course. He was so drunk that I decided the best bet would be to take him to Euston and stick him on the wrong train home, a non-stopping train that would deliver him to some distant city or cause him to pull the communication cord and suffer the consequences of his action. However, I quickly realised that that would require the purchase of two tickets and my accompanying him onto the platform to ensure he that he would actually board the train. I abandoned that idea as impracticable and hoped that I could conceive an alternative plan as I got him even more drunk with shorts whilst I drank water.

I decided that a taxi to Peckham or Brixton would fit the bill as he had revealed over dinner that he lived in Stanmore but I realised that I'd have to make sure he was not so drunk that a cabby would refuse the fare.

As it turned out a wonderful opportunity arose before Terry had downed his first drink. He staggered off to the gent's toilet and I had a need to accompany him. We stood side by side at the foul-smelling urinal which I estimated was about two inches deep in piss, as despite the smoking ban the drain in the centre of the channel was clogged by discarded cigarette stubs.

Terry stared at the ceiling, as men often do at this point to avoid completely any suspicion of attempting to look at their neighbour's dick, and started to say something about how great a shag he'd just enjoyed at the Thai Sauna. As he did so his false teeth again fell out and dropped into the trough of piss. He was startled by the dentures bouncing off his chest on their way down and stepped back a pace rocking unsteadily on his feet, his cock still in his hand and in seemingly unstoppable flow. He looked for his teeth which he suspected had been caught inside his loosely buttoned jacket but didn't spot them under the frothy surface of the urine.

I seized my opportunity. I bent down and picked them up, shuddering as my right hand was soaked by the foul liquid. I squared up to him and smiling popped the soaking dentures straight back into his mouth. He slurped as he sucked his teeth dry and unknowingly swallowed the piss.

"Olly boy, you're a gent," he exclaimed, letting go of his member with one hand to give me a comradely slap on the back.

"Indeed I am, Terry old chum. Indeed I am."

Chapter Nine
Tristan

In the early days of our relationship, Hermione's son, Tristan, was to my eyes an unlovable child and presented a major impediment to the fantasy of my future life with her. At ten years old he was I suppose of average height for his age but had already achieved through his mother's indulgence the body weight of a young teenager. She'd convinced herself it was 'just puppy fat that will burn off as he gets taller', a misguided theory she would share with all who met him, to counter any unspoken criticism that she might perhaps have over-fed the boy.

My reaction on first encountering Tristan was to wonder how such an enormous child could have emerged from that most perfect of wombs, that body so slender. Those small but perfectly shaped breasts that I longed to take into my mouth could not possibly have sustained the demands of such a suckling pig.

No, he couldn't have been breast-fed. He must have been instantly weaned on some supercharged baby milk supplement and probably from a faulty batch. Perhaps the manufacturer also produced a similar product for cattle and through an industrial accident contaminated the product with a bovine growth hormone.

I had visions too of a Sumo wrestler wiping the tears of joy from his eyes as he gently cradled his new-born son in his flabby and dimpled arms. It was clearly one of nature's cruel tricks to deliver to such a beautiful and flawless example of womanhood an alien child with no apparent trace of her angelic genes. The only plausible explanation was that Hermione had been the victim of a hospital mix up, a tragic baby swap deliberate or otherwise that had robbed her of a tiny replica of her heavenly form. These thoughts I knew were totally unjustified as I recall Hermione telling me that Tristan had been born at home.

The boy had taken an instant dislike to me I could tell. On my frequent visits to their home and on the many outings I arranged simply to be near her, he displayed a less than neutral stance. As a ten-year-old, he had no knowledge of sex yet he eyed me constantly with the suspicious gaze of a watchful chaperone. He clearly had me sussed. I sensed he was guarding his mother, protecting her from my attention, perhaps out of loyalty to a father he hadn't seen since he was a toddler.

In my presence, he assumed a number of unattractive persona. I could of course understand his preference for a younger suitor for his mother rather than someone who could be mistaken for his grandfather and initially I tried hard to encourage a warmer relationship between us. His resistance to me though seemed absolute and very soon the battle lines were drawn. I did my best to convince Hermione that I felt some affection for the boy, ruffling his hair and engaging in playful rough and tumble but he was much more clever and followed a strategy aimed at pissing me off whilst avoiding criticism from his doting mother. A game he played so well.

I'll never know whether it was part of his strategy or a pre-existing unhealthy character flaw but the boy had a most unattractive lavatorial complex and he seemed to be able to fart at will. I never once heard him do it in his mother's presence, he seemed to store it up until we were alone. He'd slowly manoeuvre himself around the room to get closer to me and then to his evident amusement take me by surprise. I might be for example reclining in an armchair reading the Sunday papers, when from an unseen position behind me he would produce a real rip-snorter. He'd then collapse in a fit of laughter. Often Hermione would enter the room at that point having heard the laughter but not the fart, and say, "You boys sound to be having fun!" It suited my strategy of course to enthusiastically confirm that indeed we were. The boy, of course, seemed to immensely enjoy the irony in this.

I have to concede that my adversary had a happy disposition and was rarely glum. Whenever he, like many children at that age, sulked himself into an unhappy mood, Hermione could instantly restore his good humour with the words, "Never mind, chops for tea!"

Tristan could also make farting noises by raising one arm and cupping a hand under an armpit. Quickly levering downwards his podgy limb would expel the air trapped in his cupped hand and produce a very realistic farting sound. Whether this artificial substitute was a skilful extension to his repertoire or simply a fall-back position to be relied upon on the rare occasions when he simply couldn't muster any gas, I do not know.

However, I had made the cardinal error of showing disgust on the first occasion, handing to him the gift of chink in the armour of my pretence of approval. He knew he could now irritate me at will.

Tristan's party piece, which in spite of its vulgarity I have to acknowledge was quite a physical achievement, was his ability to produce an extraordinary number of consecutive audible farts. He would take great delight in keeping me appraised of the latest record which reached an amazing twenty-four. I jest not and if I hadn't actually witnessed it myself, I'd have assumed it a physical impossibility.

There is evidence though that his anal performances are not exclusively aimed at my entertainment or annoyance. Hermione and her odorous offspring spent a summer weekend with me at the farm, she not in my bed alas, but one lives in hope. As I lay in the bath on the Sunday morning, I heard Tristan enter the adjoining lavatory. Through the thin dividing wall I could hear the boy talking to himself, clearly acting out some bizarre fantasy as children do. From his articulate commentary it became obvious to me that the little tyke was imagining himself as a contender in The World Farting Championships!

"The young competitor Tristan Nightingale enters the arena, raising a hand to acknowledge the welcoming applause of the crowd," said Tristan in, for a ten-year-old, a laudably accurate imitation of a 1950s' BBC radio commentator.

This sounds interesting, I thought as I diverted my attention away from *The Times*' crossword and reinvested it in eavesdropping on a ten-year-old boy acting out a disgusting fantasy in the loo. Was this really happening? Had he succeeded in reducing me to his level?

"Tristan takes the throne."

I winced at the sound of the expensive toilet seat crashing down as he carelessly knocked it into place.

"My god! He's given the signal! Yes, his arm is raised. He's going for the world record!"

Astonishingly, there was no sound of a fart, at least not one near enough to his usual standard for the sound to permeate the wall, although I did hear two loud 'plops' followed by a straining grunt before eventually a significantly smaller one.

"My god what a performance!" the plummy commentator's voice exclaimed, "That must be a world record!"

The chain was pulled and I could visualise the boy, trousers around his ankles, standing up to take a bow, no doubt interpreting the sound of the flushing water and cistern refilling as the extended applause of an appreciative crowd.

The mind games have endured throughout the six months that I have been a regular visitor to their home. He pursues a strategy of constant and often smelly resistance to my friendship, although to my surprise and great relief he doesn't communicate his evident dislike of me to his mother. Astonishingly in Hermione's presence he is polite and respectful to me and I feel somewhat intimidated at the realisation that I'm having a battle of wits with a ten-year-old, and losing on points. The contest though is far from over for I have a cunning plan.

When I eventually get her to live with me, oh and I must, I'll feign interest in the boy's future by suggesting that his life chances can be considerably enhanced by having him properly educated at a boarding school, many miles away. I'll offer to fund his education at an appropriate establishment where he would be slimmed down through a Spartan regime of exercise, rugger and cold showers and where his lavatorial preoccupation will mark him out for the rough justice of his peers. Given Hermione's nostalgia for her happy days as a boarder I feel confident she will accept.

Chapter Ten
A Game of Chance

The morning after the flight I phoned Philippa to express my hope that her air sickness had been short-lived as I was concerned the experience might have put her off seeing me again. I was assured on both counts which was a great relief.

I invited her out for a drink that evening but she declined explaining she had a case to prepare for but promised to call me next day.

It was going to be interesting. I couldn't imagine two more different women. The scholarly, articulate, strait-laced but elegant Philippa with all her evident hang ups, and Alice the fun-loving airhead drifting through life with laughter in her voice and a complete understanding of her own sexuality and the effect she has on men. I chuckled at the thought that I'd be shagging both ends of the intellectual spectrum.

I had my concerns about how difficult it might be to shake off Philippa after the conquest as she clearly wasn't the type to indulge in casual sex in a meaningless relationship but she was so different from any woman I'd slept with before that I decided to continue seeing her. I'd stick with the long game as there was always Alice to play with in the meantime. And play is without doubt the right word to describe what she and I indulged in.

In the Seventies I'd read *The Dice Man* by Luke Rhinehart, a novel that had changed my life. Get a copy, it could change yours but beware the game he describes can become addictive. It's all about daring yourself to do risky things, some enjoyable and others maybe not but leaving the decision on whether to proceed to a roll of the dice. However, once rolled the dice must be obeyed. This is as exciting as it is dangerous but by obeying the dice responsibility for your actions if not the consequences of them is not yours. The dice are responsible. The dice take the blame.

I introduced Alice to the dice game only recently and she took to it with great enthusiasm. Ken was away on a four-day foreign business trip and we were at my flat sipping a pre-romp glass of champagne and discussing what sort of sex she was up for that night. I explained the rules.

Together we wrote a list of ten scenarios, five had to be fairly tame, four very daring and one so totally outrageous that we might be frightened of the prospect of it being selected. We then applied odds to each option by agreeing whatever combination of two dice represented the appropriate risk. For example straight sex might be any odd number total, woman on top a pair of fives, simultaneous oral sex a one and a seven. Remembering that the dice must be obeyed, to increase the odds against very daring challenges the aggregate of two rolls would be required. Alice was game for anything but drew the line at anal sex. Consequently, I suggested it would require a pair of fours followed by a pair of twos, long odds that Alice even with her limited grasp of statistics was prepared to accept.

The list of ten was compiled and we nervously giggled at some of the challenges albeit at long odds.

Sex in a shop doorway required a pair of sixes followed by a five and a two.

Standing up in the shower required only a pair of threes.

A blow job in the cinema had fairly long odds attached as I wasn't sure I'd be able to concentrate sufficiently.

The rest of the list comprised various other activities ranging from the physically challenging to simply enjoying dinner and going home without having sex at all.

We rolled the dice and Alice squealed with delight as one of her own selections came up.

I would have to smother her tits and intimate parts with strawberry ice cream and lick it off. Only when it was completely removed would I then be rewarded with a blow job. Unfortunately, I had no ice cream in the apartment. I suggested that we roll the dice again but Alice was adamant that I could not break the rules as, adopting the tone of an impatient dominatrix, she asserted,

"The dice must be obeyed. So must I. Go and get some!"

I was beginning to wish I hadn't mentioned the silly game as, leaving her luxuriating in a scented bubble bath, I drove around trying to find the illusive strawberry ice cream. I visited no less than four 7-11 shops before I gave up and settled for another flavour. It was only a game after all.

Back at the flat Alice was ready for me, wonderfully naked and deliciously fragrant she reclined on the white silk sheets of my king-size bed with an even more excited look on her face than usual. She was hungry for it and readily forgave my returning without the flavour that she had demanded.

To avoid soiling the bedding I tried to slip a bath towel under her before applying the ice cream but she adamantly refused to raise her hips saying that the cloth was too rough. She wanted only silk and cream.

I stripped off ready for action, opened the tub and started to rub the ice cream into her perfect tits. Alice took a sharp intake of breath as the frozen massage oil substitute was applied and those playful inverted nipples popped out immediately and as proud as never before. I dabbed the ice cream on her lovely pink nipples, I spread it gently down her cleavage and I filled my hands with it as I cupped her ample breasts from underneath. I gently pressed a lump into her navel and probed it with my tongue.

With an unmistakeable gesture, Alice grabbed my ears and redirected me to her lower regions and as I obliged, she giggled with delight.

I slapped a handful on her knees and slowly massaged it into her inner thighs. She shivered as with the softest of touches I applied a coating of the frozen cream to the landing strip above her shaven pussy and groaned with anticipation lifting her hips to increase the pressure of my fingers as I teased her with a ten-second pause.

It occurred to me that perhaps I'd smothered her with too much ice cream when I remembered that the game she'd specified required me to 'lick it all off' before lying back to receive her expert attention. I had been more than ready too, in fact ever since I'd paid Mr Shah for the chocolate ice cream I'd been nursing a stonker.

"Now!" she said, snatching the tub from me with one hand and pressing my head towards her fanny with the other. I started with a gentle lapping motion like a kitten with a saucer of cream until the pressure of her grip around my head told me she was ready to be sucked. But suddenly I lost it. It would have been different had I managed to buy strawberry ice cream instead of chocolate but the sight of Alice's body lying there like a baby with a soiled nappy more than turned me off, it disgusted me.

I pulled away but by then it was too late, Alice had to be satisfied. Twice I retched as, with both of her hands clasping my head, she pushed my mouth harder against her mound and I was more than relieved when I heard the unmistakable little squeak of her orgasm that, like a referee's whistle, signalled the end of the game.

Even after Alice had showered off, the brown mess of chocolate I couldn't muster sufficient enthusiasm for the promised blow job and instead just drove my sexy lady home to sleep in her own bed alone, dropping her a safe distance from the house to avoid any chance of being spotted by a neighbour aware of Ken's travel plans.

I returned to the apartment, stripped the bed and stuffed the disgusting-looking sheets into the washing machine. Normally, I'd have left them in the laundry basket for Mrs Wilson to attend to but I couldn't take the risk that she might think I'd shit myself in the night. I sat there reading the Bendix instruction manual for half an hour before I could even get the bloody thing to start and had to do it all over again in the morning as apparently I'd only selected a mild rinse program, or whatever it's called.

Alice was determined that we should make the most of Ken's absence and although I'd never before seen her on consecutive nights I promised to take her out to dinner 'somewhere nice' as she put it. She drove herself around to my place and I was surprised to find that she'd brought with her a slim laptop computer. I had forgotten an earlier promise to help her set up spreadsheet software to enable her to develop some rudimentary skills in preparation for a forthcoming job interview.

She recounted an amusing incident some weeks earlier when she'd taken her computer back to the retailer to fix some minor fault. It was classic Alice.

She and her husband owned an ageing overweight brown Labrador they'd had since a puppy. Initially they named it Nobby and as he grew, he had become known as Big Nobby. As he grew fatter, no doubt owing to Alice's overindulgence, his name had then become Big Fat Nobby. This unwieldy epithet was for convenience later shortened to Fat Nob.

As many people do apparently, Alice used her pet's name as the password for her laptop. The young assistant at the computer shop had asked Alice for her password so that he could boot it up and run a diagnostic program and the poor boy blushed like a beetroot when the sexy blonde looked him straight in the eyes and said seductively,

"It's 'Fat Nob'. Something I can always remember."

The youth's embarrassment was compounded after he typed 'Knob' rather than 'Nob' and had to be corrected by Alice with mock indignation at the very suggestion that she might have been so rude.

I tried for half an hour to teach Alice the simple first steps in Excel but rapidly became frustrated at her complete inability to grasp even the basics. Worried that my impatience might send her off into one of her moods and baulk my plans for that night, I suggested that she'd done very well but perhaps that was enough for one night. We could pick it up again later.

We drove to an expensive and pretentious hotel restaurant and I parked at the far end of the car park. I wanted to kiss her sexy mouth before we dined and to grope those gorgeous tits excitingly accentuated that night by the most alluring bra and plunging neckline. I was quickly aroused by her familiar perfume and the taste of toothpaste on her adventurous tongue.

Five minutes later as we entered the restaurant's reception area, we were greeted by a smirking Maître D and a grinning waitress, and as a receptionist checked her computer for my table reservation I noticed on another screen a security camera close up of a solitary car, parked away from the others at the far end of the parking area. The area appeared to be much more brightly lit than I remembered.

We were ushered into a tastefully decorated and exquisitely furnished anteroom where we perused the extensive gourmet menu and enjoyed a Kir Royale aperitif. We made polite conversation with a wealthy looking elderly couple. The expensively dressed and discreetly bejewelled lady sat at one end of a four-seater sofa with Alice at the other and her husband and I faced them with our backs to a large marble fireplace like officers having a pre-prandial snifter on a Ladies Dining-in Night. It was all very refined.

It was all very refined that is until Alice winked at me briefly and then resumed eye contact with the lady. As she did so, she very slowly opened her legs to reveal to both the elderly gent and myself that she wasn't wearing knickers. The old boy spluttered and nearly choked on his gin and tonic eliciting an immediate sympathetic look from his wife.

"Are you all right, darling?" she enquired. Mopping splashes of drink from his shirt he hurriedly responded,

"Yes, and I do believe our table is ready, my dear."

The Maître D took our order and later showed us to our table, thankfully some distance from the people we'd just met. I wondered if he'd explained to his wife the reason for his brief coughing fit but doubted he'd find words suitable for her ears.

Our table was set for two with an impressive array of cut glassware, silver plate and highly polished stainless-steel cutlery. As the smirking MD attempted to seat Alice opposite me with an exaggerated gesture positioning a chair behind her shapely bottom, she stopped him short.

"No, I want to sit next to him, not opposite," she said as if talking to a servant. Expressionless he answered,

"Yes of course, madam, whatever you say."

I smiled instantly, recalling the dominatrix of the previous night and then put the thought rapidly out of mind as I also pictured the chocolate ice cream.

He signalled for a young waitress to attend to the repositioning of cutlery and glasses as if the task was unbefitting of his status.

I ate seared scallops while Alice with a long-handled spoon dug into an over large prawn cocktail described on the menu as 'Fruits de Mer Chambertin Classique' or something equally pretentious. Alice reached for my hand and under the tablecloth gently placed it on the bare flesh of her knee simultaneously giving me a come-on look no woman I've ever met could match.

The Maître D personally topped up our glasses, first hers then mine, wiping the neck of the bottle delicately with a white Irish linen napkin between operations. As he poured hers, far too slowly, as if dispensing the most sought-after wine on the planet, or nitro-glycerine, he looked at her, paused and asked, "More for you, madam?"

Alice moved my hand right up her skirt having parted her legs in preparation for the move and I could feel that she was moist. Without breaking eye contact with the man she whispered, "Oh certainly. All the way up please."

I tried to remove my hand from under her skirt several times but each attempt was met by a mischievously sexy smile and a tightening of her thighs to keep it captive. I was concerned that the unnatural angle of my trapped arm might make it obvious to the elderly couple across the dining room what was occurring under our table and was relieved to have the opportunity to withdraw it when the next course was served.

Alice was enjoying the food and the wine, teasing the MD with thinly veiled sexual innuendo every time he spoke. He clearly regarded her as a bimbo undeserving of quality fare, and she had him nailed as a pretentious prat. She was winning the contest hands down.

Alice steered the conversation to the dice game of the night before which she had clearly enjoyed and started suggesting in whispers treats and forfeits for a rematch. Some of the scenarios that sprang to her mind were so outrageous that in her excitement to suggest them she broke into giggles and spoke too loudly. In the undulating volume of her laughter the words 'Your Willy', 'My Tits' and 'From Behind' were unfortunately positioned at the top of the volume curve and could clearly be heard by some of the other diners. I urged her with an embarrassed expression and furtive nod of the head towards the elderly couple to speak more quietly but I recognised the signs; Alice was in mischief mode.

Through the dessert course, she continued to suggest imaginative ways and locations in which we could have sex that night.

Perhaps the most outlandish suggestion was that we should book a room there and order room service. We'd leave the door ajar and when the waiter, hopefully the MD, arrived with the tray she'd be sitting up in bed naked and I'd be unseen under the covers giving her oral sex as she told him in an unflustered manner where to put the tray.

I thought I'd scotched the scary plan when I pointed out to her that unfortunately we didn't have any dice with us but that we could certainly play again next time we met at her house.

A pretty waitress asked if we'd like to take coffee in the lounge and we retired there to find the elderly couple seated on the sofa, the scene of Alice's earlier naughtiness. As we approached, they nervously rushed to finish their coffee which was clearly too hot to drink and they left muttering between them about falling standards. I thanked God under my breath that Alice hadn't heard the words 'riff raff'.

I was somewhat perturbed that over coffee Alice was already outlining plans for the following day. It appeared that she was expecting me to entertain her throughout her husband's absence and I had no such intention. In fact I had arranged to meet Philippa for lunch as she was keen to make up for her embarrassing departure smelling of vomit last time we met. I decided that the best course of action was to nip in the bud Alice's plans for the next day before it appeared that I had consented. She looked shocked and somewhat irritated when I told her that I couldn't see her because I was meeting my solicitor for lunch. For a working lunch I added, after perhaps a little too much hesitation.

"Oh you mean Lady Philippa," she replied as if referring to her worst enemy.

"Why do you say it like that?" I responded. "She's very professional and without her help and expertise, I might have gone to gaol."

I recalled that I had mentioned Philippa to Alice and to avoid any suspicion about my plans for her had made a few derogatory remarks to throw Alice off the scent.

"Only joking darling," she said unconvincingly, "go and have your 'business' lunch. I know you've got far better taste anyway," she added with a well-rehearsed little shake of her shoulders that wobbled her tits and as always took my eyes along with them.

I breathed a silent sigh of relief as the subject was dropped.

"More coffee?" asked the Maître D, clearly embarrassed at having to serve us personally rather than direct a minion to attend to our needs.

Neither of us did and so to show him that we did know how to behave and to remind him that we were the customers and he was the servant, I thanked him for the 'excellent' meal and asked for the bill.

"Are you sure there's nothing more we can get you, sir? Madam?"

"No, thank you," I replied.

"Well, there is one thing," said Alice, looking at me as she spoke. "I don't suppose you have any dice?"

I left Alice alone while I went to reception to repeat my request for the bill as the MD and the waitress seemed to be deliberately avoiding my signals to bring it to the sofa where we sat. I'm sure it's a skill they teach at catering college, Lesson One: 'How to Avoid the Customer's Gaze.' It was as if they were wearing blinkers or wearing one of those dreadful cone-shaped collars that vets fit to a dog with a bad infestation of fleas to stop it from scratching its ears. Or perhaps it's a game played by waiters and waitresses in restaurants throughout the world. 'Bet you can't make eye contact until I'm ready.' I decided not to tip.

I settled the bill, which took about five minutes and returned to the lounge to catch Alice hurriedly replacing my phone to where I'd left it on the coffee table.

"What are you up to?" I asked suspiciously.

"Oh, I was just going to change your ringtone to something a bit more up to date," she replied with a giggle.

We made our way to the exit and were bid farewell by the MD and the receptionist both wearing the smirks they'd welcomed us with earlier. Anticipating that they would immediately dash around to the security camera monitor to watch us stroll across the car park, Alice fondled my bum as we walked and with my arm around her I cupped her right breast and gave it a gentle squeeze, just for the camera.

My plans were to drive back to the apartment, play a little music, pour a glass of wine and give Alice a good shagging on the hearth rug. She had other ideas.

"If he'd had some dice, I'd have suggested we do it here," she whispered in my ear as I started the engine.

"One dice, any number up to six," she laughed. "Just for the camera!" As we swept out of the hotel entrance and headed for home Alice unclipped her seatbelt and then mine. She turned towards me and kissed my ear, her tongue darting in and out of it as she did so. I pulled away, not just because it was so distracting but because it tickled so much. Probably taking this as a playful brush-off Alice then grabbed my left knee before slowly caressing my inner thigh in a series of strokes that moved progressively towards my crotch until she reached my zip, which she started to pick at.

"Is that alarm attached to your knob?" she joked, referring to the noise of the unsecured seat belt warning bleeper.

Here we go, I know this mood, I thought to myself. '*Alice wants to romp, and she wants it now.*'

"Let's find somewhere to park," she suggested. "You haven't fucked me in a car yet."

I favoured going back to my place as I'd planned to try to persuade her to stay the night, something which she'd steadfastly refused to do in the past. Another step too far in the infidelity stakes perhaps.

"Not tonight, Alice, let's go back to the flat and play some music. We can get the dice out if you like."

I knew already that wasn't going to happen, I knew her too well. She simply ignored me and started to remove her clothing. We were driving through the streets of town, lit by sodium lighting, in a thirty-mile an hour limit, and she was stripping off!

Alice was totally naked within half a mile and giggling like a schoolgirl trying her first joint. I imagined being stopped by the police. How would she react? How would they react? No doubt breathalyse me and charge me with being drunk in charge of a nymphomaniac.

What could I do? Stop and forcibly dress her?

Then she said it.

"So, am I coming with you and Lady Philippa to lunch tomorrow, or what?"

She was in charge of the situation now and she knew it. All I could do was find the quickest and most dimly lit route out of town.

Wow, though. What a shag! She was the best without a doubt.

Chapter Eleven
Every Other Saturday

I visited Aunt Margaret on alternate Saturdays sharing the un-resented chore with her friend Jessica who at seventy-five was ten years her junior but fit and active and importantly still driving. Margaret was keen to do her own weekly shopping and the unchanging routine had become virtually her only outing from her home in Princes Avenue where she'd now lived for fifty-three years. The old house I loved had little changed since the 1950s and was becoming difficult for her to manage even with the weekly help of a visiting cleaner.

The apple, plum and pear trees that I remember climbing as a boy were remarkably still in residence in the largely untended back garden, although now gnarled and disease-ridden rendering the fruit edible but unattractive. The greengage tree that I would often raid for its sweet fruit during the late summer holidays had sadly demised and had been reduced to a stump, a relic of happy family history.

One of my boyhood recollections is of playing in a labyrinth of numerous interconnected dusty sheds, with huge wooden workbenches each with a forged iron vice that I didn't have the strength to operate. I remember wrestling with the many stiff drawers requiring two hands and all my weight to inch them open, and handling the intriguing rusty tools I found within, wondering at their function. I recall to this day the dank smell that pervaded the high shadowy cobweb curtained chambers and the hard to reach dirty wooden shelves lined with jam jars full of screws, nuts, bolts and nails that I failed to open as the lids were rusted tight.

Returning as an adult, I was often disappointed to realise that the visions in my boyhood memories were much exaggerated. There were only two sheds and a rickety lean-to tenuously clinging to the back of one of them. There was only one workbench with just two drawers and only one small vice. The jam jars stocked for future use at least sixty years earlier by a previous occupier of the house still remained unopened, never called upon to fulfil a useful role in handicraft or household maintenance, like cherished personal possessions, just waiting to be discarded by a subsequent owner as junk when the world moves on.

I had tried for several years to persuade Aunt Margaret to move to a smaller house nearer to my home in West London and despite initially politely rejecting the idea, she finally relented.

I researched the options carefully and came up with a shortlist of six suitable properties before taking a now apparently enthusiastic Margaret on a conducted tour of the area. She reclined in the Jaguar like a queen inspecting the far reaches of her royal estate, inspecting the previously unvisited parts reserved for the tied cottages of the workers. Conveniently, three of the six prospective properties were within half a mile of each other on one residential development. As we entered the estate, Margaret made approving comments.

"Yes, Oliver darling, this looks very nice. Mmm, I can see myself living here."

We turned a corner, slowing the car to allow a man walking his dog to cross the road in front of us and suddenly both her tone and demeanour changed.

"No. It's not suitable. Let's move on. I couldn't live here."

"What's the matter, Auntie? I thought you liked it."

Margaret had just seen a sight that condemned the whole area. It was in a nanosecond very definitely off the list.

"Oh it's so dreadfully hoi polloi, frightfully working class."

"I don't think so. What makes you say that?" I asked, concerned because the next three houses I'd planned to show her were in a similar setting.

"Didn't you see that man? He had a tattoo!" Her face was a picture of indignation. It was as if the man had exposed himself. "And earrings!"

Although Tesco was two miles nearer to her home, my aunt insisted that we shop at Waitrose as she felt it offered a more genteel environment, a more middle-class retail experience. I'd take the opportunity to buy all my groceries for the week and would select one of the largest of trolleys available. Margaret, on the other hand, would take the smallest and even that didn't justify the little she bought, the meagre contents signalling the fact that she lived alone and was buying for one. Polythene bags containing ten Brussels sprouts, two apples, one 'jacket'-sized potato, a single lamb chop; perhaps a jar of Horlicks and the smallest chunk of mature cheddar in stock. We'd go our separate ways but I could fill my trolley in the time it took Margaret to select half a dozen items, so inevitably when I'd completed my shopping, I'd have to search for her shrinking body amongst the hordes of casually dressed shoppers, which year by year included an increasing number of shell-suited, working-class people. I'm sure Margaret would have supported the introduction of a mandatory dress code for customers, enforced by uniformed personnel stationed at the door to welcome the appropriately dressed with a smart salute and politely redirect the others to Asda, Tesco and Aldi.

For her weekly outing, my aunt would dress as if for Ascot. She would be immaculately dressed, behatted and bejewelled. Whilst this did cause some amusement among the more casual shoppers it presented for me the distinct advantage of making her easier to spot from within their ranks. I simply had to walk a line perpendicular to the gondolas and look down each row for the lady dressed for the races. Now Margaret, despite her intellect, hadn't quite grasped the principles of modern merchandising and would search for products in the most unlikely locations in an often-fruitless search further handicapped by her failing eyesight. I'd find her, for example, in the tinned fruit aisle, bending down, eyes closely scanning the labels searching for the next item on her short shopping list.

"Hello, Auntie, are you nearly finished?"

"Yes, Oliver darling, but I can't seem to find the bicarbonate of soda or the wire wool."

After shopping, I'd take her to Starbucks for a coffee and 'a pastry', as I was brought up to call a cake, where the pleasing ambience was for her somewhat reminiscent of the post-war establishments she'd frequented in London in the environs of Fleet Street. I was always amused at the lengthy palaver involved in the production of a simple drink in these branded coffee shops but knew enough about retail marketing to realise that the individual preparation of the coffee slowly cup by cup was more to justify the excessive price than an essential of quality control. Margaret though was pleased at the personal service and individual effort that went into the preparation of her beverage.

I recall on one occasion before Starbucks had opened in the town, I took her to a little tearoom not far from her home. It was a throwback to an earlier age and in Margaret's mind was reminiscent of the very much larger Lyons Corner Houses which at several locations in London served all classes between the wars in separate dining rooms on four or five floors. The restaurant on each floor had its own style and employed an orchestra to entertain the diners continuously throughout the day. At street level large Food Halls sold speciality dishes from the Corner House kitchens and exotic foodstuffs, wines, hand-made chocolates, cheeses and flowers. And they provided a food delivery service to all parts of the capital.

Patrons could also use telephone booths, book theatre tickets and use the services of the in-house hairdressing salon.

During the Second World War, it had become more egalitarian, the classes had learned to mix and food rationing and the great influx of foreign military personnel, particularly Americans saw the establishments through necessity adopt a more casual style.

Aunt Margaret had been in her element in those times and was very proud of her service as a civilian secretary in the press office of the ATS which she talked about frequently during my childhood and often subsequently. It was whilst reminiscing one day, not long ago, that she told me it was during her time there that she learned of the death of her fiancé. Her boss, a notable journalist of the day and the man that after the war recruited her to her first job at *The Daily Mail*, had called her into his office and solemnly closed the heavy oak door behind him. Flying Officer Peter Truelove had been missing in operations for more than a month. He'd been shot down in his Hurricane during a dogfight over the Channel just south of Cap Gris Nez and had been seen by a squadron friend in a spiral dive, attempting to make a landfall on the French coast. Margaret knew instantly from the man's body language the grave news she was about to receive. Secretly she'd been preparing herself for this moment whilst praying for better news. If he'd been taken prisoner, she knew she would eventually see him again. If he'd been picked up by Air Sea Rescue, he would have returned to his squadron and been back in the fray within days. This though was the end. The end of her dreams, the end of her plans, the end of her life. She said that she didn't cry at the time. She was told to go home and return to work only when she was ready. She turned up for work next day wearing a brooch, the silver wings worn by wives and girlfriends of RAF pilots of the day, and nothing more was said.

As we sat in the old-fashioned tearooms, she had momentarily stared into space and I could read her mind. I detected the trace of a tear in her eye and was extremely saddened at the thought that she'd carried the grief all of her life. What a waste. Why hadn't she married and had children of her own? Was it that she'd never met anyone who matched up to her dashing young fighter pilot? Or had she foolishly decided that she couldn't find happiness with anyone else, so didn't bother to look. She'd always seemed so happy and content with our life together as I grew up and I hoped to God she hadn't made a conscious decision to commit her life to raising me at the expense of her own happiness. I comforted myself with the argument that she had had a child of her own. She'd had me to herself and always would. Despite the absence of any outward expression of affection from her over the years, I knew that without a shadow of a doubt she loved me. And I'd always made sure she knew I loved her too.

Over our tea and stickies, Margaret had entertained me with an amusing story about her friend Jessica, who she discovered to her immense pleasure, was the daughter of a famous Dutch modern artist by the name of Anton Arenz.

He had enjoyed an extended period of fame throughout the nineteen fifties and sixties and his work was recognised by everyone in The Netherlands as it not only hung in galleries but was very popular on greetings cards and poster prints that decorated thousands of homes throughout the country.

It is a sad fact that an artist's work is for some unaccountable reason more valuable after his death than when he's still alive and painting.

Jessica told Margaret that well before his death in 1970, her mother had received a phone call at home one evening from a total stranger. The caller had apologised for disturbing her at home especially at such a late hour, but asked if she would mind answering a question to settle an argument.

"Could you tell me please if De Her Arenz is still alive?"

The elderly lady was somewhat stunned by the impertinence of the question but simply replied,

"Please hold the line…I'll go and check."

The story had amused Margaret greatly and, of course, she would have handled the enquiry in exactly the same way herself.

I loved to hear Margaret talking about the old days and it was clear she was always very pleased to have someone happy to listen. In a reflective moment, she sometimes would talk about her school days and on this occasion about a Latin Mistress who would have the class endlessly reciting declensions. The pedantic tutor would insistently correct their texts but whilst no doubt improving the girls' written work her pronunciation rendered them audibly unintelligible owing to her 'unseemly northern accent and irritating lisp'.

When we'd finished our tea and pastries, my aunt insisted on paying the bill of a little over six pounds. "My treat, Oliver darling. I insist."

I resisted with a hopeless gesture as I knew it gave her pleasure to feel she was the hostess and I was the guest. In her comfortable nostalgia I was again the eight-year-old boy and she was the adult whose essential responsibility was to educate me in the way respectable middle-class people behaved. The way they 'took tea' rather than 'drank' it; the importance of putting the milk into the cup before pouring in the tea, and the way one lifted both the cup and saucer from the table and not just the cup, in order to catch any drips.

"You're so good to me," she said with great sincerity, "I don't know what I'd do without you, darling."

It was a phrase I'd heard a hundred times before but never tired of hearing.

As Aunt Margaret rose from the table, she thanked the waitress, gathered her handbag and her gloves and made for the door. Looking back I noticed that she'd left a 10p tip on the table. Two shillings would have been considered generous at a Lyons Corner House in 1942 and I'm sure she felt it was an appropriate gesture today. However, I let her take a couple of steps across the pavement before making an excuse to pop back into the café and adding a pound.

Margaret was an intelligent woman and her successful career was testament to that. However, I've noticed that older people seem to exist on a different plane of logic, with different attitudes, as if they have chosen to tether their values to the point in time in which they felt most comfortable, and allow the changing world to progress without them. They still though judge the world by their outdated standards and grumble about almost everything that is new and unfamiliar.

After our visit to the teashop, Aunt Margaret advised me that she had some business to transact at the bank and would meet me at the car in five minutes.

I had been sitting in the car listening to the radio when I realised that fifteen minutes had passed so I got out, locked the door and made my way to the bank to see what had delayed her. Margaret was at the front of a queue of about six customers and I took my place at the back without making my presence known as she was deep in conversation with the female teller behind the glass screen and stooping unnecessarily to speak through the aperture at the base of it under which cash and cheques were passed.

"Is there anything else I can help you with today, madam?" the unattractive girl asked without making eye contact.

"Yes, there certainly is, my dear. I'd like you to convey to whomsoever in your organisation is responsible, my total dissatisfaction with the standard of perforation in your cheque books. It's absolutely impossible to detach a cheque cleanly without tearing."

Margaret's voice was raised presumably because she'd interpreted the girl's expression of bewilderment as an indication that she hadn't heard properly the simple message that had been so clearly and eloquently articulated.

Stooping further, with her mouth now almost level with the counter, Margaret repeated her complaint, in a louder slower voice as if talking to a foreigner without any knowledge of their language.

"It's impossible to remove the cheque from the stub without tearing one or both."

I chuckled at her exaggerated indignation and decided to limit her embarrassment by leaving before she saw me standing there and made my way back to the car.

On the drive back to her home there was another amusing example of the gulf between Margaret's world and the sanitised, politically correct one which she and others of her age find themselves having to tolerate.

Closer to her home, we drove past a parade of shops which included an open-all-hours newsagent and grocery store that had just opened called Ali's News and Booze.

"That's new," I commented.

"What, the Paki shop?" my aunt replied.

"Auntie, you mustn't say that!"

"Mustn't say what?" she innocently replied.

"Paki," I answered. "You can't say that these days."

"Why not?"

"They find it offensive, and it's not PC," I explained.

"Nonsense!" she retorted. "It's simply an abbreviation. 'Paki' is short for Pakistani."

"I know that, Auntie, but you can't say it. They don't like it and it's regarded as racial abuse."

"What nonsense!" she said in a huff. "Can't use abbreviations? Whatever next?" There was a pause of several minutes during which nothing was said and I thought the subject had been dropped, and that she'd accepted the lesson until she continued,

"Can I say Aussi?"

"Well, yes, Auntie, you can."

"That's an abbreviation."

"Yes, I agree but."

"Is it acceptable to say Brit?"

"Yes, Auntie, of course."

"That's an abbreviation too. What's the difference? I rest my case."

I gave up. I could have continued the argument but sensed she'd sit there conducting a mental world cruise, listing countless examples of inoffensive abbreviations. And she did have a point.

I'd previously had cause to speak to Margaret about Asian sensibilities after taking her to see a consultant prior to a cataract operation. He was a charming man, most articulate but with a heavy accent. After long explanation from him about the planned procedure she simply turned to me and said,

"I can't understand a word he's saying."

It was embarrassing for him and even more so for me but Margaret seemed totally unaware of the rudeness. I told him in limp explanation that she was a little deaf.

I had mentioned to her at some point the morons in the English Defence League. She looked astonished that I should be critical about such a good cause and snapped,

"But what are schools doing about apostrophe abuse! They don't teach grammar anymore."

Chapter Twelve
I'm Not in Love

I'd visited Hermione's home on many occasions, spending a summer's afternoon in the garden, perhaps helping with a simple DIY job for which she either didn't have the tools or the strength; or enjoying a glass of wine by the fireside after work on a chilly winter's evening. We were still not lovers but by then very good friends. I enjoyed her company and she enjoyed mine. I wanted more but she made it clear that she didn't. It had become a thrilling, painful, delightful, stressful, stimulating, barely tolerable but unmissable part of my life.

She'd kiss me on the cheek each time I left as if I were a departing favourite uncle, and I'd respond with a gentle squeeze of that heavenly waist, or touch her lightly in the curve of her back in exactly the place my hand rested each night in my dreams. Mindful always of the hopeless gulf in our feelings for each other I'd take great care to make the bodily contact only hip to hip, to avoid startling her and embarrassing me, with full frontal contact. This often required such an unnatural twist of the torso that I often felt a twinge of pain in my back all the way home in the car. Although I'm sure she was thankful for the manoeuvre she probably thought it an ambiguous signal or perhaps even an indication of shyness on my part.

Occasionally, Hermione and Tristan would spend a sunny summer's day at the farm and the boy seemed to enjoy it immensely, flying a kite in the paddock, jumping on the hay bales in the barn and climbing trees under the watchful eye of his mother. What he enjoyed most of all was to drive my old Land Rover Defender around the fields. This, of course, required me to sit him on my lap so that I could operate the pedals whilst he enthusiastically steered figures of eight around the pasture. He enjoyed the experience very much and would make exaggerated tyre squealing noises as we cornered on the grass and when I braked to a halt. I have to confess I did find myself warming to him although I disciplined myself not to show it as I knew he was the enemy in my battle for Hermione's affection. As he fidgeted in front of me, expertly sliding the steering wheel through his podgy hands I of course was very wary that I might at any time feel a rip-snorting fart vibrate across my lap. However, having not once heard him let off within earshot of Hermione, I was confident by then that he saved his performances for when we were alone and I simply resolved to ensure his mother always accompanied us on our rural rides.

We'd have a barbeque of scallops and prawns with a fresh salad laced with a delicious dressing made to Hermione's own recipe, followed by seabass which I'd cook in tinfoil with slices of lemon wrapped in. For dessert I toss on three large bananas and let their skins turn black before slicing them open with the precision of a surgeon and spooning out the soft hot pulp to be eaten with a tablespoon of honey drizzled over them. At this stage it would be getting dark and Tristan would slump and snore on the sofa whilst Hermione and I strolled around the garden, a glass of wine in hand watching the sunset.

"You're so lucky, living here," she once said as we leaned on a fence enjoying the last scarlet traces of the disappearing sun. "Tristan just loves our visits."

She could have said, 'We enjoy our visits,' but she didn't. She just said 'Tristan', which, of course, disappointed me greatly, but she'd probably chosen her words carefully as I was by then standing too close and feeling her slender upper arm pressing against mine.

"It's a wonderful place to bring up children," I replied after a pause of sufficient duration to make it appear a non-sequitur. She turned and gave me her by now unmistakable, 'Don't start all that again' look.

When it was time for them to leave, we'd perform the hip to hip ritual again as she kissed my cheek and I'd once more with sadness settle for my role as best supporting actor rather than co-star in the story of her life.

In my lonely bed though my actions were less constrained. Throughout my life I had found that if I really wanted something, or really wanted something to happen, I could through extra effort and total commitment make it happen. No doubt this determination and positive thinking was inspired by Margaret in my formative years. It was certainly a philosophy that helped me achieve at school in both academic and sporting challenges.

There was though an added dimension to this gift that had unfailingly and uncannily recurred. I found that if, in my half sleep, I could visualise the desired event in great detail, then it would always come to pass. Conversely if, try as I did to conjure the situation into my dreams and fail to do so regardless of how hard I tried, it would not happen. So infallible was this phenomenon that I had come to use it as a test of fortune, a sort of second sight into my future. It had never let me down.

I was so desperate to sleep with Hermione, not just to make love but to hold her throughout the night, that I would lie awake, visualising my angel at that very moment asleep in her bed ten miles away from where I lay in my restlessness. I had a clear vision of the room having helped her to put up some curtain rails a year ago. In my half sleep I'd try to impose on my addled brain a dream that would take me to her. A dream that one day must become a reality if I am to avoid spontaneous combustion, the only remaining trace of me the powdery remains of my smouldering trousers in a perfect circle around the smoking residue of my shoes. I see her not naked but in a virgin-white, light cotton nightdress, lying on her back, the folds of thin cloth outlining her lovely lap and faintly revealing the dark shadow of a neatly trimmed bush; a half smile on her luscious lips, waiting for me.

First, I'd have to transport myself from my bed to hers. I would slip from under my duvet and stand erect, often in more ways than one, and prepare for take-off. With the power of a Saturn rocket I'd then zoom up through the ceiling, through the roof, up over the ten miles of suburbia that separated our homes. Like Superman, I would fly across parks and gardens, sleeping houses and quiet roads. I'd navigate by the lights of the city until I found myself silently alighting on the landing outside Hermione's bedroom door. Composing myself I'd quietly enter her room and watch for a few moments as she lay there pretending to be asleep, now on her side, hair untidily covering her beautiful neck. She'd turn to face the ceiling, sleepily brushing her tussled locks to one side and say dreamily,

"Is that you, Oliver?"

Then raising herself onto one elbow, to knowingly give me a glimpse of a lust-swollen nipple she'd say, every time.

"Come to bed, my darling. I've been waiting for you."

My heart would race as I'd slip in beside her, anticipating her eager hot kiss and impatiently reaching for a scallop-soft buttock. And then…

And then nothing! However hard I tried, night after frustrating night my dream would stop there. As much as I tried, I couldn't force my mind to picture the next frame in the movie. Infuriatingly and inevitably, it would wander to the next topic in the worry file. Jerked awake by the disappointment I'd try to concentrate, try to regain the dream and get back into that bed on which my heart was focussed. It was hopeless and I knew it. The harder I tried the more elusive the image became, like a one-armed man chasing a cake of soap in the bath.

Always I was left with the thought that if my oft-proven superstition was again correct, it didn't bode well for my future plans for Hermione.

My unhappy happiness rolled on. I continued to take Hermione out to lunch but only thinly disguised my feelings, as she seemed to have come to terms with the unequal situation and probably felt that the minor embarrassment was a small price to pay for a 'decent lunch'.

It was early February again and I decided to enhance another Valentine card with my latest pathetic attempt at love poetry. Once more I accessed the protected file and printed out the verse, surreptitiously stapling it into a humorous card and taking care that no-one could see any reflection of the colourful card in the glass panels of my office walls. Oliver was not the type to send a Valentine; that would be ridiculous. Men of his age don't do that.

This time I had tried to raise the standard by borrowing the opening lines from Robbie Burns. Remembering her dismissive laughter at my last attempt, this meant I could pass the whole thing off as a joke if it elicited a similar reaction.

'O, my love is like a red, red rose,
That is newly sprung in June,
Petal soft her perfect skin,
Whilst mine is like a prune.

The beauty of her magnet eyes,
Deep pools in which I drown,
But if my glance becomes a stare,
She answers with a frown.

In the music of her voice is lost,
The wisdom of her words,
For such distraction is her mouth,
Oft leaves her speech unheard.

She's in the summer of her life,
For me it's late September,
I sore lament the hopeless gulf,
But the joy I will remember.'

'ANON' I added, as if she would have any doubt as to which lovesick fool had been so bold.

Shatteringly, but predictably, Hermione's reaction was exactly the same as the previous year. Unimaginatively it was verbatim,

"Thanks for your card. It made me laugh."

I had become so proficient at concealing my disappointment that I laughed it off too.

Confusingly her cool indifference to my declarations of love was always balanced with a sympathetic warmth in all her dealings with me. Whether at work or socially her happy demeanour, her smiles and laughter deceived me into hoping that she loved me too but that for some reason felt it must be held secret, that it could not be declared. However, if I ever dared to be more direct in my search for a hint of mutual affection, she'd be cruelly uncompromising in her swift rejection.

"Hermione, will you give me a yes or no answer to a straight question?" I asked when driving back from lunch one day.

"Mmmmm, depends what it is," she suspiciously responded.

"Be honest; don't pull any punches," I stupidly added.

"If you had a magic wand that could make me stop feeling for you the way that I do; would you wave it?"

"Yes," she replied without a nanosecond of hesitation or further comment. No qualifying clauses, no consoling words, no sympathetic sentences; nothing to which I could attach the faintest hope.

She was also at pains to let me know that she didn't find me attractive, not in an unkind way but by cleverly transferring the put down to a third-party scenario. For example, in my presence when asked by a female colleague if she fancied a very wealthy and over-attentive client who had been turning on the charm, she replied,

"Oh I couldn't possibly date someone over fifty."

I wanted to interject but stifled the pathetic words letting them resonate only within my head,

"Oh, Hermione, I may be over sixty but for you I can be thirty in the dark!"

I listened to the chatter between them, Hermione's contribution I felt sure meant for my ears rather than for her workmate. The conversation developed into one about the ineptitude of men in courtship, their lack of understanding about what really turns a woman on, and the laughable tactics they employ, 'to get into your knickers'. The friend illustrated her point with some very amusing anecdotes from her hectic but evidently unfulfilling love life and I was surprised at how candid she was. *Are women always so frank with each other? Do they tell their friends every intimate detail?* I wondered. *Men certainly don't, although I believe women think that we do.*

I got bored with the chit chat and had directed my attention to other matters when I heard Hermione say,

"Yes, and that pathetic thing they do with their eyes!"

What a stab. What a cruel thrust to the heart. Is that what she thinks when I look into her eyes? When I prolong the contact to see into her soul and feel the tender effervescence? She thinks it's a deliberate ploy? And she thinks it's pathetic?

God, that's awful, on two counts. She thinks it's a pathetic seduction tactic, part of some premeditated courting ritual, rather than an involuntary but compelling drive to experience a rare and wonderful gift of nature first delivered by total accident to someone who previously had not harboured a single romantic thought about her. And even worse news, it means she clearly hasn't felt it herself, for me or anyone else. When her beautiful, magnetic eyes look back, she feels absolutely nothing.

It was only a single sentence but it stabbed me deeply. I was overcome by the hopelessness of miserable one-way love.

It was clear something had to be done. I could no longer live like this, no longer bear the frustration, no longer give up ninety percent my brain capacity to thoughts and dreams of a woman who didn't care and with whom I clearly had no future. I resolved that for the sake of my sanity I too must adopt the cynical mind-set so clearly demonstrated by the two women on whose fickle conversation I had eavesdropped. I'd suppress these feelings and give up the ridiculous dream and begin living my life for me.

I'd make a start by bringing an end to the lunchtime 'dates', stay away from Hermione's home that evokes those counterfeit visions of future happiness and start making plans to get out of the chaffing manacles of my job. Freedom here I come!

Chapter Thirteen
Taking Cats to Lunch

How did I get myself into such a fix? How could I have avoided it? How would I break it to Philippa? How outrageously would Alice behave? How was I going to handle it? These questions preyed on my mind all night.

Alice had made it clear that the alternative to inviting her along to lunch next day would be to suffer her longest mood ever. She hadn't actually said so but it goes with the turf when you're shagging a bimbo. They are gorgeous, they're sexy, they're fun but they sulk like teenagers.

Don't get me wrong, I wear the trousers in the relationship, unless Alice is ripping them off me that is, but somehow she always seems to talk me round, always ends up getting her own way.

If I'm honest, I guess it might be that I just can't believe my luck. A gorgeous young woman, sex on legs, always up for it but married to someone else and determined to stay that way. It doesn't get much better than that, does it?

I'd even offered to cancel the date with Philippa. Yes, the word 'date' had slipped out before I could stop myself. Alice scented my ploy and out-manoeuvred me saying that she wouldn't want me to miss out on the 'business' discussion and how she'd be pleased to meet at last the woman she'd 'heard so much about in recent weeks'. The truth is I'd hardly mentioned Philippa but to challenge that would certainly have increased the depth of the hole I had dug for myself.

It occurred to me that there were two factors I had to bear in mind. One was that I hadn't actually bedded Philippa by then and although the indications were very positive it was possible it might not happen, so why risk losing my lovely porn star's services for however short a period? Or even permanently? The other factor was that having decided to play the long game with Philippa, the introduction of some competition and particularly from someone younger, sexier and more attractive, might just work in my favour.

I called Philippa's mobile number five times that morning to cancel our date without getting a response. I hadn't known that she would be in court until midday, and at eleven thirty I left a message to say that I'd meet her as arranged at one o'clock but that I'd just been reminded of an earlier arrangement and would have a friend in tow. That gave me just about an hour to decide how to play it.

It would be no use pretending that Alice was 'just a friend' as she wouldn't let me get away with that. Neither would she let me get away with anything less than affectionate body language as she'd question my motive for wanting to hide our relationship from 'my solicitor'. Why should I?

Philippa would be confused at any show of affection for Alice as I hadn't even mentioned her before, and she'd taken our lunch to be a date rather than the business meeting I'd described it as to Alice. Oh God!

To play for more thinking time I suggested that Alice meet me, yes I was smart enough to say 'me' rather than 'us', at the restaurant rather than picking her up from home. Who knows, she might have got lost en-route or bumped into her mother in law, or developed her first migraine, or been taken hostage in a high street bank siege or something. I was desperate. I had no idea how to handle it. I thought at one point the only way out might be to fail to turn up myself and call each of them very much later with profuse apologies for being unavoidably delayed. Of course, that wouldn't work. Alice would simply enter the restaurant and shout out, "So which one of you is Lady Philippa then?"

Philippa would be somewhat easier to handle. I could be as cool as I could possibly get away with towards Alice and then call Philippa that evening to explain that Alice was a clingy ex-girlfriend that I couldn't get rid of. Shit, no! She'd probably persuade me to take out a restraining order and even offer to arrange it for me.

I was running out of time. The more I schemed the more indecisive I became. One thing though was very clear, I had to be there when they arrived. I couldn't risk their introducing themselves to each other without my nonchalant presence. No, clearly the only way out would be to appear the epitome of politeness to both, to play 'the gentleman', the cool dude with absolutely nothing to hide.

Shiiiiiit!!!

I arrived at Luigi's at twenty to one to be absolutely certain I'd be there when the first of the two women arrived.

Who would be first? I wondered.

I hoped that it would be Philippa, so that I could have a few minutes alone with her to elaborate on my lie about a forgotten arrangement and to position Alice as the troublesome ex-girlfriend who needed to be humoured to avoid a scene; with profuse apologies of course for exposing her to any embarrassment. That would hopefully explain any slight show of affection for Alice should it become necessary to allay her fears about Philippa being in any way a rival.

If Alice arrived first I'd explain that I wanted her to act in a business-like manner in front of 'my solicitor' and not embarrass me by being kissy cuddly or talking about our wonderful relationship. I'd ask her to moderate her language too as Philippa Stapleton was 'rather strait-laced'.

God! I hoped Alice was not feeling playful.

As that nervous thought flashed across my mind, I saw them arriving together.

Philippa was first through the door. She was dressed for court in lawyers' black but wore a bright red silk scarf to add a touch of colour and had switched her sensible shoes for a pair of four-inch heels also in red. Her auburn hair looked as though she'd spent the morning with a stylist rather than a judge and her lips were glossed to match the scarf which looped loosely around her elegant neck.

Without looking behind her she briefly held the door for Alice not realising that she was the unwanted guest, until a waiter sprang to relieve her of the task. In doing so he had to pause momentarily as Philippa stopped in her tracks looking round the room before spotting me getting up from the table to greet her. The interruption caused Alice to collide with the door as it was held ajar and she bumped her nose painfully into it.

"Don't mind me!" she shouted in a sarcastic tone, looking daggers at Philippa.

"Oh, I am so sorry!" Philippa replied with equal sarcasm.

Their meeting hadn't got off to the best of starts.

Alice had clearly given a deal of thought to her appearance for the meeting with the woman she instinctively saw as a rival. However, instead of trying to achieve a classy, professional image to reflect her mind's eye impression of how a lawyer might dress, an option by no means beyond her as she had quite an eye for style, she opted for a total contrast. Alice looked like a Barbie Doll, dressed as if she'd come straight from the fancy dress hire shop.

She wore a gold-sequinned miniskirt with jacket to match over a low-cut white blouse revealing at least two inches of cleavage accentuated by what she always referred to as her 'Hello Boys' bra.

Her beautiful blonde hair was back-combed and lacquered into a ridiculous tall crown adding about four inches to her height with long kiss curls hanging down in front of her ears and across her cheeks.

This unnatural and tarty construction was complemented by more make-up than I'd ever seen her wear before and the longest false eyelashes imaginable. The total image unnerved me considerably as, having never seen her dress to any degree like that before, I had to conclude that she was dressed for a performance, the prospect of which prompted a cold bead of sweat to run down my back. Oh God! She was feeling playful. I'd seen it many times before but dreaded to think just how outrageous it was to be this time.

Perhaps I could defuse her plans by not reacting to the 'fancy dress' in any way and certainly by not appearing embarrassed by it.

I thought it prudent to greet Alice first to stave off one of her moods but had to dance a tango around the fussing waiter standing between the two women as he tried to simultaneously greet them as he'd been trained and to apologise to Alice for the little accident with the door.

"Hello, Alice; hello, Philippa," I said in as confident a tone as I could muster given my nervousness and frightening mental image of the disastrous encounter that I felt sure was to follow.

"I see you've bumped into each other already," I joked stupidly in an attempt to break the ice.

They both looked at me in disbelief at the fatuous remark, perhaps the only point of accord to pass between them that day.

I touched Alice very lightly on the hips and kissed her briefly on the cheek whilst standing about a foot away from her, a distance intended to signal the coolness of our relationship to Philippa. Alice sensed the ruse and responded with a kiss on my mouth firm enough to leave traces of lipstick on my lips throughout the meal and held me tightly.

"Hello, darling," she said with exaggerated affection and then theatrically stepped back half a pace as if startled and said, "ooooh as pleased to see me as ever, I see!"

I chuckled as nonchalantly as I could to give the impression to Philippa that this behaviour was just frivolous banter and par for the course with Alice.

I started to lean forward to give Philippa a platonic kiss on the cheek but more than half-way into the manoeuvre decided against it for Alice's benefit and went for a business-like handshake instead. It must have looked as if I'd just tripped or was trying to whisper something in her ear or sample her expensive perfume, and having already turned her head to receive the kiss she blushed a little at the apparent misunderstanding.

"Hello, Philippa," I repeated, "nice to see you."

Her face broke into a warm smile as we made eye contact, a smile that instantly morphed into one I'm sure she saves for troublesome rival lawyers as she turned towards Alice when I completed the introductions.

"Philippa, meet Alice. Alice, meet Philippa."

They exchanged glances but not handshakes and I think that nanosecond of eye contact between the two women was the longest of the entire encounter.

I led them to the table at which I'd nervously awaited their arrival where fortunately the attentive waiter helped Philippa to her seat which allowed me without any apparent favour to do the same for Alice.

"Thank you, darling, as chivalrous as ever."

The ladies settled in their seats and each responded to my invitation to aperitifs. Alice ordered a Kir Royale but Philippa asked for 'just a glass of sparkling water' and I feared she was possibly keeping her options open for an early tactical withdrawal if the lunch became unbearable. The poor woman clearly wondered what I had let her in for and conveyed this subtly but unmistakably with a single glance.

"So you're his lawyer then?" said Alice opening the painful conversation.

"Yes, that's right. And you're the girlfriend?" Philippa enquired.

"Mistress," Alice replied confidently as if there was an important distinction.

I was desperate to take control of the conversation to steer it without delay onto an uncontroversial topic of mutual interest, not that I could imagine there might be one, when I was rescued by a waiter who picked up each linen napkin in turn and with an expert flick of his wrist transformed it from the shape of a baby rabbit, ears erect and perched on the table mats in front of us into a more useful form which he respectfully draped across our laps.

Alice, of course, couldn't resist some comment about the close proximity of the waiter's hand to the high hem of her miniskirt and I cringed as in an exaggerated Essex accent she squealed,

"Hey, careful, cheeky!" Philippa glanced at me with an almost imperceptible shake of her head as if in disbelief that I could be in any way involved with such a common girl. Any hopes I'd foolishly entertained of the lunch being anything less than an embarrassing fiasco disappeared with those words. Alice was here to make trouble.

I thought I might calm her with a compliment, nothing too affectionate as to reinforce Alice's assertion that we were in a regular relationship and in weekly contact but a little flattery that Philippa might view as a mere pleasantry, and one that Alice could see as a supportive gesture.

"Have you had your hair done this morning, Alice?" I asked. "It looks very nice, doesn't it, Philippa?"

As soon as the words had left my mouth, my stupidity dawned on me. Fancy asking an elegantly dressed woman to comment on the appearance of one turned out so deliberately to look like a tart. But it was too late. Philippa replied as the hot flush of embarrassment coloured my cheeks.

"Yes, very nice," she offered, and turning to Alice added, "it really suits you."

My attempts at polite conversation thereafter proved futile, with both women avoiding eye contact with each other and in turn looking at me to break the ice. It was clear though that the battleship Cordiality was stuck firmly in the Antarctic winter freeze.

I sat helpless as Alice fired the first salvo. She faked an admiring glance at Philippa's hair before asking,

"Did you choose that colour or are you a natural ginger?"

Oh God, I thought, *here we go.*

Philippa, of course, was too practiced at keeping her cool under provocation to rise to the bait and responded calmly but with just a trace of superiority as if she were introducing a new word into Alice's limited vocabulary,

"It's 'Auburn', quite natural. And yours?"

Alice looked at me as she quipped back,

"Oh I'm a nat-ur-al blonde, darling, as Charlie will confirm."

Alice was smart enough to read the insult in Philippa's reply and loaded another question.

"Have you been to a funeral this morning or do you always dress in black?"

"No, only for work. It's a convention that we wear black in court."

"Oh shame for you. I should imagine you'd be happier in beige."

Philippa ignored the cruel quip.

To appear unperturbed by the attack Philippa responded with a question she hoped Alice might see as polite conversation and an attempt to show she wouldn't be rattled by the girl's pathetic attempt to win a war of words with an articulate superior.

"And what do you do for a living, er, Alice?"

"Why don't you guess?" Alice replied, a little unnerved by the question and playing for time whilst she thought of an alternative to the truth that she was actually unemployed. She was smart enough to anticipate that her rival would ask if that was 'unemployed' or 'unemployable'.

Philippa, after a brief pause during which she made it obvious she was studying Alice's ridiculous blonde bouffant tresses, suggested, "Hairdresser?"

Alice took a deep intake of breath lasting several seconds like a baby preparing to scream its head off but a pleading look from me surprisingly persuaded her not to react, though I knew it was just a matter of time before she'd escalate to the use of thermo-nuclear weapons in the war of words she was obviously determined not to lose.

The golden girl then changed tack with what I suspected was a flattering set-up line for a cruel insult that was sure to follow.

"You're very slim, Philippa. I bet you weigh less than nine stone."

Philippa spotted the ruse and as if duelling with a rival barrister cleverly outmanoeuvred her.

"I wish," she answered calmly, "A little over that actually. What about you?"

"Oh, eight and a half in the nude…as Charlie will confirm."

"Is that with or without make-up?"

A red-faced Alice realised that her planned punchline had been rendered unusable and was left open-mouthed in defeat.

Before she could gather her thoughts, the opening skirmish was thankfully interrupted by Luigi's arrival at the table as he handed the menus first to the ladies and then to me, along with the wine list.

"Good afternoon, sir, ladies."

He stepped away from the table as a young waitress arrived with the drinks we'd ordered together with two bottles of water, one still and one sparking, just like the two women I was lunching with I thought with an increasing feeling of doom that would I felt probably leave me unable to eat anything at all.

I was grateful for the two or three minutes of silence as my guests perused the fine menu but had been so instantly stunned by the speed with which Alice opened hostilities that I couldn't think clearly enough to determine a strategy to avoid the battle royal I felt sure was about to commence, let alone think about food.

Philippa chose an escalope of veal in a lemon sauce and when encouraged to choose a starter opted for gazpacho. I was initially surprised at Alice's selection as she had become quite enamoured with quality food since we'd been seeing each other, but of course she chose something more in keeping with today's role.

"I'll have a prawn cocktail and steak please," she said with wry smile, passing the menu back to the waiter standing on her right but looking directly across the table at me.

"How would you like it cooked, madam?"

"Well, grilled of course!" she retorted, again watching for a reaction from me.

"Is that medium, madam, or well done?" replied the waiter without the slightest recognition of her ignorance or her joke whichever it was and without any interest either way.

"I'll take medium for now," she replied and then in a deliberately audible whisper added,

"I'm hoping to get well done later."

Philippa's body language said it all. She realised that Alice was going to continue to rile her throughout the meal with thinly veiled insults and innuendo. She looked at me and sighed with a look that unmistakably asked why this was happening to her and giving me very little time to take control of the silly bitch lunching with us before she beat a rapid retreat never to be seen again.

I could see all my plans for Philippa disappearing rapidly and quickly toiled with the question of which 'relationship' I could most easily salvage if one of them walked out.

Whilst considering this I was prompted by the waiter for my order having missed his question whilst quickly pondering my sexual future.

"Oh, I'm in two minds. Erm…I think I'll have the scallops, followed by monkfish."

"Go on, have a steak!" Alice interjected, "Get yer strength up for tonight."

"Alice stop it! Please," I said, changing my tone mid-sentence from assertive to placatory in a futile attempt to show Philippa that I had some control over the bimbo without making Alice feel admonished.

I breathed an audible sigh of relief as Alice made an insincere apology,

"Sorry, only joking. You know me."

At that point Alice went over the top. She knew that her mission was already accomplished but confident she held the high ground in the battle of wits went in for the kill.

"If you can't decide, why don't you roll the dice? You have brought them with you for this evening, haven't you?"

She had delivered the coup de grace whilst fixing me with a look that unmistakably conveyed that she was fully aware of my deception and if I were foolish enough to underestimate her she would unleash the weapon of mass destruction.

"You have brought them?" she persisted.

All was lost.

"No, I haven't," I replied wearily signalling abject defeat.

"What dice?" Philippa enquired.

I made a futile attempt to avoid the graphic description I felt Alice would delight in giving and quickly cut in before she could reply.

"Oh it's just a little game we have played once or twice in moments of indecision."

Alice laughed at my pathetic attempt to wriggle out of the inevitable denouement and looking me in the eyes with the unspoken words, 'Here it comes Big Boy and you deserve it', fired her penultimate cannonade.

"Well, before we have sex, we write down a list of scenarios and ways of doing it and allocate a—"

At that point, Philippa snapped shut her menu and pushed back her chair as if making to leave.

I attempted to stop her with gentle pressure on her wrist. Although clearly upset she was far too professional to make a scene so adopted a voice she might use in court when cross-examining an untruthful witness.

"Charles, exactly why did you invite me here, may I ask? And why is this, this, this, 'person' here? I thought we were having lunch together, you and I. I'm a lawyer you know, not a counsellor. If you two have some issues, I'll leave and you can resolve them between yourselves. I have better things to do and can think of many more enjoyable ways of having lunch."

I didn't need to answer. Alice realised that she had won the battle outright but clearly enjoying my discomfort and presumably determined that I should learn from it wanted to prolong my agony further.

"Keep yer 'auburn' hair on Philly, I was only having a joke. Look, you two wanted to have a 'business lunch' as I understand it, so don't mind me, I'll just shut up and eat my food and you two can get on with whatever you wanted to discuss."

There it was. My deception clearly uncloaked. In a sentence Alice had cleverly outmanoeuvred me by informing Philippa that I'd told her our lunch date was a strictly business affair, and there could be only one reason for that subterfuge. I was undoubtedly still in a relationship and not a free agent as I'd led her to believe. I was clearly a liar and philanderer just like every other man who'd made advances to her since leaving university.

Philippa stood up and calmly positioned her chair neatly under the table.

She was clearly upset and a little flushed as if in court within moments of convincing the jury of her client's innocence, only to be passed a note from the dock saying, 'OK Guv, it's a fair cop, I dunnit.'

"I won't say thank you for the invitation, Charles, or that it's been a pleasure to meet you and your brainless trollop but next time you need a lawyer try elsewhere."

I was about to get to my feet to try to pacify her and persuade her to stay but received such a violent kick on the shins under the table from a smiling Alice that I was unable to stand or even speak other than to groan in pain.

"Don't get up," Philippa quipped enjoying my pain, "I'll see myself out and leave you both to your prawn cocktails and steaks."

All was lost but I knew Alice would want the last word and as her beaten adversary retreated called her back and said, "Oh, Philippa, just one thing that intrigues me."

"Yes, Alice?" she replied with the tone of a teacher impressed that the dunce in the class should have such a word in her vocabulary.

"Do you ever masturbate while you're driving?"

Chapter Fourteen
Keeping Fit

I had retained little contact with my RAF chums having left the service prematurely under the circumstances I explained to you earlier. However a guy I met on the day I joined has remained a life-long friend. Max Grainger, or 'Max G', to use the sobriquet he soon earned after bringing a Jet Provost back to base after a solo general handling sortie with corrugations in the upper surfaces of both wings having severely overstressed the aircraft pulling out of an aerobatic manoeuvre at very low level, remains to this day my best friend. The Royal Air Force, usually totally unforgiving of any slight misdemeanour, such as my own minor offence, chose to overlook Max's transgression, possibly recognising in him the makings of a determined fighter pilot.

Their uncharacteristic forgiveness paid dividends as he went on to become an accomplished ground attack pilot and Jaguar weapons instructor. Now out of the service and flying 757s for an airline affiliated to one of the major holiday companies Max has to relieve his frustration at the strictures of commercial flying in his little Cessna Aerobat when off duty, whilst condescendingly condemning all light aircraft with the derisory description 'Puddle-jumpers'. When he gets a bit too boastful about military jet-jockeying, I bring him down to earth with a not so tuneful rendering from Springsteen's 'Glory Days'. I also remind him that while in different ways we both had a Jaguar 'on the firm', I still have mine.

As well as meeting Max at the flying club of which we are both members, we also get together most Monday nights if his flight roster permits, at a Men's Keep Fit class in the gymnasium of a local college. I'd far prefer to attend a pukka gym offering the benefits of modern fitness equipment and decent changing rooms, let alone eligible females in Lycra, rather than the grubby school facilities with their stench of adolescent sweat and filthy abandoned sports kit in the lost property box but Max, ever one to select the cheaper option, persuaded me to accompany him. That was four years ago and we're still attending because I must confess it's a bit of a hoot.

The course has a total establishment of about twenty men of ages ranging from late thirties to mid-fifties with just one spritely member of seventy-one, although attendance each week averages around fourteen. The format is simple. Ten minutes of 'touch rugby' to warm up, ten minutes of stretching exercises, which to my mind ought to precede the rugger to avoid pulling any unprepared muscles, and half an hour around a quite demanding circuit-training course. This is followed by an hour of team games in which the skill of the players is vastly exceeded by our enthusiasm and will to win. We occasionally play basketball but more usually indoor hockey to Marquis of Queensbury Rules, which Max has dubbed 'Agincourt' in view of the extreme violence with which it's played and the often-high body count. This is always followed for the last half hour of the session by a game of volleyball, not so violent but again with scant observance of any rules.

I don't think much fitness improvement is experienced by any member of the class but all I think attend as much for the camaraderie as for any physical benefit. For me it's for the banter as much as anything else and the chance to catch up with Max.

The group is very mixed, not just in age and physical ability but also in occupation, intellect, political persuasion, articulacy, very definitely sense of humour, and confidence or lack of it.

The course leader Jake, a tall, fit, fifty-year-old schools inspector with curly fair hair, who is frequently reminded of his likeness to Noddy Holder of *The Slade*, does his best by example to encourage everyone to derive maximum benefit from the sessions by giving it total effort. His prowess at basketball is legend and although most of us hate the game with a vengeance and much prefer to play volleyball or 'Agincourt' he gets his way occasionally and runs rings around us from one end of the court to the other like a demented spider, contemptuously dodging all defenders and invariably scoring from a great distance.

The elder statesman of the group, or as Max dubs him, 'Father of the Gym' is Ernie, a retired catering manager and one-time scout leader with a remarkable likeness to the grumpy old codger in the TV series *Steptoe and Son*. Having had both hips replaced and probably a knee or two he doggedly refuses to give in to age and although useless at virtually every activity and a liability in any team game owing to his ineffective spectacles and total lack of spatial awareness, owns the affection and respect of the whole class. When the ball goes out of play during a game of volleyball and the person returning it to the server does so by means of a kick, he is with monotonous regularity chastised firmly by Ernie with a shout of, 'Don't kick the ruddy volleyball!' as if rebuking an errant Boy Scout at summer camp. This exclamation has become a catchphrase among the group and Ernie's complaint is invariably echoed by many in unison with calls of, "'arold, don't kick the volleyball!"

Another of the more senior members is David, an English and History teacher nearing retirement age at the local Comprehensive who demonstrates a lack of physical co-ordination to rival Ernie's directional instability. His eye-hand-brain co-ordination makes him a liability too and invariably Jake contrives to put them on opposite teams to even out the handicap. It's hard to imagine David keeping order in a class of teenage boys or girls as his timid persona, sloth-like movement and soft-spoken manner give him the appearance of the cartoon character *Mr Magoo* but evidently he has survived a career in the classroom without being set alight or superglued to the blackboard.

David clearly thinks I'm a flash git and continually engages me in brief conversations usually about my extensive travel, business success and trappings of wealth and believes his unsubtle and thinly-veiled sarcasm goes over my head. I delight though in responding with exaggerated examples to boost his prejudice and am amused greatly by the knowledge that it is my returns that go over his head, just as most volleyballs do when he's on court.

I very much enjoy the company of forty-something Kelvin, a burly rugby player and civilian instructor at the local prison who always greets me with a couple of blue jokes, none of which I can remember long enough to pass on, and the latest tale of prisoner misbehaviour or management ineptitude. It pays to be on the same side as cheerful Kelvin in team games as to accidentally run into this man mountain with a basketball or hockey stick in your hand will have just one painful outcome.

Amongst the younger element is Simon, a well-built Cornishman whose stature evidences a doting mother who must have over-fed him throughout boyhood and a wife who took over the duty immediately after their wedding with hefty portions of nourishing meals. Not fat by any means but 'solid' in a way that speaks of a seafaring ancestry and Celtic grit.

Simon is a true gentleman and the most caring and decent individual you could wish to meet, but put a hockey stick in his hand and he becomes a raging bull in the proverbial china shop, swinging it high above his head, in complete disregard for the rules, and producing a delivery, on the rare occasions that he actually makes contact with the puck that is, that would have the most proficient keeper sacrifice a goal rather than risk serious personal injury by attempting to save it.

Simon is a playful character and frequently quotes one-liners from *Morecambe and Wise* TV shows whilst clowning on court, emerging from successful tackles with his glasses deliberately askew and slapping the back of his head with a free hand. A regular performance from him is to grab me around the neck in a headlock and, using a line from one of their classic sketches, shouts, 'get out of that!' My unveiled annoyance at this weekly assault bizarrely never fails to amuse the whole class.

Max is without doubt the most competitive person I have ever met, which is probably the reason for his success as a fighter pilot, and is a walking example of how the 'Baby Boomers' doggedly refuse to give up and grow old gracefully. He will attend the session on most Monday nights sporting an ever-increasing number of elasticated support bandages; around both knees and elbows and probably others elsewhere but out of sight.

The part of the session that I enjoy most is the game of volleyball at the end of the evening. The winning team is the first to score twenty with at least a two-point lead.

After each point Jake shouts out the score, five-four, ten-twelve, sixteen-fourteen and so on, although very frequently getting it wrong and having to be corrected by the other players in unison. He developed the habit too in his boyish way of occasionally adding the odd comment to particular scores such as, '20-20 perfect vision' or '8-8.two fat ladies'. On one occasion calling, '18-15 battle of Waterloo'. That gave me a mischievous idea and ever since I've impressed most of the group, joyously including teacher David I'm delighted to say, by interjecting entirely spurious historical references to almost every score line.

"14-13 battle of Crecy," I'd shout. "18-19 repeal of the Corn Laws," "17-20 death of Queen Anne."

It is all complete bollocks, of course, but very satisfying to be regarded as somewhat of a history buff when we get together in the pub afterwards for a couple of pints of ale to relax and probably undo any benefit we might have gained from the session.

Chapter Fifteen
George Fights Back

George had made several references to our fateful night out and had initially asked nicely that I should delete the video and photo images from my phone, adding with mock joviality that he'd like to have copies for his continued amusement before I did so. I suspect that's a well-tried double bluff for a blackmail victim in a sex scandal, terrified at the prospect of the pictures being revealed but pretending that it would represent only a minor inconvenience if they were and certainly not an eventuality worth paying to avoid.

I assured George that both the video and the other pictures were very securely stored but I did comply with his request for copies. After all I wanted him to be in no doubt about the clarity of both the images and the sound so I despatched them to him by email with the title 'Naughty Boy!'

He was in a hopeless position and he knew it. He couldn't get tough and there really wasn't any sanction he could take against me without risking exposure. No doubt he'd pondered the spectrum of implications of my forwarding the evidence to Hilda; physical violence, separation, homelessness, divorce, financial ruin, and the ridicule of colleagues, friends and family. He had no choice but to sit and wait for the blackmailer's demands, but none came. He must have wondered what was the price he'd have to pay me; money, career advancement, collusion in covering up an 'accounting irregularity', or even embezzlement on a major scale? Might he be drawn into a criminal act that could see him sent to gaol? He must have had sleepless nights on the scale of my own.

I left him dangling. I made a conscious effort to behave as if nothing had happened, as if I considered it a trifle, an amusing one-way joke that I'd probably forgotten about, a blokeish pact that promises 'what goes on tour, stays on tour'. I never mentioned the pictures or the evening out, either directly or obliquely.

The truth is of course that I hadn't yet decided what to do with my immensely valuable prize. It was a 'long hold' investment that I would cash in when the time was right, and when the price was right.

A couple of months went by during which time the subject was not mentioned by either of us, and then one day George summoned the courage to attempt a little reciprocal blackmail. He'd been regularly receiving and signing off my expense claims for corporate entertainment which since our night out had increased considerably. I had been taking Hermione to expensive restaurants for lunch a couple of times a week for six months or more but 'til then had always settled the bill at my own expense, paying with a personal charge card. We bankers of course don't use credit cards. However, safe in the knowledge that George would not risk upsetting me, soon after his little indiscretion I started charging the pleasure to expenses, claiming it as 'client entertainment'.

George tried his luck. I'm sure he didn't regard my sin as anywhere near the magnitude of his own but he at last had some leverage and tried to use it. I suspect too that he'd been nervous at the radio silence on the subject and felt compelled to take any opportunity that presented itself to see if at best I could be persuaded to release him from my grip or at least give him further reassurance that I had no intention to expose him.

He called at my office late one afternoon. In itself that was an extraordinary occurrence as the stuffy protocol would invariably see me summoned to appear on his home turf at Corporate HQ. He marched in boldly which was also uncharacteristic as his accustomed gait was to walk tentatively, treading lightly with a slightly forward lean as if his trousers were too long and he was trying to avoid treading on them with his heels.

He leered at Hermione as he passed her workstation and swept through the open doorway and into my office. He closed the door behind him signifying that the matter he wished to discuss with me was confidential or of such great import that our conversation could not be shared with junior colleagues. He sank into and severely tested with his considerable weight the visitor's chair that faced mine across my desk.

It was the chair on which Hermione's beautiful little bottom would elegantly rest each day during our business discussions and morning coffee chats about Tristan and his schooling and her home life, the latest volume to be read and debated by the yummy mummies' book club she enjoyed so much and countless other trivial topics that daily gave me the opportunity to admire her beautiful face and look into the compelling eyes that still after all this time took my breath away. On how many occasions had that desk concealed a semi as I soaked up her presence and listened to the music of her voice?

I remember an embarrassing episode a year earlier when a self-important female director on an impromptu visit to the bank was without notice escorted into my office to be introduced to me briefly in order to receive due homage. Hermione had been facing me across the desk and as she was talking seriously to me about a client account, I had been mentally sharing a bath with her. As I laid back in my chair, hands clasped behind my head, the hot water was up to the rim of the bath. Our legs were astride each other in the close confines of the tub, her fascinating erect nipples just breaking the surface of the soapy water and her hair tied back in a temporary ponytail, secured with a simple elastic band. My upstanding member was just breaking the surface too when my daydream was interrupted by the entrance of the senior stranger and her entourage.

Unable to stand without risk of scaring the woman with the awkwardly persistent bulge in my trousers I offered her a handshake from a seated position. Her body language clearly indicated that she was unaccustomed to such casual treatment and had expected me to leap to my feet in recognition of her status if not her sex. Aunt Margaret would have been ashamed of me too.

Hermione also was surprised at my apparently disrespectful stance and I'm sure would have been even more disgusted if she'd known the reason for it.

George skipped the pleasantries to underline the gravity of the issue he'd come to discuss. There was no smile, no small talk, no disarming friendly body language. He displayed the air of a man here to deliver bad news, an ultimatum and to dish out some discipline. I was suddenly unnerved at the realisation that he was here to wreak his revenge but I couldn't imagine that he would be prepared to risk my retaliation, unless of course he'd already gone to the police with a tale of blackmail and extortion. Of course this was not possible as I had made no demands on him; yet. There was another explanation that raced through my mind. Perhaps Hilda had died, or confessed to a ten-year affair with the milkman, or had been caught shagging the vicar; or his horse, freeing him from the implications of exposure, at least as far as his wife was concerned.

George had a habit, when trying to look cool and 'in charge' of removing his glasses and rubbing them clean using the end of his tie. Evidencing this was a large dark shiny patch on every tie I'd seen him wear and today was no exception. I stared at it with an insolent grin hoping to diminish his confident stance which was intended to indicate his superior rank and undisputed position as the alpha male.

"I'm afraid I have a serious matter to raise with you Mr Purkiss," he said solemnly. 'Mr Purkiss?' Did he call me 'Mr Purkiss?' He'd never addressed me that formally in all the years I'd worked for him. It had always been 'Oliver' or 'My Boy'.

"I must have words with you about your expenses," he said with gravity, producing four expense claim forms each with a restaurant receipt neatly stapled to the top left-hand corner.

"There are a number of irregularities requiring clarification before I take the matter any further."

He probably imagined himself as a High Court Judge with the power of life or death, donning the black cap but I could still see him with a used condom dangling ridiculously from his flaccid Willy. Any traces of concern immediately left my thoughts and I started to grin the widest grin I could muster.

"What are you saying George? Are you doubting that these are legitimate expenses incurred in the service of the bank? I do hope not."

He modified his tone a little no doubt as a result of my confident and challenging response.

"You know darn well they're not. You've been wining and dining that girlfriend of yours," he said gesturing in the direction of Hermione's desk, "at the bank's expense. That's fraud Oliver, and a sackable offence."

I was stunned. Although it was my greatest wish for her to be so I was shocked that Hermione might be regarded by anyone else as my 'girlfriend'. She would be mortified. And she had done nothing to give that mistaken impression to anyone. She'd simply joined me for 'decent lunches' dozens if not hundreds of times. It had never occurred to me until then that it might look that way to others and I wondered if she'd ever considered the risk she was running of office gossip when regularly leaving the building with me at lunchtimes. Were the non-existent curtains twitching as we got into the Jaguar and drove away? The concern was quickly dispelled by the knowledge that my self-assured, sophisticated Hermione wouldn't give a toss. In her mind the fact that we were just friends would be enough. The rest of the stupid world could suffer in ignorance if they chose. That would undoubtedly be her attitude and the thought brought the grin back to my face.

George's willingness to drag Hermione into this enraged me. I felt suddenly very aggressive towards him and protective of her, but held my cool. Aunt Margaret had often used that line from Kennedy when teaching me about anger management. 'Don't get mad, get even' she'd say and 'Revenge is a dish best served cold'. I decided in an instant that it was time to play one of the aces in my hand against the amateur poker player facing me sternly across the desk.

"You're right, Ge-or-gie Boy," I said slowly, emphasising the nickname in three separate syllables, a pause between each, to instantly remind him of the last occasion on which he'd been addressed that way.

"But what are you going to do about it?"

"Well, it's a very serious matter and I could have you suspended you realise, with immediate effect, pending further investigation and a decision on disciplinary action."

"But?" I prompted him.

"Indeed, I'm sure we can sort this out between the two of us," he said adopting a more friendly tone.

"I can make this go away; provided there's no repetition, and of course provided you're ready to stop this silliness with the, er…photos and things."

I leaned back in my chair, put both feet on my desk and interlocked the fingers of both hands behind my head. My body language would demonstrate that despite the fact that he was my boss I was entirely relaxed and completely in control. I decided that to get involved in a lengthy and pointless negotiation was entirely unnecessary and would give George a glint of hope that I might waver. He had to know that his crime carried a life sentence.

"Don't be silly George. I've got your balls in a vice and you know it," I said as casually as I could.

The colour drained from his face.

"What's more I shall not desist from entertaining who the fuck I like at the bank's expense, and you George will continue to approve my expenses. I hope that's clear. To make it easier for you I will of course ensure each claim remains under your authorisation level. Just under. Now, is there anything else?"

He was defeated and his demeanour demonstrated that without ambiguity. He folded the expense reports carefully and returned them to the inner pocket of his grey suit jacket. His tone softened and he appeared to be wavering about discussing another matter with me. I think he was desperately searching for another topic so that our meeting could end on a less defeating note.

"Actually, there is one thing," he said hesitantly.

"It's not for circulation just yet, but confidentially, the decision has been taken to close this office and move some of the team to CHQ."

"Some of the team?" I responded with suspicion.

"Well, your post is of course secure, Oliver."

"Of course," I replied with emphasis, as if answering a child who'd asked if they had to go to school that day.

"Unless you'd er…you know, prefer to go early. There will be a generous package for management."

I didn't respond to the hopeful suggestion, just smiled and shook my head not in reply but in disbelief at the ridiculous proposition. He understood. "And Mrs Nightingale?" I enquired.

"Ah, now that's a problem, Oliver. It seems that entire level is being 'rationalised'. It's considered that there's sufficient capacity within General Office to cover the Chief Clerk's role."

Time to play another ace, I decided.

"Look, George, you just don't get it do you? Let me tell you how it's going to be. I will be relocating to CHQ, and you will ensure that I'm given a decent office, with a window, not a 'workstation' in a noisy open plan cattle market. And you will ensure that Mrs Nightingale is relocated too. Note I said 'relocated' George not 'redeployed' and certainly not 'rationalised'. She will continue to be my Chief Clerk and if General Office has some spare capacity I suggest you 'rationalise' one of their number instead."

He was stunned and after a long pause to consider his reply he sighed and attempted a smile.

"It will be difficult Oliver. It's not all up to me you know," he said nervously, knowing full well that I'd settle for nothing less.

"Your problem, Ge-or-gie Boy. Just fix it."

Weary in defeat, he raised his bulk from the chair and slowly crossed the room. As he opened the door I called after him,

"Oh, and one more thing George…"

Suspecting a further blackmail demand, he closed the door and turned to me without loosening his grip on the handle like a drowning man clutching a line thrown from a lifeboat.

"Mrs Nightingale is overdue for a pay rise. I appreciate there's a salary freeze at the moment, but fix it will you? Ten percent would I feel be appropriate."

His body language expressed the desolation of defeat and he meekly responded with an almost imperceptible nod of the head. I then cruelly gave the knife another turn.

"Oh, and George," I said, to ensure I had the focus of his complete attention.

I formed a ring with the thumb and forefinger of my right hand and raised it to frame my nose like a sausage peeping out of a toad in the hole. Then mimicking Tristan I blew a raspberry to remind George of the amusing fanny fart and to indicate without saying so that it was captured forever on the priceless video. Again, he got the message.

Chapter Sixteen
A Mental Illness?

My resolve to resist the powerful, magnetic, erotic, emotional vortex that pulled me helplessly to Hermione, and it's devastating effect on my peace of mind, my sleep pattern and my happiness lasted just a little over two weeks. Two endless weeks of torture during which I avoided contact with her as much as bank business would allow. It took all the determination and self-discipline I could muster but I stuck to the plan, I didn't take her out to lunch and I stayed away from her home.

I had begun to question my mental health. Why on earth would any sane man persist in his desire for a woman who not only showed no reciprocal feelings but also made it clear her lack of romantic interest with short, blunt, honest, hurtful responses to any expression of affection?

Some say love is a mental illness and they are probably right. The parallels are there for all to see however hard the sufferer contrives to conceal them.

They exhibit mood swings, ecstatically happy one moment and utterly depressed the next. They suffer sleeplessness, loss of appetite, weight loss, attention deficiency and all the other physical symptoms of mental stress. They're accused of undergoing a personality change, neglecting their friends and losing interest in the things that previously gave them great pleasure. They sulk like teenagers and withdraw into a shell where they retreat from normal life and lock themselves into an inner Trappist order of silence where thoughts can be concentrated on the only important issue in the world, the object of their love.

I recognised the utter hopelessness of the cause but I missed her. I missed her voice, I missed her face and I missed her eyes. I missed her shapes.

I had no doubt about the price I'd have to pay to enjoy her presence again. I'd have to accept that I was a hopeless fool. I knew the relationship was going nowhere but I had been stripped of the will to resist and stripped of the self-respect that would be my only means of escape. What a pathetic fool.

I knew too how it would turn out, that my quest was doomed to failure.

I recognised my future self like a man returning from service in the Foreign Legion having exiled himself for years to cauterise the wound of rejection by seeking the distraction of alternative pain through adventure.

His love was in his thoughts daily all the years he was away, fighting wars, suffering the privations of life in desert forts, overcoming impossible odds and achieving great acts of heroism. He determined to return home emboldened by his self-imposed sentence, to face his love, to end his misery and to not take no for an answer…only to find that she didn't even remember his name. His misery compounded by the realisation that his long torment was entirely his own fault and that he was the fool. He, not she had wasted his life.

The lesson was clear. The cruel inequality of unrequited love, the endless agony of time-wasting years is entirely self-inflicted. The remedy was obvious. As Hermione once put it with characteristic clarity, 'Just get over it'. Correct, sensible, simple, but easier said than done.

I started taking Hermione out to lunch again and also for the occasional dinner when she was able to arrange a babysitter to look after the young Sumo. I again wondered if he treated those trusted with his care to demonstrations of his odorous prowess, or whether those performances were reserved exclusively for my displeasure. When I drove Hermione home after an evening out, she always politely invited me in for a drink and I always made some excuse to avoid the immense pleasure of just being with her in that comfortable domestic setting that I knew would reinforce my fretful dreams.

However late the hour Tristan would always put in an appearance in his dressing gown, either opening the front door to greet his mother or showing himself at his bedroom window. He'd address a half-hearted wave to her and on occasions it felt as if they were aimed at me too. One night as I drove away, I caught a glimpse of him through the rear-view mirror as I turned out of the driveway. He was waving goodbye despite the fact that he believed I couldn't see him. No doubt he was saying to himself, 'Goodbye and good riddance', and more likely than not punctuating the words with a fart.

It was over lunch one day that I told Hermione in the strictest confidence, about the planned office closure, although such was my trust in her that I felt she'd be justified in considering the 'in confidence' clause a little insulting. We had no secrets. At least I had no secrets from her; apart from my shameful Thai experience and my insider dealing. Oh, and the fact that I was blackmailing my boss, and charging the cost of our expensive dining to the bank. I kept secret to the continuing frustration of my unrequited love for her, as I had by then given up all hope and was simply trying to regain some self-respect, whilst still enjoying the doubtful pleasure of the magic bubbles, like a junkie tired to death of his addiction but knowing he didn't possess the will to stop.

The news of the office closure seemed to worry Hermione very much. I told her that I was confident of her relocation to CHQ and that I'd been assured her role would be unchanged but as I could not reveal that her safety was guaranteed by blackmail she was unable to accept my assurances. Her confident air dissipated gradually to be replaced by a state of suppressed panic like a refugee caught in slow traffic realising that they were going to miss the last boat to safety.

When news of the closure broke unofficially, forcing the bank to put out a hastily written and ill-considered letter to employees, she was drawn into the mass hysteria that broke out across the office. Never previously one to join in the office gossip Hermione could be seen in huddles with others spending and exchanging the currency of speculation and the latest rumour. I saw her distress but couldn't do anything to relieve it apart from urging her to 'trust me, everything will be alright'.

Although it hurt me to see her growing anxiety and disappointed me to see that she didn't trust in my power to secure her future employment, the episode did have, for me at least some compensating benefit. Hermione sought my reassurance daily and started to spend much more time in my office subtly steering the conversation each time away from the business topic of the moment to the question of the office closure and her professional future. It pained me so to see her worrying and I was tempted on several occasions to explain to her just how I could be so confident about her survival. But I held back from that dangerous step. I could not risk losing the respect of the woman I loved so much.

During the meetings in my office and over lunch Hermione continued to fret despite my continued attempts to paint a secure picture of the future. I even lied to her in an attempt to set her mind at rest. I told her that during a recent visit to CHQ I had seen in George's office a draft organisation chart which included both my initials and hers. The news calmed her and she perked up. Her beautiful smile returned to reward my deceit.

Hermione also warmed in other ways too. To my astonishment and confusion she started holding my gaze, prolonging eye contact just when I had at last mustered the willpower to limit my quick darts into her soul to about three seconds a shot.

It was extraordinary and exciting too because gradually she would introduce a smile before breaking off contact. I was confused, and like a drowning man snatched at the straw I was thrown. I tested the hope by watching her carefully over several days in order to be sure it wasn't just wishful thinking on my part. It happened so often I convinced myself that somehow she actually seemed to be feeling something. Inevitably I allowed my three second hit and run raids to extend to four, and five and six and seven. The bubbles kicked in at about four and the inner sigh at seven. I was gone again. Not only did she not mind, she actually appeared to be sharing the sensation.

Sadly, I was mistaken. Over lunch one day I was so encouraged by her new-found affectionate body language that I broke my self-imposed silence on the subject and again spoke of love.

"Hermione, you know I love you desperately, don't you?"

"Yes," she whispered without emotion, looking nervously around, embarrassed that other diners might have heard my question and no doubt thinking that a one-word answer might bring the unwanted conversation to a close.

The reciprocal confession of love did not come. Was she playing with me?

I was determined that this would not turn into one of those conversations that I would later replay in my half sleep, wishing I'd pressed the matter further or said something spectacularly and perfectly apposite that would win her heart in an instant.

"Why can't you love me, Hermione?" I said in a tone of mock exasperation to conceal my deep desperation.

"I do love you Oliver, you know that. But I'm not 'in love' with you."

I knew the difference of course. I loved Margaret to the extent that I would die for her, but I wasn't 'in love' with her. There it was, the truth at last. Hermione loved me like an uncle, like a school friend, like a generous boss. But that was all.

She could read my disappointment and added,

"It's not your fault you know. It's me. I just don't feel anything…for anyone. I really wish I could, but I can't."

I didn't believe a word of it of course. But what else could she say without crushing me? What words would make me understand?

'I love you Oliver but don't be ridiculous, I couldn't shag you because you're old enough to be my father'? Or, 'I am looking for a life-partner to help me raise my boy, but I want someone who's still going to be around when he's twenty-five'?

That was it, I decided. Time at last to face the facts. I couldn't do this anymore. It was ageing me. Ageing me to death.

We ordered a second bottle of wine because for entirely different reasons neither of us wanted to leave it there. We wanted to continue to talk, to show each other that it wasn't the end of the line as friends.

The conversation continued and we stayed off the subject until, by then clearly under the influence of the second bottle, she said the most extraordinary thing. And she said it in the past tense.

"If we had slept together, Oliver, you'd have tired of me in six months."

I didn't answer. What was the point? She was either playing games or rubbing my nose in it. If we had slept together, I'd have been the happiest man alive, and she knew it. No, it was time to face the facts, time to be a man, time to regain my self-respect.

When we got to the car, we both felt the effects of the bottle of wine that we'd each consumed. We sat and looked solemnly at each other for a few moments, and then spontaneously burst into laughter.

"Oh, what a waste," I said. "What criminal waste. Some people spend their whole lives looking for this, and many never find it. What a waste to throw it away!"

I was quite drunk and I actually thanked her for being so frank with me.

"Give me a goodbye kiss," I said.

She offered her cheek as she had done on so many partings, but I didn't kiss it. I held back. She read my mind. A peck on the cheek would just not be enough on this occasion. She offered her mouth. I kissed her beautiful moist lips, for the first and I thought probably the last time.

Chapter Seventeen
Dog Day

A fortnight had passed since the disastrous lunch with Philippa and Alice and I cringed with embarrassment whenever it came to mind, which was about a dozen times a day as I wrestled with my determination not to call either of them but to await an approach from one or both. 'Treat 'em mean, keep 'em keen' had always worked for me in the past but I must confess I was really missing my little porn star.

There had been a period of radio silence from both women but I knew, or at least very much hoped, that Alice would make an apologetic advance probably just as soon as her husband departed on his next business trip. I thought it likely that I'd never see Philippa again as she very definitely didn't seem the type to be messed around by any man. She was much too intelligent for that I thought. Yes, I'd almost certainly have to abandon my plans for the elegant lawyer. Shame though, I had been looking forward to the challenge.

I'd given Alice a right bollocking as soon as her rival had departed Luigi's that afternoon.

She was grinning in triumph as Philippa walked away and wasn't in the slightest concerned that the outrageously vulgar question she'd asked had been overheard by shocked diners on the two adjacent tables.

"Do you what? when you're driving," I repeated angrily, leaving out the M word.

"What possessed you?" I demanded.

Alice was unrepentant.

"Stuck up bitch deserved it! Did you hear her?...*and you're the girlfriend?*" she mimicked in an exaggerated plummy voice. "*And why did you bring this, this, this, person?*" she continued with her nose in the air.

"And you," she added, "should have defended me! The bitch was insulting me and you just sat there and said nothing!"

My insistence that it was Alice who had picked the fight and a reminder that it had been a business lunch to which she'd invited herself was dismissed with a huff and she told me in no uncertain terms that if I wanted to 'play around' it was my choice but that would be end of our affair.

Silence reigned for three minutes or so as I gathered my thoughts and rubbed my painful shin. Alice with an intimidating stare dared our neighbours to continue looking at her whilst I hoped ruing her ultimatum.

The chilly silence was interrupted by the arrival of the first course, my scallops and a very elaborately decorated prawn cocktail for Alice delivered by one waiter and Philippa's gazpacho served to the empty place setting by another.

"Has the lady been called away Sir?"

"Yes, sadly she has." I lied.

"Will she be returning Sir? I won't offer to keep it warm," he joked.

Alice quickly answered before I could, looking me straight in the eyes.

"No, she won't be coming back," adding in a faintly audible tone, "probably frigging herself in the car as we speak."

I think two weeks without sex is probably the longest I've gone since I discovered that my Willy was not just for peeing. It was fortuitous then that, just as I weakened and was planning my overture to her, my mobile buzzed with the message, 'Alice Calling'. I could have played it cool but to be honest I was aching for it and didn't want to risk another fortnight's abstinence, from the real thing.

I decided the best course of action was to make a joke of it as to have implied that I was still annoyed at her behaviour towards Philippa would have reinforced her belief that I still had dishonourable intentions in that area, which I certainly did. I had calculated that if Philippa were to call me I'd without doubt have the upper hand in the seduction stakes but that if it were left to me to re-establish contact I'd be faced with an extended courtship process for which frankly I didn't have the patience.

"Is that the salon?" I enquired without giving her time to speak. "I was wondering if Alice has got a slot for me soon."

She giggled and delivering an astonishingly good bimbo receptionist impression replied,

"Let me see now. Yes, she could possibly fit you in this morning if that's convenient."

Her emphasis of the words 'fit you in' matched my own delivery of 'a slot for me' and triggered an immediate stiffy which would probably require dowsing in a cold shower before the journey to her place which I felt certain I'd be making within the hour.

"How are you Angel?" I enquired.

"Fine thanks. What have you been up to? Shagged that lawyer yet?"

Her words had the same effect as the imagined cold shower.

"Oh Alice, don't start that again. I haven't seen her or spoken to her since," I paused not wishing to resurrect in her jealous mind images of the excruciating lunch but had already started the ill-considered sentence, "since that 'business' lunch."

"OK, I'll believe you but there'll be a penance to pay." *'Penance?' Bloody hell, where did she get that word from,* I wondered. *Perhaps from an agony aunt column in one of those fatuous celebrity magazines she was so addicted to. Still, the way she accentuated the word did carry exciting connotations.*

"Oh yes? What do you have in mind?" I enquired.

"You'll have to come and find out."

Yes there was definitely something of the dominatrix in her voice.

"Ken has just left on one of his trips so you could get over right now." She added in the same tone.

"OK, but I only want a wash and cut," I joked to level the field a little. "And a blow dry of course."

"Possibly," she replied. "But if that's what you want you better bring the dice."

I pictured the scene as I soaped myself in the shower.

Alice has the most gorgeous tits I've ever seen let alone buried my face in. Those assets come in that most desirable combination, the ideal of most men, big breasts on a slim woman. They are completely genuine, large, round and firm with high centrally positioned nipples. And they tick the 'ten' box by meeting that rarest but most important criterion of all; they can be seen from behind. Her 'puppies' she calls them as they are large enough and soft enough to flop over each other as she lies naked on her side, like a pair of cute baby Labradors tumbling over each other in their basket. They are as playful as puppies too.

Alice is the first woman I've slept with to possess that most fascinating phenomenon, inverted nipples. Sometimes they are out and ready, like excited pets welcoming their master home. At other times, they have to be coaxed out to play with a gentle kiss, a very light touch of the tongue or a circular lick around the pimpled areola. If more subtle approaches won't tempt them to put in an appearance, an impatient suck is unfailing. It amuses me that they rarely come out together but emerge each when ready, as if in a sibling contest, sucking a sweet without chewing, to see who can hold out the longest. I'll give my attention first to one and when it's standing proud, I'll tease the other out to play. Often it will take a minute or two before both are excitedly reaching out, stiff as corks emerging slowly from a bottle of wine. Occasionally, they both pop out together instantly like stoppers from a magnum of champagne.

My erotic planning in the shower and the knob-throbbing anticipation during the drive to Alice's house simply amplified the disappointment. The moment she opened the front door to me I knew the day was about to take a different turn. She was smiling but had evidently been crying. Her eyes were red and her cheeks showed the tracks of her tears.

I wondered what disaster had befallen my playmate and as I crossed the threshold a number of troubling scenarios came to mind, all of which meant trouble for me. Had Ken discovered her infidelity and abandoned her? Had a girlfriend in whom she'd confided threatened to tell her husband unless she gave me up? God! Was she pregnant?

I hugged her affectionately causing her to burst into tears but her explanation was virtually unintelligible through her sobs.

"Oh, look what I've done," she cried.

Squatting in the doorway to the kitchen was Big Nob with a clumsily bandaged paw which he held in the air as if he'd been asked to shake hands. Although the cause of all the emotion he was totally oblivious to the fuss and apparently unconcerned at his mistress's tearful expressions of remorse.

"I dropped a tumbler and he stepped in the broken glass," she whimpered. "It's a really deep cut. We'll have to take him to the vet."

It was absolutely clear that the morning was not going to be spent romping with Alice in the guest bedroom or playing out an erotic forfeit demanded by the dice, so I thought I might as well bank a few brownie points by playing the calm and chivalrous companion.

"Of course, my angel, if that's what he needs. Let me take a look at it."

The wound was superficial to say the least as evidenced by Big Nob's apparent bemusement at having one of his paws gloved in an untidy lint and linen knot secured by a thick red elastic band of the type discarded by postmen throughout the country.

"I don't think it's bad enough to need a stitch," I optimistically pronounced as I crouched to inspect the extent of the wound.

"Yes it does!" she shrieked, anticipating that I was about to selfishly argue that her poor doggie should continue to suffer whilst I rogered her with abandon as planned.

"You should have seen all the blood!"

I hadn't seen her so indignant since I'd once teased the gullible lass that when I was a boy I used to tempt a neighbour's cat to cross the road in front of traffic by waving a prawn at it. She was really upset at the lie, as if I'd confessed to being a serial child killer who'd escaped capture so I had to quickly admit I'd been joking. I didn't mention though I had discovered that an airgun pellet hitting the tip of its tail would have a cat moving faster than any greyhound.

Big Nob rapidly switched his gaze from each of us in turn as if watching a tennis match and no doubt wondered why on earth she was shouting at me.

"Calm down, angel, of course we'll take him."

Alice realised that she'd over-reacted and apologised, embracing me tightly and kissing my neck, her cheeks still hot with emotion.

"I'll get his lead," she said and recognising the word Big Nob of course leaped up and ran to the front door, on all four legs without the slightest hint of a limp.

We drove to the Vet's surgery in Alice's car as she knew that if we were to travel in mine her precious dog would have been confined to the boot.

The waiting room was packed. Middle aged ladies with cats in baskets or plastic cages sat facing each other contriving to proudly offer an accidental glimpse of their beautiful feline child substitutes as they offered comforting words to their pets in a mixture of baby talk and chirping noises. Why not at least speak to them in their own language? I thought. An impatient man dressed in a crumpled business suit, obviously annoyed at having to bring the family's poodle for treatment during office hours, checked his wristwatch every thirty seconds as he sat next to an overindulgent mother accompanying a five year old girl nursing a Tupperware container housing an obviously dead hedge sparrow.

A Great Dane strained at the leash held by an elderly lady with half its body weight as a young schoolboy watched nervously. He didn't seem to have an ill or injured pet with him and I pondered whether he had perhaps mistaken the surgery for the dentist's practice next door, or perhaps he had a damaged stick insect or amputee toad in his pocket.

Another five or six adult humans had brought along another six or seven creatures of various brands. A pair of cuddly Labrador puppies were the most attractive by far.

"Now what do they remind me of?" I whispered, eliciting a broad grin from Alice and a sharp dig in the ribs for my trouble.

Kittens no doubt attending for their first inoculations, a Tom cat probably about to lose his nuts, a budgie lying down in its cage rather than gripping onto a perch, a couple of mangy looking dogs and incongruously a clergyman with a pure white duck made up the rest of those seeking veterinary attention.

Alice, with Big Nob firmly held on a short lead had earlier settled on one of two chairs immediately outside the consulting room and next to an elderly couple one of whom was grasping a guinea pig wrapped in a tea towel. From these seats, despite the door being closed we could clearly hear what was being said owing to the booming voice of the Vet within.

"No, I said two of the white ones every morning and one of the red ones at night! Don't worry it'll be written on the label."

A nervous looking lady emerged carrying a parrot in a cage.

"How on earth do you give pills to a parrot?" Alice whispered, breaking into a muffled giggle.

"With a catapult?" I suggested quietly.

It was a poor joke but the best response I could come up with and Alice spluttered with half suppressed laughter as if was the gag of the year.

Oh dear, I hoped she wasn't going to get playful.

Sure enough she was. I was pleased to note the change in her spirits but there was great potential here for mischief.

As each pet owner entered the thinly walled consulting room in turn Alice proffered an instant diagnosis. "Too much sex," Alice ventured as the Great Dane towed the old lady across the waiting room.

"Yes, almost certainly," I concurred. "The old girl looks exhausted."

According to self-styled veterinary expert Alice, the puppies were here for a fitting for their first brassieres, a repetitive joke between us and one that I perpetuated on most of our assignations. My contribution was that the kittens were here to be put down, the Tom cat's halitosis would correct itself in time once he no longer had his bollocks to lick and the dunnock was here for cryogenic storage.

Alice's suggestions were more imaginative and became progressively louder as her giggles progressed into belly laughs.

She quietened down a little after receiving stern looks from a grossly overweight veterinary nurse who had entered the room to receive the dead sparrow. The naive five-year-old had obviously pleaded with mum to bring the limp corpse to be saved and missing an opportunity for an important life lesson the overindulgent parent had agreed. The nurse handled the situation well and addressing the child said,

"Thank you, darling, give it to me and we'll take good care of it."

This was enough to touch Alice's sentimental heart and she smiled at me sweetly with a look that conveyed a mothering instinct that I hadn't seen the slightest trace of before. Well, at least that has quietened her down I thought but that was until the fat nurse, out of earshot of the child said to the mother,

"No charge dear, we'll pop it in the bin."

Alice, with a hand clasped tightly over her mouth, eyebrows raised, eyes wide open and no doubt biting her lips, looked at me, as if desperately seeking my assistance in stopping her from laughing out loud.

I too was close to bursting but managed a patronising look, silently commanding her to take control of herself. She managed to hold it just until the little girl had left the room and then erupted into uncontrollable laughter causing her to accidentally spray sputum on her dog, who calmly moved from between her feet and took refuge further beneath her chair.

"Alice, get a grip for God's sake." I whispered.

The embarrassment of the accidental spitting did calm her and as she wiped her mouth with a tissue she faked a look of stern sobriety, sitting up straight, hands on knees and raising her nose in the air like a Victorian lady obliged to share a railway carriage compartment and faced with a leering, lecherous fellow traveller. But worse was to come.

The penultimate patient was the parson with the white duck. Alice stared at me with a look that dared me to laugh, and I could hear it coming.

"Chlamydia," she unsuccessfully attempted to whisper but instead loudly snorted before bursting into a fit of hysterical laughter from which I feared she'd take an hour to recover.

The waiting room was now empty apart from the two of us and her uninjured dog. The elderly couple with the guinea pig were in the consulting room and we could hear the Vet delivering the results of a recent blood test.

"Yes, I'm afraid it is diabetes," he boomed.

We heard nothing more until the door opened and the desolate couple slowly passed in front of us on their way to the reception desk.

"God, what on earth can you do with a guinea pig that has diabetes?" I foolishly asked Alice, already straining to control the ultimate outburst, if she hadn't already wet her knickers.

"Cook-in-Sauce," she blurted before we both completely lost it.

Unsurprisingly the elderly couple didn't appreciate the joke let alone our juvenile laughter and scowled at Alice, whilst the fat nurse could muster nothing more damning than an outraged, 'Well, really!'

The day had turned out all right in the end. We hadn't rolled the dice and I didn't get a much-needed shag but Big Nob got a rare trip out and a canine equivalent of an Elastoplast, and we'd had a lot of laughs. Most importantly my relationship with my little sex goddess was back on track.

Chapter Eighteen
A Quick Drink

If I'd been stupid enough to believe in astrology I'd have been convinced that my horoscope for the day that Alice had called me would have forecast 'considerable advances in your love life as Venus enters a favourable juxtaposition with your birth sign' or whatever bollocks terminology they use to hook the gullible, the feeble and the loveless.

Astonishingly Philippa phoned within ten minutes of Alice's call. In fact I was in the shower preparing for my visit, making a mental note not to forget the dice and contemplating a series of options for them, not that I had doubted for one moment what would be the outcome.

I played it cool at first until she flummoxed me with an opening gambit that took me entirely by surprise.

She pretended that her call was to follow up an invoice for her earlier legal services in a tone worthy of an experienced credit controller, politely business-like but laced with an unmistakeable edge of contempt for the transgressor.

I responded by apologising in similar mode for the oversight and promised to attend to the matter without delay, until I remembered her brilliant performance with the hoax call from 'The Prime Minister' and realised of course that partners in law firms have minions to take care of such mundane matters as chasing debts. Clearly this was an attempt to re-establish social contact so I immediately abandoned the speech I'd prepared for this unlikely scenario, the one in which I apologised profusely for the embarrassment at lunch and neatly blamed it all on Alice, who of course I'd dumped within minutes of her departure from the restaurant.

Instead I asked after her health and let her make the running.

There was a pregnant pause whist she thought of something to say, no doubt having expected me to apologise immediately. Her tone softened.

"OK, if you can that will be great. It's just that Accounts keep pestering me about it. So, how are you?"

"Fine thanks, you?"

"Good. Yes, me too."

A long pause followed, each of us determined to make the other speak first. I won the contest.

"Look Charles, shall we meet for a drink? It's just that I'd hate to leave things as they are, I mean as they were. It was all very silly."

"Yes, I'd like that," I responded but without sounding too excited at the prospect of seeing her again and reactivating my seduction plans.

"How about this lunchtime?" She suggested.

"Love to but sorry I can't. I have a pressing engagement."

A vision of Alice lying naked on the guest room bed sprang to mind.

I'd lied and she knew it but her pause forced me to suggest an alternative or risk losing the opportunity.

"How about tomorrow evening?"

Philippa agreed and we arranged to meet in the bar near her office where we'd had our first drink together and where I'd encountered her frightful colleagues.

We met the following evening as arranged at eight-thirty and evidently, she had been home from chambers to change. I had been half expecting her to come straight from work dressed in black but with a few colourful accessories because apart from the day of our disastrous flight in the Pitts and the even more painful lunch with Alice, I hadn't seen her in other than her lawyer's garb.

The contrast was startling. She wore skin-hugging silk trousers, OK they were black but boy! far from formal, and a gossamer thin white blouse that would have given me a clear glimpse of the tiniest of bra's but for a white silk slip worn no doubt precisely to prevent that. The sensible office shoes she had worn on our last visit there were replaced by three-inch-high heels in red almost matching the colour of her lipstick and nail varnish. And as if to accentuate the difference her make-up was discreet but perfectly applied in total contrast to how Alice had appeared when imitating Barbie at that lunch I was optimistically hoping wouldn't be mentioned.

"Hello, Charles," she said with confidence, touching me on the elbow and reaching to give me a kiss on the cheek, a kiss I guessed that was designed to look platonic to any of her workmates still present at that hour but one intended to convey much more to me.

I responded in a way that one might kiss a favourite sister.

We talked small talk and drank champagne. We agreed we'd go out to dinner but didn't get around to it. The conversation became wider-ranging and she asked about my flying and current business projects. Glass by glass the talk became more personal.

By the opening of the second bottle of bubbly Philippa was unsteady on her feet and by the end of it unsteady in her speech too. In her eyes I saw an expression of melancholy desperation as if she were friendless in a tedious world in which everyone but her had a partner and a purpose and that she had made the decision at last to do something about it. She had gradually shifted her weight from the bar and onto my shoulder, her arm eventually finding my neck and mine her waist.

She was giggly for a while and then suddenly became serious.

"You're still seeing that little tart aren't you?" She accused. "That hairdresser," she added with a sudden laugh as she remembered what she clearly thought was the crowning insult of the exchange between them.

"What on earth do you see in her?"

I left the question unanswered whilst I pondered how graphic to make the explanation. No, better not.

She was clearly pissed and getting emotional and a gentleman would out of kindness have prevented her from going any further, but I had a letter from the RAF to prove I wasn't a gentleman and anyway I was keen to see how far she'd go. It didn't take long.

She put both arms around me and slurred,

"You do know that I'd like to get to know you better, Charles, don't you?"

Funnily enough, I was more surprised by the clumsy choice of words than by the sentiment but it was time to go in for the kill.

"And that's my strong desire too, Philippa. I think you've known that from the start but you must learn to loosen up."

I was quite pleased with that for a spur of the moment reply as I was a bit pissed too. It conveyed that I'd been serious from the beginning but had held back owing to her coolness and had given up after the restaurant episode. Thank God I hadn't called her. That would have probably meant taking months to get to this point.

It was time, I concluded, to obliquely raise the question of sex and long experience had taught me that it's best achieved via the more subtle topic, 'relationships'.

"You told me about that chap at University you were once close to, but has there been anyone since?"

"Of course!" she lied, "Do you think I've lived like a nun?"

The obvious untruth in her response together with the dramatic change in her dress since our last meeting and the unexpected physical contact convinced me that, however reluctant she had been in the past she was now for whatever reason very definitely up for it.

"I didn't mean to suggest you'd been celibate," I hurriedly replied although I would bet the profit from the current project that she had.

"I meant has there been anyone that you've been close to since him?"

"I wasn't close to him in any way at all. I'm sure I told you that," she snapped. "It was a one-off that meant nothing."

I had of course remembered that and in fact it was part of the appeal, a reason for targeting her. I was utterly convinced it had been her one and only sexual encounter with a man but I had strong suspicions that her relationship with the House Mistress at boarding school might have been closer and longer lasting. I made a mental note to probe her on that when I'd got to know her more intimately, the certainty of which I was now totally convinced.

Philippa, still the lawyer despite her inebriation, expertly turned the tables on me and asked if I'd ever been married.

"No."

"Engaged?"

"No."

"Serious about anyone?"

That was a tricky one. If I'd lied and said no, she might have thought I was incapable of commitment, which might have turned her off, and if I'd told the truth and said I had, then she might have probed for more details. Admitting I'd been dumped a month before the wedding to the only woman I've ever loved was, even after eight years not something I cared to talk about, and certainly not to someone with whom I planned a rapid seduction and short relationship, especially as this one carried all the hallmarks of a 'clinger'.

"Pass," was my enigmatic reply, leaving my options open to lie either way at some future point as circumstances might require.

"There's no one at the moment, how about you?"

"No," she replied, "but what about The Hairdresser?"

"Oh, that's just pure sex," I answered, seizing the opportunity to raise the subject.

"Anyway, she's married and determined to stay that way. Not that she's the type I'd marry."

Philippa was clearly stunned by the revelation and as she digested the information I guessed at what was going through her intelligent and respectable mind.

Why would anyone determined to stay married want to get involved in an affair or take the risk of so doing? Do people who don't love each other actually have long running sexual relationships? Why would this man enjoying a sexual relationship with a younger, albeit stupid and tarty, woman imply that he is attracted to me? Hadn't he actually said it was his 'strong desire too?'

I decided that it was time to respond to the unanswered question about 'what on earth did I see in Alice' but chose, for then, not to make it too graphic, although no doubt at some point in the future it would be interesting to do so.

"Look, Philippa," I explained, "she may be dim but she has a zest for life that I find appealing and she really enjoys sex. It's hard to imagine a happier person. She clearly loves her husband but sees sex not as something exclusive to her marriage but a capacity for joy that belongs to her as an individual and at the moment something she's happy to share with me. And until I'm in a serious relationship with someone else, can you honestly blame me?"

"Will you ever tire of her?" came the lawyer's loaded question after a thoughtful pause.

"I honestly don't know," was, I considered, the safest response.

"I just don't understand," she said. "She loves her husband but she's having sex with you. Why?"

"Perhaps if you loosened up a bit you might find out," I ventured. "Life is to be lived Philippa, to be enjoyed…and not to be taken so seriously."

At first, she looked as though she'd taken those words as a reprimand, her head jerking back a few inches in indignation. She looked down at the floor briefly before slowly raising her eyes to meet mine.

"Perhaps you're right," she said and after a thoughtful pause softly and slowly added,

"I'm sure you're right."

150

It seemed though as if she were speaking for someone else.

Now was the time to cut to the chase, to be unequivocal about my intentions. What did I have to lose after all? I had no interest in a courtship, a loving relationship, an engagement, living together, getting married! God no. I suspected though that she had.

"Philippa, what are you doing here?" I asked in a gentle manner.

"You've just said that you want to get to know me better. And I've told you I've wanted that ever since we met. But we're adults my angel not teenagers. You're a beautiful, sexy lady and I want to get close and intimate with you…and very soon."

I thought, 'close and intimate with you' was safer at this stage than, 'fuck you senseless' and I was right.

In hindsight I think it was calling her 'My angel' that did it. She looked at me and opened her mouth to answer but instead just let out a sigh.

I think the sensors within her self-preservation system had at that point alarm-signalled the receptors in that part of her brain that controlled common sense and she removed the arm from around my neck, straightened up and announced that it was time to drink some water.

For half an hour or so the conversation reverted to small talk, I resisted the temptation to suggest that I accompany her home or invite her for coffee at my place and it was clear that she regarded the evening a success.

I guessed that Philippa had accomplished her mission. She had in one 'interview' found out exactly how the land lay with Alice, established that I did have a strong interest in her but that the relationship would rapidly become a sexual one if she decided to proceed. It was her call.

For my part I was confident that before very long she'd be in my bed.

Chapter Nineteen
Margaret's Accident

One cold wet evening in November I phoned Aunt Margaret from the car on my way home, as I often did. It was perhaps mean of me to call her whilst I was driving but it was a ruse to ensure the conversation lasted no more than twenty minutes as my arrival home gave me the excuse to end the call.

If I phoned her from home, I found it difficult to break off the conversation as she could go on for hours. She was well into her eighties now and seemed to have aged considerably over the past couple of years. She was having some trouble with her feet which caused her occasionally to lose her balance and I knew that she was due for a fall. Since seeing the man with the tattoo she had resisted all of my attempts to persuade her to move to a flat, a bungalow or in fact anywhere at all.

"Don't fuss Oliver darling, I'm perfectly alright here. And one has one's friends nearby."

There was no answer to my first call and I concluded that she must be taking an early bath or that she was unusually late back from a visit to Jessica. I resolved to phone her later that evening after I'd had dinner.

I made another call about 8pm and to my surprise there was still no answer.

This was a little worrying as she was never out that late but never retired to bed that early. I decided to leave it for an hour before trying again. I called her later during a commercial break in a showing of one of the Bond films that I'd seen on several occasions over the years. A super-suave Roger Moore was battling zombies on a Caribbean island, escaping death by seconds and as ever winning the girl. Sadly I thought, working in the bank is unlikely to present any opportunities for me to win Hermione's heart through heroic acts of bravery. Whilst I might have the chance to save her job, it doesn't carry quite the impact of saving her life from voodoo sacrifice, the exploding island headquarters of master criminals or underwater caves full of hungry sharks.

It was by then ten o'clock, my third call was unanswered too and I was getting worried.

I considered driving to her house but after some soul searching decided against it. She would not welcome being disturbed by a late-night knock at the door if, as I suspected was the most likely explanation, she was already in bed. I'd had a couple of glasses of wine with my dinner and had shared a bottle with Hermione at lunchtime. And it was a cold wet dirty night. I had a ten o'clock meeting at CHQ next day and would need to get into my office early enough to collect some papers en route. I decided that the best compromise was to rise early and although it was five miles in the opposite direction, call in on her on my way to work. She would be irritated by my waking her up but at least my mind would be at rest. I'd then drive straight to CHQ, although that would mean missing the delights of start-the-day coffee with Hermione.

I had a third glass of wine and fell asleep on the sofa, missing Bond saving the world again in the inevitable pyrotechnic climax to the film. I was awoken by an intensely irritating loud-mouthed north-country comedian shouting at the top of his voice trying to sell me double glazing.

"I said yer buy won! Yer get won free! I said yer buy won, yer get won free!"

Fuck off! I made a note of the number he was urging me to ring and determined to call it next day and ask to speak to their Managing Director. I'd either give him a lesson in advertising or pretend to be a journalist from a marketing magazine congratulating him on being the unopposed winner of '*The Most Fucking Annoying Ad of the Year Award*'.

My plan for an early start next day was a failure. I'd slept heavily, dreaming that I'd beaten a clown to death with a baseball bat. There seemed to be a lot of broken glass about as well.

I got up so late that there wasn't even time for breakfast. I thought of calling Aunt Margaret on my way into the office but I was preoccupied with the business of the day and excused myself with the thought that she was still sleeping soundly. I resolved to call her around nine thirty instead.

The business of the day conspired against me and I forgot all about her until three in the afternoon. I rang again but didn't get a reply. I was by then very worried but convinced myself that she was alright and out taking tea with Jessica or another middle-class local lady, chatting about the past and telling for the umpteenth time about her wartime experiences in Whitehall and tea at a Lyons Corner House.

I rang again on my way home at seven and still there was no reply, so I extended my journey and arrived at her house at a quarter to eight. The curtains were drawn but the lights were on both upstairs and down. As I approached the front door, I could hear the signature tune of *Coronation Street* sounding the mid-programme commercial break. My concern reached critical point as I knew it was a drama that she never watched, too working class for her liking no doubt. I then heard the first advert. Oh no, that infuriating clown again!

I felt a surge of panic as I spotted a bottle of milk on the doorstep. Something was seriously amiss. I rang the doorbell. There was no reply. I knocked as loudly as I could on the door, loudly enough to hurt my knuckles.

I squatted down and peeped through the letterbox but could see nothing as the inner vestibule door was closed. I called through the letterbox in a measured voice not wishing to alarm her if my fears were unfounded and she was napping on the sofa. No reply. Then I shouted with as much volume as I could muster.

I decided to try my luck at the back of the house but the six-foot-high gate to the side passage was bolted and padlocked, a security measure I had installed myself some months earlier. I climbed the gate and whilst astride it caught the crotch of my best suit trousers on a rough edge between two of the seven planks that made up the gate. Dropping down the other side the momentum of my fall tore the cloth of one trouser leg from crotch to knee, scratching my leg painfully. I reached the rear garden and tried the conservatory door which was of course also locked. The blind was down in the kitchen and the lounge curtains were drawn. There was no point on the ground floor at which I could see into the house. I took a few steps backwards onto the lawn to inspect the upper floor windows. The curtains were closed in the guest bedroom and the blind was down in the bathroom but the bathroom window was open a couple of inches.

I searched for something to stand on but could find nothing high enough to give me access to the window. I tried in vain to reach it by placing two plastic recycling boxes on top of the wheelie bin but as both were empty they wouldn't take my weight and the lid of the blue uppermost one collapsed inside it. I realised they would be more rigid if I inverted one of them so that I could stand on the base rather than the lid. This got me high enough to reach the window with my fingertips but no closer. I started shouting again,

"Margaret! Margaret! It's Oliver, are you there?"

My shouts brought a neighbour to the bedroom window of the house next door. He recognised me instantly and seeing me standing there, in torn trousers at the foot of a makeshift climbing frame didn't need any explanation.

"Do you need a ladder Oliver?" he shouted.

"Yes!" I replied. "Have you seen Margaret today?"

He hadn't.

Two minutes later the sound of his up and over garage door opening broke the silence and a minute later I heard him in the side passage baulked by the locked back gate.

"Pass it over the top!" I shouted.

It came over slowly like the plank of a seesaw and I quickly dragged it to the rear of the house. Within seconds I had it resting a few inches below the bathroom window and scaled up it like a squirrel towards a birdfeeder stuffed with peanuts.

The partially open bathroom window was secured by a casement stay but I managed with ease to lift it and push the window fully open.

I shouted again,

"Margaret, it's Oliver! Are you there? I'm coming in through the bathroom window!"

There was no reply. I could hear only Ken Barlow reasoning with a highly irritated Deirdre.

I plunged headlong through the window scraping the buckle of my belt on the porcelain of the hand basin and accidentally turning on the hot tap with my left foot before I landed with my hands on the floor.

Getting to my feet I called again and took a deep breath preparing myself to face a real trauma. Was I to find her dead in bed? No, the television would not be switched on downstairs. Would I find her dead in a chair? That was a possibility. I braced myself.

As soon as I reached the landing, I saw her figure lying face down a couple of paces from the foot of the stairs. A dried bloodstain on the carpet framed her head and a larger damp patch of what I assumed was urine spread around her lower body. Her nightdress was up around her waist. I scampered down, my heels sliding on the rim of the last six steps of the flight and landed on my knees by her side.

To my immense relief she raised herself to rest on her forearms and turned her head to look around briefly before sinking back to the floor.

I pulled her nightdress down to cover her backside and legs and asked her if she was OK. What a stupid thing to say!

Satisfied and relieved that she was still alive I grabbed a duvet from the bed in the guest room and covered her up. Fortunately the central heating was on and so too were three bars of an electric fire. The room was sweltering. I didn't know how long she had been lying there but calculated that it was possibly twenty-four hours. She must have fallen whilst getting ready for bed the previous evening. If only I'd called round last night at the first indication of trouble. It occurred to me that her life had probably been saved by her inability, or unwillingness to master the timing switch on the central heating boiler. 'All this modern technology is quite beyond me Oliver darling' she had said on many occasions. She used to switch it on at teatime and switch it off when going to bed. She'd retire wearing woolly socks and carrying a hot water bottle to a bed pre-heated by an electric blanket.

I knelt by her shoulders and spoke to her but the only response was a groan. She was barely conscious but couldn't communicate and I suspect didn't recognise me either.

I called the emergency services and gave a concise report of the situation. A calm female voice followed the prompts on her screen gathering first the data she needed to despatch the crew. I was talking too quickly. Elderly lady had a fall, unconscious, probably been lying there for twenty-four hours, come quickly! To my total astonishment an ambulance arrived outside the house and paramedics were ringing the doorbell before I'd finished talking to the dispatcher. It turned out there was a combined fire brigade and ambulance station just half a mile away.

A bizarre looking ginger haired paramedic in green overalls and sporting an embryonic Mohican hairstyle, entered carrying resuscitation equipment in a case about the size of picnicker's cool box and started examining Margaret. As he stooped over her, I noticed that the back of his neck was decorated with an elaborate floral tattoo. It was like an Aubrey Beardsley design which bloomed at the nape of his neck and I suspected grew up his back from its roots somewhere lower down. I wondered whether it originated from his bum like a weed growing out of a crack in the crazy paving of an unkempt garden path. *How would my aunt react if she regained consciousness now?* I wondered. Despite my deep anxiety, I inwardly sniggered at the ironic thought of Margaret's life being saved by a working-class tattooed man. Perhaps that would be enough to cure her snobbery for good.

It was immediately clear though that he was a master of his craft. He exhibited the skills and knowledge of a doctor rather than a first aider and my confidence in his ability to give Margaret the best possible chance of survival was absolute. His colleague reversed the ambulance onto the drive before returning with a stretcher. I became a bystander, a useless bystander. All I could do to help was to switch off the television and close the bathroom window. After presumably being examined for broken bones Margaret was turned over, gently lifted onto the stretcher and simultaneously wrapped in what looked like a tin foil thermal blanket. Her head was immobilised between two padded blocks and she was taken into the ambulance.

The driver advised me which hospital they were taking her to and enquired whether I'd be following in my car. He added that they first wanted to stabilise her in the ambulance before setting off and that it might be a while before they were ready to go.

I knew she was in good hands and I trusted that the vehicle was equipped with whatever was needed to tend to her immediate needs.

Amazingly half an hour passed before the ambulance left the driveway and every one of those thirty minutes had me wondering what was going on inside it. How fragile could she be that it should take half an hour just to 'stabilise' her for the journey? Had she died whilst they were ministering to her?

I was distraught. I'm an atheist but out loud I promised God that if she survived, I would lead a good life from that day forward.

I'd expected 'blues and twos' but surprisingly the ambulance silently obeyed the speed limits as I followed three cars' length behind, stupidly determined not to let any other traffic get between us and separate me from it and its precious passenger.

I was very upset and replayed in my mind over and over again the events of the past twenty-four hours and counted the missed opportunities to cut short her agony.

I phoned Hermione as I drove and my emotion got the better of me. Several times I had to remain silent for a moment, swallow hard and deliberately lower my voice an octave or two for fear of breaking into childlike sobs. She was wonderful. Sympathetic and caring, she said all the right things to reassure me and keep me strong for the difficult night ahead. There was a sensitive tone to her voice that I could not remember hearing before. She is lovely. If only…

My thoughts, highly inappropriate in that situation were cut short as I followed the ambulance into the casualty bay. I swung the Jaguar into an 'ambulance staff only' parking space and caught up with the stretcher as it was rushed into Triage. My presence was tolerated only briefly before it was politely suggested that I remove myself to the waiting area and allow the professionals to do their job. I could see that it was going to be a long night, at least I hoped it would be and prepared myself with a cup of liquid masquerading as coffee from a vending machine. It was undrinkably disgusting and I dropped it into a litter bin and imagined the wrath of the cleaner whose turn it was next to lift the plastic bag with its contents from within.

A nurse approached me after half an hour to give me the good news that although unconscious Aunt Margaret had no broken bones. She had suffered very bad bruising to her face, both arms, right hip and legs, consistent with a fall. The critical issue though was that her body temperature was dangerously low and their immediate concern was to warm her up to give her body's natural defences a better chance. She was in a coma and had been moved to Intensive Care. I could see her briefly if I wished.

It was an awful sight. In my panic at the house I hadn't really appreciated the extent of the bruising to her face and arms, unless it had got very much worse in the past hour. She was unrecognisable. I felt desolate, helpless; guilty.

I spoke some reassuring words to her sleeping body before being asked to remove to a next of kin's waiting room just outside the ward where I was informed that I could spend the night if I wished. They promised to let me know immediately if there was any deterioration in her condition.

I sat there for an hour unable to sleep in the most uncomfortable chair ever built and one clearly designed by a sadist for a masochist. The rickety wooden arms were witness to its occupation over many years by sleepless, tired people fidgeting in a vain search for a comfortable position. I wondered whether it was especially configured to dissuade visitors from staying overnight.

I suffered the physical discomfort as I thought back over my life with Margaret, how she'd looked after me, cared for me and I'm sure in her own way loved me.

In my pre-school years Margaret managed to get a lot of time away from the office to look after me by working from home, a practice very uncommon at the time. I can remember it being impressed upon me how important it was not to make a sound or even approach Auntie whilst she was typing and I recall thinking how clever she was to make sheets of paper with stories on them appear from the clattering machine. I also learned the phrase 'damn and blast' delivered in a whisper as the tape ribbon curled or jammed. I instinctively knew that this was a phrase only to be used by grown-ups.

She'd take it in turns with a neighbour to do the food shopping for both families. In the 1950s this didn't entail a 'weekly shop' being before the days of supermarkets, widespread car ownership, shopping trolleys and household fridges and freezers. Neither was it one-stop shopping but a trawl around the butcher, the baker, the grocer, the greengrocer and occasionally the hardware store. Rationing too was still in force on many items. All of these factors contrived to make a shopping trip much more irksome than today but on the other hand women, and it was almost always women, were limited not just to what they could afford but to what they could carry home in two baskets on the bus. They'd complete the journey on foot, a bag in each hand like a milkmaid struggling with two heavy buckets but without the help of a yoke.

In the summer, whilst Margaret or the neighbour were shopping, I would spend the morning with the children next door who had a sandpit in the garden, as common then perhaps as trampolines are today.

The convention was that the returning parent would after unpacking the shopping present us with a 'packed lunch'. It had even by that young age already been explained to me that middle class people have lunch at midday and dinner in the evening whilst the working classes had dinner at midday and 'tea' in the evening. Each of us was given a brown paper bag containing a piece of buttered bread, perhaps with some fish paste, a biscuit and if we were lucky a juicy red plum. We'd sit side by side in the sandpit delighting in a meal that would probably have disappointed greatly had it been presented on a plate at the kitchen table.

The drink that always followed was a glass of orange juice, provided by the State which was diluted from a concentrated liquid poured from a flat-fronted bottle that looked more like one designed to dispense medicine. Identical bottles were also used for free supplies of cod liver oil, a disgusting spoonful of which was mandatory before bed each night. The present of free orange juice from government also provided those few people with fridges the means of making iced lollies, small cuboid blocks of coloured ice supported on a thin wooden cocktail stick. In the absence of these half a wooden clothes peg would suffice. Margaret, being middle class, of course had both a fridge and a plentiful supply of cocktail sticks with which I often saw her spear a slice of lemon to daintily decorate a glass of Dubonnet, her favourite tipple at that time, which sadly she drank alone perhaps transporting herself to the hotel bars of wartime London.

My junior school held an annual flower show sponsored presumably to drum up business by a local nurseryman whose son was a classmate. The school bought quantities of daffodil and hyacinth bulbs from him which they sold to the children to nurture at home before bringing them into class for the school's own spring flower show which coincided with a similar festival in the town. Auntie was not too keen, probably doubting that 'five-minute-wonder boy' would actually remain sufficiently interested to complete the project. I purchased one daffodil bulb, planted it in the appropriate bulb fibre, also bought from the school and supplied by the nurseryman, considerably over-watered it and having been briefed to put it 'somewhere dark' shoved it in the under stairs' cupboard. I monitored it daily but not seeing any sign of emerging plant life after three days got bored and gave up on the exercise. A week before the flower show my teacher reminded the children to bring their entries into school for judging on the big day. Being reminded of the forgotten plant I opened up the cupboard to reveal a painfully disappointing sight; an eighteen-inch-tall, dark-green stalk with no sign whatever of a flower on top. I brought it out and in tears of disappointment and encouraged by Auntie applied water to the parched and cracked bulb fibre. It was truly amazing that it had survived but what use was a long green vegetable in a flower growing competition?

At this point, Margaret moved to console me and pointed out a tiny embryonic bud at the tip of the huge stalk.

"Don't worry darling it might open in time."

A very wet week later on the actual day of the show it did exactly that. It popped open to reveal a large, beautifully formed, perfectly coloured flower which I gingerly carried to school on the bus with the care one would apply to an open phial of nitro-glycerine. It had been raining all week and I'd been wearing wellingtons to travel to school every day with strict instructions from Margaret to change immediately on arrival into my black plimsolls.

"Don't forget that, darling, will you? It would be so bad for your feet to have your boots on for too long."

My daffodil proved to be at least eight inches taller than any other entry and so in the school hall secured centre spot on the long trestle table covered in green baize displaying all of the entries. It certainly dwarfed the artistically arranged cluster entered by the son of the nurseryman and chief judge. A photographer from the local newspaper was there to record the presentation to me of a ten-shilling book token for first prize!

Margaret was delighted for me that victory had been snatched from the jaws of disaster and was kind enough not to mention that it was a pure fluke rather than a reward for dedicated husbandry. Her delight was tempered somewhat when four days later my picture appeared in the local paper, smiling angelically, book token in hand, centre-stage in pristine school blazer, neatly pressed short trousers, and wellington boots.

The first time I was allowed out in the evening was at the age of nine to attend the Cub pack in a wooden hut behind the local Methodist church. I was disappointed to have to wait three weeks before I was able to wear a uniform though I guess that was so that Auntie could gauge how keen five-minute-wonder boy was before buying the cap, pullover, neckerchief and leather woggle. She bought me a splendid leather belt at a jumble sale with a pukka Boy Scout emblem forged into the buckle but I had nothing to hang from it as she refused point blank to left me have a sheath knife.

"Far too dangerous Oliver darling." Within weeks though I'd acquired one by swapping some Dinky toys, a maroon horsebox and a green Austin A30 baker's van, for some roller skates and then trading those for the knife. It was magnificent and at night I'd remove it from its hiding place in my bedroom and admire it by torchlight under the blankets. Its blade was engraved with the image of a 1930s Boy Scout. The cutting edge of the blade was curved to a point and the other was flat with a serrated section presumably for some less interesting function I imagined such as grinding conkers into a pulp to make porridge. Its handle was of black Bakelite and it was secured by a tiny strap with a metal stud into a well-worn leather sheath. It was my pride and joy. On Friday evenings I leave for 'Cubs' having earlier secreted the knife into the saddlebag of my juvenile cycle bought for twelve and six saved up from birthday gifts. I'd give Margaret a goodbye kiss on the cheek making sure she could see the vacant space at the back of my belt from which others proudly displayed their sheath knives. Once around the corner I'd stop, lean the bicycle on a lamppost and thread the sheath onto the belt before continuing the journey, my symbol of manhood proudly displayed on my skinny bottom in short grey school trousers.

Cubs on a Friday night was doubly looked forward to as it marked the start of a weekend full of play; dawn 'til dusk, wall-to-wall, unfettered adventure, fun, games and laughter. My strongest recollections of childhood are not of particular events but of laughing so much that my cheeks ached. Today I often lament the lot of sullen young children hot-housed by anxious parents fixated on the belief that their priority, nay their sole mission is to give their offspring the best start in life, reinforced by the fear that they'll starve and die if they don't excel in all subjects and skills which can be achieved only through afterschool clubs and extra tuition at weekends.

'We have to prepare them for a more competitive world,' I hear them say as their children reflect the stress of their parents or escape it by losing themselves in fantasy video games, Snapchat and social media. How I'd love to give them a taste of adventure and freedom; riding bikes without crash helmets, climbing trees without a safety harness, playing conkers without safety glasses, lighting bonfires and firing airguns.

Hermione is no exception to this modern trend and I often think that if Tristan were my boy, I'd contrive to give him a taste of my carefree, deliriously happy childhood. If only I had the chance.

I was nudged awake from my half sleep by Hermione. At first, I thought I'd been dreaming, and then I hoped I hadn't been snoring. It was such a surprise to see her and the concerned expression on her face that I was overcome with emotion as I sprung to my feet.

"I'm so sorry," she said. "How is she?"

I started to speak but broke down after only a few words. She hugged me tightly and I felt the shudders of my suppressed sobbing vibrate through her fragile body. I felt her rib cage against mine, I felt her shoulder blades and her hipbones. It was the closest I'd ever been to her in all the years I'd existed on the fringes of her personal space. It was as if she'd decided to switch off the impenetrable deflector shields of her personal Starship Enterprise.

I composed myself quickly and thanked her for coming out so late. I dried away my tears on a handkerchief in a manner that implied I was simply rubbing the sleep from my tired eyes.

Hermione spared me her usual look of resigned distain that she often exhibited whenever I produced a handkerchief from my pocket in the office or when dining. She regarded them as not only very unhygienic but extremely old fashioned too. I remember once offering her an unused, neatly ironed, virgin white, brand new, straight from the box, Irish linen handkerchief to wipe away tears from her eyes during an emotional moment; one unfortunately totally unrelated to our non-relationship. The very gesture had been enough to stop her tears which were instantly replaced by a disgusted sneer.

"Oh, No thank you," she had said, preferring to scrabble in her handbag for a tissue. Her facial expression was as if I'd offered her a bogey-encrusted, bloodstained, oil-smeared, smelly rag. Instead I'd watched as she slowly unravelled a previously used but now dry *Kleenex*. It was like watching someone carefully unfold a lottery ticket that had been accidentally screwed into a ball and thrown into a wastepaper basket before realising they'd just checked the winning numbers for the wrong week.

We sat closely side by side on a small leather sofa which like the armchair was designed for a price rather than for comfort, but with barely room for two it required its occupants to tolerate, or enjoy, shoulder to shoulder bodily contact. We talked for an hour and drank tea from a cousin of the vending machine in Casualty. It was little better than the undrinkable coffee I'd discarded earlier but it was wet and it was hot.

Hermione seemed so different that night, so sensitive, so caring, so utterly loveable. I'm ashamed to say that I almost forgot about Margaret whilst we were talking. The conversation was relaxed and rambling, not about my aunt's dangerous predicament, or the dramatic events of the day, nor about the developments at the bank. We talked about nothing. It was wonderful, relaxed, meaningless chit chat. Her voice had its usual dreamy effect on me as I watched the changing shape of her sexy mouth and felt the tender vibrations it unfailingly triggered in my internal organs. It was the now familiar sensation, but that night somehow different. This time it seemed to signal it was no longer some rare and precious fleeting sensation that had to be clung to in case it disappeared for ever. It had suddenly become softer, more tender, unhurried, dependable; permanent.

I shared my gaze between Hermione's lips and her eyes but she looked everywhere else. She wasn't avoiding eye contact but dreamily stared at one point for perhaps half a minute before shifting her focus elsewhere. She noticed the tear in my trousers and as she spoke absent-mindedly gathered the edges of the torn cloth between her fingers on my inner thigh as if undertaking an invisible repair. It was extraordinary. She was touching me quite intimately but not realising what she was doing, as if she was merely flicking some dust off my lapel or picking a strand of hair from my shoulder.

Suddenly she looked very tired. She stifled two or three yawns before breathing the next very slowly through a cupped hand pressed against her wide-open mouth.

I insisted she left at around midnight and said that I would remain there until Margaret woke from her coma. I asked her to advise George that I'd be away from the office for as long as it took. We raised ourselves from the rickety chair and stood in the accustomed hip to hip embrace that had come to characterise our partings. She offered me her cheek. As I kissed her goodbye, I felt her lungs fill with a sudden intake of breath, sadly not triggered by the touch of my lips but to fuel an even longer yawn, which she let out in a series of short puffs, Huh, huh, huh, huh.

As I heard the clicking sound of her high heels fading into the distance on the polished floor of the hospital corridor I knew what I must do. I'd only once kissed her lovely mouth, but I would ask her to marry me next time we met.

Chapter Twenty
Wicked Uncle

I sat in the family room at the hospital until three o'clock. I couldn't sleep both through my concern for Margaret and my worry about how Hermione would react to my imminent proposal. As the nurse had promised to call me the instant that there was any change in my aunt's condition my stress-exhausted mind concentrated on Hermione. I was so tired of the whole ageing business of the one-sided love affair that I concluded I had nothing to lose. If she said 'yes' then my life would be wonderfully changed forever; if she said 'no' I would have to find a way to get over her. The worst that could happen was that she might laugh uncontrollably and tell me to fuck off and die. I might have to find myself another Chief Clerk but either way I would be free of this constant heartache and have the motivation at last to retire from work and go out to play.

I first considered the implications of the preferred scenario, the 'yes' decision.

I knew she would be happy to live at the farm and so too would Tristan. Ah yes, Tristan. Now there was a possible impediment. The boy clearly disliked me with a passion but despite that, over recent months I'd had to admit to myself a growing affection for the boy. I had been at pains not to show it of course but there were things about him that I liked, things that amused me and things that I even admired. As I looked back over the time I'd known him, I couldn't actually remember any incidents of open hostility. There hadn't been any arguments, or tantrums or disrespect. It was just his looks of constant, smouldering, distant hate, of ageist prejudice, of guarded jealousy.

I liked though his polite respect for his mother, I was amused by his precocious sense of humour and I was, to be completely honest, even highly amused by his farting prowess. I enjoyed too the brief glimpses into his highly imaginative fantasy world. He could play out really creative scenarios, such as his participation in the World Farting Championships without the slightest embarrassment if his dream-world mutterings were overheard. They say sarcasm is wasted on children but if my limited experience based on Tristan was anything to go by, it was definitely complete nonsense. He had a much wider vocabulary than most children his age and often surprised me with intelligent witty remarks worthy of an adult. He was still a podgy little tyke but I'd become fond of him and decided to drop my plans for his educational deportation should Hermione accept my proposal.

I couldn't let him win the battle of wits though, so I contrived to display an air of disapproval when out of his mother's presence, an act I would maintain until he was ready to accept me. He had to meet me halfway. I did though feel somewhat guilty about the deception and on reflection, perhaps sometimes I'd been the childish one.

During a visit to my home one September weekend Hermione and I were strolling through a small orchard a few hundred yards from the house with Tristan running on ahead whacking the tree trunks with a stout stick he'd found in a hedge. He spotted another of a similar length but unlike the first more slender and brittle.

"Oliver, let's play sword fighting!" he cried.

His mother showed no dissent so I agreed. The grinning boy handed me the slender one.

"On guard!" he shouted, immediately attacking. As soon as we crossed swords, mine of course snapped in two, leaving me holding but an inch of stick in my hand.

"I win!" he shouted in triumph.

I threw the remains of mine at him playfully and chased after him catching him easily before dragging him to the ground and tickling him roughly, armpits and tummy, until through his laughter he begged me to stop.

After composing himself he looked around for some other amusement.

"Can I have an apple please?" he asked as the three of us stood under a gnarled tree, perhaps the oldest in the orchard. Its heavily laden branches hung to waist height offering the boy a mouth-watering choice within easy arm's reach.

"Which one can I have?" he politely enquired.

"Any one you like," I answered. "You choose."

"That one please!" he said, pointing a podgy finger to one at the very top of the tree. "That big red one." I looked at Hermione urging her to instruct him to select one more to hand, but she just grinned at me obviously highly amused at her son's little joke. I though saw it as a cunning challenge.

I tried to get it down by shaking the tree, many fell but not that one. Would he accept the alternatives I offered, of equal size and colour? No. Hermione seemed very amused, perhaps to see how far each of us would go, Tristan in his intransigence and me in my attempts not to disappoint the boy. I sensed she wanted to see who'd win the trial of wills. With probably twenty newly dislodged apples joining a similar number of windfalls I gave up my strenuous tree-shaking efforts and not wanting to be beaten climbed the tree. With outstretched hand I managed to grab it, but it slipped from my grip and fell to the ground bruising quite badly.

As I climbed down, I slipped and painfully barked my shins but made little of it though both had noticed my wincing. Tristan picked up the apple I'd climbed the tree for and another of equal size, identical apart from the unsightly bruise. I was already planning to laugh at the boy's ingratitude, expecting him to discard the one I'd put so much effort into picking for him, when to my astonishment he looked at both, discarded the good one and sank his teeth into the bruised one. Hermione's wry smile unmistakably indicated that she'd read my sentiments and expressed pride for her boy.

There was a pond on my farm around which Tristan would spend many hours silently and unsuccessfully fishing for perch and roach. I'd bought him some tackle and showed him how to bait a hook with a pair of colourful maggots or a juicy worm he'd dug out of the soft ground at the edge of the pool. I'd stand behind him, my arms wrapped around his as I held his wrists and showed him how to cast the line into the deepest part of the pool. It was real father and son stuff which I could tell his beautiful mother appreciated very much. I'd catch sight of her smiling tenderly at the sight of me passing on the skills to her boy. This activity kept him occupied for hours whilst I had Hermione to myself a hundred yards away, relaxing in parallel hammocks hung from the long low branches of an ancient horse chestnut tree, enjoying the warm summer breeze and a chilled glass of wine.

She probably would have been less appreciative if she had known that the pond was completely devoid of fish.

In another season that pond was the scene of a dramatic incident that frightened Tristan very much and terrified his mother too.

During a day-long visit one freezing cold weekend the boy wanted to slide on the ice which covered the pool. Hermione was reluctant to allow this but relented after I demonstrated the thickness of the ice by tentatively walking across it myself. Tristan, dressed in Wellington boots, jeans and a thick hooded parka had great fun running at the pond and sliding right across it, stumbling each time as his momentum was arrested by the low bank on the far side. Eventually boring of that game he noticed a trace of weed dimly showing through the opaque whiteness of the ice about halfway between the bank and the centre of the pool.

Childishly he started stamping his foot at that spot. I can't imagine what his intention was and perhaps he didn't have one. He was possibly acting out one of his silent fantasies, perhaps as a knight giving a dragon the coup de grace or a Ninja Turtle super-hero killing a giant spider. Then he started jumping up and down on the spot.

Hermione and I were at least a hundred yards away, but we heard a loud sickening crack as the ice fractured. We watched horrified as, it seemed in slow motion, a square section of ice broke from the surface and tilted on edge as Tristan's body displaced it. As he sank into the freezing water he screamed for his mother. She grabbed my wrists and her fingernails dug deep into my flesh. I was astonished at her strength. The boy instinctively leaned forward and attempted to hold onto the unbroken surface around the hole he had created and became wedged there as the displaced sheet of ice tried to regain its original position. His fingers scratched at the slippery surface and he shrieked in horror.

"Oliver!" he screamed. "Save me, Pleeeeeeeeeeease! Quickly!"

My run towards the pond was hampered by Hermione's vice-like grip on my arm. After her initial scream she was stunned into silence, one hand clasped tightly across her mouth. I shook her free and covered the icy ground on which we stood in about thirty seconds, including the five that I spent sliding on my arse after slipping over. I paused at the edge and composed myself, not easy given the painful bruising the fall had inflicted on my bum. I needed to reassure the boy of course, but I also wanted Hermione to see me taking charge of the 'crisis' in a calm and assertive manner.

"Tristan, listen to me," I said calmly from the edge of the ice.

"You'll be OK if you don't panic. I'll have you out of there very quickly, but you must keep still."

He started whimpering.

"Tristan. Look at me," I said firmly.

"Trust me. I will get you out."

I looked around for something to span the gap between us, a branch or piece of wood but could see nothing close at hand. I took off my bright red woollen scarf and kneeling at the edge of the pond threw one end towards him. He grabbed it at the second attempt. I tried to pull him out but he didn't have the strength to overcome his own body weight and hold on.

There was nothing else I could do but boldly walk across the ice and try to haul him out. The surface of the ice, now weakened by the hole Tristan had created, cracked and collapsed under my weight, and my legs sank knee deep into the freezing water. I slipped and fell, sprawling forward, my progress checked by the large sheets of broken ice ahead of me. I was on my knees but it must have appeared to Hermione that I was up to my chest in the water. I managed to grab Tristan's outstretched hand and pulled him towards me. His progress out of the hole and his kicking feet shattered the ice between us and in a few seconds he was in my arms, clinging tightly around my neck. He clung so tightly that he was choking me and I spluttered as I made my way to the bank in a series of falls from a kneeling position, our combined weight smashing a route ahead of us like an icebreaker.

Once clear of the ice Hermione snatched Tristan from his grip around my neck and held him close to her, chastising him loudly for his stupidity whilst choking back the tears of relief.

We started our chilly walk back to the house, the wind deepening the discomfort of our wet clothing. The boy, quickly overcame his terror and stopped crying, running on ahead of us. Hermione took my soaking wet arm and hugged it, leaning into me as she had never done before. She said nothing but her body language communicated clearly her gratitude as she felt I had saved her son's life.

I of course modestly shrugged off the whole episode as a trivial incident. I also resolved to ensure neither of them ever discovered that I had known the pond was only three feet deep.

Hermione planned to spend that Christmas visiting a wealthy friend who owned a country house in Wiltshire. I had hoped she and Tristan would stay with me for a few days over the holiday and I had mentally planned every detail including a pre-lunch country walk on Christmas Day to a pub that in past years had been heaving with well-dressed ladies, and men in garish and often ill-fitting pullovers, gifts from their mothers that morning and subsequently reserved for gardening or never worn again until Bonfire Night when they could be concealed under scruffy anoraks. The place had been buzzing too with the delightful chatter of small children happily confirming that they had indeed been given the latest 'must have' toy relentlessly advertised at them since September and twelve-year-olds busy texting pointless messages to their school friends on their new mobile phones.

Sadly, Hermione had preferred the company of her friends and whilst I didn't blame her I feared she might meet some handsome and eligible bachelor twenty years my junior whilst partying with the county set. Romances so often start at Christmas.

I had heard Tristan hinting unsubtly for weeks about what he'd like for Christmas. Not for him the latest fad or electronic gadget; he was a leader rather than a follower. They boy wanted a pogo stick. I hadn't seen or heard of one for ten years and I wondered where he'd seen them. They were certainly no longer advertised on television and as I discovered not stocked by toyshops either. Hermione had already decided to buy him a Nintendo DS and I suspected she felt that a pogo stick might be soon discarded after he'd played with it for the duration of the holiday.

I decided that I would buy one for him. I knew it would give him great pleasure and also thought the exercise would help him shift some of the flab he still carried. I could see him energetically bouncing around the garden like a wallaby on steroids whilst providing a detailed commentary as he played out some Star Wars fantasy perhaps leading an intergalactic legion of super-hero warriors equipped from birth with springs rather than legs. I was sure that Hermione wouldn't buy one too, so I kept my intentions secret until I had found one. I bought it on the internet and it was shipped over from America a week before Christmas.

Two days before Christmas Eve I called on Hermione to deliver the present, using it as an excuse to see her once more before she disappeared for the holiday and hoping to find a sprig of mistletoe hanging from a light fitting in the vestibule between the front door and the hall.

Like most men I am absolutely crap at wrapping presents and had just about managed to conceal the bright yellow pogo stick inside an untidy bundle made from two sheets of festive gift wrap, two of brown paper and about five yards of Sellotape.

I timed my arrival for after Tristan's bedtime and hopefully not too long before Hermione's in the vain hope of catching a glimpse of the nightwear that decorated my dreams. This was of course complete fantasy as I had arranged to call in just after eight, but one lives in hope.

Hermione opened the door with a beautiful smile masking the extreme stress that seems to overpower all women in the days before Christmas.

She greeted me with a kiss on the cheek and an astonished look that seemed to ask, 'Why has this man bought my son an ironing board for Christmas?'

She offered me a glass of wine as I attempted to lean the unstable package against the banister post at the foot of the stairs. Its awkward shape and unhelpful centre of gravity conspired against me and after several attempts I gave up and laid it on the floor. She was more than slightly flushed and the glass of wine she held was obviously not her first of the evening.

The amateurish bundle and the obvious fact that I had grossly underestimated the number of sheets of gift wrap necessary to cover it amused Hermione immensely. She looked at it, then at me and burst out laughing. She had a habit of covering her mouth when in uncontrollable laughter in a totally mistaken belief that it showed too much of her gums rather than her perfect teeth. In fact she had the most beautiful smile and a gorgeous mouth that couldn't look unattractive in any circumstances. I imagined that her dentist might have to conceal the bulge in his trousers and concentrate hard to steady his drilling hand when in such close proximity to her heavenly bouche.

Hermione's tears provoked my own as I watched her bend double in a fit of uncontrollable laughter. She reached out a hand to touch my arm either to steady herself or in a mild gesture of gratitude before composing herself enough to ask if she could help me to wrap the present properly.

I tore the parcel open and screwed the paper and the tangle of Sellotape into a ball which I carried through to the kitchen and stuffed into a large stainless-steel pedal bin.

Hermione produced four large sheets of gift-wrap printed with images of robins balanced on the heads of smiling snowmen and I lifted the pogo stick intending to hold it whilst she applied a woman's deft touch to wrapping it.

The floor covering in the hall was of heavy-duty carpet, and perhaps spurred on by her laughter or the alcohol or both, I decided to try out the toy before it was turned again into a lumpy although this time expertly wrapped parcel.

Hermione could read my intentions and giggled, no doubt at the prospect of seeing me fail. I didn't disappoint her. I achieved just two perpendicular bounces before another at a dangerously inclined angle sent me crashing through the glass panelled door into the vestibule.

The sound of breaking glass, splintering wood and Hermione's instant scream, followed by her almost hysterical laughter brought Tristan to the top of the stairs. His disapproving frown unambiguously conveyed his utter distain at the sight of his drunken mother and the prostrate interloper lying on the floor whilst bleeding from cuts to both hands and across the bridge of his nose.

Tristan retired sulkily to his bedroom and Hermione washed the splinters of glass from my minor wounds under a cold tap in the kitchen before patting them dry with a soft towel and applying to my hands a patchwork of Elastoplast almost as intricate as the cat's cradle of Sellotape I'd used to wrap the boy's present.

I promised to arrange for someone to replace the door after Christmas and Hermione graciously accepted before pouring us both another glass of wine. She was in such high spirits and full of fun and laughter that I didn't want to leave.

"Let's take Tristan to the Christmas Fair," I said on a whim. "Tonight. Let's go tonight."

She looked pensive for a moment, no doubt weighing the need to continue packing for the holiday and getting the boy out of bed, against my most outlandishly playful suggestion. Tristan who'd heard every word from his vantage point on the landing instantly snapped out of his mood and yelled with excitement.

"Yes, pleeeeeeeeeeeese, Mum! Can we?"

To my immense surprise Hermione agreed. We swept up the broken glass and splinters of wood whilst Tristan got dressed and leaped into the Jaguar like excited children.

Hermione wore a padded anorak against the cold and Tristan the parka he'd worn the day of the ice drama now forgotten. I was more formally dressed in a navy-blue overcoat and wished it had a warmer collar as there was an icy wind that night.

We rode on 'The Whip' together in a small pod held in by a locked bar that we clung to as it flung us in figures of eight across a large rotating disc, the centrifugal force pressing us into our communal seat. I sat Tristan between us for safety and missed the chance to have Hermione's body pushed hard against mine by the g force. She laughed aloud at first but by the time the ride slowed to a stop after five minutes she was feeling ill. On reflection perhaps it wasn't the most sensible thing to do after I don't know how many glasses of wine.

Tristan spotted a traditional roundabout and made a bee line for it. His head whipped from side to side like a spectator at a speeded-up tennis match as he watched the passing horses, ostriches and other animal figures, deciding which he'd ride when it eventually came to a halt.

Surprisingly, he opted for a large pink cartoon pig which he mounted with the assistance of a scruffy longhaired youth with a cash bag hanging over one shoulder who showed him how to slide his feet into the stirrups and urged him to hang on tightly to the reins. I jumped up alongside him to make sure he was seated securely and to pay his fare.

The music started ahead of the roundabout which rapidly gathered pace reaching full speed by the fourth rotation. The pink pig and its grinning podgy rider passed by every six seconds or so, rising and falling as it went as if surfing on a rising tide. On every orbit Tristan looked for the acknowledgement of his mother who responded with an exaggerated smile and a wave. At each pass, I could see the boy searching for us and then beaming with delight as soon as he made eye contact with Hermione.

The motion of the ride and its close proximity must have made her feel sick and she distanced herself from it by a few paces. I joined her and saw Tristan anxiously searching for our new position, his face lighting up as he spotted us.

I looked out for the pink pig on each circuit and strangely began to feel that Tristan's smiles and need for acknowledgement were aimed at me rather than Hermione. It was a bizarre sensation. Why should he do that? Was he perhaps challenging me to be brave enough to ride a big pink pig too, or was he farting at me on each orbit?

I tested the theory by moving away from Hermione and sure enough it was me to whom he was looking for acknowledgment rather than to his mother.

Very strange, I thought. *What game is the little tyke playing now?* I smiled and waved each time to meet the challenge.

Hermione was getting very cold standing in the chill night air and suggested that we go home. It was way past Tristan's bedtime and she still had packing to do. I had intended to just drop them off at the house and politely decline

Hermione's invitation to go in for coffee but when we arrived at the house Tristan answered for me.

"Please come in, Oliver, I want to give you your present," he said.

I was taken aback by his words. I did of course want to go in, especially as I was about to spend ten lonely days without seeing his mother and worrying that she might meet an eligible man of her own age whilst in Wiltshire.

Tristan noisily dashed upstairs as soon as the front door was opened and disappeared into his bedroom. I suggested that I make the coffee while Hermione performed the now entirely unnecessary task of gift wrapping the pogo stick which she did speedily and expertly, after wiping a few remaining bloodstains from it with a damp cloth.

As I was preparing to leave, and dishonestly wishing Hermione a wonderful Christmas in Wiltshire, Tristan appeared in his dressing gown walking slowly like a choirboy, taking very short steps, his eyes focussed on the present he was carrying with great care in both hands. It was an old Quality Street tin which he had decorated with a band of tinsel stuck around its circumference with *Sellotape.* His vision was somewhat impaired by a large red envelope which he held between his teeth, requiring him to nod his head occasionally to both keep an eye on his precious cargo and negotiate a safe passage around the furniture.

"Happy Christmas, Oliver. Here's your present from me," he said with sincerity.

I was stunned. I had come to realise over recent months that I was very fond of the boy. I had begun to see in him some endearing qualities that I would have been proud of in a son my own, if I'd had one. However, despite this astonishing development I was convinced the boy still resented both my frequent presence in his home and my unconcealed affection for his mother. As he passed the gift to me, I silently prayed that it was not just a cruel joke.

"It's quite fragile, so keep it this way up and open it carefully, please," he added.

"You can open it before Christmas Day if you like."

In my lack of experience with children I didn't realise that was an invitation, if not a plea, to open it there and then. I took the card and the tin and thanked him. It was quite light but definitely not empty, so I concluded it contained more than just a stale fart.

"Oh no, I'll save it for Christmas morning, Tristan. Thank you very much."

I said goodbye in the hallway and prepared to savour a tender moment, but as Hermione kissed my cheek her feet crunched on some remaining shards of glass and the kiss turned into a raspberry as she snorted with laughter remembering the earlier scene. We laughed together and wished each other a happy Christmas.

I kept my promise and didn't open my present until Christmas Day. The tin contained a little cameo in *Plasticine*. Completely filling the inside base and nearly reaching the rim was an amazingly detailed model of a boy being rescued from the broken ice covering a pond. The card featured the same boy being taught to cast a fishing line. It brought tears to my eyes.

Chapter Twenty-One
Solo Flight

I wheeled the Jaguar through the airfield gates and immediately slowed to little more than walking pace as I meandered around the potholes in the ageing and neglected Tarmac which seemed to grow in number, width and depth with every visit.

I always feel excited visiting an old airfield particularly one that has seen wartime service and here at North Hellidon there are many reminders of its glorious past as a Battle of Britain fighter station, the old black hangars, the square white block of the control tower, now housing the flying club's operations office, clubhouse, bar and kitchen.

There is an Air Traffic Control radio room positioned on the roof as there would have been in the frenetic months of summer 1940, although it is now an ugly white PVC box looking more like a cheap conservatory. From this vantage point the approaches and thresholds of all four runways can be clearly seen and mounted above it is a green beacon indicating at night that it is now a civil rather than a military aerodrome. Straddling this plastic carbuncle are steel cables supporting a tall VHF radio mast and projecting from a corner of the ATC 'greenhouse' is a weather vane and anemometer sending wind speed and direction information to a display console inside the hut from where it can be relayed to joining and departing traffic.

Haunting the airfield at several points still stand the brick-built air raid shelters, damp, dark and fetid through decades of neglect. To the rear of the hangars are the remains of several abandoned Nissen huts now held captive by thickets of sycamore trees, mountains of impenetrable bramble and great plumes of buddleia. In summer, the cascading buddleia flowers attract hundreds of proud and confident butterflies; Peacocks, Red Admirals, Painted Ladies and Orange Tips providing a blaze of colour as they fly circuits around the dangling fronds, stopping only to refuel on nectar before taking off again on their next sortie. In the cold of winter the fronds hang brittle, brown and lifeless, their energetic summer visitors gone without trace remaining only in the memory of those who admired them in their all too brief existence.

One Saturday afternoon in November, the low cloud base making it impossible for me to go flying I ventured into this jungle, beating a path through the brambles with a large metal rake to reach the nearest of the Nissen huts. Made from pre-formed curved corrugated steel sheeting and assembled to form tunnels like giant, semi-circular garden cloches they had been covered with thick black bitumen paint which had largely protected them from corrosion to this day. Each end of the 'tunnel' was closed by a brick wall, with a central door between two windows at one end. The corroded metal window frames remained intact but had long ago given up their glass to winter gales, retaining only fringes of stubborn time-hardened putty and a few small shards of glass like shark's teeth in a sun-bleached jawbone washed up on a deserted beach. The wooden door had at some point been left slightly ajar, but although its timbers had rotted, its hinges rusted solid and weeds anchored it to the ground, it had denied access for decades to any intruder.

My attempts to prise it open though quickly resulted in its inevitable destruction. As I pushed the door open, it fell apart and collapsed inwards leaving only the obdurate rusty hinges fused with the screws that had held them to the doorframe in red-brown amorphous lumps.

Quite what I had hoped to find inside I can't imagine but there was nothing. Absolutely nothing. No iron bed frames, no rickety chairs, no noticeboard with faded wartime posters warning against careless talk, no abandoned equipment or fabric remains, not even any graffiti. Cobwebs of every description shrouded the open space. Some thick and dust covered like abandoned hammocks spanned the corners, some hung in great ribbons from the empty Bakelite bulb holders dangling from brown cotton-covered electric cables and others formed circular targets like the roundels on the fighter aircraft once stationed there. Evidently all that had disturbed the cobwebs over the years were the swallows that had built countless nests of mud still fused to the brick walls at both ends of the room. There were though no traces whatsoever left by the young men who'd rested and slept there after flying their Spitfires and Hurricanes on daylight patrols to intercept the Luftwaffe bombers in the skies over Sussex and Kent or sorties to stalk lone intruders in the black night void over London.

The exciting, intoxicating cocktail of airfield odours; aviation fuel, grass cuttings, rubber and oil are no doubt the same as they were in those heady, anxious days but the sounds are very different. The Rolls Royce Continental and Lycoming engines that power light aircraft today and the Rotax motors in microlights are puny in comparison with those of the mighty warbirds and this is reflected in the sound of aircraft taking off, joining overhead, landing and taxiing.

Gone is the unmistakable symphonic growl of the supercharged 12-cylinder 1720 hp Merlin powering a Mk IX Spitfire on full boost launching into the sky and the crackle of a landing Hurricane throttling back in a tight descending turn onto finals. Not then the annoying, thumping beat of helicopter rotors either.

Through these similarities and differences runs an undeniable ethereal link. I doubt whether, even in ignorance of the past, could anyone fail to sense the almost spiritual feeling exuded by these remnants of past military aviation activity or do you perhaps need to be a pilot to feel it? If that is the case, how privileged are those who fly and how deprived are those oblivious to the joys of flight.

I parked the car and entered the control tower to sign the air movement log. Behind the counter, high on the wall, was a dial showing wind speed and direction. Beneath that was a whiteboard on which was written in chinagraph crayon the runway in use that day and the circuit direction. It was 28 Right hand.

I exchanged a bit of banter with Dave, the Chief Instructor of the flying school, a droll East-Midlander with a dry sense of humour and the totally unflappable demeanour essential for training ab initio pilots and giving air experience flights and trial lessons to those dipping a nervous toe into what for some becomes a life-changing exposure to a totally new dimension but for others just a one-off jolly, something to boast about to friends and family.

I completed the Air Movement Log; date, aircraft type, registration, pilot's name, number of people on board, departure airfield, (to be completed by pilots arriving from other airfields), intended destination, planned departure time, aircraft owner's name and pilot's signature. The actual take-off and landing times would be entered when signing back in after the flight.

It is all information an airfield is required to record by the CAA, (Civil Aviation Authority, or 'Campaign Against Aviation' as it is cynically known by many private pilots) in the event of an accident or more likely any infringement of controlled airspace or other misdemeanour, to counter any claim that one was playing golf that day and certainly nowhere near an aeroplane.

I mentioned earlier that I enjoy taking women flying but nothing really compares to the thrill of solo flight. You detach yourself from the world and enter a three dimensional playground beyond the help of others in which to apply your skills and enjoy alone the thrills of flight, looking down on the world and dealing with any eventuality that might arise, totally dependent on your own skills and self-reliance to get you and your aircraft back on the ground in one piece.

Mind you there's a very exciting and challenging game we play whenever Max flies with me. We head off to a safe aerobatic manoeuvring area, he in the front cockpit me in the rear. We take it in turns to look down inside the aircraft so that you can't see ahead whilst the other has control and does a couple of aerobatic manoeuvres to disorientate the other, before handing back control of the aircraft in some crazy attitude.

The aeroplane might be for example inverted in a steep climb, slowing rapidly and nearing the stall, when I hand it over with full rudder and the throttle closed and shout,

"You have control."

Max then has to quickly orientate himself and turn the unusual attitude into a pukka manoeuvre. After a few twists and turns he tells me to look down whilst he repeats the process perhaps slowing the Pitts and entering an inverted spin before shouting, "Yours," the signal for me to resume control.

The exercise is not only great fun but builds confidence that you can recover safely at any time from any unusual attitude should the need arise.

I took a pre-flight 'nervous pee', a discipline I'd been taught in the Airforce and have maintained to this day. Not only is it uncomfortable on the bladder when pulling 'g' trussed up in a five-point harness but in the unlikely event of a crash a full bladder can present complications to the medics attending to an unconscious pilot.

I collected my flying helmet with its built-in earphones and microphone, together with my parachute from the boot of the Jag as I walked across to the hangar. I entered though a small side door before pressing a button which activates the powerful electric motor that raises the huge hangar door in less than a minute, just giving me enough time to walk over to the Pitts and gently place the parachute pack on the tailplane before returning to hit the isolation switch once the door is high enough for the aircraft to safely pass under it.

I completed the slow, routine, circular walk-round inspection of the aeroplane, looking for anything amiss. I ran my hands gently over the leading edges of each of the four wings of the aerobatic biplane, the propeller, fuselage and tailplane checking for any visible damage, tell-tale oil leaks, or disturbance to the fabric which might indicate some unseen structural fault beneath. I moved the ailerons and rudder through their full deflection to ensure there were no restrictions to these control surfaces and that there was no play in the linkages, hinges and bearings through which they were operated. I couldn't 'kick the tyres' as they're largely hidden by the streamlining wheel spats but enough of them showed at ground level to show that the pressures were OK.

I unclipped the engine cowling, unscrewed the dipstick and checked the oil level. It always needed a little top-up as, even though the engine was fitted with an inverted oil system, half an hour of vigorous aerobatics always resulted in a little oil being ejected through a drain pipe running the length of the fuselage and exiting just ahead of the tailwheel spring.

Having topped up the oil I removed the fuel filler cap and inserted a notched wooden dipstick into the tank to measure the Avgas on board and to decide whether I'd need to refuel for the planned flight. It measured three-quarters full on this crude device, more than enough for half an hour of aerobatics, largely flown at close to full throttle. There is a rudimentary fuel gauge in the cockpit which comprises a plastic tube plumbed into the fuel system and running through a graduated scale on the instrument panel. However, although reasonably accurate on the ground and in straight and level flight, the first time the aeroplane is rolled inverted it just displays a useless stream of bubbles. The only safe procedure therefore is to know how much fuel you have on board before take-off, how much you'll burn during the planned sortie and to keep a safety reserve should some emergency require you to delay your return or divert to another airfield. Another factor for aerobatic pilots to remember is not to perform aerobatic manoeuvres with less than a quarter tank of fuel, as this can result in the engine stopping, and an associated adrenalin rush.

The more than adequate fuel reading meant that I didn't have to push the aircraft to the pumps about a hundred yards away but instead could just roll it out of the hangar and close the doors behind me. Starting an aeroplane with an open hangar door behind it causes a dust storm within, accompanied by a tornado of empty oil cans, sheets of paper, cardboard and any other loose article that will almost certainly damage any aircraft parked inside. It causes a storm of furious protest too. I can vouch for that. You live and learn.

I removed the wooden seat back giving access to the inside of the fuselage behind the pilot's seat and shone a powerful torch into the void to satisfy myself that there were no loose articles that could move around in flight and jam the controls with disastrous consequences. I removed some small change from my trouser pockets for the same reason, donned my flying suit and once I'd checked its many pockets zipped them up. I picked up the parachute from the tailplane and put it on before adjusting the webbing straps as tightly as comfort allowed.

I slid open the Perspex canopy, climbed onto the port wing and lowered myself slowly into the cramped rear cockpit taking care not to kick any switches or other controls as I did so. During the walk-round I'd checked that the unused front cockpit harness, last used by Philippa on that disappointing flight were safely stowed to avoid them thrashing about the front cockpit as I looped and rolled.

I strapped in, carefully arranging the aircraft harness over my parachute harness and tightened it so that it would hold me firmly in place whatever the attitude of the aircraft. Next I plugged in the comms lead from my headset into a socket in the instrument panel. In the event that I'd have to bale out I would simply reverse the procedure. Having first jettisoned the canopy I'd pull the comms lead out to avoid being connected by the head to an out of control aeroplane spiralling earthwards, flick open the quick release device that held all five elements of the harness together, roll the aircraft upside down and fall out and away, securely strapped into my life-saving parachute. Well, that's the theory anyway.

I fired up the engine, called the tower for a radio check and to be given the local and regional barometric pressures with which to set my altimeter and taxied to the hold for runway 28. Once the engine had reached operating temperature, with the fuel/air mixture fully rich I increased the pressure on the toe brakes to stop the aircraft moving forward as there isn't a parking brake on a Pitts and advanced the throttle. With the propeller 'fully fine' I set 1800 rpm and checked the two magnetos by switching each one on and off in turn to satisfy myself that the engine would continue to run, albeit at slightly reduced rpm should one fail. I then increased it to 2000 rpm and 'cycled the prop' to check that the variable pitch control was working as this would be needed immediately after take-off.

As I did so the expected drop in rpm occurred as the propeller blades went into coarse pitch indicating all was well.

"Let's go flying," I said to myself out loud after an excited intake of breath.

After being given clearance to enter the runway I positioned the Pitts on the centre line, gave the engine instruments one last scan to ensure all was in order; cylinder head temperature, oil pressure and oil temperature and then steadily pushed the throttle forward to full power. As the aircraft accelerated, I pushed forward slightly on the stick to lift the tailwheel off the ground and checked the airspeed indicator as it rushed towards the speed at which the Pitts would lift off. With the engine on full power and indicating nearly 3000 rpm as it roared away in fine pitch I established 100 mph in the climb before reducing rpm to 2500. With the propeller now in course pitch the crescendo of noise in the cockpit abated considerably and about half a minute later I levelled off at 2000 feet. As I did so, the aeroplane accelerated to 170 mph in the cruise. I leaned off the fuel mixture and trimmed for level flight. Oh joy!

I turned back in a wide arc over the airfield and set course for my chosen aerobatics practice area, well away from towns and as far as possible from villages. As I passed directly overhead the runway, I rolled the aircraft inverted momentarily before resuming straight and level upright flight. Many fliers at North Hellidon think I'm a flash bastard and the non-aerobatic pilots amongst them believe this overhead manoeuvre is yet another example of unnecessary showing off. In fact it has a serious purpose. If any fault in my harness or in the inverted systems of the aircraft should occur and the engine cut I'd rather be directly overhead the airfield and better placed for a forced landing than out over some boggy farmland or worse still woodland.

To the south of the airfield that day was a line of fluffy white strato-cumulus clouds with their base at three thousand feet and tops at about seven. Looking like massive dollops of mashed potato or huge soft, white cotton wool mountains they attract adventurous pilots like moths to a candle. I headed for them in the climb arriving alongside at four thousand feet. Whilst the regulations state that under VFR, (Visual Flight Rules) aircraft should remain a prescribed distance clear of cloud both vertically and horizontally, in the same way that Jaguar drivers are exempt from complying with road speed limits, that rule is clearly made to be broken by those in high performance aerobatic aeroplanes. You see, flying straight and level in clear-blue sky one gets no real impression of speed owing to the lack of any static reference point. But as you fly close to clouds, with your wing tip barely brushing the edges at a hundred and eighty miles an hour, zooming around, up and over them, slowing at the peak of the climb as the aircraft runs out of vertical energy then accelerating in a steep dive down the other side you really do feel the speed. It is to my mind the very pinnacle of flying enjoyment. It's simply what aeroplanes are for. The joy is more than doubled when two aircraft tail-chase, the leader trying to lose the chaser by perhaps diving for speed before zoom climbing and rolling inverted over the top of a cloud then pulling steeply down the other side with the follower cutting corners to catch up, trying to get within fifty yards when he can imitate machine gun fire over the RT, "Tacka-tacka-tacka-tack."

All harmless fun provided you maintain some discipline such as agreeing with the other pilot that today you will both only circle the cloud clockwise or anti-clockwise to avoid meeting head on.

The only real risk I guess is if you were to meet a glider coming the other way as they tend to seek out cumulus clouds to benefit from the rising thermals around them.

Well, like I think I said before, with aerobatics you either get it or you don't.

Having enjoyed five minutes of exhilarating cloud flying I headed to an area I often use to practice my aeros routine. After a good look around to ensure there were no other aircraft in the vicinity and having made a few pre-aerobatic checks within the cockpit I dived to a hundred and eighty miles an hour. From level flight I pulled up into a loop, pulling 4g on the first quarter, easing off over the top, checking the wings were level by reference to the horizon whilst I hung weightless, inverted, before gently pulling the stick back to let the nose drop and pulling hard again on the fourth quarter to ensure the loop was perfectly round. As I resumed level flight at the bottom of the loop the Pitts shuddered as I flew through the vortex of disturbed air I'd created as I initiated the manoeuvre. I did it again but this time flicked on the smoke system as I entered the loop, painting a beautiful white circle in the sky which I then flew through again with smoke, just like threading the eye of a giant needle in the air. Within minutes the air sculpture had dissipated.

I flew a few more loops, Cuban eights, stall turns, rolling circles, humpties, four point and two-point rolls before finishing the session with a four-turn spin from four thousand down to two thousand feet.

Feeling very elated and good to be alive I set course back to North Hellidon.

About halfway back I had a close encounter with a glider, not near enough to cause either of us even a quickening of heart rate but enough to cause me to alter course to pass a safe distance to one side. In the air as at sea power gives way to sail and for good measure I gave him quick squirt of smoke just to be sure he had seen me. It is not an uncommon occurrence locally as there is a very active gliding club at a neighbouring airfield about fifteen miles to the south. Mid-air collision is probably the only real danger these days if you're flying a well-maintained aircraft in good weather conditions and on top of your game. Even that risk can be virtually eliminated simply by always maintaining a very good lookout, left, right, above and below, although of course the below bit is the most difficult.

I returned to the airfield, joined the circuit in the overhead and descended 'dead side' to circuit height, slowed the Pitts to a hundred and twenty, called the tower downwind after a few cockpit checks and pushed the prop fully fine as I made a curved descent onto finals. I brought the speed back to a hundred 'down the slope', side-slipping in to improve my view of the runway and to eighty-five over the threshold before setting her down with a tiny, satisfying squeak from the tyres.

I taxied back to the hangar and came to a halt in front of the huge doors. I let the engine idle for a minute with the mixture fully rich, I don't know why but that's what the manual says you must do. I switched off the radio and released my harness. Once the minute was up I pulled the mixture fully lean and the engine rapidly stopped. The roar of the engine that had been with me for the last half hour was replaced by a relaxed hush broken only by a quiet 'tick tick' from the hot engine. I sat for a moment as I always do and enjoyed the silence, as relaxing as a post-coital cigarette.

And to think, some people just play golf.

What joy! I shall do this until the day I die.

Chapter Twenty-Two
First Time with Philippa

I had decided to give Philippa a week to make the next move before I'd call her. I wanted her to have to contact me first but I didn't want to leave it too long in case she'd come to regret the advances in our relationship made during the boozy session last time we met, or with her 'sensible head' on even changed her mind altogether.

I was convinced that she was interested in starting an affair. Had she not said, *'You do know I'd like to get to know you better Charles, don't you?'* Even allowing for the alcohol, what else could that mean other than that she was looking for a relationship but wanted to take it steadily rather than rush into it?

And I'm sure I detected an involuntary fraction of a smile when I'd replied, *'And that's my strong desire too Philippa. I think you've known that from the start.'* And had I not added, *'You must learn to loosen up'* and *'I want to get close and intimate with you'*, evidently without instantly scaring her off'?

Yes, if she called me first it would mean she was definitely up for it and I'd have nothing to lose by speeding up the seduction. If it had been left to me to make contact, it would require an investment in time and tactics that I wasn't sure I could be bothered with.

She called me at lunchtime five days after our meeting in the bar, suggesting that we got together that evening, perhaps for dinner. I was amazed. There was such a change in her voice, so different from our last phone conversation. Gone was the cool, aloof, self-confident voice replaced by a familiar, affectionate tone as if we'd been dating for months. I detected though a slight note of nervousness in her voice, almost breaking at one point and although she was very friendly, I got the impression that she wanted to keep the call short.

I suggested we meet in a pub close to my flat for a 'sharpener' before deciding where we'd eat. Actually I didn't mention that it was near my home but it was somewhere she'd seen while driving to work and was happy to make her own way there.

We'd arranged to meet at seven-thirty but she didn't arrive until ten to eight. I saw her through the pub window, checking her hair in the mirror of her Mercedes sports car's sun visor and touching up her lipstick. I watched as she crossed the car park and I rose to greet her as she entered the bar. She looked fantastic. She was wearing the same tight-fitting black silk trousers that she wore last time we met, the same loose sheer, white blouse too but there was no slip this time to hide any trace of her tiny bra. I kissed her on both cheeks which she offered willingly with a smile but I detected a slight shiver as I touched her gently on both hips as I did so.

Philippa looked amazing. I guessed that she'd spent the afternoon at her hairdresser as her auburn locks looked and smelled freshly crafted as I'd not seen them before. Her make-up was again discreet but expertly applied and her nails immaculate in the same red gloss as last time. She wore the same red high heels too.

I ordered a couple of gin and tonics and we settled around a corner table for some preliminary small talk before discussing where to eat. She seemed nervous and pre-occupied as we spoke, so much so that that I asked if she was OK.

We talked about the weather and work, and flying and her pitiful colleagues, but made no mention of our inebriated conversation at the bar less than a week ago. I'd steer the conversation around to it after some more alcohol. Her nervousness evaporated at the same rate as the level in her glass decayed. It was empty before mine so I necked the rest of my gin and asked if she wanted another. She declined and asked where I planned to take her for dinner adding that she'd prefer 'something light'. I thought better of suggesting Italian and cringed for a nanosecond as I remembered our excruciating high drama lunch at Luigi's.

I ran through a few options and we settled on a local bistro a walkable distance away after I'd asked jokingly if she could manage two hundred yards 'in those shoes'.

"I'll take them off if I need to make a run for it," she quipped with increasing confidence.

I laughed at her little joke but wondered if it was perhaps a subconscious slip betraying her earlier nervousness. Did she feel she might have to escape at some point? Was she embarking on a journey about which she hadn't yet fully made up her mind, one from which she might need to cut and run?

'Monet's' was situated in a large cellar beneath a Regency terrace in the high street, opposite the offices of the pretentiously named advertising agency where Alice had briefly worked and made such a lasting impression, no doubt still laughed about by management, staff and clients alike. I drove past it every day and always had to look up at the window boxes on the first-floor balcony and chuckle as I pictured Alice over-watering them whilst deliberately treating her male colleagues to a glimpse of her scanty knickers. At times like that I have to admit that I do love her in a way, a joy to be with and ever happy, my little airhead, so different from the woman I was dining with that night.

The bistro is approached down a steep flight of steps from the pavement lined with tall, black railings topped with ornate gold-painted spearheads. It has a surprisingly high ceiling for a basement and is cheaply furnished in a style favoured by the achingly trendy metropolitan ladies who lunch. The dozen or so scrubbed, bare wooden tables are supplemented by a smaller number of converted antique sewing machine stands which although fitted with flat table-tops still feature the ironmongery that once supported the treadles that powered them. Diners sit on old rickety wooden chairs of various designs, though all make the same painful screeching sound as they scrape against the bare York stone floor.

The walls are decorated with prints of popular Monet paintings and some of his lesser known works together with reproduction 1930s Riviera travel posters, unrelated rustic artefacts, crudely framed mirrors, inconceivably large wooden spoons and ladles, stone liquor jars, and empty classic French wine bottles, all no doubt bought at car boot sales just outside Calais; or perhaps Camden Market.

High on the wall behind the bar is a large, artificially distressed, painted wooden sign bearing the name of the establishment. Beneath it is a five feet wide mirror reflecting, from the opposite wall an almost equally sized print of the famous impressionist work, *A Bar at the Folies Bergere.*

The effect created is that the late nineteenth century waitress reflected in the mirror appears to be serving behind this bar too.

I'd in the past been impressed by this clever visual illusion until Philippa pointed out in a whisper that the painting in question was actually the work of Eduard Manet rather than Claude Monet.

The restaurant wasn't busy but I selected a table in a corner away from the three or four couples already dining. I wanted to get the conversation round to 'relationships' again as soon as I could and to persuade Philippa back to my place for coffee and sex after the meal. It would be much easier if we didn't have to whisper.

"G&T?" I asked after seating her at the table.

"Yes please, just a single."

I went to the bar to collect a couple of menu cards and I ordered a gin and tonic for her but secretly just a tonic water for myself.

I returned to the table with the drinks which we sipped as we perused the limited offering.

We both selected scallops to start and whilst I opted for the thinly sliced calves' liver with green beans, Philippa decided on a crab salad.

I asked the waitress for a bottle of Chilean Sauvignon but before she could jot it down on her order pad Philippa interjected. "Oh no, just a glass for me, a small one and water."

"Still or sparkling?" was the gushingly attentive waitress's programmed response.

"Tap water will be fine thanks," said Philippa as the girl hid her disappointment with an affected smile.

I was surprised and a little concerned that this might indicate a determination on her part not to get as inebriated as she had been on our last date. A slight tremor in her hand as she raised the glass to her lips had again betrayed her nervousness.

I asked for a small carafe instead of a bottle, stressing the word 'small' as that implied I was sensitive to Philippa's request, although I knew it would contain a generous half litre, most of which I'd contrive that she would consume.

As we awaited the scallops, I got to work.

"You're looking particularly gorgeous this evening, angel. Love the hair."

I reached out meaning to tenderly touch her hand but at that instant she picked up a piece of bread and dunked it into a little dish of balsamic vinegar and olive oil. She spotted the gesture and seemed amused at my clumsiness. It put her at ease though and she giggled and touched my fingertips briefly to indicate that the advance was not unwelcome. It meant though that she'd had to change hands to meet my right with her left and in doing so dropped the balsamic-soaked bread against her breast leaving a dark brown stain on her delicate white blouse.

"Fuck!" she snapped, dabbing the mark with a red paper napkin.

Her chair screeched on the stone floor with the sound of fingernails being scratched down a blackboard as she rose to her feet. She excused herself from the table and hurried to the ladies' toilet to clean up after apologising for the outburst. It was the first time I'd heard her swear.

She returned to the table after five minutes looking a little embarrassed. The dark stain had been reduced to a lighter coloured damp patch but in attending to the impromptu laundry, no doubt by rubbing a wet paper towel inside and outside of her blouse, she had neglected to fasten up all the buttons. As she leaned forward to settle back into her chair, I was treated to an intimate glimpse of her tiny cleavage created more it appeared by the design of her bra rather than the very limited amplitude of her breasts.

Philippa drank the remains of her gin and immediately took a gulp of the white wine which had arrived whilst she'd been in the loo. After a second sip I topped up her glass from the carafe.

We ate and talked and drank. A second carafe followed during the main course and we chose coffee rather than desert. During the meal I'd steered the conversation around to our last meeting and our mutual desire for a relationship. She concurred rather than backing off so I took her hand and kissed her fingertips to cement the decision. As we talked our prolonged eye contact caused stirrings in both of us. At least I assumed it was in both of us as I sensed Philippa was aroused because she kept modestly looking away before regaining my glances. At the appropriate moment I took both of her hands in mine, leaned forward and gently kissed her lips. It was very brief and she did not resist.

Sadly, she wasn't as drunk or clingy as she had been last time and although the meal was almost over I hadn't managed to reach the point at which a sexual proposition was likely to succeed.

Later we walked slowly arm in arm towards the pub where we'd earlier left our cars, Philippa leaning on me from time to time as she struggled in her high heels to match my pace. She slipped her arm from mine and took my hand. Hers was slim, long-fingered but dwarfed in mine. I thought ahead to the possibility of an imminent parting in the pub car park and the disruption to my amorous plans and as the distance was so short took perhaps my last opportunity to get her alone. I steered her into a dimly lit shop doorway and held her in a full-frontal clinch. I kissed her gently and I felt what I took to be a shudder of excitement flow through her. As I released my grip on her, she sort of belched and pulled away. I think it was a belch, or possibly a retch as she produced a tissue from her handbag and wiped her mouth. She was embarrassed but continued to hold my hand until we reached the cars.

"My place for coffee?" I suggested. "It's just two minutes from here."

She looked nervous and didn't answer.

"Come on, angel," I pleaded in a tone making clear that more than coffee was at stake. "Let's get this relationship started."

"Yes…OK," she sighed after an interminable pause.

I persuaded her that we should take my car, that hers would be safe there and that I'd walk her back later to allay any fears she might have that it was an overnight invitation.

We got into my car and kissed again. We drove in silence the short distance to my apartment and through the automatic barrier into the underground car park.

Once into my flat I selected some soothing music on *Spotify* and started to brew coffee as Philippa wandered around the place like a nervous animal tentatively exploring its new quarters at a zoo. I watched her unseen from the kitchen as she looked up at the ceilings and through the windows, ran her fingers over the furniture and opened doors to survey adjoining rooms before sitting upright on the sofa, hands on her knees.

Her body language appeared so defensive that I cracked a joke to put her at ease.

"It's alright, you can leave as soon as we've had sex," I shouted from the kitchen.

She laughed.

"Oh, that's a relief. I was worried you might hold me prisoner."

The exchange brought about an amazing change in her demeanour. Having kicked off her shoes, she slowly drifted into the kitchen, approached me from behind and hugged me as I stood at the sink.

"I don't want coffee, Charles. Let's just do what we came here to do," she whispered. I was stunned at the ease with which we'd got to this point.

I turned and kissed her again and led her into the bedroom, pointing out the en-suite.

"Do you want to be first with the bathroom?" I enquired, as I moved to turn back the duvet. It was a question I had asked many women before in that room.

I returned to the kitchen and selected a bottle of champagne from the fridge returning with two glasses between the fingers of one hand the neck of the bottle grasped in the other. I dimmed the lights, removed my jacket and hung it in the fitted wardrobe. I unlaced my shoes and kicked them into a corner. I was unbuttoning my shirt excitedly anticipating the sight of Philippa emerging naked from the bathroom or stripping slowly for my pleasure when the bathroom door opened barely an inch.

"Charles, I'm not sure I can do this," she said, her voice barely above a murmur.

I was stunned into silence. I've been taken close in my time but this took the biscuit. I was still thinking of something to say to recover the situation when she suddenly sprinted from the bathroom in her lacy knickers and bra, leaning forward as if to make herself less visible and made a dash for my bed to conceal her embarrassment, slipped in and pulled the duvet up close to her chin.

"The bathroom's free," she offered as if inviting me to have a wash or perhaps just to delay the proceedings.

I popped the cork and poured her a glass of bubbly which I offered with an outstretched hand. She was though evidently not prepared to let go her grip on the guarding screen of the duvet and simply indicated with a nod that I should place it on the bedside table.

I took my turn in the bathroom where I found Philippa's clothes neatly folded in the bath. I stripped off and had a quick wash but had such a hard-on that although I tried I couldn't pee. My JT was simply pointing the wrong way. Never mind.

I'd never done this before for other women but I found myself putting my pants back on before stepping into the dimly lit bedroom, my erection making it look as if I had a loofah down my underpants.

I approached the bed and untangled myself from my pants which in my haste I'd twisted into a figure of eight when hurrying into them but lost my balance and fell sideways onto the bed. My embarrassment was reduced considerably when I noticed that Philippa had been studiously looking away.

"At last, my angel, we're alone," I whispered.

I slipped rampant into bed alongside her, holding her close and kissing her mouth and neck. She shivered with what at first I mistook for pleasure. I lifted the duvet a little to steal a peep at her slender body. She was tall and of fragile build, with a minimum of flesh to cover her bones. In the potting shed of life she'd probably have been pricked out as an under-developed seedling.

I slowly unclipped her bra and dropped it to one side of the bed. I pulled down her panties just far enough to be able to hook my toe over the elastic and with my leg slipped them down and over her feet. I reached for them and pinged them like a catapult across the room. I was ready. She was not.

What followed was the most unsatisfying sexual encounter of my life. It was as astonishing as it was embarrassing for both of us. She had willingly agreed to sleep with me but was so tense that she could not have taken any enjoyment from it at all. My gentle foreplay actually seemed to make her less prepared. I cuddled her affectionately for more than ten minutes but the proximity of my member seemed to worry rather than excite her. I asked her if she wanted me to stop but she looked in my eyes probably for the first time since we'd got into bed and shook her head.

"Sorry, I'm fine," she said. "It's all right. Honestly."

She looked away as I rolled on a condom as if frightened or disgusted at the sight. We did start to have sex but she was so rigid that it brought no joy to either of us. It seemed, I thought, that she was straining for an orgasm but was so tense she even squeezed me out a couple of times.

I realised it wasn't going to happen for either of us so I withdrew and to make her feel better made a joke of it, blaming the alcohol.

"Don't worry, angel, perhaps it was a bit too rushed and we've both had far too much to drink."

Whether out of affection or embarrassment I'll never know but instead of escaping my bed in a hurry as she might have done, it appeared she just wanted to be cuddled while lying on her side facing away from me. I removed my arms from around her but straight away she reached behind her, found my hand and returned it to her waist. I slipped it up to cup a breast but she immediately grabbed my wrist and returned it to her hip. Perhaps too much territory had been surrendered too soon. I'd never before experienced this reaction from a woman.

I left her in bed after a while and went to make some tea. Before it had brewed, she was dressed and joined me in the kitchen, again approaching and cuddling me from behind.

"I'm so sorry, darling. Don't be cross," she whispered.

I was pissed off but I decided for now to keep my options open and not let it show. Philippa had after all called me 'Darling' for the first time, suggesting that for her at least this didn't mark the end of our relationship.

"Don't worry, angel. Have some tea and I'll walk you back to your car."

I returned to the apartment after she'd driven away and lazed in a bath while I drank the glass of champagne Philippa had left untouched at the bedside. The champagne was as flat as my spirits and I began to analyse the events of the evening. It had been a fiasco from start to finish and perhaps it served me right for rushing things, for being too eager to get her into bed. But as I contemplated Philippa's joyless reaction and non-participation my mind inevitably drifted to Alice. It was impossible not to draw a comparison. How differently she would have performed, how enthusiastic, how energetic, how demanding, how downright ball-drainingly sexy.

Why was I bothering with Philippa? What was the point exactly? OK, she was intellectually stimulating but I didn't want a relationship. It was just a sexual adventure and the sex was clearly not going to be worth the trouble. And certainly not worth the risk of losing my lovely, sexy, perfect little porn star. Now there's a thought. I could lose her and instead be left with just a clingy lawyer who doesn't like sex! I held thoughts of Alice as I settled into bed and switched off the lights.

In my half sleep Alice was astride me, leaning forward with her ample breasts gently stoking my chest as she gyrated rhythmically back and forth, when I was jolted awake by the phone at my bedside. Could it be Alice calling me to a late-night assignation after Ken had departed to catch an early flight to USA for ten days? If so, I could be with her in less than half an hour.

No, it was Philippa. Philippa in tears. I glanced at my watch; it was 2 am.

"Charles, I'm so sorry," she sobbed. "I wanted it to be perfect but I don't know what came over me. I should have stayed and..." She didn't finish the sentence.

"What? Stayed and persevered?" I suggested cruelly.

"No, just not left in such a hurry. To talk about it, to explain. I'm so sorry to have disappointed you. You will see me again, won't you? Don't let this be the end."

What a character change; no longer the assertive, confident, professional woman but belittled, submissive, pleading.

"I love you, Charles, and I so want to be with you. Please can we try again?"

I could have dumped her there and then but decided it might be interesting to play along for a while provided I was careful not to let it interfere with 'the main attraction'. I'd keep my options open and in fact it might be an awful lot easier now that I well and truly had the upper hand.

"Philly, darling!" I said, adopting the uninvited diminutive, "Don't be silly, I fully understand. Don't worry. What do you think I am? I told you, we simply both had too much to drink."

"Yes, it was that, wasn't it," she replied, her sobs subsiding and her tone becoming more composed.

It was perhaps a little unkind but I couldn't resist it.

"And I'm sure you'll join in next time."

There was a long pause and I sensed she had perhaps lost it again before she answered in a faltering voice.

"I'm sorry, I'll try to please you. I'll do anything for you, Charles…but don't …let me down."

I'm sure she'd been about to say 'Don't hurt me' but felt that would be too demeaning. Still, no matter. I knew where I stood and I looked forward to the next stage in the seduction of Miss Philippa Stapleton LLB (Hons).

Chapter Twenty-Three
Take Me Home

Aunt Margaret was transferred from intensive care to a general surgical ward after two days and awoke from her coma exactly a week following her admission to hospital. I'd shared the vigil with her friend Jessica who did the afternoon shift, handing over the watch to me at six in the evening and I would stay until midnight. It was the longest week of my life. At first, I just sat by her bed holding her hand and thinking back over our years together. When I was told she was out of danger, I occupied myself with other thoughts and simply waited for her to come round. I really wanted to be there when she emerged from the long sleep. She was connected up to various tubes. If conscious she might have tolerated the twin oxygen lines that entered her nostrils, crudely secured in place with what looked like masking tape, but would have been mortified to find herself being drained by a urinary catheter into a plastic bag hanging from her bed frame for all to see.

She was initially fortified by a glucose drip which entered her arm through thin tubing concealed by an adhesive bandage. A few days later this was replaced by another tube which fed her an unappetising looking grey liquid through her nose. I asked a humourless staff nurse if the fluid came in a range of flavours, suggesting that if so my aunt would I'm sure prefer the lobster bisque.

Margaret was given the lightest of blanket baths by the nursing staff and her eyes seemed to be continually sealed with sleep so I took it upon myself to gently wipe them with a damp tissue.

I was told it might be helpful to talk to her and did so until I ran out of family memories, stories she'd told me about wartime London, and idle chit chat.

I whispered to her,

"Come on, Auntie, I know you can hear me. You're nearly awake, aren't you? Just make that extra effort and open your eyes. Come on now, do it for me."

After the umpteenth time I was beginning to doubt the theory and in desperation raised my voice slightly and said,

"Margaret, for fuck's sake wake up, will you!"

To my astonishment there was a flicker of her left eye lid and then the right. She was straining against the sleep-encrusted lids to open her eyes. I wiped them again and she opened them fully.

"Hello, Auntie," I said, struggling to overcome the lump in my throat, "Welcome back."

A nurse noticed her awakening and busily took over. She grabbed Margaret's right hand and slapped it quite vigorously and spoke to her loudly as if she were stone deaf. She shook Margaret's shoulder so forcefully that I was almost moved to intervene. I became quite cross and decided that the best course of action was to go for some tea at the hospital visitors' cafeteria that I had discovered on day two of my vigil and leave the nurse to do whatever she'd been taught to do to in that situation.

I had a little difficulty swallowing the tea owing to the lump in my throat and was worried that if anyone spoke to me I might burst into tears. It was a very emotional moment, a mixture of relief and elation swept over me. In my ignorance I assumed that her emergence from the coma had guaranteed her survival.

When I returned to the ward, the curtains around her bed space were being drawn back. She was sleeping and seemed somehow more peaceful. Remarkably her severe facial bruising was fading fast and it appeared that the nurse had brushed her hair and tidied her clothing. The pillows behind her had been plumped up and she looked serene. Margaret was no longer a comatose body. The character had re-entered her. I smiled at the thought that she'd soon be keeping the callous nurse on her toes, and no doubt correcting her grammar too.

I returned next morning to find Margaret sitting up in bed drinking a cup of weak tea and eating a biscuit. It was thin and sugary and she ate it hesitantly, breaking off very small pieces before offering them to her mouth as if they were foul-tasting tablets. I made a mental note to bring some of her favourite *Peek Freans* shortbreads on my visit that evening.

My aunt had no recollection of her fall or the events that had brought her to hospital. She was totally lucid but had difficulty believing that she'd been there for eight days. I gave her a sanitised account of events; that she'd had a fall without breaking any bones and had been very well looked after by the ambulance and triage staff. I didn't mention my break-in, or the carpet ruined by blood and urine, or the twenty-four-hour delay in my finding her.

In fact I had already tidied up the living room, stripped out the carpet that was beyond cleaning and attended to the bloodstained floor beneath it. I had by then ordered a replacement carpet which was to be fitted a couple of days later. I had also gathered a few personal items of clothing for her at the hospital's request, nightclothes, a shawl and toiletries. I'd felt extremely uncomfortable going through her bedroom drawers and whilst doing so made an extraordinary discovery, one that gave me an astonishing insight into her personal life that shocked me greatly. But I'll tell you more about that later.

"Oliver darling, I want you to do something for me," she whispered, signalling me to come closer.

"I want you to take me home. Today."

"I can't do that, Auntie, you're not well enough yet, but I will just as soon as I can."

"I want to go home now," she insisted. "It's dirty in here."

"Dirty? Auntie. What makes you say that?"

Margaret touched my arm and drew me closer before whispering,

"I asked to go to the loo, but they wouldn't take me. Just told me to go ahead and do it in the bed!"

"That's alright Auntie, you have a catheter fitted." I replied trying not to snigger. "Didn't the nurse explain that?"

Margaret's face was a picture of disbelief, and horror as she realised how intimately she'd been handled in her sleep. She sat quietly for a moment before saying that she felt fit enough to go home and would anyway be more comfortable in her own bed. She then demonstrated her mental rather than physical recovery by telling me that she'd put six pounds in an envelope for the milkman and that I'd find it in her bookshelf between copies of *Wuthering Heights* and *Rise and Fall of the Roman Empire.*

I visited Margaret the next day, after calling at her home as requested to collect any mail and to roll the envelope containing the six pounds into a tube and poke it into the neck of an empty milk bottle placed on the doorstep. It looked like the fuse on a Molotov cocktail. To my astonishment Margaret was out of bed and sitting in an armchair at her bedside. She looked very tired indeed, and very unwell. The nurse explained that it was policy to get patients out of bed as soon as possible as this aided recovery and prevented bedsores and other complications. One didn't need any medical training however to see that the act of moving the frail old lady had set her back considerably. She was fatigued to the point of tears and pleaded to be put back into bed. I'd never seen her so low. The nurse ignored my request with the arrogance of a surgeon faced with a self-diagnosing hypochondriac, but I went over her head and the Ward Sister could see at a glance that my aunt had taken a serious turn for the worse.

The green curtains were once more closed around the bed space and I stood helplessly listening to Margaret's squeals of pain and protest as she was repositioned back into bed. The Sister emerged through the curtains like a pantomime dame to announce that the show was being brought to a premature close as the leading lady had in fact broken the proverbial leg.

"Your aunt is very tired. I think it's best we let her sleep. The doctor will see her on his evening rounds. Why don't you come back tomorrow, I'll give you a call if there's any need."

I had a deep feeling of impending doom and stood there for a moment searching for an excuse to stay. But found none.

I recalled an occasion a year or two earlier when, over coffee after a Saturday morning shopping trip to Waitrose, Margaret had raised with me the hypothetical question of her future infirmity. She made it clear that if incapacitated she wanted to be nursed at home rather than in hospital and extracted from me a promise that I would never, put her in 'one of those frightful establishments in which people smelling of liniment sit around all day weaving baskets and waiting for death'. I began to plan for the recruitment of a suitable live-in nurse and wondered how many hundreds I'd have to interview to find one with the right mix of medical knowledge, manners, intellect and class to pass muster with my aunt.

The thoughts drove me to go once more to Prince's Avenue and conduct a cursory preliminary study of how the place might be adapted to accommodate a live-in nurse. It also occurred to me that I'd better give some serious thought to the documents I'd need to get Margaret to sign in order that I could manage the many investments, both mine and hers, in the event that she became too infirm to do so later. These thoughts were not just influenced by the awful sight of her deteriorating condition but also by what I'd found at her house the previous day. As I looked for a nightdress and shawl in her bedroom I found in the wardrobe several bundles of documents together with two shoe boxes of family photographs, many of which I could recall seeing at some point in my childhood.

The parcels were marked either with the words, 'Letters – Destroy Do not Open' or 'Various Documents – Read if you like, then Destroy'.

In the Utility Room I found a cardboard carton labelled, 'Old Magazines 1947-53'. There were several more catalogued with various other dates. Another contained old Christmas and Birthday cards dating back over five decades.

There was a 1930s' style cabin trunk with reinforced corners that reminded me of the elbow patches on my headmaster's sports jacket, seen only at Saturday afternoon rugger matches, or when he was encountered in town and impossible to avoid. It was simply labelled, 'Oliver'.

Inside was every single painting that I had ever brought home from school. I'd always felt a pang of disappointment when they were removed from the walls of the kitchen or the door of the fridge after only twenty-four hours, when in my friend's homes theirs hung proudly for weeks. I had always assumed that Margaret had binned them after dutifully playing the proud guardian role for just as long as she could manage before they made the place look untidy.

The birthday and Christmas cards I'd at first made for her and later bought for her, were there also, all filed in chronological order.

I felt so saddened. My aunt had clearly been busy putting her affairs in order in preparation for death.

I returned to the bedroom to collect the clothes and toiletries that I'd accumulated on her bed when I spotted on the bedside table the ever-present framed photograph of Peter. Peter the tragic, ever-smiling, ever-youthful fiancé.

I thought it would please Margaret to have it with her in hospital, as I felt it safe to assume she'd rarely spent a night in her life without it at her side. It would also give her a conversation piece with the nurses and fellow patients in the ward.

As I picked it up, it slipped from my hand and fell to the carpet, breaking into several pieces. The glass didn't shatter but the four pieces of the frame and the backing card separated like the bones of a skeleton dropped onto a museum floor. I carefully picked up the pieces wondering whether to take just the photograph and reveal my clumsiness or wait a day or so until I'd had it repaired. I then found a seventh component of the relic. A carefully folded one-page letter had been hidden behind the picture held in place by the backing card. It was well thumbed and torn in places through regular unfolding and refolding. I felt compelled to read it.

I hadn't in the past considered my aunt capable of any physical love and had always assumed that, as they were never married, that she and Peter had not had sex. I'd seen her as a virgin spinster, a victim like myself of unrequited love. But the letter painted a very different picture.

Tangmere, September 4th 1940

My dearest Maggie,

I miss you so much and can't wait to see you again my darling.

Leave is out of the question at present as the weather is perfect. It's all too bloody.

We are all exhausted and God, how we pray for rain!

I'll get up to see you when we next get a 48, which please God will be soon.

When I see you I'm going to fuck you and fuck you.

The sentence continued over both pages before ending with:

...and then I'm going to fuck you again.

Your everloving,

Peter
XXXXXX

When I reached the hospital that evening, I was told that Margaret had taken a turn for the worse and was again in a coma. A doctor took me into a small, untidy office and told me that my aunt was very frail and that her chances of survival were quite slim.

"She's very weak, and her body has taken a serious shock. You should prepare yourself…" He didn't finish the sentence.

"But she was sitting in a chair a few hours ago!" I protested. "To aid recovery the nurse said!"

"Well, yes. But at her age…"

They'd clearly cocked up. She hadn't been ready to get out of bed and the stress of being manhandled had been too much for her. I was furious, and frightened.

I sat with Margaret throughout that evening and most of the night.

At one point she started to have difficulty breathing and developed a worrying rattle in her chest. A pair of nursing assistants came and drained fluid from her upper respiratory tract using a suction tube which appeared to be plumbed into a vacuum system running around the ward and serving each bed through a terminal above the headboard. The relief lasted only about half an hour before the awful sound of her restricted breathing started again. Over the course of three hours the nurses repeated the process once more on their own initiative and twice more at my insistence. They were clearly expecting her to die in her sleep and I realised in horror what the term 'death rattle' means.

A doctor was called to examine her and to explain to me that Margaret was fading away and wouldn't last the night. I challenged him on the need to keep her comfortable, to ease her breathing but he answered by telling me it was 'the sound of her body shutting down'. They humoured me by repeating the suction process again later that night before she passed quietly away in the early hours of the morning. I held her hand as she died. She took one last gasp of breath that filled her lungs and raised her ribcage either in joy or defiance I'll never know, then exhaled very slowly for the last time. Sadly Peter wasn't there at her bedside.

I kissed her and left.

Chapter Twenty-Four
The Wake

Two weeks had passed since Hermione turned down my proposal of marriage. She hadn't been at all surprised by the question. I think she'd been expecting it for some time and was perhaps even relieved that I'd given her the opportunity to finally make it clear she wanted no change in our friendship, no advance in our relationship, and to end my hopes forever. She was characteristically unemotional about it and explained dispassionately that in truth I was her perfect man. She liked me and loved me and respected me. But she wasn't in love with me. That damning phrase again.

There was no one else in her life and whenever I'd heard her talking to a friend or to her sister on the phone, her answer to the obvious but unheard question was, "No, there's no one at the moment, it's a desert out there." Once when I expressed disbelief that such a beautiful woman didn't have a legion of suitors waiting in line, she'd unguardedly responded, "Well, you're a hard act to follow." A hard act to follow? Did I miss something? Had we had an affair so torrid that my brain had burst in ecstasy leaving me in a permanent state of amnesia?

The only consolation I could draw from the enigma of our continued close friendship in the face of my irrepressible expressions of love, was that she did love me but was simply too sensible and too practical to contemplate marriage to a man so much older than herself. The moment passed, the episode seemed forgotten and she just carried on as before being warm, and friendly, and determinedly independent. And I continued to be aged by the suppressed emotion.

Hermione was tirelessly helpful in the arrangements for Margaret's funeral. She made phone calls to strangers to spread the word, as I was initially too choked to do it myself. She ordered the flowers, recorded music to be played at the service and booked a private room upstairs at Luigi's for the small group of mourners which because of our much-pruned family tree comprised of many more friends than relations.

She looked so elegant in her stylish coat and little black dress and Tristan was a model child in a smart suit and black tie. Not a single fart broke the solemn silence in the chilly chapel of rest. He was the only child in attendance and rose to the occasion perfectly. At one point I saw him chatting politely and intelligently to Jessica after lunch as they sat at the dining table as other guests were departing, and I caught him maturely patting her wrist in a sympathetic gesture between the empty coffee cups and discarded napkins. I was proud of him. Perhaps given the chance I could have cared for him as Margaret had for me.

I expressed my gratitude to the vicar for his word-perfect rendition of the eulogy I'd written in praise of Margaret's character and thanking her for raising me and educating me, for her patience and her love. I thanked her too for her wit and good example, for her unfailing support and loving me and treating me as her own. I owed her everything I had and everything I would ever have. I couldn't thank her enough.

As my words left his mouth, I said silently to myself that the only thing she didn't give me was the warm physical affection I'd always craved from her.

Hermione and her boy were the last guests to leave. Luigi had insisted we have a private drink with him whilst a middle-aged waiter made a fuss of Tristan. He may have appeared to me more grown up than I'd ever seen him before but the playful Italian lifted the heavy boy and carried him off to the kitchen like a bambino over his shoulder.

Hermione went home to her house and I returned to the farm, exhausted by the stress of the previous weeks and emotionally drained by the events of the day. I returned to work the following morning to the predictable pleasure of Hermione's smile and comforting 'first coffee' ritual. Where would it all end? When would it all end? In two short months in fact.

Chapter Twenty-Five
The Happiest Day of My Life

You won't believe this! It's incredible. Has Margaret had a word with God? Has she bustled into his outer office and brushed past his stern bespectacled gate guardian, demanding an immediate audience? Did feathers fly as angel wings were flapped in panic at the intrusion? Did the upstart newcomer point out to him the evident shortcomings in the zodiac? Had she persuaded him to pull himself together and sort things out?

Hermione called me last night. It was just before ten thirty and I was about to retire. I'd just completed the nightly walk round, locking the front and back doors and checking the windows, switching off the outside lights that illuminated the driveway and the stable yard. I was loading the dishwasher when the phone rang.

It was a pleasant surprise to hear from her at such a late hour and as we exchanged pleasantries I pictured her standing there scantily clad and ready for bed. She would have removed her make-up and brushed her hair, and her lovely breath would have smelled of toothpaste. Oh my God, Superman would be flying again tonight.

I thought perhaps she'd received a worrying call from a workmate passing on some unfounded rumour about the office closure and was calling me for reassurance so that she could sleep in peace. Or perhaps Tristan was ill and she was calling to say that she wouldn't be at work next day. She knew I was planning to be at CHQ in the morning and not expected into my office until lunchtime.

After inconsequential chat about the smell of paint from the newly repaired vestibule door she came straight out with it. "Oliver, if you still want me, we will come to live with you."

I was stunned into silence. Was I dreaming? Did I hear her correctly? Had all my dreams come true?

"I don't mean marry you," she continued, "but if you want we can just live together and see how things go."

We'd arranged to meet at Luigi's for lunch at twelve and I'm already thirty minutes late because that idiot George kept droning on about the move. I hardly heard a word anyone said at the meeting as I was so happy and so excited thinking about the future. Life is going to change so much. I'll give up work, and so can Hermione if she wants to. The world is going to be our scallop at last!

I phoned to say I'll be there in twenty minutes and told her to ask Luigi to put some champagne on ice. I can't wait. I can't wait! I'm so excited and strangely nervous too. How different it will be when we meet. At last I can hold her properly, from the front, breast to chest rather than hip to hip. Yes, lightly hold her by both hips, and gently kiss her mouth at last.

Oh joy! I'm the happiest man alive.

I'm late. I better get a move on.

Chapter Twenty-Six
Woman on Top

The vision of Alice in my early hours' half-sleep that night materialised in every detail a couple of days later. Two days in which I'd received no less than six calls from Philippa, four emails and several texts, all suggesting we meet again soon and most containing pitiful apologies for the non-event. I had, after a tactical delay of course, replied briefly to all of them, each response attempting to put her at ease in order to keep my options open rather than to make her feel better but I hadn't committed to a firm date to meet. I explained I was 'extremely busy sorting issues with the current project but would see her again very soon.' I held back from telling her that frankly I'd rather have sex on my own or that I doubted she'd ever loosen up enough to enjoy it herself because I had a strong feeling that there was no point in writing her off completely just yet. What a bastard I am.

Alice had summoned me to call on her for some 'afternoon delight' with a suggestion that I should have a restful morning as I'd need all of my energy and added a reminder to bring the dice.

On the drive over I recalled an earlier occasion on which I had been similarly summonsed to attend for an afternoon session. I laughed out loud at the memory. She would normally greet me at the front door to speed me inside but on this visit I'd had to ring the doorbell to get her attention. She didn't respond but a buzzer sounded and the door automatically unlocked and inched open.

Alice's disembodied sexy voice tempted me from above.

"I'm waiting for you Big Boy, come and find me."

What a delightful little tease. A trail of clothing led up the stairs, a skirt, a blouse, silk stockings, panties, a bra.

Anticipating encountering her naked, lying on the bed and ready for action I instead found her sitting in an armchair fully clothed.

"Sorry," she said, "I just dropped the laundry basket, you might have picked them up!"

This time I arrived to find her in a white towelling dressing gown of the type provided by decent hotels usually with a polite note attached assuring that they were freshly laundered but reminding you they were available to purchase at reception, no doubt to reduce the number stolen by guests when checking out also carrying a month's supply of shampoo, conditioner, body lotion and shower cap, leaving only the shoe shine pad and the useless little vanity kit containing a ready-threaded needle and neutral coloured shirt button. *Do people ever use those?* I wonder.

Alice was horny, so much so that she didn't mention the dice until after we'd romped. Within five minutes of crossing the threshold I was flat on my back in the guest bed being teased by those playful puppies.

What a contrast!

She took my member into her mouth as she invariably did during our foreplay but this time held it more tightly than usual, using her teeth a lot more than her lips and tongue. In fact, it hurt and I yelped. She looked me in the eyes and smiled.

In the post-coital glow she lay alongside me with one leg between mine and an arm across my chest whilst gently biting my earlobe and talking the delightful nonsense that alternately amused and annoyed me. She wittered on for ten minutes; the lull before the storm.

I doubt the small talk was a diversion as Alice was not that devious but she had an astonishing ability to ambush me with a sudden change of subject or outrageous comment.

She gently combed with her fingers the hair on my chest for several minutes as we talked. Then, as she often did at such times propped herself up on her elbow and pointlessly played with my limp willy, waggling it from side to side like a floppy rubber toy.

She looked down at my penis but whispered into my ear.

"Well, Mr Wibbly-Wobbly, have you shagged the lawyer yet?"

I was stunned and took so long to answer that my silence betrayed me.

"What?" I shouted. "For God's sake, Alice, don't start all that again. No I haven't and if it helps, I don't want to either!"

"Bet you have," she replied in a baby voice as if talking to Big Nob but still addressing my willy. And although her tone made it clear she wasn't looking for an argument she firmly gripped my scrotum in an unmistakable warning.

"Because you know what would happen if you did."

"Alice, for the last time!"

"Alright, but you are intrigued by her, aren't you?" was her next gambit.

"No, for God's sake, how many times must I say it? She's a flat-chested Plain Jane and as sexy as a plank. Now can we stop this nonsense before I get cross?"

To my relief she dropped the subject as quickly as she'd raised it but left me unconvinced that it was the end of the matter.

Alice slipped slowly out of bed and walked over to the adjoining en-suite taking exaggeratedly tiny steps, clenching her buttocks while covering her bum cleavage with a protective hand and keeping her knees together in a much-repeated little joke. The 'bed to loo shuffle' she called it. I'd seen it many times before but it still made me laugh and I was grateful that she seemed to have dropped the accusations.

I heard the flush of the toilet and the gush of the power shower. A bare leg seductively appeared around the door followed by a finger beckoning me to join her. I needed no further invitation and moved into the cubicle alongside her. She wore a very large flower-patterned shower cap pulled down to her eyebrows and covering all of her hair and neck and giving a very good impression from a Victoria Wood sketch pulled a face and said in a Lancashire accent,

"I'm looking for me friend… Kimberly…'ave yer seen 'er?"

We laughed and cuddled in the shower and soaped each other. I pampered the puppies and in return and she gave Mr Wibbly Wobbly a gentle soaking.

She was a joy. Such fun to be with. I'd have to be careful not to fall in love. I didn't want to go through all of that again.

I dressed but Alice slipped back into her dressing gown and made a pot of tea which we drank sitting at the kitchen table. Big Nob, unseen and unheard until that point, made his presence felt with a long lazy yawn as he awoke in a large dog basket in the adjoining utility room. He trotted up to the table, made a beeline for me, plonked his nose onto my lap and wagged his tail in welcome as I ruffled his ears and gave his neck an invigorating scratch. He must have wondered who was master in the house.

I took a sneaky delight in the fact that the dog always approached me at the table rather than Alice, something that she'd often commented on.

"Dog's will always seek out the leader of the pack." I asserted.

"Yeah, or the one who'll secretively slip him a biscuit when I'm not looking," she quipped. "You mustn't do that, Charlie, you know he's on strictly two meals a day now."

"How's your poor paw old pal?" I asked as if addressing an elderly soldier and stressing the alliteration.

Alice started giggling as she recalled the childish banter we'd enjoyed during the recent visit to the vet.

She took a gulp of tea which in a sudden involuntary eruption she then sprayed over the dog as she burst into laughter. Just as he had in the waiting room Big Nob immediately sought refuge under her chair.

"What?" I enquired.

"Cook-in Sauce!" she blurted.

We chatted for half an hour during which time I was updated on Ken's latest DIY disaster.

He'd spent four consecutive weekends building a kennel for Big Nob, insisting that the dog would prefer to spend summer nights sleeping in the garden. At least that was his justification to Alice who wasn't fooled as she was well aware that her husband wasn't happy unless he had one of his 'projects' to work on.

Ken had made detailed drawings; front elevation, side elevations, rear and plan view. He first attempted a scale model in balsa wood, cutting out each element carefully with a razor-sharp craft knife but had to abandon the approach when it became difficult to manage the tube of superglue with three fingertips of each hand crowned in Elastoplast and wearing a thumb bandage.

Ken went to the same store for the timber as he had for the chipboard used in his previous ill-fated attempt at boarding the loft. He was recognised there as the man to whom you could sell any equipment remotely associated with the job in hand. Consequently Ken had come to regard the staff as friends, helpful beyond the call of duty, as they were ever ready to discuss his needs, review his drawings and make suggestions for subtle design changes, and of course to ensure he had all the hardware, adhesives, wood treatment chemicals and most importantly power tools necessary to complete the task.

On this particular occasion he'd been persuaded to upspec his plans to include fully insulated cavity walls, which almost doubled the amount of timber needed, and to purchase some 'premium high-thermal-value' polystyrene pellets which unfortunately were only available in a 100 litre 'Value Pack'. Still, he imagined they'd come in handy should a future project involve insulating the garage.

The kennel had been completed the previous Saturday and was without doubt her husband's proudest DIY achievement. It stood four feet high at the peak of its bituminised fabric roof and the outer walls were finished in shiplap boards. Five feet long and three feet wide it was mounted on four-inch stilts to keep it clear of the ground. It was to be entered through an arched opening through which his master had no doubt visualised the happy dog energetically wagging his tail in gratitude. And there certainly would be room to wag his tail as the starting point in Ken's plans had been to measure the dog using a spring-loaded metal tape measure. Alice's eyes filled with tears of laughter as she described how her husband had attempted to measure Big Nob from his healthy wet nose to the tip of his wagging tail. After many fruitless circuits the pair together stretched out the dog on the terracotta tiles of the kitchen floor, Alice holding his front paws and Ken the rear as he marked the extremities with chalk lines on the ground whist attempting to immobilise the wagging tail. Ken then measured the distance between the two lines and was astonished to find that Big Nob appeared to be six feet long.

To say that the construction was over-engineered would be an understatement. It was so heavy they couldn't manage between them to move it and Ken had to enlist the assistance of a neighbour to help him relocate it from the garage into its place of honour in the garden, a spot from which it could be admired from the living room window.

I enquired whether it had been one of the neighbours who'd earlier rescued her husband from the scrotal trap on the new clothesline post and went to the window to inspect the edifice. I had to admit that it was a very fine dog kennel, indeed one that I would myself have been proud of.

"Well Alice," I enquired, "What does Big Nob think about it?"

"Ungrateful Mutt," she snorted. "He wouldn't go near it. He dug his paws in and couldn't be dragged within a yard of it. Ken was so disappointed. He blames it on the man at the store who told him he must give it a good soaking in Crearyosoak or something. It smells awful and Ken had to buy ten litres of it."

I managed to suppress a laugh.

Although we've never met and I'll do my damnedest to ensure we never do, I must confess I'm beginning to feel some not inconsiderable empathy for Ken.

I can understand why she feels comfortable with the man and why in her own way she is loyal to him. Extraordinary. How lucky I am.

I was just thinking about leaving when Alice gave me an alarming ultimatum. First, she announced that in a fortnight Ken would be away on an extended business trip leaving her alone for four nights.

"Excellent," I replied, "Have you anything in mind?"

"Well, yes I think I'm available," she teased. "Let's do something really exciting."

"Do you have anything particular in mind?" I asked again.

"Yes. You did bring the dice?"

I began to get excited as I sensed Alice had something really outrageous to suggest. I knew that look. There wasn't much that she could ask that would concern me, apart perhaps from driving around town naked or putting on a show for that restaurant's car park video cameras, although I wouldn't put it past her.

"Well, let's make the list," I suggested.

"OK, but it's just a short one."

"Intriguing. How short?"

"Just one forfeit actually. One dice. Any odd or even number between one and six."

Why did I feel a sudden trepidation? There really wasn't anything she'd be up for that I couldn't handle. In any event whatever it was that she wanted to do would inevitably end in sex of some form in whatever location.

"Come on then, let's have it. But remember the dice must be obeyed."

"OK. I want three-in-a-bed sex."

"What!" I exclaimed, terrified that she might mean with another man.

"Don't worry. With a woman I know. You'll love it I promise."

I was astonished. This was something that she had specified as the 'forfeit' but with stone-bonker odds of it happening, even though she'd never in the past given any hint that a lesbian encounter might interest her in any way.

"Tell me about her."

"No, that's not the game. You're either up for it or you're not. And I've never known you not to be."

With that she opened her knees just wide enough to treat me to a glimpse as she had done to the spluttering old gent and I that evening in the restaurant anteroom.

"If it makes you feel any better, I can tell you that she's really hot and if I fancy her I'm absolutely certain you will."

The challenge had been laid. It was crazy. I could never have imagined she would want such a thing or could suggest it but she had. And what did I have to lose?

I withdrew the dice from my trouser pocket hampered not a little by a growing erection. I had done this once before but not with Alice and the thought of a total stranger joining in made it all the more erotic.

"Well?" she enquired, in a tone implying that she was totally in charge and offering me a once in a lifetime opportunity.

"Certainly," I replied, "if you're sure?"

I don't know why I bothered rolling the dice but I did so unnecessarily on the kitchen table.

"Five!" Alice screamed. "Excellent."

"Wow. So, when, where and who?"

"Oh yes," she replied casually as if they were unimportant details. "One of the four nights. I'm not sure which yet, I'll let you know nearer the time…your place…Ms Philippa Staplewhatserface."

"Ha ha! Very funny. Don't be ridiculous Alice. You can't be serious."

"Never been more so," she retorted.

"But Alice, she's not that way inclined and anyway I've just told you I don't fancy her."

"Mmmm. You were willing to fuck a perfect stranger two minutes ago."

"Alice. Forget it. It's nonsense. It can't be done."

"Well, that's up to you Charlie. If you're right you've just shagged me for the last time."

Her tone I'd never heard before and the look she gave me left no doubt that she meant it. There'd been no indication in the past that she had any leanings that way. The ludicrous challenge would be impossible to deliver and she must have known that. It must have been a devious plan to end our affair, to ditch me.

"But Alice, Angel, please, be reasonable. It's just not possible!"

"You're forgetting something darling. Your rules. The dice 'must be obeyed'."

Chapter Twenty-Seven
Indecent Proposal

I drove home from Alice's house, my head spinning.

The prospect was exciting but the odds impossible. It was ludicrous: a non-starter. Her suggestion was utterly outrageous but her ultimatum I felt sure was serious. There must be an ulterior motive behind her demand.

Did she really, in her wildest dreams, believe that Philippa would do such a thing? Of course not. And even if she could be persuaded Alice must be the last woman on earth with whom the highly intelligent though sexually inexperienced Philippa would do such a thing. They clearly hated each other.

What was behind Alice's insistence? Did she know I'd already got her rival into bed? That must be it. I remembered the words she'd spoken to 'Mr Wibbly Wobbly'. Not to me but to my penis for God's sake! *'Have you shagged that lawyer yet? Bet you have.'*

She must know, but how could she?

Could Philippa perhaps, in her desperate state during the past few days have made contact in an attempt to baulk my relationship with Alice? No, impossible. She wouldn't have known how to reach her.

On the plus side, perhaps Alice has been influenced by some scatterbrain drivel she's read in one of those pathetic celebrity magazines she's so fond of.

'Style icon soap star shares her secret fantasies.'
'Is bi-sexuality a modern woman's true freedom?'
'Agony Aunt suggests Curious of Kingston takes the plunge'.

Of Course! I've got it! Doh! She's suspicious of my intentions with Philippa and knows that such an outrageous proposition will ensure her rival never speaks to me again.

OK, don't panic. Think clearly. What are my options?

I could tell her that Philippa was outraged and refused point blank but that I've come up with an alternative but willing participant. I'm sure I could find one in the local paper's Personal Services columns.

I could play a waiting game, ignore her, wait until she's feeling horny whilst hubby's away and simply refuse to accept the challenge. She'll come around.

I could tell her that Philippa is not answering my calls but that I'll try again in a week or so, or that it's all arranged but then Philippa fails to turn up.

I could take her out to dinner on the first night of the potential four-day shag fest and simply say that I didn't believe for one moment that she was serious.

On the other hand; I could give it a try.

What have I got to lose?

If I ask Philippa and she refuses, she'll never speak to me again. Do I care? Not really. She's desperate and clingy and doesn't like sex. So what's the point of continuing the seduction? And then gone is the risk of losing the sexual favours of my lovely little bimbo.

But; just supposing she's desperate enough to agree. I'll get to shag them both with no comebacks, if you'll pardon the expression, because the melange a trois will have been Alice's idea. If it all gets frightfully messy it'll be her fault and I can take the moral high ground and insist she coerced me into it by threatening the only meaningful thing in my life, our intimate relationship.

Sorted.

Next problem; how on earth do I put it to Philippa?

My scheming was interrupted by a call from the lady in question. I let the phone ring for ten seconds whilst I gathered my thoughts but miscalculated the delay and it switched to voicemail before I could pick up.

I then noticed that there had been seven missed calls whilst I'd been with Alice.

I heard Philippa's emotion filled voice begging me to call her back as soon as I could. I waited five minutes and returned the call in a friendly and affectionate voice explaining that her call had come through whilst I was in a petrol station and unable to answer.

Sensing her distress I got in first and laid on the charm.

"Hello Angel, how are you? Sorry I've been so busy, I was just thinking of you, when can we get together?"

There was a long pause through which I could sense her relief.

"Well, I'm free this evening as it happens," she replied with affected confidence. "Can we meet for a drink or something?"

It was the *'or something'* that made me hesitate before replying. If the *'something'* was her desire for another attempt to demonstrate her desire and ability to have sex I had to avoid it. Not that it wouldn't significantly increase the even very remote chance of her accepting the indecent proposal, if I found the courage to make it, but quite frankly I didn't feel I could manage it after the energetic romp with Alice of a few hours earlier and the stress of her ultimatum. Just imagine Philippa's reaction if I couldn't get up for it.

"Oh darling I can't. I've just this minute agreed to meet Max and a couple of ex-RAF friends who are in town just for one night. Tomorrow's good though, how are you fixed?"

"Tomorrow's fine. Would you like to come to mine for dinner, about 8 o'clock?"

"That would be lovely," I replied, "Can you text me the address?"

I spent most of that evening and in half-sleep most of the night planning how to raise the subject of the threesome demanded by Alice. My rehearsed speeches came to nothing. There was no easy way to put it, no discreet reference, no euphemism, no double entendre from which I could retreat in humour claiming a misunderstanding when the inevitable outrage was shrieked. My nerves must have got the better of me as I simply couldn't come up with a plan. It would almost certainly be my last meeting with Philippa so perhaps I should wait until after we'd had sex if indeed she was able to manage it this time. I felt sure that it was her intention to try and if successful perhaps in the afterglow she might be persuaded. Perhaps I could sell it as the next stage in a specially tailored programme of sex therapy in which I would selflessly assist her to shake off her inhibitions. Or would that be too arrogant, even for me?

I concluded simply to play it by ear, see how the evening developed and if necessary, just blurt it out.

I arrived at Philippa's house at a quarter past eight next day, a bottle of wine in one hand and a bunch of flowers in the other. The latter was a bit of an afterthought, so I'd had to buy them at a petrol station and with great difficulty pick the £3.50 price label off the cellophane wrapper.

When Philippa's text had appeared giving me her address it occurred to me that at no point since we'd met had I learned anything of her domestic arrangements. I assumed that she lived alone and hadn't considered that she might have been sharing with a female colleague or other housemates. It turned out though that she had originally shared a rented terraced house in a trendy part of town with a girlfriend, Annie, who'd subsequently decamped to move in with a mysterious boyfriend to whom Philippa had never been introduced nor of whom had she ever seen any photographic evidence. Following her friend's departure she'd bought the property and had it extensively refitted and modernised.

The late-Victorian house was small but expensively furnished and tastefully decorated. The front door boasted its original colourful stained-glass panel and opened to a central hall off which was a large living room to one side and a small dining room and modern fitted kitchen to the other. Stairs led from the mosaic-tiled hall to an upstairs bathroom and two large bedrooms, one of which I was to have the dubious pleasure of visiting that night.

Philippa was much more animated than I'd ever seen her in the past, her staccato speech and rapid change of subject betrayed her evident nervousness. In one sentence she greeted me, told me how much she'd been looking forward to getting together again, thanked me for the 'gorgeous' flowers and complimented my choice of wine whilst simultaneously offering her cheek for my embrace. That too revealed her anxiety as having first offered a cheek she evidently decided that was insufficiently intimate for the occasion so tried to kiss my mouth instead, the result being that we did little more than wipe moist lips over each other's faces. The absurdity though caused us both to laugh after which she relaxed and let out a long-exaggerated sigh.

"I'm sorry Charlie, I've been so nervous!"

"Don't worry Angel, come here."

I gently took back the bottle from her and placed it alongside the flowers that she'd laid on a small table behind her. I held her gently around the waist with both hands and said,

"Shall we start again? Hello Angel, good to see you. I've been looking forward it."

I kissed her on the lips gently and briefly and then let go.

Philippa led me into the dimly lit dining room. The large black-tinted glass dining table reflected the only light source in the room, a table lamp professionally converted from a once beautiful antique oil lamp. Rising from a heavy black ceramic base edged in gold was a highly decorated, tapered brass pillar supporting a cylindrical coloured glass reservoir about ten inches in diameter and six inches tall. This would have once fed a pair of wicks drawing from a pint or two of paraffin prior to its conversion and been crowned with a tall, narrow glass flue before it's replacement by a white plastic bulb holder trailing a flex. A pure white, stylishly modern lampshade completed the desecration.

The white walls contrasted with the charcoal grey wooden flooring and were each hung with a single, very large, black-framed print. Each picture was of a single flower in monochrome shades of grey with a splash of colour just to define the petals.

It reminded me immediately of how Philippa had dressed on the first few occasions we'd met, in her lawyers' smart black with a red chiffon scarf and fingernails painted to match. It was not at all as I had expected to find her home. It seemed more like a bachelor pad.

On the drive over I had been anticipating the bedroom scene as I expected it would develop that evening, visualising pure white bedding, with neutral coloured carpet, curtains, bedside tables and dressing table all colour co-ordinated in no doubt pretentiously named off-whites, 'Egyptian Cotton' or 'French Putty' or 'Angels' Flax' and an uncomfortable 'Artisan' chair monopolised by a big-eyed rag doll unnervingly staring at me with stern disapproval.

As it turned out, with the exception of the doll my mind's eye had it almost to a tee.

The table was set for two with place mats at opposite ends and a pair of stainless-steel candlesticks in the centre. Two sparkling clean plain wine glasses had been placed in precisely the same position for each setting. I'd have expected cut glass but clearly that would have been incongruous alongside the cutlery that was far from traditional. A shallow plain glass dish in which floated a handful of rose petals was the only other table decoration.

Philippa invited me to take a seat in the living room whilst she retreated to the kitchen and poured us both a beer. The room was furnished in a minimalist style, the same grey wooden flooring, the same white walls, a white leather sofa and two matching chairs, a pair of chrome-plated uplighters and a modern glass-fronted electric fire designed to look like a wood-burning stove in which artificial flames danced and licked at the door.

The only wall decoration was a very large portrait, about five feet by three, of a naked female form in various shades of aquamarine. It was beautiful. The standing figure's magnetic eyes looked out from a melancholy unsmiling face. Her relaxed bowed arms framed her bosom pushing her breasts together very gently as they fell in front of her and the slender fingers of her cupped hands concealed her vulva. She was breathtakingly beautiful and held my gaze.

"You've met Beryl, I see," said Philippa entering the room with a Peroni in each hand. "Lovely, isn't she?"

"Yes, gorgeous. But Beryl?" I protested. "Surely she deserves a more heavenly name."

"Such as?" she responded. "Such as Philippa," I answered, inwardly congratulating myself on the quick thinking.

"No resemblance sadly," she replied with genuine modesty, "I'm a redhead with freckles and no boobs to speak of but I've learned to live with it," she continued turning the reaction into a joke.

Philippa wasn't one to fish for compliments, it was but the self-effacing humour of a confident woman who despite her undoubted intellect simply wished she had the body that glossy magazines present as the ideal attractive to men.

I took the beer from her outstretched hand and kissed her cheek.

"Nonsense, you're gorgeous. You do it for me, and you know it."

"I do hope so."

"So who's the artist?"

"I don't know, it's unsigned."

"Where did you buy it?"

"I didn't. It was a leaving present from Annie when she moved out."

I sensed from her suddenly hurried tone that she didn't really want me to continue this line of questioning but I was curious. It seemed strange for the person leaving to give a present and it wasn't the sort of gift I'd expect one woman to buy for another.

"So why not call her Annie?"

That was clearly a step too far and Philippa expertly brought the matter to a close in a barely concealed sarcastic tone that implied I'd been slow to grasp the point. "Because it's aquamarine. Blue-green. Sea green."

I relaxed on one of the armchairs whilst Philippa sat upright at the far end of the sofa, nervously sipping at her lager and unconsciously pulling the hem of her dress down closer to her knees. She'd decanted hers into a half pint tumbler but she obviously felt I'd be more at home drinking straight from the bottle.

We exchanged small talk but Philippa's eyes urged me to talk of love. I could read her mind. I felt sure she wanted me to raise the subject of sex sooner rather than later, to refer to our earlier attempt and to give her the opportunity to signal that she was tonight up for it and determined to make it a success.

Convinced of that, I decided to talk about work. I asked her about any recent court appearances but she quickly ducked the subject with a dismissive gesture saying only that it was too boring to relate. I launched into an update of my current renovation project with a gripe about a building inspector's intransigence on the routeing of a drain that I intended to pass under a garage to avoid shifting a wall by a metre to one side. My disappointed hostess was saved by the bell as a timer sounded in the kitchen.

Philippa attended to the oven leaving me to my beer and to stare at Beryl's perfect body. If only she looked like that, I thought. A thought that inevitably drifted to my sexy, sensuous, eager Alice. With that the stirrings started as I wondered what my lovely was up to that evening. I was reminded of my mission and that I'd earlier concluded that one option was simply to blurt it out at an appropriate time, post-coital. Time therefore to prepare the ground with Philippa.

I went into the kitchen and found her standing at the stainless steel sink which was situated in a central island, an essential feature of today's trendy kitchens but totally out of keeping with this building. A Belfast sink would originally have stood under a window in the rear wall looking out to the back yard and an outside toilet. The entire wall had been removed and a full-width extension built to provide more room but at the expense of the garden which was now limited to a small patio approached through glazed bi-fold metal doors. It was mostly paved in York stone with gravelled areas around an incongruous water feature the centrepiece of which was a concrete nymph pouring from a pitcher a dribble of water over sea-polished stones into a shallow basin. Expensive looking plants in large terracotta pots provided a minimal touch of colour. I half expected to see the discarded Belfast sink sprouting parsley, sage and thyme with a tuft or two of chives but it had no doubt been committed to the skip along with the displaced masonry. I was surprised to see that the outside toilet building remained. The brickwork had been nicely repointed inside and out, the door removed and the internal walls whitewashed. The Tippler lavatory has been removed and in its place was a willow-green wooden chair. I smiled at the thought of Philippa sitting there reading The Sunday Times where years ago a man in a cloth cap would have read the racing pages of The Daily Express whilst sucking on a Woodbine waiting nature to take its course.

I approached her from behind wrapping my arms around her in a firm hug, brushing her hair to one side with my nose and kissing her neck, causing an immediate involuntary shrug which broke the embrace. Then, as if to indicate that her reaction was not a rejection, she turned and kissed my mouth with a brief peck whilst raising her hands to touch my cheeks. Whether this was a spontaneous loving gesture or a manoeuvre to put some space between my chest and hers I was uncertain.

"Shall we make love before dinner or afterwards?" I blurted.

She was clearly taken aback by the directness of the question and paused so long before replying that I thought for a moment I'd completely misjudged the invitation and her intentions.

"It'll have to be afterwards," she said hurriedly and then after a pause, "But only because the souffle is already rising."

The souffle was not the only thing that was rising so I released her from the hug and stepped away to cast a less critical eye over the back yard.

"I love the er, outside space," I lied, "very stylish."

"Well, it's the best one can do with such a limited area. Luckily, it's a real sun trap in one corner. Please take a seat, this one's yours."

We ate the soufflé and sipped the Chablis Grand Cru I'd chosen for the occasion. Both were superb although Philippa insisted on diminishing my praise by insisting the dish had sagged. It hadn't. It was truly excellent.

Throughout the meal we shared our thoughts on all-time favourite menus and found much in common.

Perfectly cooked sea bass fillets followed, served with boiled Jersey Royals rolled in butter, sprinkled with chopped herbs and accompanied by small fronds of broccoli.

Mmmmm, so she loves good food but doesn't like sex, I thought. Strange, in my experience they normally go together. Visions came to mind of Alice with playful, smiling eyes seductively tapping a langoustine on her lips before very slowly sucking it into her sexy mouth.

"What?" Philippa enquired in reaction to my sudden smile.

"Oh, er just wondering what delights you could possibly come up with to top that."

"We'll see. I hope you won't be disappointed."

By the end of the main course, my hostess had quaffed almost three glasses of Chablis to my one but seemed no more relaxed. She removed the dinner plates to the kitchen and fussed around there for far too long before returning to the table wiping her hands on a napkin. She regained her seat, almost drained her glass and put it down on the table heavily with a shaky hand and in doing so knocked it over.

"Sorry!" she exclaimed, as if it were my treasured table rather than her own under attack, and leapt to her feet to mop up with the napkin the tiniest drop of wine that had been spilt.

"How clumsy, I'm so sorry Charles."

Philippa was clearly still very nervous and the reason was obvious. How was I going to fulfil my mission and raise the outrageous question when evidently she was terrified of even what was planned to follow the meal that evening?

A gentleman would have been sympathetic to her concern and have put her at ease by indicating that there was no rush, that he understood, that it could wait 'til another evening, wait until she was completely sure and absolutely ready. Instead I said,

"Do you want to have sex before dessert or afterwards?"

She was clearly startled but I sensed in some way relieved that the point of no return had at last been reached.

"It's up to you," she replied. "Do you want to do it now?"

I was astonished. These were not the words of an adult lawyer but more like the vocabulary of a teenage virgin spurred on by peer pressure from friends who'd already 'done it' and feeling bound against her instincts to commit this uncomfortable but mandatory rite of passage. "Only if you're ready, Philippa."

"Let's do what you came here to do," she replied. I remember clearly that she said 'you' rather than 'we'.

Her outstretched hand gripped mine and she looked me in the eyes, holding my gaze for perhaps the first time that evening.

"Charles, I'm so sorry about last time. I don't know what came over me. I just sort of froze. I do want you and I so want you to love me. It will be different this time I promise."

"Angel, I told you, it was the booze. Don't worry."

With a twist of the head and a glance at the ceiling I suggested that we move upstairs.

Philippa slowly got up from the table smoothing the creases from her dress as she rose.

Then silently she led me to the stairs and as we climbed, I watched her pert bottom and mentally undressed her. I was certainly ready but feared she was not.

"That's the bathroom," she said with the tone of an estate agent conducting a viewing. "I'll go first if you don't mind."

She pushed open an adjacent door and said,

"We'll use this bedroom, if you'd like to wait in there."

This was so different from the normal early relationship pre-coital preambles. No petting on the sofa, no groping, no sliding of hands up skirts, no outrageous suggestions whispered into ticklish ears, no girlish giggles and boyish mild obscenities, no fumbling fingers searching for fly zips, no unfastening of bras, no trail of abandoned clothing.

I stood in Philippa's bedroom and although relieved not to encounter the doll with the accusing eyes was somewhat at a loss about what to do as I waited for her. Should I strip off and jump into bed ahead of her, my member raising the duvet like a tent pole in welcome? No, she'd certainly think that unhygienic. I'd been invited to use the bathroom 'after her' unlike encounters with Alice which often involved mutual splashing, primping, priming and dabbing with fluffy white towels.

Philippa took so long in the bathroom that I decided to undress at least down to my bulging briefs. I'd kicked off my shoes, slipped out of my trousers and unbuttoned my shirt when she emerged fully dressed. For a nanosecond I thought she'd changed her mind.

"Bathroom's free."

She stood by the bed as I paused to watch her slip out of her clothes but she waited motionless with her hand behind her feeling for the zip on her dress and clearly waiting for me to leave.

"Let me help you with that."

"No, I can manage. Just go and use the bathroom."

I had a pee, which if Alice had been waiting in the next room would probably have been a physical impossibility at this stage, splashed my bits around in the hand basin and towelled off.

I re-entered the bedroom to find Philippa just as she'd been last time, the duvet up to her chin in defensive mode and I could tell simply by their absence from the hurriedly piled clothing that she was still wearing her bra and pants. Was this to be a repeat performance? I wondered.

It was. It was. It was.

I slipped into bed but not into Philippa as despite my patient and gentle foreplay she remained as stiff as an ironing board and tight as clam throughout.

After ten or fifteen minutes we gave up, she in tears and me in silence.

I lay back, my hands behind my head on the pillow and stared at the ceiling which I was pleased to see still retained the elaborate Victorian plaster ceiling rose and coving which delineated walls and ceiling on three of the four walls. An uncaring decorator had completed the square using a non-matching modern polystyrene substitute to the fourth. The original panelled pine doors had been replaced with the ubiquitous modern one-piece fakes and at the windows the vertical strips of the blinds fluttered in the breeze linked together by beaded chains.

Philippa's sobbed apologies continued and I did my best to persuade her that the problem was again the wine. She remained implacable until, seeing my mission in tatters, I suggested that 'next time' perhaps we'd get together in the afternoon without any alcohol.

"I'm surprised you want to see me again after the two failed attempts."

Yes, she actually used the word 'attempts'. Did that imply that it was for her a trial? If so, what exactly does she want from me? She says she loves me, wants to be with me and wants a relationship. How can that be if, as it seems, she doesn't want to be intimate?

The thought suddenly dawned on me that she and Alice were diametric opposites. Philippa was in love with me, was looking for a lasting relationship but evidently doesn't like sex, and Alice wants nothing from me but regular, energetic, uninhibited sex. Love is never, ever mentioned and her commitment to her husband is absolute. A loving relationship is the last thing she wants and I fear if I ever got to the point where I did, and I must confess that lately I'm getting more and more fond of her, she'd probably kick me into touch.

These thoughts reminded me of Alice's ultimatum. If I failed to achieve the impossible and deliver Philippa to her she'd withdraw her services forever and I'd be left with the clingy one who doesn't want to fuck. The little minx. She's got me by the balls. I'm done for. Perhaps her sixth sense had alerted her to my interest in Philippa and she'd already decided to ditch me but not without first subjecting me to the humiliation of an inevitable, screaming, relationship-busting finale with her rival.

I was in two minds. Should I withdraw defeated and hope to persuade Alice to accept she'd demanded the impossible? Should I defer the indecent proposal to a later meeting? Or should I continue with my plan and just go for it?

I did what I normally do and made a mental throw of the dice. Two dice, any total between two and twelve and I'll go for it. Nine! Game back on. I turned to Philippa, now facing away from me, slipped an arm under her and held her momentarily in a gentle embrace. She responded by gently breaking loose, rolling onto her back and facing the ceiling.

"Don't be silly Angel, of course I want to see you again. It'll be fine but you must learn to loosen up."

"I know, I do try. I do want you. You do believe that don't you?"

"Of course I do. Don't get hung up about it. You once told me about the guy at college you slept with. That worked out alright didn't it?"

Philippa remembered the lie but paused with a noticeable shiver whilst planning her response.

"Yes, fine. I told you I'm just so nervous with you, it's all been so sudden. Things have moved on at such a pace."

"How many men have you slept with Philly?"

She paused at the unfair question but obviously realised that such a conversation had to continue if I were to accept her excuses. "Oh, several, over the years, but none lately. I've been so busy with my career and just the one actually."

So there it was, a full admission of her long-term celibacy but coupled with a genuine desire for a sexual relationship with me.

I felt a momentary pang of guilt at being the one who had re-awakened her interest in men when my intentions were so dishonourable. I soon got over it though, I had so much to lose.

We lay side by side in the bedroom with its many incongruous architectural features that reflected the many differences between us and our desires.

"You will give me another chance, Charles, won't you? I do want to be with you but it's just that I get so tense."

"I know and I'll help you through it, angel. I think your problem is that you take sex much too seriously. You must come to look at it not as something you're giving away but as something you're sharing with someone and not necessarily just someone you love. It's a gift to give you pleasure when you're alone."

Philippa blushed at that but her lips cracked into an almost imperceptible smile.

"And there are so many ways in which couples can please each other. Abandoning your inhibitions is the first step."

"More easily said than done in my case," Philippa said but turned towards me letting the duvet slip to reveal her breasts no doubt in an attempt to communicate that she was at least willing to make a start.

"You're not by any means a 'skinny redhead with freckles and no tits'," I paraphrased. "You're a beautiful, intelligent woman with a sexy body and the most enchanting eyes. You just have to learn to loosen up."

"And what exactly do you recommend, Doctor," she replied, her spirits clearly lifting.

"Just do what comes naturally and don't think too much about it. Love your body and get used to the idea that others will love it too. Walk around the house naked in daylight when you're alone; strip off and admire yourself in the mirror; go skinny dipping at night in the park—I'll come with you; have sex in a car; let me watch you slowly undress; let me give you oral sex if you're not ready for penetration; there are so many ways."

I heard Alice's voice in my head prompting me with, 'Masturbate while you're driving.'

I think it must have been the mention of oral sex that did the trick as after a pause of nearly a minute she said,

"Naked night swimming doesn't really do it for me Charlie but maybe next time you could just give me oral."

Encouraging progress, I thought, but although we'd been lying naked in her bed, she had stressed *'you could give me'* and *'next time'*.

Chapter Twenty-Eight
Degrees of Persuasion

I spent the night reflecting on the events of that evening. I'd not exactly failed in my mission, in fact I felt I'd made good progress. It would mean another date with Philippa before I could pop the question but with nearly a couple of weeks to go there was still plenty of time.

As I lay in bed wondering, as I often did, what my lovely playmate was doing at that precise moment it dawned on me that things had changed gradually but significantly in my feelings for both women. Philippa I realised was a hopeless case and, but for Alice's challenge, I probably would not have bothered seeing her again. She clearly didn't enjoy sex so there'd be absolutely no point in pursuing the seduction. I felt sure too that getting rid of her would prove difficult if the relationship became more steady. She would demand fidelity, constantly want to know where I was and who I was with and likely as not become jealous and possessive. She had the potential to become a real bunny boiler.

It was significant too that throughout the evening with her my thoughts had kept returning to Alice.

How different they were. Every fault and frustration I found in Philippa was not present in Alice. Every joy in Alice was unknown to Philippa.

She'd come to mind as I sat in Philly's sitting room being aroused by the beauty of Beryl, when during the meal I'd imagined her seductively sucking on a langoustine, and as I'd contrasted their preparations for bed and their motivation and performance once in it. Most troubling of all was the real risk of losing her should this crazy, stupid, pointless dare fail as it doubtlessly would. The thought produced the cold sweat of fear and the realisation that despite all the rules of our game I had fallen in love, something I had promised myself never to do again. I wanted to be with her and only her. I was ready to give up sleeping around and settle down, if only I could persuade Alice to come and live with me.

Next morning, having waited until after nine to be sure Ken had left for work, I phoned Alice, not for any particular reason but just to hear her happy voice. Optimistically I hoped too that it might prompt an invitation to visit for some afternoon delights and present an opportunity to persuade her to abandon the impossible challenge she'd laid.

I dialled. She took longer than usual to pick up.

"Hello Alice, it's Charles, can you talk?"

"Yes, have you asked her yet?"

No pleasantries, no small talk, none of the familiar sexual innuendo, she just came straight out with it.

"Not exactly but I will very soon."

"Well, either you have or you haven't."

She spoke in a tone I hadn't heard her use before in all the time I'd known her.

"We'll, I've sort of prepared the ground."

"And what's that supposed to mean? Is she going to be up for it or not?"

"Honestly Angel, I have my doubts. It's just not her scene. She's virginal, uptight and probably frigid."

"Oh, really. And through what sort of 'business' discussion did you establish that?"

"Alice, be reasonable. You laid down the stupid forfeit, you chose the odds to ensure it must be paid. It's not my fault you nominated the wrong woman."

"I seem to recall Charlie that you were just as excited at the prospect."

"No I wasn't! I told you that I don't fancy her but you wouldn't believe me. Look Angel, don't let's fall out over it. If this is something you really want to do let me find someone else, someone who'd more readily be up for it."

"Oh, you've got a long list of eager sexual partners, have you?"

"No of course not! But we could easily find someone advertising in the personal columns. You should know, you used to take the ads in that job at the Echo."

I hoped that reminding her of the hilarious trail of disasters she'd caused by misdirecting mail might get her laughing and into a better frame of mind.

"Oh you think I'd stoop that low, do you?"

"Alice, stop it. Why are you being like this? You know I love you."

There was a long pause and then, in a much softer tone, she said,

"Please don't say that. You know the rules, and anyway it's not true."

She was right about the rules. We had long ago promised each other it was just for fun, no ties, not to let it get serious. But she was wrong on the other point and I couldn't deny it to myself. I had fallen in love with her but to declare it too soon would be a mistake that would almost certainly drive her away.

"Angel, this is silly, why are we arguing? Why don't I pop round and we'll make up and talk about where you want to go and what you want to do whilst Ken is away next week? I can bring the dice if you like."

"It's not next week, it's the week after and no don't come around. I told you last time, fix it or you won't be shagging me ever again. Your rules, the dice must be obeyed, remember? He's away Tuesday to Friday, I'll let you know which night but it's your place at eight o'clock and bring Lady Philippa with you or it's over. Just let me know when you've sorted it."

With that she hung up.

What on earth had come over her and what was she planning? What could she be thinking would happen even if I could get Philippa there and even if her rival had miraculously transformed into a bi-sexual nymphomaniac prepared to take part in a threesome? Obviously it wouldn't get that far. She's probably planned an embarrassing confrontation, one that will end in Philippa's humiliation and my losing both of them forever.

I had to face it, I was between a rock and the proverbial. Make or break, shit or bust, there was only one course of action. I'd have to face the biggest challenge of my philandering life and corrupt the strait-laced, sexually inexperienced lawyer and persuade her to accept what she was bound to see as the most sordid proposition she'll ever encounter, and all within two weeks. What could possibly go wrong?

I had to make a start and I decided to throw all my efforts into it as the stakes were now higher than ever. My future life with Alice depended on it. Just like one of my building projects it would require a detailed timing plan. Assuming it could be at the earliest the Wednesday I'd have just ten days.

Say two days to get Philippa used to being naked with me and give her the oral sex she'd sort of already agreed to; pop the question on day three allowing her a few days to freak out but then get used to the idea and accept it as the price she'd have to pay if she wants a meaningful relationship with me; fuck her on day eight leaving me two days to rest up for the big night.

It was a tall order and perhaps the only chance I had was to exploit her single weakness, that she desperately wants me to love her.

228

There was no time for delay so I resolved to call her early that evening as soon as she got home from work.

I spent much of the day rehearsing my speech. I made some notes about what to say and what not to. I'd have to be careful not to get ahead of myself but lead her there gently.

I called Mrs Wilson to see if next week she could switch her usual Friday visit to the Thursday morning to make sure the place was perfectly tidy and to change the bedding for the new white silk sheets and pillowcases. My mood was a mixture of excitement and panic, of joy at the thought of settling down with Alice contrasting with feelings of impending doom. Although I was going to try my hardest to arrange it I knew the threesome with Philippa was not going to happen. My only real hope was that Alice would then be happy that her rival had been seen off and secure that having made her point she could be sure of my exclusive attention. When things got back to normal I'd just have to hope that eventually I could persuade her to leave Ken and come to live with me, even marry me.

At seven o'clock I poured myself a large gin and dialled Philippa's number. There was no reply and so I left a voicemail message asking her to call me back to arrange to meet for a 'drink or something'.

She didn't reply and I tried again the next night, my crib sheet close at hand on the coffee table. Again she didn't pick up and I began to get worried. It was the end of Day 2 and time was running out.

I sent her a text which also went unanswered.

Her mobile went unanswered on Day 3 too so in desperation I called her at work mid-morning. The receptionist at the chambers explained that she was out on business but back later although tied up in meetings until six o'clock. She put me through to a female colleague whose name I remembered as someone Philippa was quite friendly with and she agreed to take a message asking Philippa to call me as soon as she was free.

"Yes, I'll ask her. I know she's got your number Charles." There was something about the way she said 'got your number' that intrigued me momentarily, but I thought nothing more about it.

As I waited for her call, I pondered the reasons for her not responding to my messages. I really was getting paranoid but as it turned out for no good reason.

Philippa called at a little after six, breathless and seemingly anxious to speak to me and launched straight into an apology. She told me she'd been working late at the office both nights preparing for an up-coming trial and had lost her phone amongst a myriad of file boxes and it had only just come to light.

"Sorry Charlie, I've only just got your messages."

"That's OK, I was wondering if you'd like to come out to play."

"I'd love to Darling but I can't, not today. I'm deadbeat and just need a glass of wine in a hot bath and an early night."

"Alone?" I gambled.

"Sorry, yes I'm afraid so," she giggled.

Well, I thought, at least we've now started some vaguely suggestive banter.

"OK, but I'd really like to talk to you. Why don't you call me when you've had your bath?"

"Yes all right but it won't be late. I really must get to bed."

"Better still call me once you're in bed."

"OK Charles," she said breezily, "speak to you later."

I poured myself a Peroni and flicked on the TV to catch the news but my mind was still spinning as I tried desperately to find a way to make up the lost days on the timing plan. I was still mentally scheming when her call came through.

"Hi Charles, it's Philippa."

"Hello, angel, are you nicely tucked up in bed?"

"I am."

"I've been thinking a lot about the other evening and what we resolved."

"Me too Charlie and I'm so embarrassed about what happened, again."

"Don't be, especially as we've decided what we're going to do about it, yes? About helping you to loosen up."

"Yes Charlie and I really do want to."

"I know you do and I'm so pleased."

"And I'm pleased you're pleased."

"Good. So there you are relaxed and naked in your lovely comfortable bed."

"Yes. Well, no not exactly, I'm in my pyjamas."

"Really. How about just slipping out of them?"

"Why?"

"Just for me. I want to imagine you lying there, all lovely and pink and perfumed."

"Ooh, Charlie, OK just for you."

We were making progress, and I certainly could imagine the scene.

"If I could be with you I'd be lying up close and kissing your ear, and your neck, and gently, very gently touching your nipples with my finger-tips."

"Yes, OK, I get the idea."

"Now I'm licking them very gently. Can you feel that?"

"No, not yet."

"I'm sucking them now and running my tongue around your cute little areola, dabbing very gently."

"Mmmmm, what next I wonder?"

"I'm moving down slowly, very slowly. Now I'm kissing your navel, probing it with my tongue."

"My navel? Why on earth are you licking my navel?"

"Now I'm down to your hip bones, alternately kissing one and now the other."

"OK."

"I'm stopping short of your pussy though, saving that for a little later."

"Moving South steadily in fact."

"Of course, angel. I'm slowly sliding my hand up from your knee now, caressing your lovely white thigh, inching closer and closer."

"Yes, I get the picture."

"Now, tell me, are you getting moist?"

"Hang on, I'll just check. Er, sorry, no I'm not."

Suddenly I could picture her there, probably fully clothed and sitting on the sofa or at her desk. This was a complete waste of time.

"Philippa, you're hopeless. It's not going to happen is it?"

"Charlie, don't get angry with me. I can see what you're trying to do and I appreciate it but I'm just so bushed."

"It's not that, Philippa, is it? You're just not interested in sex and probably never will be."

"Don't be cruel to me, Charles. I will try, honestly."

"No, I don't think so. I don't believe you can. I don't think you want me enough."

She started sobbing.

"Don't be so cruel. I've explained it's just all been so sudden. Please give me more time. I love you Charlie and I'd do anything for you, anything. Please don't ditch me, not now we've got this far."

'*Cruel?*' I thought. *Try this for cruel.*

"So you'd do anything for me would you Philippa?"

"Yes!"

"OK, well it'll take something drastic to get you to loosen up, if you ever can. So here it is."

"What Charlie? What do I have to do?"

"You have to sleep with me and Alice, a threesome."

"What?" she shouted. "You mean have sex with you and that brainless bimbo? Are you serious?"

"Absolutely serious."

"Well, who the fuck do you think you are? You fucking arrogant bastard! Now just fuck right off!"

That exchange ended the call.

Well, that could have gone better, I thought as I quaffed the rest of the lager. *Still, good riddance. All I've got to do now is break the news to Alice and hope to God she's satisfied with the outcome.*

I went out for a drive to collect my thoughts but ended up in a bar and getting so pissed that the landlord insisted on keeping my car keys and ordering a cab to take me home. The episode of course hadn't cleared my thoughts at all and although I'd nodded off in the taxi, once in bed I slept the disjointed, interrupted, troubled sleep of a condemned man.

I awoke next day without a plan. I was dithering and anxious and I really missed my lovely little blonde and her limitless sexual repertoire. I sensed the end of our affair now made more certain by Philippa's predictable refusal. My only hope was that Alice would be satisfied at her rival's departure from the scene and admit that that had been her sole intention all along.

I showered, had a strong coffee and a stale croissant. I needed thinking time to plan the best way to break the news to Alice. I decided to spend the morning at the airfield, not to fly as I was too hungover but just to do a little work on the Pitts. During the last couple of flights I'd detected an occasional unfamiliar rattle inside the rear of the fuselage. I suspected a loose article, foreign object debris or 'fod' in aeronautical parlance, perhaps a small screw or washer or even a stone that had perhaps been brought into the cockpit stuck to the sole of my trainers.

I'd previously tried to find the source of the noise by tilting the rear seat forward and shining a torch into the dark space through which the elevator connecting rods and rudder cables were routed but could see nothing. There were many nooks and crannies where fod could get trapped and from which they might later work free. Whatever it was it had to be found as something even as small as ten pence piece could in extreme circumstances jam the elevator controls with disastrous results.

It was impossible to reach far enough into the fuselage to pick things up but I had a telescopic metal rod with a magnet on the end to recover such things provided they were made from ferrous metal and of course provided they could be located. Failing that another method was once airborne to roll the aircraft inverted, push and pull on the stick to rock the nose up and down until the offending object miraculously appeared in the Perspex canopy above my head or rather beneath it when upside down, where it would be recovered and slipped into a zipped pocket.

En route I found myself making a sudden detour past Alice's house. I wasn't ready yet to admit to myself why but I remembered from long ago the obsession and irrational behaviour that is part of being in love.

I drove past her house half hoping to catch a glimpse of her walking the dog or pruning roses in the front garden but not wanting to be seen and having to later explain my presence in the area. *Oh God, here we go again.*

I looked left as I sped past and noticed a black Mercedes sports car in the drive, the same model as Philippa's.

It couldn't be! Of course not, I told my racing imagination. I didn't know Philly's registration number but found myself making a U-turn and driving past again to make a mental note of this one.

It's impossible, it can't be hers!

I couldn't imagine a scenario in which Philippa might be visiting Alice. The more I thought about it, the more ridiculous the possibility seemed. No, I concluded, it was a co-incidence there must be dozens of that model around, thousands in fact, if not tens of thousands.

Yet it played on my mind. I remembered the paranoia that preceded the break-up of my engagement years earlier. The pain and anguish of doubt, the unfounded suspicions, the rows, the guilt and then the absolute determination subsequently to not ever get that close to anyone again.

I didn't find the fod but spent the morning tinkering with the aeroplane and joking with a hangar mate whose immaculate but puny Cessna was stabled next to my beautiful, powerful beast and then made my way home planning my report to Alice.

My hangover had dissipated and I had in my mind the words which I hoped would placate her. I dialled and she picked up after a short delay.

"Hello, angel, how are you on this lovely afternoon?"

"OK thanks but it rather depends on what you've got to tell me."

"I was hoping we might get together for lunch tomorrow, how are you fixed?"

"Charles, I've told you, we're not 'getting together' until we meet at your place with the lovely lawyer. Have you asked her yet?"

"I have and not surprisingly she told me to fuck off. Now can we forget this nonsense and get back together? I really miss you…and so does Mr Wibbly Wobbly," I added hoping she'd change her icy tone.

"Mr Wibbly Wobbly is going to stay wobbly until you've fixed it so what are you going to do about it?"

"You've got your heart set on this, angel, haven't you?"

"Yes I have. You promised and remember, the dice must be obeyed."

She was being obstinate and I was at a loss at what I could say to talk her round. Earlier in our relationship I'd have been more assertive and called her bluff but now I was in love with her I couldn't take the chance. I couldn't risk losing her.

"Angel, what more could I do but ask her? I did and she refused. She's just not the type to fulfil this fantasy. If it must be done, we'll have to find someone else."

She didn't respond. After half a minute of silence I had to find something to say as to let her hang up without further talk would almost certainly have been terminal. I had to change the subject and keep her on the line.

"I drove past your house this morning. I was on my way to look over a property for sale up on The Grange."

"Well, it's a good job you didn't call in because Ken was working from home this morning having a meeting with his boss before going to a client together for a presentation this afternoon."

"Oh, I wondered who the Merc belonged to."

"Yes, that's Bruce's."

My relief was immense. How could I have imagined that it was Philippa's?

"Darling, what's happened? A few days ago things were wonderful between us. Now you seemed to have gone cold on me. Do you want it to end? Is this impossible challenge your way of driving me away?"

"No, of course not. I'm really fond of you and I love what we do together. It's different, and it's fun and since you introduced me to the dice game it's been really exciting too. I've told you before, I love you but I'm not 'in love' with you. I'm in love with Ken. I'll do anything with you but nothing to hurt him."

It crushed me. Alice may be a delightful scatterbrain but she was without doubt a unique and complex individual. All the women I'd known, with the exception of the scrubbers I fucked on one-night stands, eagerly sought the eternal progression from friendship to romance to love to commitment. Now that I was ready to settle down the woman I'd fallen for was telling me she wanted nothing more from me than fun and sex.

"So where does that leave us? Do you want to carry on seeing me?"

"Yes, of course I do, Charlie."

"But unless I achieve the impossible and persuade Philippa to have sex with us both you won't see me again. And I can't persuade you to accept a substitute?"

"No substitute. It has to be the lawyer and it has to be next Thursday."

"But Angel, I've tried. She told me to fuck off and die. What more can I possibly do?"

"I'll tell you what I think. I think you should ask her again."

Chapter Twenty-Nine
A Lonely Week

It was the Monday before the appointed Thursday, and I hadn't heard from either woman during the weekend which I'd spent fruitlessly plotting ways of getting back with Alice. I'd also thought about life without her and it hurt. I berated myself for not being more romantic, for shagging her rather than wooing her, for treating her as a sex object, even though she didn't mind. I was sure I could have made her love me but the whole time I was just counting my lucky stars that she didn't want to. Philippa had used the words, 'please don't hurt me' and now, suddenly I knew exactly what she'd feared.

I doubted I'd hear from Philippa ever again but desperately hoped hour by hour during the weekend for a brief call or text from Alice.

I drove out to an industrial estate to meet with a building supplies company which had initially under-delivered on a shipment of laminate flooring and then followed up with a batch that simply didn't match. I was ready to vent my frustration on someone and they would certainly do.

On the way I entered a roundabout intending to turn right. Straight on would have taken me towards Alice's home. I made three complete circuits, on each one asking myself if I was man or mouse, before finally acknowledging that I had indeed become a mouse; a mouse with a breaking heart.

I drove past her home at speed and to my astonishment it was there again, the black Mercedes sports car, parked on her drive. In my befuddled state I had forgotten both registration numbers, Philippa's and the one Alice had told me belonged Ken's boss. It hadn't after all been necessary for me to remember following Alice's immediate and plausible explanation. Another home meeting perhaps. But two in a week?

The returning pain of paranoia again gripped me.

It couldn't be Philippa. It was Monday, she'd be in her office or in court. She was a very busy woman, with a currently very high workload, or so she'd said.

No, it couldn't be, particularly not after the events of the last week. The thought of her sipping coffee in Alice's kitchen brought an involuntary snigger. They hated each other. 'Keep yer 'auburn' hair on, Philly!'

"Pull yourself together man!" I shouted out loud. "For fuck's sake what's happened to you?"

I doubled back and resumed my journey to the building supplies outfit and entered in a foul mood.

I was rude, arrogant, unreasonable, bullying, sarcastic, patronising and by the time I'd finished totally embarrassed at my over-reaction to a problem to which they'd already found a solution. I very nearly apologised but wasn't in a mood to break the habit of a lifetime.

On the return journey I made another pass only to find that the Mercedes had gone.

I pulled into a lay-by and sent Alice a text.

Hi Angel, Good weekend? C.

Yes, you? A.

Free for a coffee? C.

Have you asked her again? A.

Didn't bother. Absolutely no point. C.

I see. A.

Is he still off from Wednesday? C.

Yes, Why? A.

Because I want to see you of course. C.

Old ground. A.

Angel, there's nothing I can do! C.

There is. Ask her again or forget it. A.

It's pointless. C.

She didn't respond.

It was lunchtime and I needed a beer. Rather than drink alone I gave Max G a ring to see if he was free and was delighted to find him at home, not on stand-by, which would have precluded a drink but on leave. We arranged to meet in the pub we frequent after the weekly Keep Fit class, although I hadn't attended a session for months, since I'd met Philippa in fact. A bit of male company would certainly cheer me up, get me firing on all cylinders again.

I was ashamed of myself and had to buck up before Max arrived. I'm Charles Trelawney. What the fuck was I doing letting any woman give me the run around? Philippa was a hopeless case and I should have spotted that straight away. In fact I'm sure I did. I reminded myself that it was just the long odds challenge of bedding a Plain Jane blue stocking lawyer that made me set my sights on her in the first place. Good riddance. And Alice; maybe it was time to face facts and move on. All good things come to an end and I had to admit I'd had one hell of a run. A beautiful, sensual, ready-for-anything sex partner who couldn't get enough of me but vowed she'd never leave her husband. How unique is that? How lucky was that?

Max had long known about Alice but over lunch I told him about Philippa, about how we'd met in the police station, about her pathetic workmates and their unbelievably stupid names, about her spoof call from the 'Prime Minister', about the truncated flight and about the disastrous lunch with Alice. I didn't mention the failed attempts at sex or about Alice's challenge that had brought it to an end. I just told him that she was getting too clingy and possessive so I'd kicked her into touch. I told him that I was getting bored with Alice too and looking for pastures new.

He'd listened in silence, gestureless apart from raising his eyebrows and shaking his head in disbelief at my account of the lunch at Luigi's and then looked me in the eyes and said,

"Charlie Boy, when are you going to grow up?"

We spoofed for the bill. He won, I paid.

As we parted, he suggested that as it seemed I'd be getting less exercise of a certain kind in future I should start coming to the gym class again.

He hadn't raised my spirits at all and I drove home feeling as depressed as ever.

I'd already briefed Mrs Wilson on the now unnecessary preparations for Thursday, the extra cleaning of the en-suite and the new white silk sheets. I thought about telling her not to bother with the change of bedding but decided against it.

No, if Alice didn't want to romp, I'd find someone who did. I'm a bit old for clubbing but there was a great new wine bar in town full of silly giggling girls. If I arrived late in the evening there'd be a few too pissed to bother about a ten- or fifteen-year age gap. That was my plan; cauterize the wound and move on.

I tried hard to fantasise that night about the prospect of new young flesh, the chatting up, the proposition and the conquest but my thoughts kept returning time and again to Alice. I knew that the fantasy was born of disappointment, frustration and revenge. I knew she'd be alone the next three nights and that knowledge increased the ache in my stomach. Despite the best laid plans I'd be sleeping alone on Thursday, between the new white silk sheets.

On Tuesday morning I phoned Alice to test her resolve at the prospect of dining and sleeping alone for three consecutive nights. It would be a challenge for her I knew, and I desperately hoped that as the time got closer, she'd relent. She loved good food and I'd never before dined out with her without ending up in bed, or the back of the car, or even having sex somewhere al fresco.

My cunning plan was to invite her out for dinner, making clear it was just dinner. I would acknowledge that I'd failed in the challenge, despite strenuous and embarrassing efforts and so couldn't expect to bed her afterwards. I'd just drive her home, kiss her goodnight in the car and go back to my apartment alone. I knew darn well of course that after a glass or two of wine and an empty house to go back to she'd get horny as hell and be toying with my zip before we got halfway there.

There was no reply.

Her phone went unanswered throughout the day and that evening. On Wednesday morning, Day 9 on the abandoned timing plan, I called again and this time she picked up straight away.

"Hi Alice, how's things?"

"OK. You?"

"Yes, fine thanks. Missing you though."

"So what are you doing about it? Have you asked her again?"

That icy tone had returned to her voice. How quickly people can change.

"No Angel, I told you. You are asking me to achieve the impossible. You might as well have asked for Mother Theresa. There's no way she'd change her mind, in fact she'll never again answer the phone to me, of that I'm absolutely sure."

"You said you'd ask her again," she snapped.

"No I didn't. I asked her because you wanted me too. Her refusal was emphatic."

"What does that mean?"

"It means that she'd rather appear in court naked with a thorny-stemmed rose gripped between her tight little buttocks and tassels on her tiny tits."

That raised a laugh and so I thought I'd continue with the humour to brighten Alice's mood and maybe get her to change her mind.

"She'd rather be caught masturbating in her car by speed cops and the film posted on YouTube."

That got a giggle and Alice's tone softened. A few more had her laughing out loud.

She recapped on her husband's schedule for next few days and how wasteful it would be to miss the opportunity.

"And I hate to think of you lying there all alone Angel," I gambled, "Let's get together, it's been so long."

"Yes, how long is it now?"

"Well, it's getting longer as you speak Angel."

"OK, I'll give you one last chance."

"You will? That's my girl."

"Yes, I'll give you one more chance to ask her again and have her there for eight o'clock tomorrow night."

"But."

The rest of my sentence went unheard.

So that was it. After all this time it had come to an end.

I spent Wednesday poking around the latest property I'd just acquired for renovation. It was a 1930s semi with overgrown gardens and 1950s décor throughout. It was also fully furnished, a veritable museum to that period. It was a probate sale following the departure of an old lady who'd been suddenly taken into care before dying less than a week later. Her only relatives, a son and his wife lived in the USA and had made one very brief visit, presumably to search for any valuables before putting it on the market lock, stock and clutter. They sold it to me it with the proviso that anything of value subsequently discovered would be shipped to them at my expense.

There was sad evidence of her last day in residence. The bedding was turned back, the remains of a breakfast atrophying on plates in the kitchen sink, half a mug of tea capped with a crust of mould and dirty laundry twisted in careless knots in the washing machine. The relatives had not made any attempt to clear up in their haste to check for anything of value. The bureau had been hurriedly searched and every drawer in the house had been turned out as if ransacked by vandals. The cushions had been removed from the sofa and armchairs which had all been turned over and even had their under-linings cut with a sharp knife or scissors to retrieve any small change or other items that might have accidentally slipped from pockets over the years or been hidden there more recently.

Cupboards full of crockery and kitchen utensils, wardrobes full of clothes and ladies' shoes, a display cabinet full of porcelain, bedside table drawers full of pills and spectacles and lace handkerchiefs, all abandoned.

I was astonished and saddened too to find that a number of family photograph albums had been discarded too. Black and white images of a newborn baby, buckets and spades on a beach by a pier, an oversized sun hat on a grinning toddler, a nervous boy's first day at school and proudly posing on his first bicycle. Colour photos of family groups, weddings, holidays and cheeky children pulling faces and poking out their tongues. To me an invaluable pictorial record of a family's life, probably once the most cherished possession to be saved in the event of a house fire, now discarded along with the detritus of a lonely life.

I wondered if that's how I would eventually end up. An elderly bachelor living and dying alone in dementia-fuelled untidiness, uncleanliness and squalor with no-one to care or even remember.

That evening I sat at home alone drinking lager and watching a couple of DVDs, *Top Gun* and *The Battle of Britain*. What was it about flying that had so consumed me? From boyhood I'd wanted only to be a fighter pilot. The speed, the thrust, the 'g', the three-dimensional freedom, the sheer brutal power, the self-reliance, the bravery, the achievement and the glamour. I'd had a taste, not the full career but more than most. Now I had my beautiful Pitts and access to the pure joy of flight whenever I wanted it and without the restrictions, discipline and bullshit of Her Majesty's Royal Air Force.

There's a scene in *The Battle of Britain* film in which supporting actors Christopher Plummer and Susannah York, a married couple are interrupted by an air raid when about to hop into bed for some much delayed conjugals. He's lying on the bed fully clothed in uniform and she's partially undressed wearing a WAAF officer's blouse, frilly knickers, stockings and suspenders. All very sexy but she's coy about undressing in front of him with the lights on.

The parallel with Philippa immediately sprang to mind and emboldened by the beers I decided to have one last crack at it and although it was late texted her.

You still mad at me? C.

Hell yes! What did you expect? P.

Will you ever forgive me? C.

There was no reply for an hour. I'd fallen asleep slouched on the sofa at the point where Susannah hears about her husband's horrifying burn injuries and I was awoken by the buzzing of my mobile as the closing titles rolled. Another text from Philippa, the shock of which had me bolt upright and sober in an instant.

Do you still want me to do it? P.

It took a minute for me to decide how to reply.

Yes, but only if you're happy to. C.

Was it your idea or hers? P.

She was testing me.

Does that matter? C.

Yes it certainly does! P.

How should I answer? If I said it was my idea, then she'd think I'm a real perve. If I said it was Alice's she'd think I'm under her thumb or suspect foul play and maybe think she'd be walking into a cat fight. I took too long to reply as I pondered the motive behind the question.

Well? P.

It was hers. C.

OK. If it was hers, I'll do it. When and where? P.

My place at eight o'clock tomorrow. C.

Had I dreamt it? How could it be true? Surely, she was winding me up. Yes, that's it, a parting kick of disappointment straight in the balls. And I deserve it.

Chapter Thirty
White Silk Sheets

I called Alice first thing next day and gave her the news she'd been hoping for but not expecting I'm sure. Her fantasy might after all be fulfilled, unless Philippa chickens out at the last minute, I added under my breath.

To my astonishment she answered in a matter of fact way, with not a hint of excitement in her voice.

"OK, good. Your place at eight then. Don't pick me up, I'll make my own way there."

Could her bluff have just been called? Had she demanded this stupid, near impossible challenge in the certain belief that I'd fail to arrange it? Had her plan simply been to ruin the relationship she'd long suspected I was having with Philippa and then to ditch me. If so, had it just backfired? Well, this was going to be interesting, either way.

I sat around whilst Mrs Wilson tidied the apartment, cleaned the en-suite, hoovered the carpets and changed the bedding. She gave me a grandmotherly look of disapproval, muttering something indiscernible to herself as she smoothed down the white silk sheets and plumped up the pillows. The reason for her mumblings and old-fashioned look became apparent when, as she left, she handed to me the crib sheet I'd prepared for my call to Philippa that she'd found under a cushion. *'...now I'm licking your navel.'*

After she'd departed, I made a shopping list and headed for the supermarket.

I bought champagne, white wine, mineral water, orange juice, lager and condoms.

The thought then occurred to me that the ladies might be expecting dinner as well. That could significantly delay the proceedings so I decided to buy food that could be cooked quickly; very quickly. I selected some scallops, French bread and soft cheese but was dithering about the main course when I decided to forget the whole thing and if necessary take them out to dinner afterwards instead, depending of course on how the evening progressed and whether or not one of them or both had walked out before that point.

I returned to the flat and considered how the early manoeuvrings might play out. I rearranged the furniture by removing one of the two armchairs complete with its scatter cushion from the living room and into the bedroom, leaving just one opposite the sofa. If I made sure I occupied the remaining armchair, the ladies would be forced to sit together on the settee, no doubt at either end. I could then, after passing each a glass of champagne, take a seat between them and cosy up to both.

What was Alice planning? The thought played on my mind throughout day apart from the equal time I spent thinking about Philippa's likely reaction to any physical attention whatsoever from either of us. I looked at various scenarios from Alice's point of view. If she seriously thought we could get Philippa into bed for sex, she clearly was going to be disappointed at her rival's nervousness, nay frigidity. If she wanted to fuck me in Philippa's presence and send her off in tears, that was a more realistic outcome. If she wanted to come onto Philippa and scare her off, with me an accessory to the assault and thus end any relationship real or imagined, that too was highly likely. And what of Philippa? Was there really any chance that she'd show up? No, of course not. It was a wind-up for sure.

With that at last out of mind I concentrated my thoughts on how to handle the transition from Alice's hoped-for threesome into a regular, familiar, long-overdue twosome. We'd give the lawyer an hour before concluding that she wasn't coming, during which time I'd get a drink or two down Alice and rebut her inevitable accusations that I'd lied about Philippa's agreement to join us. At least then I'd have a chance to get things back on track. I'd have the dice at the ready.

I was showered and changed by seven and polishing glasses in the kitchen when the phone rang. It was Max. After some small talk, he came to the point of his call.

"Listen, matey, you and I go back a long way, yeah?"

"Yes, Max, we certainly do."

"And you know I'd always take your side in any trouble."

"Yes, buddy, what's on your mind?"

"Look, it's none of my business but…"

"Come on, Max, spit it out."

"I don't want to fall out with you."

"I know that…and it's not going to happen. What is it? Say your piece."

"OK, mate, I think you're being a complete cunt."

"What? What are you on about?"

"You're kicking Alice into touch you say, 'cos you're bored with her'. You're making a big mistake. She's the best thing that's happened to you in years. I've never known you as happy since you took up with her. It's time you took a long hard look at yourself and your lifestyle and recognise what you've got, then settle down before it's too late. You're so far up your own arse with all the womanising and it's time you grew up."

What could I say to that? He was my oldest friend and if things had turned out differently, I'd have been honoured to be his wingman. He was wise and worldly and of course I knew he was right.

"Max, you don't need to tell me that. The truth is I know she's the one for me and I'd settle down with her like a shot, if I had the chance. Trouble is whilst she's happy to shag me senseless, she'll never leave her husband. It's hopeless, mate, and there's absolutely zilch I can do about it."

"Ah, I see. Shame. Sorry. OK, matey, good luck. See you soon. Cheers."

"Cheers."

Eight o'clock passed and neither Alice nor Philippa had shown up or made any contact. I rang both but their phones were switched off. I didn't leave messages as I was beginning to suspect that I'd been set up and appearing anxious would have just compounded the ridicule. I was depressed and Max's frank words kept ringing in my ears. *'You're so far up your own arse with all the womanising and it's time you grew up.'*

My hand wavered over the champagne in the ice bucket but I settled instead for a Peroni which I necked in four or five swigs straight from the bottle.

The front door video phone buzzed and I leapt to my feet to answer it. Pictured on the screen were both Alice and Philippa, cheek to cheek their faces distorted by their proximity to the camera. A coincidence that they should both be late yet arrive together I thought.

"Helloooo. We're here," they shouted in unison.

"Come on up," I replied pressing the door release button.

What a contrast to their arrival at Luigi's a few short weeks ago. No overt animosity; quite the contrary. They looked like a couple of dizzy girls out on the lash.

I opened my door to them and as they entered, they simultaneously kissed me on the cheeks, one each side.

Philippa seemed so different from the last time we met, and it wasn't just her appearance that had changed. There was something about her demeanour too, something unnerving, even threatening. A new confidence had banished the nervousness I'd expected to see. Had my defence lawyer suddenly turned prosecutor? The uncanny feeling though passed as soon as she spoke.

"Hello, Charles. This is exciting, isn't it?"

Alice echoed the sentiment.

Philly was wearing the tight-fitting silky black trousers I'd seen before, what looked like a sleeveless lacey black top and she held a small matching clutch bag gripped loosely under her armpit. Her red high heels again matched her lipstick but her eye makeup was much more adventurous than I'd seen her wear at any time in the past.

More surprising was Alice's appearance. Not a repeat of the tarty caricature in gold she'd performed at Luigi's but 'smart sexy' as she often described it when attending events for which the suggested dress code was 'smart casual'.

She wore a white blouse, short black skirt, black stockings and black high heels. The blouse although not see-through permitted more than a glimpse of her lace-edged black bra which strained to hold the lovely round puppies in check and defeated all bar three of its buttons, although it revealed barely an inch of cleavage.

Alice was carrying a large carrier bag of the type posh dress shops give away but when I reached out in an attempt to politely relieve her of it, she whisked it away as if it contained a 'Not-to-be-opened-'til-Christmas-Day' present or some secret merchandise.

"Just a little treat for later Darling. Let's not spoil the surprise."

The girls giggled loudly at that, very much giving me the impression that they'd both already had a measure or two of Dutch courage. I was both astonished and relieved at their demeanour. I began to think that the evening might not after all turn out to be the unmitigated disaster I'd been expecting.

I ushered the pair towards the sofa and invited them to select some music on *Spotify* whilst I prepared the drinks. From the kitchen I heard them making suggestions to each other about a play list for the evening. They were twittering like a pair of school friends.

"No, he won't like that one." Alice snorted with laughter echoed by Philippa.

"I know Alice… Vivaldi. Are you OK with Vivaldi?"

"Don't know any of their songs to be honest," Alice joked.

Again they laughed. It was extraordinary. I watched them through the jamb of the door as they put down the remote control having made their music selection and settled on the sofa. I listened as they started exchanging girly chit chat.

"I like your top," said Alice.

"Thank you, yours is nice too."

"Were you working today?"

"Yes but I took the afternoon off. You?"

"No, I'm sort of between jobs at the moment."

"What sort of work do you do…when you're working?"

"Oh, an eclectic mix," Alice replied. *'Eclectic mix!' Where on earth did that one come from?* I wondered. Alice was clearly upping her game.

"I used to be in advertising and before that in newspapers."

"Oh that must have been fun. Not like the boring old law."

This was marvellous. They were both making an effort to be nice to each other. I began to get excited.

I could see Philippa's eyes drawn to Alice's stocking tops which were clearly on view as they sat at either ends of the sofa.

"Victoria's Secret?"

"No, Intimissimi but my basque is."

"Mine too," Philly replied.

Good God, she was actually wearing a basque. Jesus! Loosening up or what?

"Champagne or cocktails?" I shouted from the kitchen.

"Champagne for me please," Philippa replied.

"Have you got any Cassis Charles?" Alice enquired.

"Yep."

"Then I'll have a Kir Royale."

It was obvious to me that Alice was trying hard to eradicate the bimbo image she'd deliberately presented to Philippa at their last meeting and appear to be sophisticated. Philippa for her part was responding with great tolerance and forgiveness. My thoughts suddenly returned to the black Mercedes. Could they possibly have got together since that dreadful lunch and made friends, or were they both just trying hard to get on for my sake?

There was a moment of silence and then while I was still occupied in the kitchen, I heard Philly's lowered voice. Barely above a whisper she said,

"What's this? Alice, take a look at this!"

A further moment of silence followed.

Intrigued, I popped my head around the door and saw Alice hurriedly stuffing something into her carrier bag. They both looked a bit shocked and I concluded that perhaps the bag had been found to contain an additional item that Alice hadn't bought, a bonus freebie, possibly a sex toy slipped in unnoticed by the shop assistant.

I brought the drinks in on a tray and placed them on a coffee table an arm's stretch from the sofa where the girls sat separated only by the posh shopping bag. Philippa took a peep into the bag and laughed the dirtiest laugh I'd ever heard from her; in fact, one I wouldn't have thought was in her laughter repertoire.

"Wonderful, Alice. Just wonderful." I moved to settle in between them but Alice quickly lifted the bag onto her lap and shifted along to sit closer to Philippa baulking my planned manoeuvre.

"Come on, Alice. What have you got there?" I asked, beginning to suspect a joke at my expense.

"We'll show you later, darling. Don't worry, you're going to love it."

I was intrigued though somewhat suspicious, particularly as she'd said, *'We'll show you,'* implying some collusion between them. I was past caring though as I was by then confident that Alice's fantasy was actually about to be acted out. The trouser snake was sensing it too.

I sat for a while at the end of the sofa as we drank our first drink but was cut out of the conversation as the two women chatted away and moved progressively closer and closer to each other. To break the two-way conversation, I returned with the second round of drinks to sit in the armchair opposite them. But still they ignored me, intent on continuing the girlish twitter.

"I like the way you've got your hair tonight," Alice whispered as she gently brushed Philippa's hair back across her cheek to hook it behind an ear revealing more of her neck.

"It really suits you. Do you ever wear it back?"

Philippa blushed but didn't flinch as I'd have expected and smiled at the compliment.

"Only at home, scragged back while I'm working in the evenings but not in the office, we have to be so prim and proper."

"You're certainly not looking prim and proper tonight, Philippa. You're looking very sexy."

"Thanks. You are too."

"Do you think our basques are the same?" Alice asked. "Probably. Still it's not as bad as turning up in the same dress."

They laughed. I watched in amazement and growing frustration.

"Yes, I think they are the same," Alice said, gently picking at Philippa's blouse and touching the lacey edge of the basque now just visible.

She then undid one button of her own blouse to confirm the point.

"Yes, look. Identical."

"Yes, but yours is a bit bigger in the … 'er top," Philippa tentatively joked.

The lawyer was now showing the effects of the booze and seemed to be getting bolder with every passing minute.

"I've always wanted a bust like yours, Alice. In fact, I'd have a boob job if I was brave enough."

"Oh don't ever do that, Philly, yours are in perfect proportion to your slender figure. And be careful what you wish for. You won't believe some of the difficulties of carrying these around all the time."

With that Alice took Philippa's right hand and for several seconds held it against her own left breast. Philly blushed again but didn't seem phased by the advance. "And another thing. Blokes just stare at them when they're talking to you. What is it about men and tits?"

"I know what you mean, Alice, but I'd enjoy a bit more up there. A thirty-six maybe. You can wear such nice dresses when you've got enough to add some shape."

I feared it was in danger of turning into a girls' night in, so I decided some intervention was needed to get our plans back on track. I pondered for a few minutes on whether to ease into the subject of what we'd come here to do or just blurt it out.

Philippa's reaction so far had been encouraging but I was worried that she might take flight once things got steamy.

"Philly, are you entirely happy with…what's planned…I mean with…coming to bed with us?"

I thought that had the right blend of concern and consideration.

Alice replied for her.

"Of course she is. We've talked about it and it's OK if we take it slowly."

"You've talked about it? When?" Alice paused long enough for me to suspect a lie was to follow.

"We met as we arrived here and went for a quick drink."

"Oh, I see."

Lie or not, I didn't really care. It was still on and we were about to make a start at last.

"Happy, Philly?" Alice whispered.

"Yes, happy Alice."

They kissed briefly, just a tiny peck and got to their feet, Alice leading the way to my bedroom taking the carrier bag with her.

The two girls entered first and I followed but as I got to the doorway Alice turned and stopped me with a gentle push to my chest.

"I'm sure you'd like to see some girl on girl action first Charlie, so go and slip out of your clothes while we get ready." She kissed me briefly to prevent any argument, smiled and raised her eyebrows as if to say, *'Well, we've actually done it.'*

I took my black silk dressing gown with its gold Japanese motif from the peg behind the door and went to the main bathroom to undress leaving the en-suite for them to use in their preparations. When I returned, naked under the silk I found Philippa sitting on the bed with Alice standing close by. Both were fully clothed.

I gently embraced Alice and moved to undress her but she took my hands in hers to stop me.

"No, Charlie, we'll do that…you can watch for now and join in later, when we're ready."

She then walked across the room and repositioned the armchair about a foot to one side of where I had placed it and adjusted the cushion.

"What are you doing?" I asked.

"I want you a bit closer to the action, darling. Sit there."

I sat down extremely excited at what was in store. Mr Wibbly-Wobbly was now Mr Stick of Blackpool Rock and I had to adjust my dressing gown and use the cushion to cover up, embarrassed as the girls were still fully clothed.

Alice produced the carrier bag and theatrically revealed its contents one by one.

"Now what have we here?"

The first item was a pink feather duster.

"This one's for the girls," she announced dabbing it gently on Philippa's bosom like a fairy with a magic wand and gave an exaggerated squeal of delight. "Ooooooh!"

Next out was a shiny chrome-plated vibrator about eight inches long.

"And so is this one."

Philippa smiled.

A black silk blindfold was next.

"And this is especially for you."

I frowned.

"Bear with, bear with. You'll like it."

Next to be revealed were two pairs of toy handcuffs.

I frowned again.

"Just to make sure you don't jump the gun until we're absolutely ready for you to join in. We know what you're like don't we Philippa?"

"We certainly do," Philly replied joining the banter.

Alice reassured me with a firm kiss and I willingly accepted the handcuffs binding my wrists together. She then moved behind the chair and offered up the blindfold which she tied in a tight knot behind my head. That done she nibbled my earlobe and whispered.

"Remember, the dice must be obeyed."

I felt her move past me and towards Philippa.

I could tell that the girls had started undressing each other. Familiar exaggerated fake breathless gasps of delight came from Alice and I sensed genuine ones from Philly. It was too good to miss so I pushed up the blindfold with my captive hands to catch a glimpse of them both stripped of their overclothing and down to the basques.

Alice was sitting on the edge of the bed with Philippa standing between her knees as she fiddled with her shy playmate's lingerie. Philippa's pert little bottom looked incredibly sexy in the scanty underwear and she seemed quite content with Alice's close attention. Not the embarrassed dash for concealment under the duvet that had characterised our two disastrous previous sexual assignations. No, on the contrary, she seemed to be participating freely and enjoying it. Well, I thought, as long as it loosens her up.

At that point Alice spotted that I'd removed the blindfold and got hurriedly to her feet.

"Not yet! Not Yet! You naughty boy."

She picked up the feather duster and the second pair of handcuffs as she approached me. In a speedy action as if premeditated she snapped one end of the handcuffs around the small chain that linked those I was already wearing and the other around a central heating pipe feeding a radiator behind me. So that was why she'd repositioned the chair; not to 'get me a bit closer to the action' but to ensure I couldn't participate until invited.

Next she reapplied the blindfold, tying it even tighter than last time. I was unable to get out of the chair and deprived of seeing what the girls were doing. I couldn't see and I couldn't touch. I could only listen.

I could hear them sighing and purring and panting. It was erotic torture. I could only guess that they were by now naked but I could tell from the sound of the mattress that they were definitely now lying on the bed.

"Alice, OK, I'm ready. Let me join you," I pleaded.

"Ready you may be, but we're not ready for you just yet. Shall we see how he's getting on?"

I heard one of them get down from the bed and approach my chair. Whoever it was first pulled away the cushion and threw it to the ground before opening my dressing gown to expose my eager member. Was it Alice or was it Philippa? It must have been Alice, but the uncertainty added to both the eroticism and to my embarrassment. Next I felt the feather duster tickling my scrotum and then being rubbed very gently up and down my throbbing willy, all in total silence. I strained against my chains but couldn't move.

The silence was broken by girlish giggles from both of them and I was suddenly gripped by suspicion and fear. Were they going to deny me the chance to join in? Was that their plan all along? Were they going to leave me here all night, or even all week, to be found by Mrs Wilson naked, soiled and starving like a tortured war zone hostage?

I then felt breath on my face. Next a breath in my ear. Was it torture or foreplay? It could be either, but I didn't like it.

"OK, girls, that's enough. Come on, this isn't what we came here for."

I then felt hands on my knees and the weight of someone leaning forward towards me; then soft breasts being gently brushed left and right across my chest and then across my face. They had to be Alice's judging by the size although the nipples were erect, almost hard. They hadn't needed teasing out this time evidently.

"All good things come to those who wait. Don't you trust me, darling?" It was Alice's voice.

"Not too long now. Be patient."

I heard her re-join Philippa on the bed. I heard them kissing. I heard them sighing. I heard murmurs of pleasure. And then I heard the sex talk.

"I'm lying up close and kissing your ear, and your neck, and gently, very gently touching your nipples with my fingertips."

"Lovely. May I touch yours?"

"Now I'm licking them very gently. Can you feel that?"

"Mmmm yes, that's wonderful, Alice."

"I'm sucking them now and running my tongue around your cute little areola, dabbing very gently."

"Oh that's exquisite, Alice."

"I'm moving down slowly, very slowly. Now I'm kissing your navel, probing it with my tongue."

"Oh don't bother with that, Alice, move on down."

"Now I'm down to your hip bones, alternately kissing one and now the other."

"That is unbelievably sexy."

"I'm stopping short of your lovely little pussy though, saving that for a little later."

"Not too much later I hope."

"Of course not, angel." Alice's voice stressed 'Angel', a clear reprimand for my using the name with both of them.

"I'm slowly sliding my hand up from your knee now, caressing your lovely white thigh, inching closer and closer."

"Oh, Alice, pleeeeeeeeeease don't make me wait any longer."

"Now, tell me, are you getting moist?"

"Positively soaking, darling!"

They both broke into fits of laughter and I heard the ripping of paper as my crib sheet was torn into tiny pieces and showered over my head like confetti.

I was straining at the handcuffs and becoming fearful that they might be planning to do me a serious injury.

"OK, girls, very funny. I asked for that. But, Alice, you did keep pestering me to persuade her. You kept telling me to ask her again."

"Did you, Alice?" Philippa asked softly.

"Yes," she replied equally softly after a pause of a few seconds.

For the next five minutes the silence was broken only by heavy breathing and panting which reached a crescendo with a familiar noise, the unmistakable timid squeak of Alice's orgasm.

Five minutes passed in total silence.

"We're both ready for you now, Charles," said Alice.

I heard her getting down from the bed and felt her brush past me to place herself behind my chair. I felt a surge of anticipation expecting to be released from the handcuffs. Instead she roughly gagged me with a thin silk scarf which she tied painfully tight behind my neck before quickly pulling the chair from beneath me.

"OK, you self-centred, arrogant bastard, it's payback time," she muttered in a low voice.

I was left in a kneeling position desperately tugging at the handcuffs fearful of what cruelty was sure to follow.

Alice's voice again.

"We've decided what we want you to do for us Charlie...if you're capable of it that is."

An unseen hand then slapped a slop of KY Jelly between my bum cheeks and instantly I knew what was coming next. I thrashed about with all my strength to free myself but became wedged between the bed and the armchair. Philippa restrained me by sitting across my calves and ankles whilst Alice slowly slipped the thin chromium-plated vibrator into my arse and switched it on. It hurt like hell and I strained to push it out as if constipated. I succeeded at first but then she shoved it even further, to the point that I realised that my struggle might cause some serious damage.

"You fucking bitches," I shouted. "What's got into you! Why are you doing this?"

Philippa's voice now, "We want you to just lie there and think about all the women you've treated so badly, all the lies you've told and all the pain you've inflicted in your selfish life. And this is for Oliver too."

"Who?" I cried, "Who the fuck's Oliver?"

Next I felt Alice astride my hips riding me like a seaside donkey and I felt her writing something on my back in what turned out to be lipstick.

She leaned forward and whispered in my ear,

"Well, my darling, you conniving bastard. You've got half an hour to get free. We've invited some of your gym friends round for a party here at ten."

They had a last laugh at my humiliation and left the apartment leaving the front door propped open.

Chapter Thirty-One
Slipping the Surly Bonds

I drove to the airfield next day smarting with the embarrassment, humiliation and loss of the previous evening.

Embarrassment at the realisation that I'd been well and truly stitched up and hadn't seen it coming. I didn't believe for one moment the girls had met at my front door and slipped away for a drink before calling. It was obvious that they'd met several times previously and planned the whole thing. It all now fell into place. The Mercedes on Alice's driveway, Philippa's sudden agreement to take part, Alice's veiled threats to Mr Wibbly-Wobbly during our last romp and her insistence that I should persevere and proposition Philippa again after her blunt refusal.

Humiliation at the thought of them chaining me naked to the radiator and reading out loud my banal crib sheet. Humiliation too when the only three guys to accept Alice's invitation arrived to find me still captive with the words 'Insert here Big Boy!' written in lipstick on my back with an arrow pointing down to the crack of my bum, surrounded by a scattering of gay men's porn magazines. And loss. The loss of my lovely, lively, luscious, little porn star, now gone forever, just as I'd realised that I'd fallen in love with her and yearned for a different kind of relationship.

Max was right, I'd been a complete cunt; an arrogant, exploitative, conniving fool. I had looked at women as playthings and shown them no respect. I'd treated it as a game and now, for the second time in my life, it was a game I'd lost.

I harboured no hopes of reconciliation with Alice and no desire to rapidly replace her with the next in line, to cauterize the wound by speedily finding another lover. I was numb and desolate and sexless. Some phantom doctor had visited me in the night and surgically removed my libido. I was spent.

All I could think of was to do what I often do to relieve stress and cheer myself up; go flying and slip the surly bonds of earth.

It was Friday morning and the aerodrome was remarkably quiet which surprised me as the conditions were perfect. Three eighths of alto-cumulous with their base at about seven and a half thousand feet bubbled upwards forming great white mountains in the azure blue sky to their tops at around ten. A perfect day for some cloud flying.

I rolled the Pitts out of the hangar, pushed it to the pumps and filled the tanks to about three-quarters full. I walked around the aircraft and conducted the essential pre-flight checks. A note I'd left myself in the cockpit reminded me to have yet another look for the loose article that had caused the puzzling rattle on recent trips. I found nothing so whatever it was must have shaken free, slipped out and fallen to earth.

I removed the front seat cushions and again secured the redundant harness straps so that they couldn't interfere with the controls as I threw the aircraft about the sky.

I strapped in, ratcheted up the five-point harness and plugged in the twin comms leads that linked the headset in my canvas helmet to the radio and intercom.

The starting procedure really requires two feet, both knees and three hands. The absence of a parking brake makes it necessary to keep one's feet pressing firmly on the toe brakes. When the starter is activated by turning the ignition key with one hand whilst with the other advancing the mixture control smoothly once the engine fires, one is an arm short because the control column must be held fully back at this point. The only solution is to tightly grip the stick with your knees.

I flicked on the master switch and checked that the alternate air control was in the 'off' position. I set the prop governor to high rpm and switched the fuel selector to 'on'. I exercised the throttle lever fore and aft then set it a quarter open. Next I pushed the mixture control to fully rich and primed the fuel system with three strokes of the wobble pump situated below and to the outside of my left calf. I pulled the mixture back to 'idle cut-off', shouted, "Clear Prop!" and turned the key cranking the engine into life with a deafening roar as I returned the mixture steadily to fully rich. My spirits rose as the instruments in front of me sprang into life.

I taxied out to the hold of the duty runway and turned the Pitts into wind holding it stationary on the toe brakes as I monitored the oil pressure and waited for the oil temperature to reach the minimum for take-off.

Whilst waiting I checked the flying controls for full and free movement and that the trim tab on the elevator was functioning properly then set it to 'neutral' for take-off. All OK. I further tightened my harness with the ratchet until I could no longer lean forward in the seat or lift myself off it and double checked that the canopy was closed and locked.

With the engine oil and cylinder head temperature within limits, I checked the magnetos at 1800 rpm before increasing to 2000 and cycling the prop. As the propeller moved momentarily into coarse pitch, the aircraft strained against the brakes like an impatient thoroughbred in the starting stalls at a racetrack. I spun the Pitts round on the spot to give me a better view of the approach and having satisfied myself that there were no aircraft on 'finals' I called the tower and announced my intention to enter the runway.

"Nothing known to conflict," they answered, "wind two eight zero, ten knots."

I entered runway 28 which stretched just short of a kilometre ahead of me, scanned the engine instruments to confirm 'temps and pressures' were within limits, double checked the mixture was fully rich and the prop fully fine, positioned myself on the centreline and smoothly opened the throttle to full power. Applying rudder to counter the yaw as I accelerated, I lifted the tailwheel after two seconds, giving me a much better view of the runway ahead and after five seconds I was airborne.

What joy!

I pulled the prop back to coarse pitch and at a thousand feet banked left into a 270-degree climbing turn at a hundred and twenty miles an hour taking me back over the airfield at two thousand feet. I levelled off, throttled back to cruising power, leaned off the mixture a touch, trimmed the aircraft for level flight and rolled inverted for a few seconds to ensure my harness was holding and that no loose articles were in evidence.

I headed out towards a great stack of cumulus and entered a spiralling climb around it. At five thousand feet I levelled off but continued to circle it running my port wing tip into the fluffy white vapour like a knife into candyfloss.

I dived to a hundred and eighty miles an hour and then in a zoom-climb converted the speed back into height, rolling as I climbed vertically. As the speed decayed almost to zero, I kicked in full left rudder, applied a little right aileron, reduced the throttle slightly and the aircraft pivoted on the spot in a perfect stall turn. I held the vertical down line for a few seconds as the velocity increased and then pulled up into a 45-degree climb and again advanced the throttle to full power.

I romped for fifteen minutes in that exclusive aerial playground, sating my eager appetite with the sheer joys unknown to most, understanding precisely what J.G. Magee shared through his faultless verse.

I well and truly *'danced the skies on laughter-silvered wings'*, literally laughing out loud. "Yippeeeeeeeeee!"

I *'climbed, and joined the tumbling mirth of sun-split clouds'*, and wondered at their contrasting pure virgin-white uplands and warning grey valleys.

I flicked on the display system and on full power pulled up into a vertical roll drawing an upward corkscrew trail of thick white smoke until, *'High in the sunlit silence, hov'ring there'* the aircraft stopped momentarily, gravity fighting the horsepower until gravity won as she inevitably will. I smoothly closed the throttle, eased the stick forward and firmly held it there. The aircraft slid backwards a few lengths before flipping canopy downwards into a vertical descent.

I climbed again, *'Up, up the long, delirious burning blue'*, rolling, flicking and looping. I'd once more, *'topped the wind-swept heights with easy grace'* until, light-headed I'd had my fill and the euphoria melted into an all-consuming feeling of contented relaxation, an aerobatic pilot's post-coital glow.

With playtime over and relaxation returning, at five thousand feet my thoughts drifted back to Alice and what might have been.

I decided to descend down to two thousand, the height at which procedure required me to arrive over the aerodrome, by the most enjoyable if not the fastest route, a flat spin.

The speed decayed as I closed the throttle and pulled back progressively on the stick to maintain level flight until the stall. I felt the pre-stall buffet vibrations and kicked and held in full left rudder. The nose dropped to port and as the Pitts spiralled down, I controlled the speed of the violent rotation by applying varying degrees of in-spin and out-spin aileron. Recovery would be simple. Check throttle fully closed, apply full right rudder and after a brief pause push the stick forward until the rotation stops.

Chapter Thirty-Two
Seeing Her Again

It was a glorious day. The sun shone above a cloudless blue sky and songbirds sang their little hearts out as if it were spring rather than the first week of October. I manoeuvred tentatively along the unfamiliar tree-lined drive, looking out for directions to the car park. I felt happier than I can ever remember, in fact I'd say without doubt I'm now the happiest I've ever been in my entire life.

I'd arrived fifteen minutes early but remained in my car in the parking area waiting for Alice to appear and felt very excited at the prospect of seeing her again. A number of people, mainly men, were gathered in huddles at various points in the wooded park decorated by leaves in yellows, reds and browns, some already falling, some underfoot and others hanging on for the first gales of winter just a month or two away.

Then I saw her. She was talking to a group of men but it was clear from the constant movement of her head that she was listening to them but looking out for me. She caught sight of me and her face lit up.

Isn't it amazing how suddenly life can change? How you can see a person in one light and then in a flash your view can change, utterly.

It was an absolute joy to be with her. Beautiful, vibrant, excitingly unpredictable, full of life, full of humour, yet so tender and loving; not at all the sex-mad bimbo that Charles had led me to believe.

We'd met several times a week during the three months since he'd been killed and made love a dozen times or more. His funeral had been delayed following the post-mortem and uncertainties surrounding the air accident investigation which ultimately concluded that he'd been unable to recover from a spin because of a serious control restriction.

My sole reason for attending the funeral was not to pay my respects but because it presented yet another opportunity to be with Alice. I felt nothing for

Charles and not even the merest smidgen of guilt on learning that the cause of the control failure was found to be a silver bracelet jamming the elevator linkage. I'd often wondered where I'd lost it. I must also confess to a snort of laughter when I heard about the difficulty the authorities faced when attempting to recover the wreckage. Charles's garishly painted stunt plane had crashed at speed into a pig farm, burning it down and killing forty-five pigs and a horse.

I watched her every step as she walked towards my car, dressed all in black, a stylish three-quarter length coat, black high-heeled knee boots and her lovely blonde hair tied up beneath a spikey fascinator. She looked beautiful. My love, my darling, my angel. I owe her so much.

Sex with her that day at Charles' apartment had shocked me, thrilled me, awoken me. Our precious, tender lovemaking since has enhanced my being, and made me realise the potential I have rather than lament the wasted years of my other life. I have become a new person.

Alice had found my phone number in Charlie's mobile and called me at home one evening. She wasn't looking for a fight, was cool and matter of fact and simply wanted to know whether or not I was having affair with him. She added that she didn't really care either way but needed to know. I told her the truth, in part; that I was 'interested' but wouldn't be strung along if he was in a relationship with someone else. In that we found some common ground. I sensed it would be a contest to see who would back off and at that point I was still keen that it should be her particularly as she appeared somewhat ambivalent.

We then traded his indiscretions. She said he'd told her that for him it was strictly business, denied any interest and that he'd called me a flat-chested Plain Jane and as sexy as a plank. I returned that he'd described her as an air-headed bimbo of the first order. I then told her she was welcome to him as I'd had enough of his lies and that after all her need was apparently greater than mine. Alice asked what I meant by that and before I could stop myself, I lied that he told me her need for him was because her husband was impotent.

Her silence was so long that I had to ask if she was still on the line. The expected explosion didn't occur. Instead, very calmly she asked if we might get together for a coffee. We did so next day and later met twice at her home. On the first occasion Alice outlined her cunning plan to humiliate Charles and the realisation that he'd been cruelly grooming me from the start led me to agree.

The woman I went to meet turned out to be not the tarty Barbie Doll of our first meeting at Luigi's but a wonderful, funny girl with an irrepressible joy for life. She really made me laugh, a breath of fresh air to one whose social circle has been for so long populated by dull lawyers and intellectually challenged policemen.

Her original plan had not of course involved us getting naked together though I must confess that the thought of stripping down to our underwear and the role play she suggested had both scared and excited me in equal measure.

I probably couldn't have done even that without the earlier drinks and the champagne Charles served but once she started touching me I almost immediately wanted more and I sensed very strongly that she did too.

I think it started when she was picking at my blouse as we sat close together on the sofa. Then later in the bedroom with Charles unsighted by the blindfold and handcuffed to the radiator I felt a sudden desire to see her naked and touch her, and I wanted her to touch me. We undressed each other in silence and slipped between the cool silk sheets and in an instant I knew where my future lay. It had been a new experience for Alice too which made the moment so much more poignant, more precious.

Alice's plan had worked perfectly. He was so crestfallen, the stupid, arrogant tosser. How had I ever imagined I might be in love with him when in hindsight he epitomised all I despise in men? Had I been so desperate to find someone to love that I convinced myself that he was the one?

Alice climbed into the car, sat beside me and smiled her wonderful smile.

"Hello, gorgeous. You look wonderful."

"I know," she joked, "Black suits me, doesn't it?"

I was so keen to kiss her that moving too quickly to do so I was painfully poked in the eye by a feather in her fascinator. My eye immediately began to water.

"Sorry, Philly, does it hurt?"

"It does rather, but it'll be OK in a minute. If Charlie's looking down, he'll think I'm crying tears of sorrow."

"I'll let you know if I smell bacon."

We composed ourselves and joined the other mourners filing into the anteroom of the crematorium prior to entering the chapel, as those attending the earlier service were ushered out into the garden of remembrance beyond to admire the floral tributes. It was Charles's turn in the non-stop process, one out, one in, one waiting. It was like a drive-through stairway to heaven; his turn in the departure lounge.

It was only the second time in my life that I'd been to a crematorium. On the previous occasion, for the funeral of an elderly client I was quite fond of, I arrived twenty minutes too early and not recognising any of her relations sat through the complete service for a total stranger surrounded by weeping relatives and then had to go through the whole rigmarole again.

It was a small assembly of about ten men and two elderly ladies one of whom I understand was his cleaner. Charles would no doubt have been disappointed in not seeing a gathering of tearful past lovers but I doubt he ever left them with fond enough memories to justify their attendance. The mostly middle-aged men were I later discovered from his weekly gym class.

A guy called Max approached us solemnly to offer his condolences to Alice, introducing himself as Charles's best and lifelong friend. 'He often spoke about you Alice. I know you meant a lot to him.' Such kind words.

Alice smiled sweetly and nodded in acknowledgement. We were both surprised I think to find that the Charles we knew could count such a decent man amongst his friends.

During the service, a number of Charlie's friends made short speeches, most of which were upbeat and delivered with humour.

A Jewish man called David was first to offer a eulogy after making a bad joke about a Catholic priest and a Rabbi in a strip club but fluffed the punchline creating perhaps more laughter than the joke properly told might have deserved. He damned Charles with faint praise referring to his business acumen, implying speculator, his generosity, implying flashness and his humility, implying arrogance, before finally describing him as an enthusiastic amateur historian, which raised a laugh from all bar Max. Apparently, Charles would add historical references to volleyball scores. Everyone knew they were incorrect David explained, often by as much as a hundred years but no one wanted to embarrass him by letting on.

Max spoke of glory days in the Royal Air Force and the loyalty of his trusted friend. He read the poem, High Flight, his voice breaking at times with long pauses and coughs whilst he composed himself.

A Cornishman called Simon recounted tales of Charlie's playfulness and their shared love of *Morecambe and Wise* comedy sketches. He told of how he'd often re-enact a catchphrase by holding Charles in a headlock and saying, "Now, get out of that!"

The sniggers turned to belly laughs when he finished by turning to the coffin and saying, "Now, Charlie…get out of that!"

A small man sitting at the back shouted,

"And don't kick the ruddy volleyball!"

The Vicar cleared his throat noisily, thanked 'Charles's true friends' for their contributions and resumed the formal service. During 'two minutes of silence for reflection about our lost friend' I turned to look at Alice sitting close to me, our arms touching and savoured the thrill of the tender eye contact.

We stood for the final hymn, *From all who Dwell below the Skies* and I discreetly touched her gently in the small of her back. She moved away to break the contact but softened the blow with a look that unmistakably said, 'please understand.'

The clergyman gave the blessing and at his signal a pair of small doors opened mechanically, and the coffin slipped slowly through them and out of sight to the tune of *The Magnificent Men in their Flying Machines.*

I heard the Jewish chap, who'd by then resumed his seat in the pew in front of us, whisper a question to Simon.

"What do you suppose is in the coffin? There can't have been much left of him, especially after the fire."

A Cornish voice replied, "Ashes to ashes, mate, ashes to ashes."

My love affair with Alice lasted another six months. She remained devoted to her husband, Ken, yet shared with me a joy in sex I never thought I'd experience. It sounds corny but I found myself in her.

It ended when foolishly I asked her to leave her husband and come to live with me. It was a step too far for my lovely and her refusal marked a gradual cooling of her feelings for me. I'd broken the unspoken rules and asked too much. We have remained friends however and meet on rare occasions for coffee or lunch.

She discovered a new-found determination to better herself and was excited about the future. I knew I had to let her go and the realisation hurt, it really hurt.

I've been asked to be godmother when eventually she has children and after the initial pain, I've come to think I can do it. I'm at peace now. I'll always love her, and I owe her my new life. She showed me a new exciting, fulfilling, dimension and if I'm lucky maybe there'll be someone just like her for me awaiting around the corner. Who knows, I might even get married one day if I find another Alice. If I do, I'll see if I can track down my mother and invite her to the ceremony. She's bound to ask me about the man I've found but I'll keep that a surprise until the wedding.

Chapter Thirty-Three
Looking Back

I can't believe it's been so long.

Ten years spent listening to emotional waifs and strays, addictive personalities, those with low self-esteem, bereavement and loss issues, relationship problems, anxiety, depression, anger management difficulties, sexual fetishes and countless other conditions real or imagined.

I've counselled with a sympathetic face and calm reassuring voice a continual stream of those with marital problems, separation and divorce trauma, poor parenting skills, uncontrollable children, OCD, self-harming and eating disorders. Unlike many of my clients though I can at least say that I've had some variety in my work.

After my affair with Charles and my curious, exciting dabble into the 'other side', my fling with Philly, I did some serious soul-searching and concluded that it was time at last to grow up and put my carefree live-for-for-today attitude behind me, settle down and actually achieve something worthwhile. Something that would make Ken really proud of me. I was spurred on particularly by Philippa telling me that the selfish bastard Charles had referred to me as his 'air-headed bimbo'. I'll show him I thought and although he wasn't around to see it I'm sure he'd have been surprised at my achievements as were many others too.

I owe it all to Philly. She changed my life. To think I actually hated her with a vengeance even before we'd met and my performance at that lunch with Charles at Luigi's was something she and I laughed about for months. Well, to be honest she would laugh, and I would just cringe. We became good friends. I know it was very much more than that for her and I do believe she really loved me. For me it was something much more important, much more liberating. I was so impressed by her intellect, her confidence, her vocabulary, her professionalism and what she had achieved in her life compared with mine. It was she who encouraged me to make something of myself, something to satisfy me more than just being a wife, a lady of leisure.

She really helped by advising me to look for a career that would play to my strengths. God, I didn't know I had any until I met her. Philly actually felt that I had more confidence than her and that I was more intuitive and had more empathy. I can even remember having to look that one up. She helped by suggesting some options that would suit me. I chose to train for counselling and took to it like a duck to water. I think it was absolutely right up my strasse. I'll confess to being somewhat unconventional in the role and haven't always necessarily followed recognised procedure, which I'm sure won't surprise you but I did generally achieve positive outcomes.

In training it was impressed upon us the importance of remaining detached, of not getting too close to the client, of letting one's natural empathy draw you into a situation in which one absorbs the stress and emotional pain of those sitting opposite in the *'Comfy Chair'*. I've managed that with ease but several contemporaries on the course failed miserably and departed the profession, some requiring therapy themselves as a result. I though am made of sterner stuff and feel justified in saying I've made a real success of it. It all seemed to come quite naturally to me.

I'm pregnant with twins after years of trying and Ken, although very proud of me, is keen that I should give up work for good. As I sit here on my last working day, shredding client files and clearing my office, I have no regrets at all about my decision to do as he suggests.

My office, or consulting suite as we describe it in our brochure, is one of just two attached to a very fragrant shop and 'Wellbeing Clinique' offering homeopathic remedies, holistic counselling, alternative medicine, acupressure, aroma therapy, crystal healing (for fuck's sake!), massage with essential oils and Reiki. When I say 'attached to', I must stress that I mean positionally rather than professionally as I have absolutely no belief whatsoever in all that catch-penny nonsense. My partner and I simply rent consulting space in the establishment. We'd be at pains to disassociate ourselves from the rest of it altogether but so many of our clients are referrals from the shop, we suspect when perhaps the crystals and essential oils have failed to fulfil the carefully worded claims on the packet.

If you think I sound cynical, well, maybe I am. If you wonder how someone with that attitude can actually be a success as a counsellor and help a client, well, it's because I've come to the view that there's very little more to it than use of the appropriate facial expression whilst giving the impression of total absorption in the subject's outpourings. In my experience, they invariably talk themselves out of the problem, unless of course we suspect mental illness in which case we suggest quite diplomatically that they should perhaps see their GP as, 'we believe there's a medical causal factor in the issue that's troubling you' and leave it to their doctor to refer them to a psychiatrist.

My business partner Dr Melanie Nose, who of course tired of the obvious joke whilst still at infant school, is not a medical doctor at all but has a Doctorate in Biblical Studies. She doesn't make the distinction clear unless asked directly as the unintended subterfuge adds a certain comfort and reassurance to some 'patients' as she misleadingly refers to them. Her educational background has though over the years equipped her to assist the not insubstantial number of clients suffering from what I call, 'the negative effects of religion.' I've been inclined to refer them to her at an early stage to avoid any further damage should I inadvertently reveal that in my view religion is the scourge of the planet.

Melanie can get a bit superior at times, justifiably perhaps as she has a whole raft of relevant qualifications rather than my single diploma. I do though have a rather large impressive-looking framed certificate which hangs in the consulting room on the wall behind my chair. The bold headline is worded, 'Qualified Senior Practitioner'. Every morning when I enter the office it makes me smile. It represents my greatest personal achievement.

Dr Nose as well as being a bible thumper has taken the time to acquire relevant qualifications and add many strings to her golden bow with membership of numerous notable professional bodies. She's a fully qualified Cognitive Behavioural Therapist, COSORT accredited and trained as both a relationship and a psychosexual therapist with Relate.

Melanie Golden Halo accuses me of being cynical and unsympathetic but I've learned that in this job true empathy is fatal. You could get so depressed if you really shared the pain so I've found it's best to treat it all as a drama on telly such as *Eastenders*, engrossing 'til it's over then switch off, forget it and make some tea.

You might wonder why Melanie has been prepared to work for so long with a less-qualified partner, a situation of which she finds it necessary to remind me at regular intervals.

The answer is our longstanding close friendship, reinforced a little perhaps by my knowledge of her many extramarital affairs and her current cocaine habit.

My task today is to clear my desk, empty my filing cabinets, delete computer files and consign all of the remaining confidential clutter from my office into the bin. I've already passed on the current files relating to those who've agreed to be transferred to Dr Melanie together with all of the relevantly titled reference books conveniently visible from the clients' perspective in the bookcase behind my black leather swiveller. Ten of them I've read, being textbooks from my Counselling Diploma course but the rest of the impressive array I've picked up for display purposes only from car boot sales and charity shops.

I'm making a start by disposing of the contents of a filing cabinet full of obsolete promotional leaflets, many dating back to our early days. I've had a good laugh at the ridiculous gobbledygook in many of them, which were produced by the agency that once fired me, Shutter Tomlinson Rounce Edwards Welch Taylor Hampton, a more self-important bunch of twats you'd be unlikely to encounter. Although I would have enjoyed playing the client and seeing them bow and scrape, I decided it would be better if Melanie took that role. I'm a different person now.

Between them they came up with some cringeworthy materials, a mix of Melanie's professional buzz words and their pretentious advertising bollocks. Just listen to some of these.

'Many of us suffer depression, anxiety and low self-esteem. You are not alone.'
'A phobia shared is a phobia solved.'
'Addiction, Action, Reduction, Redemption.'
'Trained to listen, born to care.'

Oh God! I remember this one.

'We provide a confidential and supportive space with a caring expert trained to listen and make you feel better.'

Unfortunately, there was an unnoticed typo in the final artwork and two thousand brochures were printed saying, *'make your feet better'*. The shop received numerous calls from existing customers asking if we'd added chiropody to our offering.

So, here we go, all that lot into the bin for recycling, hopefully to be pulped and processed into something of much more use to the world such as paper cups or party hats.

My client records are somewhat unconventionally filed. Two drawers for current cases, one for past and a fourth for those who felt we'd gone as far as we could in resolving their issues but whom I'd been certain would return in time. The cover of each folder carries the assumed name under which they'd registered. It's common practice to recommend prior to the first appointment that they select a *nom de scene* both for confidentiality and to perhaps make them feel a little more at ease, as if anonymous away from *The Comfy*. The practice is also followed by therapists who operate under an assumed name, mine is Marjorie and Melanie's is bizarrely Rose. We do this to avoid any risk of troublesome clients seeking us out in our private lives.

After the first appointment, I add a coloured tag to the folders indicating the general nature of the subject's problem and their personality type. Blue for anxious or depressed, green for affairs of the heart, white for addiction, (I must have been thinking of Melanie when I selected that one), pink for self-confidence issues, black for anger management and red for downright weirdos. More complex cases remain untagged.

Regardless of the individual problem they all fell into one of two categories and another indicator reminded me of whether they were *'Talkers'* or *'Taciturn'*. Talkers were easy. I just had to turn my imaginary hearing aid down a touch, stay awake and look concerned, nodding at intervals or raising my eyebrows and shaking my head when their body language signalled it appropriate. I became quite expert at that. I did though often find myself saying things under my breath when they were droning on. *'For God's sake woman, ditch the useless bastard, he'll never change.'*

The Taciturn were much harder work and of course required more pre-planning for the session. I found that ten minutes quoting from my notes what they had said last time would get them started, although that as often as not resulted in the 'greens' reaching for a tissue and dabbing away tears with that pathetic little wipe just under the lower lid to preserve the eyeliner.

The folders contain my aggregated notes made during and after each session, a resumé of my diagnosis and strategy for future appointments. I usually spent ten minutes re-familiarising myself with each case prior to their visit but for some this was totally unnecessary. For the 'reds' there was simply no point.

My clients have come from all walks of life, both sexes and all socio-economic groups although there has been a predominance of forty-something middle-class ladies. The only common factor was that they all willingly paid the sixty pounds I charged for a forty-five-minute consultation.

Initial appointments were made by phone and I always asked who had referred them. It was sometimes past clients but if it was a GP a different approach was required and my notes were more fastidiously taken. Often it was a close friend no doubt sick to death of tear-sodden shoulders and chats over coffee that continually drifted to the same boring issue rather than children's schooling, holidays, clothes and new kitchens.

Our clients have a wide variety of reasons for seeking help but in my experience the vast majority suffer anxiety, anger and depression caused by relationship problems. The 'Love-Wounded' I term them, victims of abandonment, broken marriages, ended affairs and unrequited love in its many forms. What sympathy I have is reserved for these sufferers rather than the others who generally just lack the backbone to accept that life is imperfect and get on with it. I've also found the former easier to help as generally, however long it takes, the answer is simply to give them a glimpse of the future without their errant lover and let them see how futile it is to waste time on someone who never did or no longer cares. It helps too to paint a picture of someone much more deserving waiting just around the corner. I once suggested to Melanie that we could generate an additional revenue steam by forming a business association with a dating agency and making discreet referrals. She was furious and went off in a huff so I let the matter drop.

Right; time to dispose of the remaining client files but I'll tell you about the more interesting cases, as I feed them into the shredder.

Oh, here's a red one. This'll make you laugh.

What a co-incidence. It was the vicar that Charles and I saw in the vet's waiting room when we took Big Nob in for treatment to his paw years ago.

The reverend made no attempt at anonymity and actually attended our first session complete with dog collar. I did suggest this client should see his doctor as he was displaying the classic symptoms of what even the most tactful medical practitioner might term 'stark raving bonkers'. He bluntly refused though, insisting that it would cost him his job. He didn't want to end up in the care of the diocese which had homes for barmy clergy and although he'd heard they were very comfortable they had a policy of 'no pets' and he was sure they wouldn't accept that his pet duck Jesus from whom he appeared inseparable, was the true manifestation of the second coming.

I did think in view of the religious connection that I should refer him to Melanie but on one of her cocaine days she might well have suggested that he bring the duck with him next time so she could check it out for herself with a few obscure references from the New Testament.

Farewell Reverend. Rest in pieces.

This was a sad one. 'Christina', who came to see me during my first year in practice.

I didn't tag her file as she was so enigmatic, a complex mix of green, blue and black. I think she was love-wounded but she would never have admitted it. There were subliminal layers of melancholy and more obvious traces of anger. Insular I'd have said if having to sum her up in one word.

Christina had just one session with me but revealed that she had consulted another counsellor two years earlier. A woman abandoned by her husband, she was left with a young school-age boy to raise. Telling me about her earlier counselling she said that initially she sought help both for anger management and concerns about her inability to love a most caring and generous man utterly devoted to her and a perfect role model for her son. She seemed unable she said to breakdown an impregnable emotional castle wall she'd constructed around herself soon after her divorce. I suspected she'd had serious issues with her father in childhood and together with the abandonment had developed a deep-rooted mistrust of men but she was totally dismissive of the suggestion, even angry.

She'd felt guilt that the man had been totally besotted with her when she could not find it within herself to feel any love for him. The relationship though had reached a point at which she decided she would move in with him as she felt it would be in the long-term best interest of her young son who worshipped the man. Tragically however the friend had been killed just days before they could get together.

She had very easily got over the unwanted suitor but sought help from me not about her own problems but over concern at the impact of the man's death on her son. The young boy, previously outgoing became withdrawn and inconsolable and showed little improvement after almost three years. All I could think of was to suggest a trip to Disneyland which was met with a hail of abuse and questioning of my professional competence. Christina left in a huff without paying my fee. I do hope the boy got some help elsewhere though.

Cheerio Christina, in you go.

'Gloria'. Now she was strange!

A spinster in her early fifties who I initially tagged blue but quickly reassessed to red. I really should have passed her to Melanie after the first session as her problem was very definitely psychosexual. She was menopausal, quite attractive but had become utterly convinced that she was changing sex. She had developed an embryonic moustache which is certainly not uncommon in middle-aged women and the occasional stray whisker would appear on her chin from time to time. Not an issue for most ladies as appropriate cosmetics could easily mask the former and the latter could be simply addressed with a pair of tweezers as and when necessary. I suffer from the same inconvenience myself but it's not a problem for the sane.

On the second session we talked round and around in circles but I was unable to convince her that her fears were totally unfounded. She asked me if I thought her voice was getting deeper and became extremely agitated when I assured her that it wasn't. Gloria then revealed that her chest was 'becoming hairy' and undid a few buttons of her blouse to convince me. Sure enough there were a few tiny blonde hairs above her cleavage but again nothing unnatural. She seemed determined to have her self-diagnosis confirmed but I held back from asking if they went all the way down to her balls. It was when she expressed deep concern at becoming an avid watcher of *Match of the Day* that I decided I could do nothing more for her and suggested that she see her doctor.

I would have referred her to Melanie instead as she showed all the potential of being a long-term diary filler but unfortunately my partner was taking a brief spell of sick leave at the time. She'd started punctuating her speech with an annoying sniff every thirty seconds or so which was becoming embarrassing for her when listening to her patients' ills and woes. It was clearly not hay fever as she at first claimed given that we were just a few weeks off Christmas. Chronic rhinitis was her next excuse but it was obvious to me that the golden girl had foolishly snorted away her nasal septum, a severely limiting factor for one so often counselling those abusing drugs.

Goodbye Gloria. Gimme a man-hug.

'Geraldine'. Tagged white, a true addict.

Geraldine was a wonderful person, happy and jovial but as fat as a pig. She weighed in at twenty stones and had elected to seek therapy for her eating disorder rather than be fitted with a gastric band. She was a hopeless case and confessed to me in our first session that her disinclination to be fitted with a band was because she'd heard that it seriously reduced one's appetite.

Her problem was simple. She loved food and wanted to lose weight but didn't possess the willpower to diet. She fully understood the calories in calories out equation but hoped someone could help her with a miracle cure that didn't involve giving up the foods she loved. Remarkably though she was the happiest of my clients and we'd laugh so much together that I actually looked forward to her appointments. She had a great sense of humour and appeared impossible to offend so on one occasion I felt confident that I could mention her rather strong body odour. She feigned outrage at the perceived insult and then raised each elbow in turn to sniff her armpits before asking through her laughter if I could recommend a reliable low-calorie deodorant.

Her first visit was at three one Friday and I was just enjoying my afternoon Earl Grey as she arrived. I offered her a cup and we talked about what she hoped to achieve from our sessions, why she couldn't cope with diets, her horror at the very thought of a gastric band and her commitment to doing whatever it took to lose eight stone. The enormity of the challenge was such that I thought I'd better start with a few words to manage her expectations when she interrupted me to ask if we had any chocolate biscuits.

Ciao Geraldine, I hope this hurts less than a gastric band.

On that happy note I think it's time to commit the rest of these files with their problems, their pain, their hang-ups and their loneliness to the *Powershred*, as metaphorically I'm confident I have helped most of my clients to do.

When I said earlier that I'd found there's very little more to counselling than use of the appropriate facial expression whilst giving the impression of total absorption in the client's outpourings, I was perhaps being a little too flippant. I am confident that with sensitivity, good old-fashioned common sense, an infectious positive attitude and straight talking I've helped the vast majority of those I've counselled over the years.

Throughout my career, I can count in the thousands those I've helped through anxiety, depression, bereavement, anger and all of the other emotional ills. Many have been easy, some difficult but those I've felt for most were the love-wounded, the people put through pain and torment by others not deserving of, or for whatever reason not able to return their love. I've given the subject a great deal of thought and it has led me to question the value of love in one's life. I've pondered the difference between loving someone and being 'in love' with them. What is more comfortable, what is more durable, what is more rewarding, what is more stressful?

In recent years it's been noticeable that the men and women sitting in *The Comfy* have been getting younger; marrieds in their twenties and thirties, teenage girls, even some still in school.

So many seemed unable to recognise the natural progression through attraction, lust, being in love and loving or recognise and accept the durability of each phase and the causes of change. Some would experience all states, some just a few and others sadly nothing at all.

It's such a shame that wisdom comes later in life, long after the young have made their mistakes.

I've railed at the way 'love' is sold to each generation of young girls and women through magazines, romantic pulp fiction, music videos and television drama. I've seen how it drives the lives of many to the point that they convince themselves they must search for it and that they are inadequate if they don't have a boyfriend, a partner or a husband. Many are those who through impatience convince themselves they've found it and settle for a lesser state, usually with tragic consequences.

I've seen the effects of non-nuclear family structures, the absence of good male role models in the home and in schools, the selfie culture, the fixation with body image, sexting and the pornography that corrupts young men and condemns many of them to a life of insensitive ignorance and inevitable disappointment. The media no longer reflects our culture but steers it.

You might think that's a bit rich coming from me but I do lament the speed of change in our society and the levels of stress and anxiety it causes. I have dealt with that daily and perhaps Ken is right in saying it's time for me to go.

If I were to continue in this field, my advice to the love-wounded, based on a career listening to the joys and misery love brings would be simply this:

Life is for living, not just loving.

Enjoying life is what's most important, with or without love.

Don't search for it. If it comes along, embrace it and try to make it last.

If it doesn't find you, console yourself with the certain knowledge that you've probably saved yourself a lot of grief.

If you lose it, don't waste the rest of your life in despair.

And most important of all, if you've found your perfect soul mate, then, without telling them so, make them the star of the show and make your role that of the best supporting actor. They'll then certainly do the same for you.

I often think of Philly and wonder, if I'd known then what I know now, whether I might have helped her better understand the roots of her issues and to come to terms much more easily with the new orientation in her life.

During our exciting little fling, which I know in her eyes was a true love affair, she opened up to me about her past in the most disarming way. Just before our humiliation of Charles, she'd only recently re-established a close relationship with her sister and in so doing discovered a tragic misunderstanding which had led them to have little contact in adult life. Her sister, Hermione, had been abused as a child by their drunken father who was often left alone to care for the two of them by a wife totally focussed on her career and often absent from home on business. At the age of fifteen, she reported the incident to her mother who refused to believe it and suggested that persisting with the claims might result in both children being put into the care of the local authority. The compromise was Hermione's agreement to be sent to a boarding school.

Returning to the family home for the summer holidays her innocent ten-year-old sister complained that her father still insisted that they bathe together as they had as toddlers with plastic ducks and soapy fun. Reporting this to her mother resulted in an acrimonious divorce and Philippa's terrifying despatch to boarding school, a move she not only failed to understand but one for which she held her sister totally responsible. So often longstanding emotional issues in women have their roots in unhealthy father-daughter relationships more often through a betrayal of trust than sexual abuse in my experience.

I do believe though that Philippa was damaged by an early sexual encounter at university. She told me of a terrifying incident following persistent pestering by a male flatmate to whom out of little more than curiosity she agreed to surrender her virginity when very drunk on cheap cider. As they lay naked together in her room, he tied her wrists to the brass bed rail despite her protests. He though through excess alcohol couldn't get it up and her screams for help brought two male students from the adjacent flat banging on her door. The flatmate let them in to silence the commotion but instead of rescuing her, they just sat on the bed and made rude remarks about her unshaven pussy and tiny tits. After what seemed an age, they departed for the pub in laughter leaving her to eventually wriggle free of her bonds. She suffered the humiliation in silence rather than reporting the incident and moved back into the Halls of Residence.

The other revelation from her sister was I think the deciding factor in her willingness to collaborate with me in the humiliation of Charles Trelawney. Hermione told her of her friendship with Oliver, a middle-aged bank manager killed in a road accident on the very day that they'd agreed to live together and the devastating impact on her son, Tristan, who'd formed a very strong attachment to the man. Philippa was astonished at the coincidence and mortified at the realisation that not only had Charles killed the man by reckless driving but that she had been unwittingly complicit in getting him off by assisting him to conceal the evidence in his phone.

I've cleared my desk and emptied the consulting room of all personal effects. My framed Qualified Senior Practitioner certificate is neatly wrapped in brown paper for the journey home and there remains not a trace of my nearly ten years here. It's the end of my involvement in the practice and the close of an interesting and rewarding career. I leave in the certain knowledge that I've improved the lives of so many individuals, improved the parenting skills of countless and sorted out many a dysfunctional family. I shall take nothing else with me but the memories.

Not such an 'air-head bimbo' after all eh, Charlie.

I kissed goodbye to Melanie at lunchtime, inadvertently inhaling a trace of white powder from her left cheek as I did so. Poor dear, she really should seek some counselling.

Well, that's it. Career over. I'm off home now to Ken to become a housewife and a mother to our twins and who knows maybe a few more babies in the years to come. Time at last for the next phase in life.

Although I owe her a great debt, I've decided it's best for all of us if I break my promise to Philly and not invite her to be godmother. I don't want to see her again or run any risk of Ken learning what passed between us. I'm a new person now with the past behind me, Charles, Philippa and the others. When I last heard from Philly, she told me she was 'deliriously happy' in a relationship with a woman called Annie and was hoping soon to be married.

I'm sure some of you will be thinking that my transformation into a sensible, balanced, family-oriented individual stretches credibility more than a little. Well, perhaps I can convince you by revealing that despite the excitement it brought to my life, I didn't once recommend the dice game to any of my clients and I haven't played it myself for more than ten years.

There's nothing to stop you giving it a try though. Take care.